Redemption
on
Red River

by

Cheryl R. Cain

REDEMPTION ON RED RIVER

Copyright © 2014 by Cheryl R. Cain

ISBN # 978-0-9555283-6-1

First published in Great Britain in 2014 by Sunpenny Publishing
www.sunpenny.com (Sunpenny Publishing Group)

MORE BOOKS FROM THE SUNPENNY PUBLISHING GROUP:

Blue Freedom, by Sandra Peut
Brandy Butter on Christmas Canal, by Shae O'Brien
Breaking the Circle, by Althea Barr
Bridge to Nowhere, by Stephanie Parker McKean
Dance of Eagles, by JS Holloway
Don't Pass Me By, by Julie McGowan
Embracing Change, by Debbie Roome
Far Out, by Corinna Weyreter
Going Astray, by Christine Moore
If Horses Were Wishes, by Elizabeth Sellers
Just One More Summer, by Julie McGowan
My Sea is Wide, by Rowland Evans
Someday, Maybe, by Jenny Piper
The Mountains Between, by Julie McGowan
Uncharted Waters, by Sara DuBose

This book is dedicated to:

My sweet friend, Debbie Frantz Turpin, who encouraged all my crazy plans. I miss you.

My husband and his never ending support for this endeavor and all the others he so kindly allowed me to try.

My handsome and talented sons, who let me write continuously for 30 days to accomplish my NaNoWriMo goal.

My parents, brothers, nephews, sisters-in-law and other relatives who gave me ideas for characters and stories, yet to be written.

To the readers - may you find eternal hope, a friend who sticks closer than a brother, and peace beyond comprehension by having a relationship with God.

Chapter 1

Oberlin College Commencement
August 28, 1837: Oberlin, Ohio

Anna's chemise clung to her back, adhered by rivulets of perspiration. Tendrils of hair, carefully pinned two hours earlier, now plastered her neck. She changed her position in an effort to dislodge the clothing and to stir some breeze under the heavy woolen gown. Even the shade of the tall, ancient trees in Tappan Square proved unable to lessen the stifling heat during the ceremony.

There, in the center of the Oberlin campus, lush green hedges and flowering plants fringed the edges of the open common. Large gatherings such as commencements, rallies, and celebrations were held there not only because of the size, but also because of the inherent beauty and dignity of the place, a result of the tall columns and greenery. But that day, immersed in the heat and humidity, Anna could see no glory in the surroundings.

She leaned forward in her seat amongst the other graduates, fidgeting again to try and release the clinging chemise from her skin. To her left she saw her mother, father, brother Caleb, and Aunt Maggie. Caleb wrinkled up his nose and stuck his tongue out at his big sister. Anna rolled her eyes and giggled as she saw her mother pull his ear, forcing him to direct his attention to the speaker.

Anna sighed. Looking around, she was overcome by a strange mixture of regret and satisfaction: sorrow because she was destined to miss her friends, her favorite professors, and the activities of the little community; and satisfaction at having completed one of her goals, for she was now officially an educated woman.

When Anna had first mentioned attending college, her mother had accused her father of planting such 'wild' notions in her head. Anna and her mother frequently disagreed when it came to Anna pushing beyond what was considered proper or normal for a lady.

Anna often accompanied her father to their grocery business on the days when merchants made their deliveries. While her father checked the flats of produce, bags of flour, and sacks bulging with coffee, Anna walked among the newly delivered trunks, filled with men's trousers and ladies' fancy hats, topped with feather plumes. She ran her fingers over folds of taffeta and silk fabrics and imagined the delicate china cups, embellished with petite pink roses, filled with fragrant tea, being held in the hands of refined women. Anna quizzed the delivery men with questions about the towns to which they had travelled, imagining herself in exotic places.

Her mother chastised Anna for her impertinent questioning. "Prudie, she's just curious," her father always said in Anna's defense. "There's no harm in our daughter wanting to know about the world. Someday, she will have to live in it."

A movement on the platform jerked Anna back to the present. She looked down both aisles to the edges of the common and bit her lip when she still didn't see her fiancé, Martin.

The speaker was rounding up. "Finally, Class of 1837, we salute you, and we charge you to go out and make an impact upon your world!"

Roars erupted from the graduates as they realized the sweltering ceremony, and their education at Oberlin College, were finally over.

Anna grabbed her best friend in a tight embrace. "Best wishes, Gretchen!"

"You too!" Gretchen wiped her eyes. "I'll miss you, roomie."

"Oh, you'll soon find some rich and handsome banker, get married, and have so many children you won't know what to do! But don't you dare forget about me amidst all that pittering and pattering of tiny feet!" she urged. "Tell me we will keep in touch."

"Of course we will! Oh, there are my mother and father." Gretchen waved to her parents and turned quickly back to Anna. "I'll write as soon as I get home." As her mother approached, she grabbed the woman by the arm. "Oh, Mama, do take me away from this intolerable heat," she pleaded.

Anna removed the blue cap and shoved several stray hairs back under her tortoiseshell combs as she walked between the chairs, dodging friends and their families to reach her own. At the edge of the common, she finally spied Martin, standing by a rather sizeable lilac bush. Anna stood on her tiptoes. "Martin!" she shouted, waving her mortarboard to get his attention. "Martin, over here!"

But Martin was far too immersed in a conversation with a professor to see or hear his love's beckoning call.

From behind Anna, there came another male voice to greet her. "Well, there you are! Congratulations, honey."

Her father's embrace caused her damp clothing to cling to her skin once again. She grimaced, slowly pulled away, and removed the oppressive robe, silently wishing she could also free herself from those flesh-melting petticoats and boned bustier, which trapped the heat against her as if she was a pastry in a baker's oven. "Thank you, Father, but I am so miserable in this horrendous heat!" Anna declared. "I am not sure I can stand it for a minute more."

"Yes, it is quite awful out here," Mr. Collins said. He removed a handkerchief from his vest pocket and dabbed his perspiring brow. "Your mother is waiting by the fountain, and she's just as miserable as you are. Are you ready to leave, dear?"

"I saw Martin by the hedge. I thought for certain that he would sit with you during the ceremony. Didn't he see you before he sat down?" she asked, looking over her father's left shoulder toward the lilac bush where Martin was still conversing.

"No. We waited as long as possible, but didn't want to risk losing our seats. You go on and find him. I will escort your mother, Aunt Maggie, and Caleb to the carriage and then return for you."

"I'll be quick," Anna said with a smile as she marched off toward Martin at the side of the green.

He had a blank stare glazed across his face, and he stood motionless, with his hands stuffed deep in his pockets and his head bolted toward the ground. Anna thought that if it were not for his maroon vest and gray trousers, he might be mistaken for a statue.

"There you are!" she said as she neared him. "Where were you? I thought you'd sit with my family," she asked, attempting to prevent disappointment from coloring her words.

He looked up from the grass, seemingly a bit startled. "Uh, I am sorry. I didn't wish to intrude on your family's special time." His focal point changed to the side of the green, and it was quite obvious that he was avoiding direct eye contact with his fiancée, though she wasn't sure why.

Anna deliberately moved into his line of vision.

"Besides, I arrived only shortly before the commencement began, and I didn't wish to cause a disturbance. From where I stood, though, I could still see you receiving your diploma. I'm so proud of you! Congratulations," he said with a quick hug, and then he released her abruptly. "You are now among the very few female college graduates in the world."

She frowned, sensing his uneasiness. "What's wrong, Martin?"

"Nothing. I suppose I am just a bit out of sorts today, that's all. My mind has been on business matters, and it's difficult to change my train of thought."

"Business matters? What business? The law firm hasn't released you from your new position, have they?" Anna asked anxiously. She took Martin's arm and held his unresponsive hand.

"No, no. I assure you, dear, that my arrangement of employment is in no jeopardy whatsoever. It's nothing to concern yourself with. Please pay it no further regard."

"Ah, so she found you," Mr. Collins said, interrupting the uncomfortable silence that had taken hold between them. "I hope you weren't upset that we didn't wait for you, Martin." He shook his future son-in-law's hand firmly.

"No, sir. I was just telling Anna that I was delayed. I

arrived just before the ceremony began."

"Fine then, just fine. We're going to the hotel now for the reception, along with the other graduates and their families. Would you care to travel with us?"

"No, thank you. I have my own carriage."

Anna's father turned to her. "Anna, are you coming with us?"

Anna looked to Martin, expecting a request for her to accompany him, but he simply stood there, stone-faced and silent. When she got no answer from him, she muttered to her father in a confused tone, "Uh, yes, Father. I – I suppose I shall ride with you."

She turned back to Martin. "Are you certain you're well?" Anna asked. She took his hand and gazed into his eyes, trying to read his thoughts.

Martin allowed Anna to hold his hand, but he looked away. "I'm sorry, but I won't be able to join you at the reception after all. Forgive me. There are matters we need to discuss, Anna, but now isn't a good time. Please go with your family and bask in the celebration of your great accomplishments. I'll meet you at the stagecoach tomorrow for the journey home."

He bent to kiss her, but to Anna, his lackluster peck felt quite like the kiss of a stranger.

D ear, we're so proud of you," said Prudence Collins as Anna and her father climbed into the carriage. She paused. "Will Martin not be joining us?"

"No, Mother. He cannot attend the reception, as he has business matters to attend to."

"That's odd, dear."

"Yes, I know. He looked worried, but he wouldn't tell me why." Anna looked out the carriage window, hoping to catch a glimpse of Martin as she blinked back stray tears.

Mrs. Collins patted her hand. "My darling, men often suffer from narrow-mindedness where business is concerned." She winked at her husband. "He's probably fretting over his new position with the law firm. I imagine Martin will be back to his senses again tomorrow."

"I'm sure you're right. Men can be difficult to understand," Anna agreed.

"It's best that way, darling. We all know that if we can keep the womenfolk a bit off kilter, you will be putty in our hands," Mr. Collins said teasingly, squeezing his wife's hand. "Isn't that right, dear?"

The family slowly made their way to the intersection of Professor Street and Tenth Avenue to enjoy the reception at the Briton Hotel.

Chapter 2

Sunlight floated through the slit between the shade and windowsill. Tiny dust particles catapulted and whirled, trapped within the beam. The ray alighted on Anna's sleeping eyes, and suddenly they darted open.

Anna bolted upright in bed, swung her legs from under the blankets, and stood up. "Oh, my! What time is it? I've overslept again!" She rubbed her face and blinked to clear the fuzziness from her eyes and the confusion from her mind, then sat back on the bed and laughed. "Wait... I don't have to go to class today. I've already graduated!" Anna crawled back into the cozy hotel bed, broad and comfortable, and let the thought sink in. "I'll just lie here and enjoy the decadent laziness," she said, sighing in contentment. "Oh yes, this *is* marvelous!" She closed her eyes, allowing her mind to fill with scenes from her graduation, the celebration at the hotel, and visiting with her classmates and their families.

"Anna, are you awake, lazy bones?" a chipper voice called from the keyhole, interrupting her daydream.

"No, Caleb. I'm still slumbering, basking in the absence of any chores, classes, tests, or having to ponder even one weighty notion!"

"Well, that's wonderful, but Mother said to tell you breakfast is ready in the parlor, if you'd like to join us."

She groaned. "Tell her I'll be there shortly," she called back at the keyhole voice. "Well, at least I *did* enjoy those few minutes of laziness," she comforted herself. Anna pried herself from the luxurious bed, pattered to the closet and chose a pale green lightweight cotton dress, hoping it would be appropriate for the heat. She poured water from the jug into the matching floral-pattern basin and washed her face with the lilac-scented soap beside it. Then she toweled off, dressed, and pinned up her hair with the tortoiseshell combs Aunt Maggie had given her as a graduation gift. She splashed rose water on her neck, slipped her feet into her shoes, and joined her family in the parlor of the hotel suite for breakfast.

"*There's* the most beautiful graduate in the world," Anna's father exclaimed warmly as she entered the parlor. He stood like a proper gentleman and kissed her cheek.

"Let us say grace and enjoy this wonderful fare," Anna's mother said as she reached for Anna's and Caleb's hands and bowed her head.

Anna's father completed the circle and began his prayer. "Lord God, we appreciate Your protection and provision and thank You for being with Anna during her education. Now we ask you, Father, to bless her life and marriage. We thank You for this bounty and ask that You will bless it to our bodies and our bodies to Your service."

And they all said Amen, thought Anna – as indeed they did.

"Caleb, calm down. There will still be food left when the plate reaches you." Prudence laughed at her fidgeting ten-year-old son.

"I'm hungry, Mother," he said. "Growing men need nourishment."

The family laughed at his proclamation of manhood, though he seemed to be completely serious in such a declaration.

"Nevertheless," said Anna, "you must use restraint, brother, or people may think you a rude pig." She passed him the plate of fluffy, light biscuits, and he quickly snatched two for himself.

"I wish your biscuits were like these, Mother," he said, drizzling honey over them. "If they were, I do believe I would never leave the table."

"That's precisely the reason I make my biscuits hard, square, and flat, my boy. I don't *want* you lingering around my table at all hours." Mrs. Collins smiled. "And in a pinch, they can be used for fuel in the winter."

They all laughed, and Mr. Collins winked at his wife. "Dear, we are all fully aware of your secret plot, in spite of your effort to hide it. You *are* capable of making fine, feather-light biscuits, but you keep your talent hidden for the sake of our waistlines."

As Anna packed her satchel, she reminisced about the past week. Graduation was exciting, but it was simultaneously sad, for she knew she would likely never see most of her classmates again. Her main regret, however, was Martin's absence.

But perhaps if he is still in that morose mood of his, she thought, *perhaps that is for the best.* Oh, never mind. She knew that once they were home, there'd be ample time to discuss the final details of their wedding, now only four weeks away!

Aunt Maggie interrupted her daydream. "Anna!" she called from the parlor. "When does your term at the academy begin?"

"It commences on October 23," Anna said as she exited her room and entered the parlor, where her aunt was sitting. "Why?"

"Well, dear, I was simply thinking about whether or not you shall have any time for enjoying being a newlywed before you settle into your career," stated Maggie.

"There will be two weeks after we return from our honeymoon before I must report for teaching duties at the academy," Anna replied.

"Very good, dear. It is very important that you both have adequate time to become better acquainted before adding the stresses of everyday toils and labors." Maggie smiled and looked far off, as if she were remembering her own honeymoon. "After Garrett and I married, we travelled for two months before we settled into our home. It was a wonderful time for us, and I want to you to enjoy your marriage as much as Garrett and I enjoyed those precious early weeks."

Anna sat down and took her aunt's hand. "You and Uncle Garrett were great role models for married folks. I always admired the way he treated you – with tenderness and kindness – even the time you almost burned the barn down trying to keep the newborn kittens warm!"

"Yes, that was a true testament to his character!" Maggie laughed as she remembered the charred hay and the smoke-filled barn. "He *was* patient, but I have to admit it took a great degree of patience on my part to put up with *his* antics too. That's what makes a good marriage – a little give and take on the part of both husband and wife."

"I know you miss him. He was a dear man," Anna said.

"Well, dear, we'd best not dawdle longer, or we will try your father's patience! I am sure he will take no delight in us sitting here talking instead of preparing to leave." She smiled at Anna. "You're a very precious girl. Don't let anyone tell you otherwise, and do not listen to those who intimate that you should be of a different mind, have different goals, or appear to be anything other than what, and who, you really are. There," she said, patting Anna's hand, "that's all this nosey busybody will advise. I won't speak another word of it."

"I'll remember your wise words, Aunt Maggie, and I truly will take them to heart. Thank you." She kissed her aunt's soft, scented cheek, and returned to her packing.

At the stage office, Anna saw Martin standing by the door, looking so distinguished and handsome that she wished she was to wed him that very night. She hurriedly smoothed her dress and dabbed her face before the carriage door opened. As they climbed out, Martin walked over and helped her down. His warm smile allowed Anna to relax, and she was relieved to see that he was back to his normal self – or so it seemed.

"Mrs. Collins, Aunt Maggie," Martin said. "You ladies are even more lovely than usual."

"Oh, Martin, you do go on," Mrs. Collins said, her cheeks blushing with his flattery.

They joined the rest of the family in the stagecoach for the bumpy, two-hour trip over a well-worn, rutted trail to East Liverpool, Ohio. From there, they would board a Cincinnati-bound steamboat.

As they journeyed, Anna chatted to Martin about the wedding, as excited as any girl would be about her upcoming nuptials. He kissed her hand, and Anna's mother and aunt smiled. Caleb crossed his eyes and pretended to retch; his mother swatted his hand, but Anna didn't notice his mockery anyway, for she was much too happy and lost in the eyes of the man who would soon be hers. She laid her head on Martin's shoulder, closed her eyes, and daydreamt of her future: her marriage to Martin, settling into their home, and becoming established as a teacher at last.

Anna's notebook, which was filled with plans for her classes at Barton Academy, stuck up out of her satchel. As the time passed on the journey, she contemplated in silence all that lay ahead. Martin dozed off as Anna's aunt and mother discussed the fashions they had witnessed during the graduation week, while Caleb and Mr. Collins amused each other by mocking the women.

"Oh, Father, did you see the gorgeous blue, brocade gown Mrs. Crowder wore?" Caleb offered in a high-pitched voice.

"Yes, son. I simply *must* have one for the next ball. Oh, can you imagine how it will set off my blue eyes," his father retorted in a matching falsetto.

The women looked at the two and couldn't help but laugh. Prudence slapped her husband's arm playfully, then quickly adjusted her gaze back to her daughter. "Anna, who was that nice young man who sat beside you at the ceremony?" she asked, adroitly changing the subject.

"Henry Walpole, Mother."

"And what are his plans?"

Anna thought for a moment. "I believe he took a pastorate in Illinois."

"And what of your classmate, the young lady from New York... Sophia? What will she do now?" Her mother continued to inquire about other students, and Anna answered. Fortunately, just as she was growing tired of her mother's inquisition, they pulled into East Liverpool.

Mr. Collins arranged for their luggage to be loaded onto the steamboat *Alexander* and shepherded his family up the boat ramp. They entered a sumptuous parlor lined in dark walnut paneling and carpeted in burgundy. Large fans swirled overhead, stirring the air and offering some relief from the ever-present warmth.

With a broad smile, the waiter greeted them and led them to a table next to the windows. They ordered iced lemonade, then sat and enjoyed the sonatas being played by a handsome young pianist, which added romance to the beautiful surroundings.

Stirred by the beauty of the parlor, Anna's thoughts flew again to her wedding. She and her mother worried their choices in color and decorations were too simple and they vacillated up to the last moment in their final selections. Even now, with only a few weeks before the event, they fussed aloud over the decisions.

"Martin," Mrs. Collins said. "We arranged for white rose *boutonnieres* for you and your groomsmen. I hope you won't think them too delicate for men."

"No, I – I'm sure whatever you've chosen will do."

Anna thought herself fortunate that Martin accepted and supported her choices – even the roses, which she knew weren't his favorite. Nevertheless, the would-be groom had clearly wearied of the discussion and fidgeted, much to Anna's chagrin.

"Now, Martin," Mrs. Collins continued, oblivious, "the string trio agreed to play twenty minutes before the ceremony and during the recessional, but I'm afraid they weren't available for the reception. I sent your parents a message, but I haven't yet received a reply. Would you speak to them? Perhaps they know of another group."

Martin tightened his jaw and stood abruptly. "I don't care!" He breathed deeply. "I mean, I don't know if they've received your note, Mrs. Collins, but I'll mention the matter when I see them." He stretched. "I believe I would do well with some fresh air. Please excuse me."

"May I join you?" Anna asked.

"If you wish. My stomach is a bit unsettled. Seasickness, I suppose."

Anna quickly walked with him outside and to the back of the *Alexander*. Martin took her hand. Anna sighed gently, and allowed the sun to warm her face. The couple held hands and watched as the river slid together in continuous reparation of the boat's incision.

After a quiet moment, with nothing but the sounds of the rippling water, Anna moved her gaze from the river to

Martin, only to find that his face now held the same blank stare as it had at graduation, when she'd approached him near the lilac bushes. "Martin, what is it? Are you still worried?"

He slowly released her hand and grasped the railing with a white-knuckled hold.

"Please tell me what is wrong, Martin."

"I – I... well, I..." he stammered, then subsided. "Nothing. There is nothing wrong," he said with a slight shake of his head. "I'm sure it is just fatigue from my many late nights studying for the bar exam and worrying over my duties with the firm." He took her hand again, allowing Anna to relax a little, but his grip felt like more of a resigned, forced touch, lacking its earlier tenderness.

They walked back to where her father and Caleb now sat on a wooden bench, and Anna could hear her father speaking of his family's journey to Ohio. She and Martin sat down across from them.

"My parents were both born in Connecticut, and her parents feared they'd never see or hear from their daughter again when my father decided to take his new bride all the way to Cincinnati. But together, they started the bakery, which has been quite successful – as you both well know!" he teased.

And they did well know. Anna remembered the hours she'd spent sitting upon a stool next to Caleb, the two of them watching as their grandparents rolled and kneaded thousands of lumps of dough into loaves of bread, hoping they would be offered a rich, hot, buttery slice.

"Too bad they didn't teach Mother to make biscuits," Caleb said with a mischievous grin.

His father tousled his hair. "Don't say that too loudly around your mother, son," he said. "It's one of the things I quickly learned after a few evenings of oatmeal dinners!"

"That's just awful," Caleb said.

"Thanks for the warning," Martin chuckled.

"Ah, look! We're finally nearing the dock," Anna said. She got up to retrieve her mother and her aunt from the parlor.

When the women arrived on deck, Caleb ran up to his mother. "Mother, the band's playing. Come and listen!"

He took her hand and led her to the side of the boat. The melody rang in the clear evening air, enhancing the mood offered by the rippling river and the setting sun. Against the darkening horizon, the illuminated dock was a mass of twinkling diamonds.

Together they all disembarked. At the bottom of the ramp, Mr. Collins hailed a carriage and gathered their luggage. With a brief bow, Martin said goodnight and departed, leaving Anna with her family, ready to return home.

I love coming home," Mrs. Collins exclaimed as the barouche turned into their street.

"I know. Whether returning from a holiday or a great excursion, the familiar sight of one's own home is always comforting," Maggie agreed.

"I'd rather travel all the time, eat in fancy restaurants, and see exciting sights," Caleb piped in.

"Yes, Caleb, I know. Of course, you only like the restaurants for their fluffy biscuits," Anna teased.

"We're home!" Caleb said as they pulled up in front of their house. "Anna, does it still look the same to you?"

"Well, it does seem larger than I remember, but that's probably because I've been living in a ten-by-twelve-foot room with another student for four years!"

When the carriage finally stopped, the family climbed out (with the help of the driver and Mr. Collins), and made their way along the gravel path and up the steps of the large porch that surrounded the house, their footsteps echoing on the wooden floorboards.

When they entered the white two-storey house, Anna breathed in the familiar scent of her home, letting fond memories flood her mind. "It *is* wonderful being back!" she said as she bounded up the stairs to her bedroom like the carefree twelve-year-old she had once been.

Chapter 3

In the study of the Garvin Residence: Cincinnati, Ohio

Well, Martin, did you speak with Miss Collins yesterday?" A tall, stout man, Wilson Garvin's mere presence commanded attention. Black hair ringed the back of his head, and, overshadowed by a thick, black mustache, his lips held a fat cigar. From it he exhaled gray halos of smoke that floated around his head. He turned to look at Martin, who had taken too long to respond to his question. "Well, boy, did you?"

Martin stood with his head down, studying the thick wool carpet. "No, Father. I never had occasion to speak freely with her, I'm afraid, but I plan to meet with her tomorrow."

"Don't dawdle, son. Get it done today! You must tell her the truth so you may both get on with your lives," Mr. Garvin said firmly. "Your future success at MacGregor and Jameson depends on your ability to make wise decisions, to follow through without delay and without looking back. You cannot be a man of regrets, son, or you will not make it in this business."

"I'm aware of the need for prompt action, Father, but – but when it comes to hurting someone I care about, it's difficult. I –"

"That's precisely why your mother and I warned you when you first became involved with Miss Collins." His father stood. "However, you refused to listen to our advice. You had to go on and do what you wanted, and now we must take action to clean up this mess you've made." He leaned forward on the desk. "I will not – *you* cannot – let this – this *infatuation* destroy your career with the firm. This opportunity is a rare one, son – the once-in-a-lifetime chance every man dreams of, and matters of the heart cannot interfere with business. Choices are painful sometimes, my boy, but they must be made." He straightened and pulled a heavy book from the wooden shelf behind the desk.

"Father," Martin started, "I didn't think it would go this far, but I do –"

Mr. Garvin slammed the book on the desk with a heavy *thud*. "You know the firm is staffed by well-bred men of high character. Their wives must be of equivalent status, and frankly, Miss Collins is not of the same ilk as the likes of Mrs. Abbott or Mrs. MacGregor. She could never hold her own in a conversation with women of that caliber. How would she fare at the annual gala? Really," he said, leaning forward over his desk in quiet emphasis, "releasing her is the best thing for *her*, son. If you go through with this union, that poor girl will be a very small fish in a pool of piranha, devoured without mercy. If you truly care anything for her, you will put an end to her misery before it has a chance to take hold."

"I suppose so," Martin said in a low voice, "but it *isn't* infatuation. I really lo –"

"Boy!" his father interrupted. "There'll be time later for social relationships, after you've been made senior partner. Any sensible, unselfish woman would understand and applaud the fact that you are willing to work to provide a secure future for her." He drew long on the cigar and blew a gray stream of smoke up at the gilded ceiling.

The stench of the cigar and the futility of the situation choked Martin. "Father, I just don't know if I can –"

"Martin! Would you give up all we've done for you? The schools, the connections, the sacrifices we've made, all for you? And for what?"

Martin looked at his father's florid face, veins bulging out at his temples.

"A mere girl, Martin? A pretty *child?* Sure, she might look good on your arm for a few years, but she will be nothing more than dead weight for you and your career, an embarrassment in your circles, an impediment in your business, keeping you from all you deserve." He shrugged, turning his hands upward in frustration. "But it's your choice, son."

Perspiration dotted Martin's pallid face. "I'll meet with her today," he said, defeated.

"Good, good!" Martin's deflation satisfied Mr. Garvin's controlling persona. He awarded his son with a disingenuous nod. "You go and get it done. There are far more important matters to deal with, son, and you – we – need no further distractions. Be a good lad and run along and clean up this mess you've made."

Martin and Anna had first met in the summer, after he finished his law degree. Caught in a sudden downpour while walking downtown, Martin had sought refuge from the rain and hail at Collins Bakery.

When the bell rang as the door opened, Anna rose from behind the counter. Martin stood just inside, wiping the rain from his face with a handkerchief. In spite of his wet and messy hair, his soaked hat and jacket, and his obvious displeasure at being caught in the storm, Anna thought him handsome. Flustered by the sudden invasion of her space by such an attractive – though sopping wet – man, she fumbled with the tray of warm scones and bit her lip, wondering what to do.

Should I just keep working and ignore him, so I don't seem foolishly desperate to speak to him, or should I offer him some assistance? The last thing I want to do is give him the impression that I'm some silly, giggly schoolgirl.

As she noticed his frustration with his handkerchief's inability to absorb any more water from his wet attaché, she plopped the tray down and grabbed a towel from the cupboard handle. "Sir, perhaps a dry towel would be more effective." She walked out from behind the counter and held up the cloth.

Martin looked up. "Oh – er – thank you," he stuttered. "Are you sure you don't mind?"

"No, really. Please take it." Anna smiled shyly as a raindrop appeared at his hairline, streamed down his forehead, and fell to his cheek.

"Well, it appears this handkerchief will do me no more

good, so I do appreciate it." He took the towel and dried his face, then his attaché, then glanced down at the floor. "Oh! I'm afraid I've made a puddle on your floor, Miss... um..."

Anna felt the heat of a blush rise up her neck when he looked at her. "Collins," she said. "I'm Anna Collins."

"Miss Collins? Very well then. If you would be so kind as to offer me another towel, I'll clean up the mess I have made here."

"No, no, don't worry about it. I have a mop, and I'll tend to it later. Besides," Anna said, gesturing for him to look out the window, "you might need to go while the rain has stopped."

"So it has! Well, Miss Collins, I do thank you for allowing me shelter from the storm... and for your kindness."

Anna felt him study her for a moment, and she didn't know whether to stand still or run away. She was stricken speechless by his gaze.

"Well, then," he repeated, and started to hand the towel back to Anna.

"Why don't you keep it? The sky is still dark in the west," Anna said. "It might rain again, and you might need it."

His smile caught her breath. "Yes, I – I suppose I should leave while it's still dry. Thank you again." He opened the door, nodded to Anna, and was gone.

Anna watched through the storefront window as he stepped off the boardwalk and into a puddle on the street. Muddy water splashed the back of his trousers, and she couldn't help but giggle. *He needs a woman to take care of him,* she thought, and then she sighed. *No, I'm sure a man like that probably already has one.*

The following week, Martin dropped into the bakery again.

"May I help you?" Sarah Collins asked.

He looked startled. "Er – yes, please. Last week... uh... well, I – I..." he stammered. "Is – is Miss Collins here?"

Anna's grandmother smiled back, a mirror image of Anna's grin, and he blinked. "Anna?" she asked. "Why, yes. She's in the back. Wait here for just a minute, and I shall fetch her for you."

Martin watched Anna come around the corner, wiping

her hands off on her white apron. She raised her head and brushed a few loose hairs away from her face, smearing flour across the flawless skin of her forehead.

"Oh, good morning." Anna smiled, surprised. "Are you all out of towels? Is it raining again?"

Martin chuckled. "No, but it seems *you* might need this one back," he said, gesturing at the chalky white powder on her forehead. "Was there some sort of a flour storm explosion back there?"

"Oh! Oh, no. I'm sorry. I'm a mess," Anna said, laughing as she took the towel. "Thank you." She mopped away at her face, wishing she had a mirror and hoping she didn't miss any of it. "Apparently it's impossible for me to knead dough and remain clean!"

"Well, in any case, I thought I should drop the towel off and again express my appreciation for your kindness the other day," he said, noting that she'd only succeeded in making the flour smudge worse. He wished he was bold enough to wipe it away for her, but any lady might construe that as too forward, so he abstained.

"That's very thoughtful, but you didn't have to, Mr...?"

"I'm sorry. It's Garvin. I'm Martin Garvin." He held his hand out.

Anna took it and felt the familiar heat rising from her fingers to her face. "I'm glad I could help."

Martin looked down at his feet and then back up to Anna. "Miss Collins, I have been invited to a dinner Saturday evening, and it seems my escort has taken ill."

Anna held her breath for a moment as he paused.

He quickly rushed on. "It's a tedious affair with stuffy, boring people, and I can't promise any rain, but I can assure you there will be no dough-kneading involved. I wondered if you would care to serve as my escort?"

"Why, I'd love to, Mr. Garvin," she said, trying to keep from smiling too much.

"Perfect! May I send my driver on Saturday, around 7 o'clock, to take you to the Grand Billings Hotel Ballroom, where the Cincinnati Legal League dinner will be held?"

"I will be ready and waiting," Anna said.

"And should my driver pick you up from here?"

"No – thank you. Please send your driver to my house,

at 13 Linwood Lane."

"Till then," Martin said, and took her flour-dusted hand and kissed it.

Anna felt lightheaded, and she knew it couldn't be blamed on the heat from the ovens. She watched Martin leave the shop, climb into a large barouche, and drive away.

M artin left his father's study, shaking with apprehension, remembering the awkwardness of the ball; how Anna had blushed painfully several times when she had misunderstood or been put on the spot, and the looks he had seen some of the women exchange about her. He had thought at the time that she could learn to fit in, but now...

And then there were the dinners at their home. No matter how sweet and lovely Anna had always been, his parents had never warmed to her, simply because of the status of her family.

His father was right. It wasn't fair to put her through all it would take for her to become accepted by their circles.

Unbidden, her image came into his mind. He loved how Anna's brown hair curled into tendrils framing her face in the summer humidity. He smiled, thinking of how often she would grab an unruly tress and tuck it behind her ear, frustrated it would not obey...

The smile faded as he thought of what he had to do. He felt as if he was heading for his ultimate doom, but his father, in all of his persistence, had succeeded.

Thus convinced, he made his way to the large foyer and had Davis, the butler, call for his carriage. As it arrived at the front steps, Martin gathered his jacket, hat, and gloves and left for Anna's home.

They traveled from the large manor Martin still shared with his mother and father, through the tall, wrought-iron gate emblazoned with a large "G." They coursed through Johnson Heights out into the town and passed the building where Martin would soon join the ranks of the associates. The horses' hooves clopped on the cobblestones in a cadence, which drummed out his father's words: *Get it done... Get it done... Get it done!* It was Wilson Garvin's mantra, used whenever he felt his son needed coercion to complete a task.

The carriage entered Gateswood, a middle-class neighborhood lined by tall, stately elm and birch trees. The avenue held modest two- and three-storey homes, the dwellings of men of reputable nature, albeit not high class.

On Linwood Lane, Martin instructed the driver to stop in front of Anna's home. He paused, remembering how often the Collinses had greeted him as a member of their family. They were kind people of great integrity, though they were not fortunate enough to be of the same class as his parents. He sighed, stepped out of the carriage, walked up the path, and climbed the familiar steps leading up to the wide porch. He knocked and politely waited for an answer, his stomach turning knots at the thought of what he was about to do.

Mr. Collins opened the door. "Ah, Martin! Come in, come in, my boy." He shook Martin's hand and ushered him into the foyer. "Please have a seat in the parlor. I'll tell Anna you're here."

Mr. Collins loped up the stairs and left Martin alone in the small, modestly decorated front room. He sat stiffly on the small, high-backed sofa. The rigid cushions made it much harder than the one in his own home, and that, coupled with his nervous and jittery legs, convinced him to stand once again. He positioned himself before the window and tried to gather his resolve. He looked around and caught sight of the heavy velvet drapes, faded from the sunlight. Worn carpet covered the floor beneath the well-used wingback chairs posed beside the fireplace, with ecru doilies on their backs; his mother abhorred such home-spun decorations, called them 'peasant's lace.' He grew uncomfortable in the room, and he was surprised to discover that he had not taken notice of the shabby décor before.

"Martin! I'm so glad to see you!" Anna ran into the room and took his hands. "I missed you." She turned her face up to him, expecting a kiss, then realized he was standing in the same rigid manner as he had at her graduation ceremony. His hands even felt stiff in hers. She stepped back, uncertain.

"Could we talk somewhere – privately?" he asked.

"Martin, there's no-one here but us. Father left to pick up Aunt Maggie and Mother from the flower shop, and

Caleb is visiting a friend. What is it"

"So we're alone. Good, good. Anna –" he started, then faltered. With a deep sigh, he blurted out the words: "Anna, I'm concerned about our future." He took her hand, led her to the sofa, and sat beside her. He looked down at their hands, hers so small within his. "I think it best that we postpone the wedding. With my job at MacGregor and Jameson I feel it is better if we –"

"What? Postpone the wedding? What do you mean?" Anna interrupted, staring at him in disbelief. "Why? Has something happened? Have I done something wrong?"

"No, nothing has happened, and you most certainly have done nothing wrong. Please just hear me out. I know this may seem... well, sudden to you, but it's been on my mind for a while." He breathed deeply. "I think it would be unfair to you – to us, as a new couple – to be hampered by my long work hours as I endeavor to become established at the firm. It will take a great deal of my time to make the right contacts, keep the appointments, study the cases I'll be given, and –"

"Are you sure I have done nothing to offend you?" she asked, stunned.

"No, I just –"

Anna felt her heart thudding in her throat. "Martin, everything is already planned! I have my dress, the brides-maids' gowns, the flowers and cake – all ordered and deposits paid." She shook her head. "No! I – I just – I don't understand. Why would you want to wait? Don't you love me anymore? Have you found another woman to love? Tell me the truth, Martin!"

"Another woman? Don't be ridiculous, Anna! It's simply as I said. I believe it would be best for me – for us – to wait until I'm settled in my career. It will just be easier for every-one if... well, it will take the pressure off." He stood and walked to the window, leaving Anna alone on the uncom-fortable sofa.

"Pressure? Off whom? Off you? You think our being married and you working at the firm will be too much pressure?" she asked, astonished and hurt that he would consider her a source of stress. Her panic made her desper-ate. "If that is the case, Martin, then don't take the position at MacGregor and Jameson! There are other jobs you can do that will not require such long hours, surely there are!"

He gestured impatiently at the absurdity of her remark. Just as his father suspected, she was truly naïve about such things. "I have signed a contract with the firm, and it cannot be broken," he said, emphasizing each word.

"Contract? Our engagement is a contract with *me*." Anna stood, walked to the window, and faced him. "You said we would be married, that you love me, that you want to be with me forever! What of *those* promises?" She walked away from him and sat in the wingback chair, the doily creating a halo behind her dark hair. "This cannot be happening!" She closed her eyes. "Martin, I – I *want* to be your wife! I want it more than anything in the world" And finally, Anna placed her face in her hands and sobbed.

Martin remained at the window and did not move to comfort her. "Anna, this delay does not mean we can never marry – only that we must wait a while." He paused. "I do not mean to hurt you, but I have thought much about this, and I think it would be best for – for *both* of us – if we postpone our union."

Anna raised her head from her hands. Her face was red and streaked with tears. Suddenly, she was angry. "Fine. FINE! I wouldn't want to be the cause of *you* being overworked and put you under extra strain by forcing you to be married to *me*. Oh, no. No! That would be too much for you to bear!" She stood, ran out of the parlor, and shouted back at Martin as she started up the stairs: "Please just leave! Go and take care of your precious career!"

And with that, Anna was gone, leaving him to drown in a well of silence. Moments later, upstairs, a door slammed.

Martin let out the breath that he discovered he had been holding. He picked up his hat and left the house. "Take me to MacGregor and Jameson," he instructed Johnson, his driver, as he climbed into the waiting carriage.

He took one last look at the house where Anna lived, turned his head, and said through gritted teeth, "There, Father. Are you happy now? I got it done."

Anna watched him go from her bedroom window, then stumbled backward, fell upon her bed, and wailed.

When she raised her head she could see the bag that held her wedding gown. Her veil sat in a box on top of her bureau. Just today, her mother had paid for the flowers and checked with the caterer. They had settled on the dark blue decorations.

She put her head back down on the bed. Overwhelming sorrow overtook her. *What will happen now? Mother and Father spent much of their savings on the wedding! We reserved the church and the hotel ballroom several months ago!*

Martin had insisted that the palatial Grand Billings Hotel was the only proper site for their wedding reception. Anna knew his aristocratic parents were the reason for his decision; she imagined they feared it would be held in a saloon had they not suggested an appropriate venue!

Tears of sorrow turned into sniffles as she finally fell asleep. If she cried forever it wouldn't rid her soul of the rejection and misery within.

S tirred from sleep by footsteps upon the stairs, Anna awoke, raised her head, and remembered what she'd just dreamt.

She and Martin were standing before the minister in a church as he pronounced them man and wife. Martin laughed, and continued to laugh. His parents laughed. The whole audience of guests, her family and friends, all fell into great spasms of laughter. She ran from Martin and the minister, down the aisle, seeing the faces of those she considered her closest friends. They looked at her with pity. *"Poor, poor Anna,"* they said. *"Left at the altar. Now no-one wants her!"* Anna ran out of the church, and at that moment was mercifully wakened.

She heard a knock at her door.

"Anna? Anna, are you asleep?" her mother asked. "I found the most darling shoes for your trousseau. May I come in and show you?"

"Mother!" Anna immediately began crying again. She crawled off the bed, opened the door, and fell into her mother's arms.

"Dear, what *is* wrong? Are you ill?" her mother asked in alarm as she led Anna back to sit on the bed.

"Martin d-doesn't want to m-m-marry me!" Anna gulped, and collapsed once more into racking sobs.

"What are you talking about?" Bewildered, Mrs. Collins brushed the wet hair out of Anna's eyes. "He said he wouldn't marry you? When did he tell you this?"

"He – he came by this – this morning and he – he said he worried that being m-married and w-working at the firm would be too – too difficult on our marriage. H-he said it would be unfair to me, and t-too much pressure on – *on him!*" She snatched a handkerchief off the bed, dabbed the fresh tears from her face, and wiped her running nose.

"No! I can't believe he'd be so cruel and heartless!" Anna's mother was horrified. "Perhaps... did he discover that the firm doesn't allow junior associates to be married? Why else would he change his mind this late?"

"No, no – he said it would be too stressful for him to be married while trying to become successful at the firm. He made it sound as if I would create a burden for him!"

"Oh darling, I'm sorry!" She embraced her daughter. "I would never have expected such behavior from him." Mrs. Collins shook her head angrily.

"What of the money we've spent – your savings? It's all lost!" And she wept fresh tears.

"Oh honey, don't worry over the money. That isn't important now. We'll find out what Martin was thinking. Something *must* have happened to cause this! Perhaps – perhaps he's ill, and wants to spare you from some catastrophe that has come upon him!" she said with sudden inspiration.

"I don't think him so gallant," Anna said bitterly.

Her mother sighed as she held her broken-hearted daughter. "What can I do to make you feel better?"

"Just... hold me. Hold me and tell me you love me, and always will!"

"You know I do, Anna, you know I always will. And so does your father, and Caleb. We will always be here for you."

But it was the thought of the one who would be there no longer for her that made her inconsolable, and both women knew it.

Chapter 4

The sun rose and lay down, as it had for centuries. Anna thought it bad mannered of the world to maintain its course. It should stop ; the moon and stars should dim and the skies darken and become heavy, burdened with low, waterlogged clouds, as waterlogged as she herself felt. The Ohio River ought to honor her sorrow and halt its flow. Birds should dare not sing!

But if the world felt her distress, it did not let Anna know.

Her parents canceled the wedding with Reverend Flaherity, who was shocked that such a lovely girl as Anna had suffered such treatment. They released the caterer, florist, and ballroom of their obligations. Anna's dress had been altered, and could not be returned. Mrs. Collins and Maggie thought that with a little handwork and dye it could be made into a charming evening dress, although they doubted Anna would ever tolerate wearing it again.

Martin's parents sent a succinct, businesslike note by post and enclosed a check 'for any financial losses incurred'. Anna knew it far exceeded her parents' expenditures, but it could never compensate for the emotional damage caused by Martin's betrayal.

One morning, sitting in the breakfast room, Anna's parents ate in virtual silence.

"Ethan," Mrs. Collins said suddenly, thinking to disperse the cloud of sorrow around them, "we should take Anna somewhere on – well, what would have been her wedding day. If it were me, and you broke our engagement, I wouldn't want to be near the church, or even in the same town, on that day."

"I suppose you're right." Mr. Collins swirled the coffee in his rose-covered china cup. "What do you have in mind?"

"Well..." She thought for a moment. "Let's all go to Montgomery and spend time with your sister and family on the farm. I'll send a note today and tell her to expect us next week. Your mother and father had already planned to close the bakery for a few days off. They could join us, too. It would be good if we spent time together, and it would help take Anna's mind off her circumstances."

"Good idea, my dear." Mr. Collins reached over and took his wife's hand. "The past two weeks have been very trying for us all." He leaned over the table and gave his wife a tender kiss.

"Ooh! You're always kissing!" Caleb feigned a retching attack as he entered the room.

"You're just jealous," Mr. Collins said to his theatrical son. "You secretly *want* a girlfriend who'll adore you."

Caleb pulled out a chair and sat at the table. "Oh, no, Father. Girls are too strange." When he noticed the pointed silence, he stuttered hastily: "Well, except for Mother of course... and Aunt Maggie, and I guess Anna..."

His parents laughed as he backtracked. "Don't worry, son." Mr. Collins bent over and whispered loudly into Caleb's ear, "It's our little secret, but women *are* perplexing." He winked at his wife, who smiled serenely back as though she hadn't heard.

Caleb grew quiet as he poured juice from the pitcher into his glass. "Why *did* Martin change his mind about marrying Anna? I know she's one of those 'perplexing' creatures, but he did want to marry her at first. He proposed to her, didn't he?" Mr. Collins raised his eyebrows and shook his head. "Yes, he did. We aren't sure why he changed his mind. I believe he is worried they will grow apart and that she would be lonely and upset with him because he will have to put in so many long hours at the law firm." Mr. Collins sighed. "I imagine if that is true, then it's best for Anna to not endure such agony."

"She's in agony now, Papa," Caleb said, looking over the

breakfast at his father. "I hear her crying every night. How can Martin even think that breaking off the wedding would be any kind of a relief to her? I know I am not a man yet, but it seems to me that he's doing something very foolish, even though he's grown."

Mr. Collins smiled at his son. "I'm a bit confused about that too, m'boy."

"Will Anna ever be happy again?" Caleb asked.

Mrs. Collins got up from the table. "It will take a while, honey, but your father and I are sure she'll be herself again in time. We must be patient and understanding and try to help her keep her mind off the wedding." She poured more tea into her cup and returned to her seat. "We have discussed going to Aunt Ethel and Uncle Arlis's next week. Maybe the trip, along with preparing for her teaching position at the academy, will focus her attention on something other than her heartbreak and disappointment."

"I think she'll be a great teacher," Caleb said, reaching for the breakfast platter. With an exaggerated sigh, he looked at the flat biscuits. "I *really* miss those fluffy biscuits, Mother."

He ducked as the napkin tossed by his mother just missed him and landed on the floor.

Anna didn't come down for breakfast or for lunch. Worried for her daughter, Mrs. Collins climbed the stairs, knocked on Anna's bedroom door, and waited for a response. Footsteps could be heard in the room, as well as a drawer being closed, before the door was opened. "Anna, dear, I thought you might like to come down to have tea with us."

"Thank you, Mother, but I'm not hungry. I'm cleaning my room, getting rid of some of the garbage I've collected," Anna said with a sob.

"I'm sorry, honey. I know this isn't easy for you."

"Oh, I'll be fine once I get rid of a few things," Anna sniffled. "Really, I'll be better. Soon."

"If your father and I can do anything to help, please let us know."

"You've all been wonderful – supportive and kind and I appreciate that you have not been prying into my affairs.

But then again, your kindness has just made me feel worse, I suppose."

"Oh? Dear, I'm afraid I don't understand. How could our kindness make you feel worse?"

"Well, Mother, it is the fact that I *need* pity and kindness. It's just – just shameful and pathetic," Anna said. "I have determined that I'll allow myself one last day of lamentation, and then I'll rise up from the ashes and go on. I cannot allow this – or Martin – to destroy the rest of my life."

Her mother bit her lip. "I would never consider your life a pile of ashes, dear."

"Well, perhaps you wouldn't, Mother, but that is how I feel about it. My dreams just burst into flames, and all that is left is smoldering dust and debris." Anna sat down on the bed. "Still, I'll be like the phoenix. I will rise up from my death!" she exaggerated, flailing her arms dramatically like the mythical bird of fire.

"It reminds me of someone from the Bible," Mrs. Collins said. "He had all his dreams – and even his family – taken from him, but he also rose from the ashes."

"And who was that, Mother?"

"Job."

"Oh, yes. Job. I remember that story."

"Even though he lost everything, including everyone he loved, he still believed and knew that God was in control. He still worshipped God, no matter what. I think you might give Job's method a try." Mrs. Collins touched her daughter's hand. "God still loves you, dear, and He thinks you a worthy bride, you know."

Anna sighed. "I *have* prayed. At first, I asked God for retribution and revenge upon Martin, but then I was convicted about such a vengeful, hateful attitude. Maybe it was God, or maybe it was just fatigue, but I wondered what would have happened if I *had* married Martin and it turned out as he feared. It is far better to be disappointed now than to break commitments later, after a marriage before God and man."

"You're quite right. Although we'd rather never suffer disappointment or setback, we can always be assured that God has a plan for us. He can change even the most dire or upsetting of situations into positive results."

Anna sighed. "Well, I cannot imagine this ever turning out for the best." She paused. "I think I *will* come down for tea, Mother." She gasped as she spied herself in the round mirror over her vanity bureau. "Oh dear! First I must mend my hair and my face! I am nowhere near presentable, even for Daddy and Caleb."

"Wonderful! We have blueberry scones." Mrs. Collins paused and noticed her daughter's arched brow. "Oh, please don't fret, dear. I didn't bake them. Your grandmother dropped them off this morning on her way home from the bakery."

As she closed the door behind her, Anna giggled.

She didn't see her mother look upward and whisper, "Thank you for small blessings, Lord."

The next morning, Anna descended the stairs dressed in a blue day gown edged with lace along the high neckline and around the cuffs of the three-quarter sleeves. Her hair was neatly pinned, and her clothes crisply pressed, which accounted for the fresh, bright red blister on her index finger. Her walking boots shone and her stockings were freshly laundered.

"Would you like breakfast, dear?" Mrs. Collins asked.

"Thank you, Mother, but I already had a biscuit and coffee earlier. Right now, I am off to Barton to meet with Mr. Cavendish to discuss my plans for the upcoming term. I want to enter the semester and my new position confident and with a well-thought-out curriculum. I am determined not to allow anyone to claim that I am inexperienced."

"Anna, anyone who's known you even for a little while – including Mr. Cavendish – will know you've already planned your lessons for the whole year." Her mother chuckled. "Nevertheless, your father is going into town soon to pick up a few staples at the market. Maybe you can catch a ride with him." Mrs. Collins removed the dishes from the table and took them to the kitchen to place them into the deep sink basin for washing. "Hurry out back to find him, dear, and you may catch him before he leaves."

Anna scurried from the kitchen, and burst through the screen door, allowing it to slam shut behind her. She moved hurriedly down the walkway, her eyes darting to and fro, on her way to check the stable. The carriage and Gerty, the pert gray mare, were gone. *Well, I suppose a stroll in the fresh air will do me good anyway,* she reasoned and walked back into the house. "I missed him, Mother, so I'll just walk." Anna picked up her parasol and gloves and kissed her mother's cheek. "Maybe I'll find Father in town. Have a good morning."

"You too... and be careful, dear!"

With an air of confidence, Anna sauntered down the porch steps and off towards the downtown area, where the academy was located. The cool morning air rustled the leaves, and the accompanying melodies of a few meadowlarks enhanced the beautiful day. Children chased each other through the lawns of the homes along the lane. The sunlight, filtering through the boughs of the tall oak trees along Linwood Avenue dappled the ground beneath. As Anna made her way out of the neighborhood, she crossed to 38th Street.

"Good morning!" Marshall Avery called, waving. "It's nice to see you, Miss Anna." He propped the broom against the wall of his grocery store and stepped over to meet her, smiling broadly.

"How is Mrs. Avery?" asked Anna. "I heard she has been under the weather."

"Well, she's finally on the mend. I keep telling her she's too old to try and keep up with the young'ns, but you know how stubborn she is. She won't hear of slowing down. Says those grandbabies aren't going to remember their grandmother sittin' around and rockin' her life away. And, bless her heart, those little ones do adore her."

"She is a feisty one." Anna laughed, remembering the many times when she and Caleb had played hide-and-seek with Mrs. Avery and her children. "No-one would ever think of her sitting around."

He shook his head. "I told her that the next time she falls, she might break something, and then I'll have to wait on her hand and foot and the grocery will go to pot."

"And what did Mrs. Avery say to that?"

He laughed. "She said she knows there is no way she'll

ever come between me and my store!"

Anna giggled at the man. "In any regard, please give her my love and wish her a quick recovery." And with that, she left Mr. Avery sweeping the walkway.

Several minutes later, Anna rounded the corner of Main Avenue and spotted Mrs. Godfrey outside the millinery shop, her nose pressed against the window, gazing at the display of new autumn hat designs, squinting to catch a glimpse of the price tags.

When Mrs. Godfrey heard Anna's footsteps on the walkway, she leaned back from the glass. "Anna Collins! Why, precious, it's wonderful to have you back. You are even lovelier than the last time I saw you," the little woman said, hugging Anna warmly.

"Thank you. You're looking well yourself, ma'am. Looking for a new hat?" Anna asked. She couldn't remember ever seeing Mrs. Godfrey without a hat of some kind perched atop her curly gray hair; she even wondered if the woman slept in one, and the vision of such a thing threatened the escape of a private giggle.

"My, yes. Just look at these adorable creations," she said, gesturing toward the window. "Unfortunately, I'm afraid the prices are a bit outlandish. Of course, we cannot expect a hat fashioned in Paris to be as inexpensive as the plain old ones from New York, now can we?"

"Yes, I suppose that makes sense. The plum feathered one on the right is very attractive."

"Of course! You have good taste, my dear, for that one caught my eye right off." Mrs. Godfrey squished her face against the window again. "Do you think it too ostentatious for the First Church's annual bazaar next week?"

"Not at all, Mrs. Godfrey. In fact, I think it would look wonderful with your coloring."

"Dear, you should work here," she said, flattering Anna in spite of the fact that she'd decided upon the plum number before the girl even approached.

"Oh, but Mrs. Godfrey, I'm teaching at Barton Academy next term, so I'm afraid I won't have time to help you choose a hat after September."

Mrs. Godfrey wiped the dust off her nose after her intimate contact with the storefront window. "Barton, you say?

Marvelous!" she exclaimed. "I am sure you'll make a fine teacher. Why, when you were in my Sunday school class, I was tempted to let you take over. I could just sit back and have a little catnap! You were always prepared, always knew your memory verses, the lesson, and scriptures backwards and forwards." She sighed. "But I suppose Reverend Flaherity might have frowned on that!" She laughed. "Well, I'm going in to purchase that divine chapeau. Good luck with the new position, dearest."

"Thanks, Mrs. Godfrey. It was good seeing you again, and I'll see you next Sunday."

Anna continued along the cobblestone walkway, her boots making a steady *clip-clop* against every brick. She turned east and ascended the steps of the Greek-style portico of Barton Academy. At the top of the steps, she closed her parasol, smoothed her dress, checked her hair in the reflection of the door window, and pulled the heavy door open to enter the massive marbled foyer.

She inhaled the cool air, scented with the smell of ancient books – an odor she recalled from the old library downtown. Turning left, she walked to the headmaster's office.

The large, dour lady behind the desk looked up and eyed Anna over her glasses, which seemed to be rather precariously perched on the pointy tip of her pencil-thin nose. "May I help you?" she asked in a pinched-off, nasal tone, the result of the compression from the glasses.

"Yes, I do hope so. I am Anna Collins. I am scheduled to teach next term, and I am here to speak with Mr. Cavendish regarding my assignment."

The bespectacled secretary inhaled slowly through her obstructed nostrils. "Let me check." She pointed at the wooden settee across from her desk. "In the meantime, please have a seat."

In quick obedience, Anna stepped to the seat, moved her skirt behind her, and sat down. She placed the parasol on her lap, adjusted her skirt, and smoothed it over her boots.

Shocked at how much dust they had collected during her walk, she rubbed the tops of each boot on the back of her hosed legs.

The swishing of Mr. Cavendish's corduroy trousers

heralded his arrival. "Miss Collins? Um... this is a surprise," the tall, mustached man uttered before he'd barely stepped inside the door of the room. "Come on into my office." He stepped out into the hallway and led Anna to the small office. The room was painted in a pea-green color, and the walls were adorned with a variety of immaculately framed diplomas and certificates. Mr. Cavendish sat at the table, which Anna assumed to be a desk, hidden successfully beneath tentative piles of papers and books. "Please, Miss Collins, have a seat there."

As she sat in the large leather chair, it emitted an embarrassing squeal, as if it was none too happy to support her small frame. Anna felt the heat of color rising in her cheeks, and she wondered if the usual scarlet shade she deplored now mottled her neck as well. *How utterly embarrassing,* she scolded herself.

"What can I do for you today, miss?" he asked as he drummed his long fingers against one another in a tent shape in front of his face.

"I am here for some information about my teaching assignment for the upcoming term, Mr. Cavendish. I like to be well prepared, and I have planned my lessons, so I would like to talk to you about –" Anna began excitedly.

"Well, uh – ahem..." Mr. Cavendish interrupted, clearing his throat and holding a hand up to stop her. "It's a good thing you dropped by." Mr. Cavendish played with the end of his squared chin. "There've been some, uh – some recent developments that you should be made aware of. I'm afraid our enrollment numbers shall not be as high as we initially anticipated."

"So does that mean I will be teaching smaller classes? That is not a problem, sir. In fact, it is sometimes easier if the student-to-teacher ratio is –"

Again, he held up his hand to stop Anna. "I'm afraid this has led to a decreased need for teachers." He looked at the desk as he massaged his chin; clearly, the news was difficult for him to break with her while making eye contact. As stern as he was, the headmaster was not keen on dashing anyone's hopes and plans.

Anna held her breath.

After a strident inhalation, he continued. "Miss Collins,

to be blunt and frank about the matter, I must inform you that our administrator has informed us that Barton will not engage new educators this year. I am so sorry, but I was just informed yesterday of this decision, and I planned to write a note for you this afternoon, but then you showed up here just now and –"

He had spoken the words that would shatter Anna's future, even more so than Martin's cruel tirade, and this time it was Anna's turn to hold up her hand and interrupt. "Mr. Cavendish, are you telling me I will not have a position here when the school term begins?"

The headmaster nodded grimly, wincing. "I am so sorry, Miss Collins, especially after you have poured so much time and energy into your commendable preparations."

"Sir, with all due respect, when I spoke with you during spring break, you assured me I had secured a teaching position at this school for the upcoming term." She felt her pulse quicken. "I was counting on this job." Anna's heart began to thump hard, to the point where it resounded in her ears. "I – I'm afraid I just don't understand." Her mind raced to find the reason for the change in plans, even though he'd already explained it. "My marks were excellent, Mr. Cavendish. As far as I know, all of my professors held my teaching ability in high regard. Why, sir, I was even able to –"

"I am truly sorry, miss, but please know this is by no means a reflection of your abilities. You cannot take it personally, as it is an executive decision." He looked over the desk at her. "I'm sure this, along with your broken engagement, may seem a bit disheartening, but let me encourage you to –"

"Excuse me? How did you know of my engagement being postponed? It happened only very recently."

"Ah, well... the head of our administration here at Barton is your fiancé's – er – your *former* fiancé's father, Mr. Garvin."

Anna felt the blood drain from her face. "An *executive* decision, Mr Cavendish? I *knew* of Mr. Garvin's involvement with the school administration here in Cincinnati, but I was not aware that he oversees Barton Academy. Did he file some kind of grievance or complaint against me?

It wasn't *my* idea to postpone our marriage, if that is the problem?"

"No, Miss Collins. It is a case of simple logistics and economy. As I said, it's nothing personal. We simply do not have need of additional faculty when we have less students to educate here." He stood and signaled the end of their conversation – the end of yet another of Anna's dreams. "I am afraid I must leave you now to attend a meeting," he said as he led Anna out of his office and back into the hallway of the school.

Anna looked around, mystified and stunned at the turn of events.

"Miss Collins, with your impeccable references and your high marks in your classes at Oberlin, I'm confident you'll have no trouble finding employment elsewhere. Good day," he said. Then he turned on his heel and walked back to his office, closing the door and leaving Anna standing alone in the hall.

She shook with fear; within her being a burgeoning anger boiled. She stomped down the hallway to the foyer. Tears accompanied her trembling, and great sobs burst from her as she stepped into the bright sunlight outside the academy. She fumbled with her parasol and finally opened it; she was more concerned about shielding her dismay from others' questioning glances than shielding her eyes from the sun. Blinded by the tears and distress, she grabbed for the handrail, felt her way down the steps, and at last reached the sidewalk.

"Martin!" she said aloud. "*You* did this. How could you?"

Chapter 5

With her gloved hands, Anna wiped her face and tromped down the street towards the law firm of MacGregor and Jameson. She was astounded that Martin had the audacity to not only smash her dream of being married, but also her dream of becoming a teacher. His cruel antics both grieved and infuriated Anna. Bolstered by anger, she was determined to stand up to Martin. *How could he be so cruel? Why would it matter to him if I teach at Barton, especially now that he has let me go?*

Anna climbed the four steps up to the entrance of the three-storey brown brick building in which the firm was located. In cruel mockery, it sat across from the very boutique store where she had purchased her wedding gown. The heavy door was decorated with a fancy leaded glass inset engraved with 'MacGregor, Jameson, Morgan, & Abbott Law Firm'.

A tinkling brass bell announced her arrival as she opened the door.

The assistant looked up and arched an eyebrow at her. "May I help you?"

"Martin Garvin, please. I wish to speak to him this very moment."

"Do you have an appointment, miss?"

"No, I do NOT have an appointment. Just tell him Anna is here to speak with him... NOW!" Anna enunciated the words to prevent the woman from misunderstanding.

"I'll have to check. He may not be available."

"Fine, check, but know that I refuse to leave until I have

had a word with him."

"And you are?"

"As I told you, Anna – Miss Anna Collins. Trust me when I say he will recognize my name."

The secretary rose from her station and motioned her to the waiting area. "Please have a seat, Miss Collins," she directed before she exited the office.

Anna's hands shook, her fingers tingled, and she worried that her legs might not cooperate when she stood to meet with Martin. Gazing at the attractive secretary, Anna toyed with the idea that perhaps *she* was the reason Martin had changed his mind. The lady seemed older, appeared very confident, and her red hair afforded her an exotic look – one Anna decided Martin might have found more interesting than her common, boring, dark acorn hair.

The secretary seemed to sashay back into the waiting area. "Mr. Garvin says he has five minutes to spare. Please follow me."

Anna followed the woman down the hallway, which was decorated with portraitures of the law firm founders and a few large hunting scenes encased in garish golden frames. At the door emblazoned in gold with, 'Martin Garvin, Attorney at Law' the lady knocked.

"Come in!" Anna heard through the door.

"Five minutes only, Miss Collins," warned the exotic, flame-haired, man-stealing secretary as she opened the door.

When she stepped into the room, Anna's stomach turned, particularly when she caught sight of Martin, dressed in a dashing gray woolen suit and standing behind a massive cherry desk. Along a wall stood a large bookcase, filled with impressive volumes of law statutes. The collection of watches she'd helped Martin complete was perched atop the shelf.

"I have only a few minutes. What do you want?" Martin asked, betraying no emotion whatsoever.

"I lost my teaching position at the academy. Mr. Cavendish said your father is the administrator who decided my position was no longer needed." Anna stopped to take a breath and steady her voice.

"Really? I had no knowledge that Barton would be eliminating positions."

"Martin, please tell me your cruelty has not extended to snuffing out my future career. Did you tell your father not to hire me just so you would not have to see me anymore?"

"Anna, please," Martin said, as if she was some petulant child who was being ridiculous. "Why would I care if you teach at Barton – or anywhere else, for that matter?"

"It doesn't appear to be a coincidence. Your father decided they didn't need a new teacher, and that teacher just so happened to be me, your former fiancée!" She looked at Martin with a fury she'd never felt before. "Did you ask him to get rid of me?"

Martin threw his hands in the air. "That's ludicrous, Anna!"

"I would have thought the same before, but now? Now I'm not sure I ever knew you at all. How could you be so mean, so spiteful? What did I do to deserve such hatred and contempt from you?" She tried to stop the tears from falling, but it proved to be a futile effort. "Did you ever really love me at all, Martin? And if you did, tell me what happened. What did I do wrong, Martin? Why did you stop loving me?" Anna walked over to him.

He backed away from her, skirted around the desk, and stood behind it to place room between them.

"I deserve the truth, Martin. Please tell me what happened."

Her eyes bored into his; those green orbs that had mesmerized her before now seemed cold in their sockets. "You want to know the truth? Fine. If it hadn't been for my good word to my father, you would never have been offered a teaching position in the first place. I begged him to take you under his employment." He moved towards the door, as if to dismiss her now that the fatal wound had been administered.

The words sank in, and Anna felt the room tilt and spin. "What? You had to beg that man to let me teach? Is that what you're saying?"

"Yes. I'm sorry to have to tell you this, Anna, but believe it or not, not all institutions are convinced that a woman is capable of educating the fine students of our day."

She rolled her eyes. "Martin, you know as well as I do

that I received a superior education. I achieved excellent marks in classes taught by very prestigious professors. I also have a deep-rooted passion for education. What more do they require?"

A knock interrupted her, and Martin opened the door.

"Mr. Garvin, your 11:30 appointment is here."

"Thank you, Miss Swartz. I'm nearly finished." He shut the door and faced Anna. "Maybe it was that you didn't fit the administration's ideal for the, uh, *type* of teacher they want to employ in the academy. Perhaps they desire a more, shall we say, cultured, seasoned educator who can instill their students with fine manners and precepts."

"Cultured? Oh, I understand." Anna shook her head in disbelief at his harsh words. "I'm not cultured or refined enough, but a man such as Delbert Adams, who spits in a spittoon while giving instructions in Greek, is considered refined and cultured?"

"I'm afraid I can't help you. There are other, more suitable endeavors for women such as yourself to seek, and you should pursue –"

His words were cut off by Anna's angry outburst. "Women such as me?" She closed in on him until she was standing eye to eye. "Do you know what I think, Martin? I think you're a very foolish man!"

He backed up, stunned into silence for a moment before he stuttered defensively, "Women should... well, they should stay at home and take care of their husbands and children."

"Oh, really?"

Martin began to recover himself from her attack, and defend his corner. "Yes. A wife should support her husband's career instead of stepping into areas where she doesn't belong." A smug look emerged on his face. "To be truthful, I doubt you will ever find a teaching position without help from me or my father. You don't have what it takes, Anna. You never did."

Anna lowered her eyes, gathered her wits, and looked up at him. She had to accept that she really had never known the real Martin. The Martin she had fallen in love with was a fake. "I'm absolutely amazed," she said.

"About what?" he snapped.

"God's grace, His sovereignty. I now realize the grief and despair He really spared me from when you broke off our engagement, Martin. You are pathetically threatened by a woman like me – a woman who won't settle for being a doting, worshipping, dutiful wife. It's a pity you feel so insecure, Martin."

"Blah," Martin said as he snarled and waved his hand at her, dismissing her like a common housefly. "You flatter yourself. I'm not threatened by the likes of you, Anna. In fact, far from it." He walked to the desk, picked up a heavy volume, and slammed it on the desk. "The fact is, Anna, you would have been a hindrance to my career with this firm. It is best for me that we did not get married. Father, Mother, and everyone I know advised me as such in the beginning, but I chose not to listen. In the end, I realized they... well, they were right."

Martin ran out of steam then. His head hung, and he planted his palms firmly on his expensive-looking desk. In that moment, he appeared defeated, beaten down. "Just go, Anna. Go find a husband who'll love you for who you are and have a family with him. Please go," he muttered as he leaned on the desk.

Anna grabbed the back of the chair to steady herself and prevent the roaring in her ears from overwhelming her consciousness. Tears streaked down her cheeks and puddled in her neckline.

The door opened and Miss Swartz peeked in. "Mr. Garvin, your appointment is here, and –"

"I'm leaving. I will no longer detain your fine patrons," Anna said as she rushed past the secretary, with her head down and her shoulders slumped, out of the door and out of Martin's life forever. She fled the office, ran through the foyer where the 11:30 appointment waited, and jerked the door open. The momentum caused it to slam with a loud *bang* against the wall.

Anna hurled herself out the door, down the sidewalk, and towards 38th Street and her home. With her head still down, she let the tears fall unconstrained. Thoughts whirled inside her head, and she was still dizzy from the wrangling with Martin. She wasn't aware how long she had been walking until she looked up and found herself in front of her grandparents' bakery, now closed for the afternoon. Stumbling to the bench in front of the display window, she plopped down onto it and dissolved into throes of despairing sobs.

Anna wondered how a person's life could dissolve so completely in such little time. Earlier, she had gathered her resolve, and she was determined to complete her plans – without Martin. She had marched to the academy ready to plunge herself into her work, ready to be a successful, effective teacher. Now she sat by a deserted bakery, drowning in the shadows of despair and the ashes of her incinerated dreams.

"Job," she mumbled, recalling her mother's talk. "I'm just like Job!" Tears fell again as she was overtaken with fear that she might lose the one thing she still had – her family. "Please don't take them too," Anna prayed. "I – I couldn't bear it." She placed her face in her hands, wet with her tears. "I'm not holy like Job, God. My devotion would not run as deep as his. I simply couldn't take that kind of loss. Not after all this."

"Anna? Anna, what's wrong?"

She looked up and saw her father standing by the carriage in front of the bakery. "Oh, Papa! It's – it's just that he... they..." Anna couldn't finish her sentence.

Without saying a word, Mr. Collins hurried and knelt before his daughter, wrapped his arms around her, and let her cry.

Chapter 6

T he bumpy road jostled Anna to consciousness. She stretched as much as possible in the crowded carriage that was stuffed to the seams with Aunt Maggie's sewing notions, Caleb's fishing equipment, and gifts for the relatives.

"You're awake!" Mrs. Collins reached over and swept a strand of hair from Anna's face. "Are you feeling well, dear? You seemed to sleep quite soundly, for a while."

Anna groaned. "I'm fine," she said and continued to stretch, "but I am stiff and very thirsty. I think the sleeping medication Dr. Benton prescribed makes me thirstier than usual." She yawned.

"I imagine anyone would be thirsty after a five-hour nap," Mr. Collins said. He reached into the bag of food that they had prepared for the travel and retrieved the canteen and gave it to Anna. "I wondered if we should wake you."

"Father, are we close yet?" Caleb whined.

Mr. Collins pulled his gold pocket watch from his blue pinstriped vest and looked at it. "Hmm. Seems we'll arrive in about forty minutes," he said. "The driver has made good time."

"Good. I'm so bored." Caleb looked at Anna. "You should be glad you were asleep this whole time. I wanted to sleep, but your snoring kept me awake."

Anna swatted him playfully. "Ladies do not snore, Caleb. We *purr*."

"Oh, dear sister, if that was a purr, you must be very a large cat."

Anna rolled her eyes, wrinkled her forehead, and pointed her finger at him. "Just wait until we're free of the confines of this cramped carriage, Caleb Collins, and I shall pounce on you like the biggest of jungle cats!"

"Oh, look at the beautiful field of black-eyed Susans!" Aunt Maggie beamed, interrupting the sibling rivalry.

"They are so pretty," Mrs. Collins agreed

"A deer!" Caleb yelled.

"Please don't yell, son," his mother admonished. "Where do you see it?

"On the left side of the field of flowers. See?" He pointed just as the doe and a small fawn sprinted out of sight into a nearby grove of trees. "I've never seen a deer in the wild before." Caleb grinned with delight. "I guess it was a good thing Anna's snoring kept me awake, or I'd have missed it."

"Look – the sign for Montgomery. Thank goodness. It won't be much longer now," Mrs. Collins said. "I believe I'll have to walk for days to get my body out of this position."

Twenty minutes later, the carriage pulled into the Carson, Ohio Stage Depot on the south side of Montgomery. Mr. Collins's sister Ethel, and her husband Arlis, awaited them, waving excitedly as the family dismounted from the carriage. Many hugs, handshakes, and exclamations of amazing growth and outstanding beauty were exchanged.

"I am so glad you decided to visit, Prudence," Ethel said as she hugged her sister-in-law. "You arrived at the perfect time."

"How so?"

They walked to the carriage that was prepared to take them to the farm.

"The annual summer fair is this Wednesday, and the ladies in my quilting group just finished a large quilt," Ethel bragged. "May I add that one of my own creations – a work of art, if I do say so myself – will be auctioned off? I can't believe you'll be here for that. We'll have such fun, and..." She lowered her voice and whispered into Prudence's ear, "... we'll have plenty of diversions to keep Anna's mind off her troubles. Poor dear. How has she held up since all this trouble came upon her?"

"Well, of course there are moments when she is deeply distressed and miserable, but as of late, her mood seems to be better. I'm inclined to think it the work of the medicine the doctor gave to ease her insomnia rather than a true lessening of her sorrow," Mrs. Collins said.

Ethel shook her head. "It's a shame she was treated in such an abominable way."

"We're all shocked at Martin's removal of his affections and his father's involvement in her losing the teaching position."

"Such despicable behavior for grown men – for anyone, really," Ethel said.

"Well, we're here to take her mind off it all, and I am sure you and Arlis will be able to help with that."

"You have my word, Prudie. The subject won't be broached again."

The ladies climbed into the carriage, and the families headed for the farm.

Your bedrooms are upstairs," Ethel said to Mr. and Mrs. Collins and Anna. "Caleb, you can sleep in the third floor attic with Marcus and Eli." As they entered the white clapboard farmhouse, she continued, "Maggie, you may sleep in the guest porch behind the kitchen. That way we can talk without disturbing the others."

"That sounds great, Aunt Ethel!" Caleb said, thrilled to know he'd be sharing a room with his cousins, all while taking a break from the incriminating glare and constant rules cast upon him by his loving parents.

Anna entered the room where she was to stay; it was situated in a corner of the home. Several windows banked the light and airy room. The dotted Swiss curtains batted gracefully in the calm breeze. A quilt of blue cotton print and yellow gingham covered the high bed. She placed her hat on the tall bureau and gazed at her reflection in the mirror above it. "Gracious, what a mess," she scolded her reflection. Dark circles ringed her blue eyes, still puffy from all the crying spells.

Anna rearranged her hair and poured water from the pitcher into the basin. She washed her face, arms, and hands, and changed into a fresh dress. She pinched her cheeks to add color to her pale face. She couldn't help but smile when she heard the chatting, laughing, and childish giggles of Caleb and their cousins coming from the upper floor. From across the hall, where her parents were situated, Anna could hear her aunt's excited banter.

"You will find fresh water and soap and linens on the washstand. Just help yourself and take your time." Ethel chatted away all the while, puttering around the room and straightening things. "Dinner will be ready in about an hour. If you'd like to help, just come on down whenever you're ready, dear."

"We're so grateful for your hospitality, Ethel," Prudence said and hugged her. "I'll be right down to help."

"Fine, fine. Don't worry yourself. I'm used to solitude while preparing meals. It gives me a moment to reflect and concentrate. My, I get some wonderful sermons while chopping potatoes!" She giggled as she walked out the door. "As if I'd ever get to preach to anyone but Arlis."

"My sister can be a bit peculiar at times," Mr. Collins said closing the door behind Ethel

"She is a dear, sweet woman, Ethan. Still, to this day, you just haven't gotten over the fact that she can best you in a fight!" Prudence laughed as she poked her husband's chest.

"Woman, how dare you taunt me? I know it isn't proper to wallop a girl, and that's the only reason why my sister won so many fights!"

"Yes, dear. You are always a gentleman, even to your bossy sister."

"Flattery will get you nowhere now." He pretended to be hurt, but he failed to stifle the mischievous grin that crossed his face. "I'll brood for days now. You've ruined my fine mood."

"I am sure I can set your mood right." She kissed him. "Now go wash your dusty face!" While she changed clothes, Prudence thought of Anna and the grief that threatened to engulf her. "I'm worried for Anna."

"Dear, it'll take a while for her to recover from all that's happened," he said putting on a clean shirt. "The best thing we can do for our dear daughter is to give her time... and space."

"For one to have hopes dashed like that can lead to such despair. It saddens me to know that her heart has been broken."

"Let's give her a while longer before we consider her to be in real danger." He sat down on the bed.

"I know it hasn't been that long, and she does need to get through this week, but I know that if one has no plans or anything to look forward to – when hopes are dashed – they may wander aimlessly. You know our Anna. She has that penchant for organizing and planning. Sometimes people who've lost their focus follow the wrong people and make poor decisions, trying to fill the emptiness." She removed the dress from her bag and hung it in the wardrobe.

"Prudence..." Mr. Collins walked over to comfort his wife and placed his strong hands on her trembling shoulders. "Don't worry, love. I'm not afraid for Anna. I am sure our daughter is not the sort to surrender herself over to total despair and grief for the rest of her life. She must be made aware of and accept the fact that her steps are ordered by God. She's His child, and He cares far more for her wellbeing than even you and I are capable of."

She nodded and laid her head upon his chest.

"He leads us through difficult times, through valleys, and you and I both know that God is faithful to provide what we need to survive. Prudence, our Anna will recover and find someone to love her as she should be loved, as she deserves to be loved." He raised her head up and looked into her eyes. "We won't let her run off and become a saloon dancer. If it comes to that..." He paused and smiled. "If it comes to that, we'll set Ethel on her!" Ethan laughed.

Prudence just rolled her eyes and hugged him, grateful that she had a man in her life who could always cheer her up. "I'd better get downstairs and help your sister."

"Of course. And I'll hurry and rescue Arlis from the kitchen."

Anna?" her mother said, knocking on the door. "We're going down to help Ethel with dinner. Will you come along?"

Anna sighed and heaved herself off the bed, where she had been sitting since she'd changed her clothes. She opened the door and nodded. "I'd love to, Mother. Just let me put on my shoes." If Anna had truly had any choice in the matter, she would have preferred to sit there alone, rather than being forced into pleasant conversation over trivial matters. It seemed too much to endure at times – the loss of her plans and being coerced into obligatory behavior that she was not at all inclined to perform. Nevertheless, she put on her shoes and her best false smile, joined her mother, and decided she would try to survive another day of meaningless and futile polite conversation.

A t dinner, Anna quietly sat as she listened to stories of her father's childhood mishaps and scrapes with farm animals. She was thankful when the family retired early, for she was finally released from her duty of maintaining a pleasant façade. She trudged up the stairs and quickly got herself ready for the night. She crawled into the high bed, pulled the quilt over herself, rolled over, and wept into the fluffy, down-filled pillow, which managed to muffle her sobs very well.

A rooster crowed somewhere close by, very proud of his ability to warble without a break. With her senses dulled by the sleep medication, Anna felt as if the rooster was actually right there in her room. Another cacophonic shriek confirmed that it wasn't a dream; the annoying bird trumpeted atop the roof, very near the open window of her room. Although the medication helped her sleep, it failed to dull the sadness and heartache that were now her constant companions.

Sunrise crept along the side of the farmhouse and slowly peeked into Anna's room. If the rooster's strident call hadn't awakened her, the brightness of the dawning day alone would have been enough to demand her eyelids to open. Anna pulled the sheet over her head to block the sunlight's intrusion into her dark world. She wadded some of the sheet in front of her eyes, trying to fight off the brilliance. After several minutes of scrunching her eyes, she gave up. "Gracious!" Angrily, she set upright in bed. "Do country people never sleep late?"

She pattered over to the window to confront the offensive bird and the obtrusive sun. "I wish you two would go away and leave me alone. I'm tired, and I don't wish to be up yet. This was... it was to be my wedding day." Anna fell into a heap beneath the window and cried. "Can't you just leave me alone?" She sat on the cool wooden floor for several minutes and let the anger, sorrow, and rejection wash over her once again. Everyone had tiptoed around the fact that it would have been her wedding day. No-one had dared speak of it for fear that Anna would dissolve into a mass of quivering flesh, and that was exactly what she was doing.

Ethel planned for the family to join them at the annual summer fair that evening for the quilt auction, basket dinner, and dance. Knowing this, Anna sighed, closed her eyes, and tried to squelch the ever-present sorrow. She had decided she'd allow herself to cry only once a day but she'd been unable to follow the plan. With no other course set for her future, the scheme at least assigned her something to work towards. Still, even that small benchmark seemed outside her reach.

The aroma of fried bacon wafted up the stairs. In Anna's room, the yellow curtains flapped lazily in the cool breeze. Outside, birds twittered and chirped, and she heard her brother and his cousins running down from their third-floor bedroom and crowding into the hallway, eager to get downstairs to stuff their faces with bacon and anything else they could find. The boys whooped, yelled, and argued over who would catch the biggest fish later that day.

Anna rubbed her eyes with the front edge of her night-gown. She raised herself to look out the window and watched the boys run to the pond. She plopped back down below the windowsill and wept. It was inevitable that her mother would soon come knocking, requesting her to join the happy throng downstairs for breakfast. Again, she would be forced to talk about, think about, and discuss stupid things she cared nothing about.

"I must get up... but why? What have I to do besides prepare food and talk of quilts, chickens, and dried-up cows?" Her eyes stung with tears. "No – not again. I most certainly shall not subject myself to such torture."

Anna reached into her bag on the floor and removed her Bible. She turned to the bookmark placed at Jeremiah 28:19 and read: "I know the plans I have for you, for good and not of evil." Her mother and father had prayed and shared those scriptures with her after Martin so callously and selfishly broke off their engagement. The verse seemed to touch her the most, though, after she'd lost her job. Her parents encouraged her to believe that even though her dreams were nothing but rubble, God could and would still work things for her best – that what the enemy intended for harm, God would turn to good. She prayed every morning for strength and courage to face the day; that was her day-to-day survival method. She just had to get through one day and then start another.

She couldn't help thinking that it was completely unfair. Martin had gone on with his life. He had a job, a family, and a future, and she had been left with nothing. *Well, I suppose I cannot go that far,* she reasoned. *My family is a far better treasure than Martin's.*

At that thought, she became even angrier with him. *Why should I let that selfish, lying scoundrel taint my world another day? I won't! Today is the last day I shall allow Martin to ruin my life! I shall bid him farewell once and for all, along with all the heartache he and his nosey father have caused me,* Anna decided. *No more after today. Martin Garvin, no longer will you and your pompous family tinge my life with your loathsome, self-satisfied, sanctimonious, judgmental opinions.*

Anna raised herself again to the window and stuck her head out. "Do you hear me, Martin Garvin?" she yelled out to the livestock. "After today, I will no longer waste my time on one solitary thought of you. Never again will I expend one speck of energy on you. You are no longer a part of me, my thoughts, or my heart." With that declaration, Anna fell back into the room and laughed, freed from the burden of Martin's rejection.

She quieted her laughter when she heard her parents' door opening and closing across the hall. Anna imagined her parents, standing with ears stuck tightly against the door, straining to hear what she was doing.

She couldn't help but smile. *Now they know I'll be all right.*

Anna entered the dining room. "Good morning," she greeted her family.

Her father, Uncle Arlis, grandfather, and cousins stood. Mr. Collins flicked Caleb on the back of the head, and Caleb joined them like a proper gentleman.

"Good morning, sweetheart," Anna's grandfather said to her.

Her father scooted a chair out for his daughter and greeted her with a kiss on the cheek, a tender act that threatened to evoke tears from Anna.

"I'm sorry I'm late and didn't come down to help with breakfast."

"Oh, I had plenty of help, dear," Ethel said. "We enjoyed the stories Caleb shared with us about your journey here. Pass your sister the food, Caleb," she said. "We've already discussed our plans for the evening," she said with a gleam in her eye. "We need to travel to town between three and four o'clock this afternoon. I'm so excited you're all here with us for the summer fair!"

"What shall the proceeds of the auction be allotted to?" asked Mr. Collins.

"We hope to raise money for a mission school somewhere in Indian Territory. That's really all I know about it, other than the fact that *my* quilt will bring the highest bid, I'm sure." Ethel giggled like a schoolgirl.

"They're building additions to the school and need funds for the supplies," Arlis explained while passing a plate of eggs to Anna. "They say it's a great opportunity to reach the savages."

"Oh, yes," Ethel added. "One of the missionaries dispatched to the area will speak at the auction. I'm sure it will be interesting. After that, we'll hear the results of the quilt competition with the auction following. Then the basket dinner and afterwards there'll be a square dance."

"Oh no! A square dance? Ma, do we have to go?" whined Marcus and Eli in unison.

"Of course you do. It is intended to be a family outing, especially since all of our family is here visiting. We will go together, and I shall not listen to another peep from you two about it."

"Do we hafta dance with a girl?" Marcus asked in falsetto.

"No girl wants to touch you!" Eli said. "They'd probably rather dance with one of the goats because they smell better!"

Marcus scrunched up his brow and ducked as his brother hurled a buttery napkin at him.

"Boys, outside... NOW!" Arlis ordered. "And yes, both of you will dance like proper gentlemen with every girl at the party – twice if you don't behave." He followed the boys outside and left the family in an uncomfortable silence.

"Please forgive them. They're a little rowdy at times," Ethel said.

"Don't fret," Prudence said. "We're accustomed to children and their behavior. Don't forget we have a boy of our own," she said, casting a grin at Caleb.

Anna's grandfather cleared his throat. "Well, I could sit here for hours and share some stories of three other misbehaving young'ns I know, if you'd like." He grinned at his adult children, who sat about him.

"No, Father," Maggie said with a grin. "That's not necessary. How's the bakery doing?" she asked, attempting to change the direction of the conversation.

Anna and her mother laughed at the embarrassed adults, truly wishing he'd go on with his tale.

Filled with baskets of fried chicken, potato salad, blueberry cobbler, and corn on the cob, the wagon jostled down the furrowed path. Tucked in among the food and the family were several blankets, cushioning the dishes on the journey and ready to be sat upon during the basket dinner. Lanterns hung on the side of the wagon to provide lighting for their journey home later that evening.

The family, dressed in their Sunday best, rocked gently as the wagon made its way towards the schoolhouse. Uncomfortable with their hair, which was combed neatly and stuck in place with pomade, the thick, hot vests and noose-like ties, the boys grumbled in misery. Caleb often reached to pull some hair down onto his forehead, only to have his hand slapped by his mother.

"My, you fellows look dashing," Grandmother Sarah said. "I'm proud to call you family."

"Eli smells funny," Marcus teased. "I think he fell into some of Pa's liniment."

"Hush, Marcus, or I'll tell big Angelina you think she's

beautiful and you want her for your girlfriend."

"Oh, you'd better not," Marcus retorted. "I'd rather marry a hog!"

"But no hog will have you with that funny scent of yours."

"Why, you –" Marcus said, punching his brother lightly in the arm.

"Eli! Marcus!" Arlis warned. "You boys had better get your dance cards out."

The threat instantly rendered them silent.

Brightly colored quilts hung on ropes strung in the front of the school. Many baskets of food sat atop tables placed alongside the building. On a makeshift platform and dance floor, a quartet strummed out melodious, happy dancing tunes. The sun began lowering in the western sky, and the evening heat waned as the heavy growth of trees blocked its incandescent rays.

Anna walked among the numerous quilts and let her fingers trace along the soft cotton of the stitched patterns. It felt nice to be away from people as she looked at the lovely patched works of art. Her aunts, mother, and grandmother studied the competition to see if any were of high enough quality to capture first place and raise a higher bid than Ethel's; Anna smiled at her aunt's excitement.

Eventually, her stroll took her to a display of the Indian mission, the would-be benefactor of the funds from the quilt auction. A drawing outlined the schoolhouse, and beside it there was a small building intended to be used as a barn. On the other side was a structure labeled 'Dormitory.'

A young woman about Anna's age walked up to the display. "A wonderful arrangement, isn't it?" the girl asked.

"Yes... well, I suppose so. I don't know much about either architecture or missions," Anna smiled at the girl.

"I'm Mary Dickinson," the girl said as they continued along the line of quilts.

"My name's Anna Collins. It's nice to meet you, Miss Dickinson. Is one of the quilts your handiwork?" Anna asked.

"Oh, not at all. I'm not much of a seamstress, I'm afraid. I'm from the Oak Hill female seminary in Indian Territory, and that drawing is a rendition of the mission where I teach."

"Really?" Anna stopped, shocked that such a young, waif-like girl would be sturdy enough to survive life in the wilderness, among the savages.

"I came to Ohio with a lady from our mission who is here to visit an ill relative. I heard about the fundraising here in Montgomery and decided to visit myself." In front of Ethel's quilt, she halted. "Oh, my! These colors are certainly attractive on this one, and the stitches are so intricate and even. This one will likely bring in a high profit for the school supplies we need."

Anna smiled as she realized it was her aunt's quilt that brought the compliment. She turned her attention back to their conversation. "I can't imagine living in such a primitive place. It's amazing that you can survive there, and it's admirable that you are a teacher, Miss Dickinson."

"The people aren't savages, though I am sure that is what you have heard." Miss Dickinson continued, "Truly, the Indians are very intelligent, passionate people."

"Oh, I am so sorry. I meant no harm in referring to them in that manner, and I would never speak ill of anyone. Unfortunately, I only know what I've heard," Anna said.

"Our Mr. Byington is a fine man, and he has a great concern for the children there."

"How many students attend your school?"

"There are thirty-nine living in the dormitories. The funds raised here will assist us in constructing new larger rooms for additional boarders."

"I was to be a teacher also," Anna said in a saddening tone, "but my position in Cincinnati did not work out, I'm afraid."

"Oh, I am so sorry to hear that," Miss Dickinson said.

The mayor walked up and interrupted their discussion as politely as he could. "Miss Dickinson, it shall soon be time for your presentation for the audience," he said with a smile.

"I truly enjoyed our talk," Anna said, "and it was so nice to meet you, Miss Dickinson."

"Same to you, Miss Collins. I do wish you all the best in finding a new teaching job."

"There you are!" Ethel called to Anna. "We were worried when we couldn't find you, young lady."

"I'm sorry, Aunt Ethel. "I was just admiring all these quilts, and I had a chat with Miss Dickinson, who teaches at the Indian mission where the profits will go."

"How exciting, dear! I heard she'd be here today. It won't be long before we see whose quilt brings the highest bid!" Ethel sniggered with excitement. "Come and sit with us, darling."

"Of course." Anna followed her aunt and joined the rest of ladies of the family.

The auction brought in nearly $200, and according to Miss Dickinson's speech, that would provide shelter and food during the school year for thirteen of their students.

The sun hastened its descent behind the trees, and the family settled on a blanket to enjoy their basket dinner.

"Ethel, your quilt received second place in the competition AND the second highest bid in the auction," Arlis said as he opened a basket of tasty fried chicken. "That's wonderful, dear."

"Well, I know the money shall go to a very good cause, but of all women to beat me, Sadie Larsen? She has such irregular stitches and poor sewing ability. That poor quilt isn't going to last ten years."

"Dear, you mustn't be bitter or so critical of others."

"Aunt Maggie, this chicken is great," Caleb said, wiping a greasy crumb from his chin with his forearm. "And your biscuits are... um... well, never mind." Caleb stopped when he caught his mother scowling at him, her brow furrowed, daring him to make yet another complaint about her own tough, flat, tasteless biscuits.

The chatter of the families decreased as they began to eat. After a while, the band gathered again on the platform and began to play the *Virginia Reel.*

"I love that song," sighed Ethel.

"I love it too," agreed Maggie. "Garrett and I loved square dances. Of course, now that he's gone and I live in the city, I no longer have a chance to enjoy such things."

"Why, I imagine your brother or my husband would be glad to accompany you for a round or two," Ethel encouraged. "Surely you can still promenade with the best of them!"

Maggie blushed. "It wouldn't seem... proper," she said.

"Not proper for a lady to dance with her brother or brother-in-law? P-shaw!" Ethel looked at Arlis, who was sitting next to Ethan. "Would one of you fine gentlemen partner up with the elegant Maggie for a round of square dances?"

"Well, dear, I haven't danced in quite a while, and I think I might be a bit out of shape for it." Arlis started his list of excuses, but when he saw the look on his wife's face – those arched eyebrows and that pouting lip – he quickly recanted out of pity, or fear, or a little of both. "But I guess it's about time I wake up these tired old feet again." He wiped his hands and face with a napkin, stood, dusted off his trousers, and reached his hand out to his sister-in-law's. "Maggie, may I have the pleasure of this dance?"

Maggie smiled at Ethel and looked up at Arlis with a sheepish grin on her face. "Why certainly, kind sir. I would be most honored."

"You should also go, dear," Anna's mother said to Anna, elbowing her. "We haven't many opportunities in Cincinnati to enjoy a square dance. Go on! Surely you can find a dashing young man to accompany you."

"Mother!" Anna said, slightly embarrassed but secretly amused at the idea. "I don't know anyone here."

"I would consider it a privilege to dance with you," said a voice from behind Anna and her mother, "if it is not too bold of me to ask."

Anna looked up at a tall, blond-haired young man of about twenty years of age, but she was too stunned to answer him right away.

"Oh, where are my manners? Please allow me introduce myself," he said as he reached to shake Mrs. Collins's hand. "I am Gideon Abernathy of St. Louis. I am here with my cousin, Miss Mary Dickinson."

"Well, Mr. Abernathy, it is surely our pleasure to meet you," said Anna's mother. "I am Mrs. Collins, and this is my daughter Anna."

Anna was beyond mortified. "Thank you for your offer, but I'm not very good at square dancing, I'm afraid," Anna said to the handsome young man. "It is not uncommon for me to inflict pain upon my partner and myself."

"Oh, Anna, that's nonsense! Now you go on and have a dance with the kind Mr. Abernathy here." Her mother touched her arm and whispered into her ear, "It looks like this young man could weather a dance with you without too much complaint."

Anna started to argue with her mother, but when Gideon took her hand, she felt compelled to oblige. The last thing she wanted to do was make a scene. "Sir, I'm sure you will regret this," she said. "When you are icing your feet later, please remember that I warned you."

"I understand, but it would be a shame to miss out on such a lovely evening and a chance at obtaining some exercise."

"Yes, I suppose you're right," Anna said, stepping into the line of dancers.

The two enjoyed the camaraderie of the other couples and laughed as Gideon's foot caught the brunt of several missteps from Anna's.

"Miss Collins, thank you for the dance. I am rather ashamed that I have tears in my eyes from that last do-si-do!"

"I'm sorry, but I did warn you. Any pain you endured was by your own design." Anna laughed. "Thank you again though. Truly, I did enjoy myself."

"Have you lived in Montgomery long?" Gideon asked while they walked back to the refreshment table.

Anna shook her head. "We don't live here. I'm from Cincinnati. I'm here with my family, to visit my aunt, uncle, and cousins."

"Oh? Wonderful! So you're on a holiday, of sorts."

"I suppose you could call it that." Anna looked down at her feet.

"Have I offended you, Miss Collins?" he asked when he noticed her distracted reaction.

"No. I'm sorry. The last few months have been very upsetting and discouraging for me, so my parents arranged this – this *holiday* – to take my mind off my problems."

"I'm sorry, my prying had dredged up unpleasant thoughts for you. Would it help to discuss things with an impartial, unbiased person whom you'll never see again?" Gideon asked with a look that provided Anna the courage and willingness to discuss her grief with a complete stranger.

"I'm afraid I'd only bore or depress you, Mr. Abernathy," she said.

"Please go on, Miss Collins. And now that we have shared the intimacy of injuring each other's feet, please call me Gideon."

He led her to a glade where they sat upon the low, gnarled branches of a large, primeval-looking tree. While they watched fireflies dance in the darkness, Anna poured her heart out to Gideon. She was relieved that only a few random teardrops fell down her cheeks instead of the fountains and rivers of despair that usually accompanied her heart-wrenching memories.

Gideon pulled a handkerchief from his vest and gently wiped her cheek. "It's a shame someone treated you so poorly."

She took the handkerchief from him, shocked to discover that she welcomed his touch. "The true shame is the fact I let his opinion of me change my feelings about myself. He led me to believe I am a failure, worthless, unlovable, and doomed to a sad life."

"Well, how do you feel now?"

She sighed. "I'm determined to find the place where I belong, the place where God wants me to be, to serve. Although I have no idea at this moment where that may be, I have hope that He will provide me with direction soon." She shook her head. "But enough of *my* drama. Do tell me of your life in St. Louis. It must be exciting."

"Me? My story is much like the humdrum stories of others. I work, I go home, I sleep, and I wake and start over the next day. And you thought you would bore me!"

"What's your occupation?"

"I am a journalist, a reporter. I write for the paper in St. Louis, *The St. Louis Herald.*"

"That does *not* sound boring to me," Anna said. "It seems to me that such a career would be rather adventurous and exciting."

"There are those moments, but for about three hundred

and sixty-four days of the year, my job would better be described as ordinary – perhaps even downright dull."

"I guess any occupation could become ordinary or mundane if one lost motivation. If the reason to work is only for financial gain, then it would be easy to become disenchanted with a job."

Gideon nodded and smiled at her. "You are very perceptive."

"Yes. Perhaps that is why I can see from my father's stance that he's ready for us to leave. I appreciate your kindness to me tonight, Mr. Abernathy... Gideon."

"No problem. If you ever make your way to St. Louis, please stop by the paper. I would be glad to give you a tour and show you how it all works." Gideon took her hand and kissed it.

Anna felt a tingle she hadn't felt in a long while. Embarrassed by it, she quickly removed her hand from his. "And the same goes for you. If you find yourself in Cincinnati, please stop by and visit."

A nna met her family and joined them in the wagon for the trip back to the farm. The pleasant ride home was filled with reminiscences of the evening's events. No-one mentioned Anna's long talk with Gideon, and she hoped they didn't think it improper.

"Maggie, Mr. Lynchfield is a most affable man," Ethel said with a coy grin.

"Please!" Maggie said. "Yes, he is a very nice man, and a fine square dancer as well."

Anna watched the stars and the fireflies dashed in and out of the wild rose bushes along the road. Her mind travelled back to her conversation with Gideon and the emotions his touch had stirred.

A feeling of shame lingered for a moment, but when Anna realized there was no reason for such an emotion, she relaxed. She was no longer tied to anyone, and her innocent interactions with Gideon were no cause for guilt or remorse. The enjoyment of other gentlemen's company was something else that she refused to allow Martin to take from her.

That night Anna lay in her bed and prayed, "Father, please give me direction. I want to work and make a difference in the world. Thank You for this evening, which turned out to be pleasant. Before this week, I didn't see this day filled with anything but sadness and heartache. Amen." And with that, she pulled the sheet over her shoulder and turned on her side.

Outside, the wind softly stirred the leaves of the tall oak trees into whispers, and a dog barked in the distance. Anna fell asleep alone, on the evening that would have been her wedding night, but she was content and at peace, and she had dreams of her conversations and dances with Gideon to carry her through the darkness.

Chapter 7

Father, I've decided to write to Professor Ford at Oberlin," Anna announced.

Mr. Collins put his book down in his lap. "Oh? For what purpose?"

Anna sat across from him in the rocking chair on the wide porch. She looked out at the cornfields and watched the tall, green-leafed plants wave like the ocean, caressed by the wind. "To inquire if he knows of any teaching positions for which I could apply."

"You have decided to look for another position?"

She faced him. "I can't sit still forever, Father. I want to be a teacher, and even though some have implied that I have no ability, I believe I will be a good one someday. I have a passion for children, and I want to teach them."

"I agree." Mr. Collins smiled at her. "We'll ask Arlis to take us into town this afternoon, and you can send your letter," he said, smiling again at his daughter before returning to his book.

Anna stood, reached over, and hugged her father. "Thank you so much. I love you, Daddy."

He returned her embrace. "I love you too, dearest."

In the calm of the evening, the family sat around the porch for tea. The boys ran around and squealed, trying to catch a large, green frog that promptly hopped away to hide under the porch. The cool breeze carried the sweet scent of the lilacs which grew along the front of the house.

"I could stay right here forever," Maggie said, rocking in

the large wooden chair.

"You should stay longer!" Ethel exclaimed. "Arlis, help me persuade her to stay," she said to her husband, then turned back to Maggie. "We'd have a wonderful time. We could put up the vegetables and make jam from the plums. We could sew and make a new quilt, even better than the last, and –"

"Please stay with us, Maggie," Arlis said. "I fear she will not leave me be if you don't." He smiled pleadingly at his sister-in-law.

"Yes, Maggie," Prudence encouraged her sister-in-law. "You'd have a lovely time."

"You did enjoy meeting the widower Lynchfield," Ethel added.

The remark resulted in a bright blush on Maggie's face. "Oh dear! You're embarrassing me!" Maggie said. "But I would enjoy being able to visit longer. Would you mind much if I stayed on, Prudence? Ethan?"

Both assured her she'd be missed, but a longer visit with her sister and family was fine with them.

"It's settled then! You'll stay, and we can quilt and visit night and day," Ethel said, as giddy as a schoolgirl. "Finally, there shall be someone who is willing to talk to me while I prepare our evening meals. I am growing tired of talking to myself, and Arlis is far too busy with more manly endeavors."

"It will be wonderful for me too." Arlis laughed. "I can have some peace and rest and get things done while she has *you* tied up in her apron strings instead of me."

The next morning the entire family loaded into the wagon and sat on the dew-dampened bench. They travelled down the gravel road into Montgomery to meet the stagecoach that would transport them back to Cincinnati.

At the stage depot the families bid each other farewell. Mr. and Mrs. Collins, Anna, Caleb, and their grandparents climbed into the coach and watched as Arlis, Ethel, and Maggie waved goodbye. Eli and Marcus ran alongside the coach until it reached the end of the street.

"I'm a little surprised that Maggie wanted to stay longer," Grandmother Sarah said.

"Mother, did you not *see* Mr. Lynchfield at the auction?" Prudence asked.

"That old widow man?"

"I don't think he could be considered *old*," Prudence said. "He's a year younger than I am."

Grandmother laughed at the reaction. "No, I suppose I don't consider that old either, dear. I'm sorry. I did meet him, and he seemed to be a very amiable gentleman... and also quite handsome."

"Mother!"

"Sarah!" Grandfather said.

"Well, I still have my eyesight, and poor Maggie has been grieving and lonely for quite some time now. Maybe getting away from Cincinnati will be good for her."

"I'll miss Aunt Maggie though," Caleb said.

His mother gave him a pained look. "Don't you dare say it, Caleb!" she warned.

"But, Mother, I only mean because she makes the best –"

"Caleb Collins!"

"The best peach pie, Mother. That's all," he teased with a grin.

"Good job, son," Mr. Collins said, nudging the boy.

Thursday morning, the Collins family was back in their Cincinnati home, *sans* Maggie. They missed her, but the family knew she would enjoy being out of the city and spending some time with her sister for a while.

Mrs. Collins talked of nothing other than her hope of Mr. Lynchfield and Maggie becoming better acquainted; she was certain, of course, that it would lead to a more permanent arrangement between the two. Mr. Collins always reacted to her romantic notions with a sigh and cautioned her about starting rumors whenever she began another parade of possibilities.

Anna's mind wandered while her mother chatted on of their recent trip. Mrs. Collins had to repeat questions for Anna more than once before noticing Anna's distracted state.

"Anna dear," her mother said, placing her hand on her daughter's shoulder. "You seem preoccupied since we returned from Montgomery. Do you wish to talk about anything?"

"Oh, I really am fine, Mother. It's just... well, it seems whenever I decide what step I'm going to take next, an obstacle presents itself. I feel... well, I guess *confused* as what to do next."

Mrs. Collins smiled at her daughter. "It does appear that way, doesn't it? But think of the successful steps you've taken so far. You've stepped through the grief and despair you felt from all that has happened and Anna, if that's all you accomplish in the next few weeks, then dear, that's enough."

"I don't think you and Father will think so kindly when your forty-year-old spinster daughter is still living with you," Anna said. "Perhaps Professor Ford's reply will arrive soon and offer me some direction."

The second week after the family had returned from Montgomery, the letter from Oberlin arrived. But it did not herald a plan which Anna was to follow, but carried only more frustration. The job in New York had already been filled.

Disappointed, she walked from the mail depot to her grandparents' bakery. The little bell jingled when she opened the door, and her grandmother looked up.

"Good morning, Grandmother."

"How are you, dear?" She kissed her granddaughter on the cheek. "What brings you to my shop today?" she asked, and returned to sweeping the floor.

Anna sat on a high stool at the tall counter. "Well, Grandmother, I received the reply about the New York teaching position."

"And?"

"It's been filled by another candidate. I'm not sure what I should do now." She drummed her fingers on the countertop.

Her grandmother walked to the door, locked it, turned the sign to 'Closed', and pulled the shades down. "Dearest, I know all will be well." She looked up as Anna grimaced. "I know it seems a ridiculous statement in the face of all you have suffered of late, but I've found it to be true." Her grandmother sat on a chair across from her. "There is always a reason for a door to be closed, even if we cannot see it." She smiled at Anna. "Something else will develop, dear. Maybe it will not be the specific answer for which we have prayed, but you will have another opportunity, and it will be the one that will result in the refinement God has intended."

Anna wrinkled her brow as if it was nonsense. She was growing weary of waiting for promises to be fulfilled. Nevertheless, she continued to listen.

"God will open a window now that the door of this opportunity has closed for you. You must look for another opening, in a different and unexpected way."

Anna sighed. "Well, Professor Ford did mention there is another position for which I could apply, but even if they offered it to me, I am not sure I would want to accept it."

"And why's that, love?"

"The school is in Indian Territory, at a Fort. It may as well be across the ocean, Grandmother. Is that the window I am to enter? I'm worried it might slam on me! How do I know what God expects, which way He wants me to go?"

"Put a fleece before the Lord."

"Doesn't that mean admitting that I lack faith?" Anna asked.

"If you trust that God will answer and believe the answer to be His, it could be nothing other than faith, m'dear."

"Hmm. Perhaps you are right. Perhaps I should apply, and if they accept, I can take that as my cue to go."

"If the opportunity knocks on your door, you will have a decision to make. When you make that decision with prayerful consideration, be it yea or nay, I believe your spirit will be calmed."

"I haven't experienced calm in quite a while. I suppose if I do feel that, I shall know it is a divine calling." Anna sat with her head in her hands, pondering her grandmother's wise words and trying to decide her next steps. "I'll send a letter to the Fort and apply for the position, and wait for the calm. Thank you, Grandmother. Would you like me to walk you to your apartment?"

After her grandmother was home safe and sound, Anna penned a letter to the school at Fort Towson, in Indian

Territory. She placed it on the vanity. She looked at it for several moments. When it did not exhibit a divine glow or burst into flames to signal God's approval or disapproval, Anna felt nothing other than fear that her application might be accepted.

She fell to her knees and prayed. "Oh Father, here I am again, asking for Your favor and guidance and anything else You desire for me to have. I surrender my desires to You and leave it all in Your hands. Amen."

On her walk the next morning, she prayed every step of the way for peace and assurance and wisdom to make the right decision.

Chapter 8

"Anna, are you positive it's what you must do?" her mother asked, somewhat panic stricken.

"I don't wish to remain unemployed, Mother, so while I am not absolutely sure it's the thing to do, what other opportunities do I have?"

"I understand your desire to become a teacher, darling, but if your application is accepted, do you understand the dangers and toils you'll face?" She turned and walked to her husband. "Ethan, talk to her! Make her see what might happen if she goes there, if she wanders off into the wilderness."

Mr. Collins looked at Anna and then back at his wife. "Only a few weeks ago, you were fretting about Anna's lack of ambition, worried that she'd spend her life aimlessly drifting about in despair. Now our daughter has a plan, dear, and we should support her in it."

"Are you suggesting this foolish idea is *my* fault?"

He chuckled. "No, Prudie. On the contrary, it is what *we've* been wishing for, praying for." He took her by the shoulders and looked into her green, tear-filled eyes. "Prudie, she is a grown woman."

Prudence Collins looked over at her daughter. "Perhaps, but she's only a *young* woman, Ethan. No woman of any age should willingly go alone into such a desolate, savage, dangerous country," she said through gritted teeth.

"Mother, I won't be alone. I've corresponded with Miss Dickinson – you remember her, from Aunt Ethel's quilt auction? Immediately after her visit to Ohio, she was

69

dispatched to teach at Fort Towson. She wrote that if I'm chosen, she would stay there for awhile to assist with my integration into the school and Fort. She wrote she has been safe during her endeavors."

"If *she's* there, why do they need another teacher?" her mother asked.

"Miss Dickinson is only an interim teacher until the Fort secures a permanent replacement. Then she will return to her students at the Ebenezer mission."

"I'm afraid to ask what became of the Fort's first teacher."

"Mother," Anna said in exasperation, "the first teacher married a soldier from the Fort, and they moved away. They're not savages, Mother, in spite of what everyone believes."

"Anna will be fine," her father said. "We have a few months to help her prepare for the environment before she leaves." He looked at his wife. "And we WILL support her decision to follow her heart and go the way she feels she should."

Two weeks later, the letter arrived from the Fort confirming that Anna was selected for the position. With it came the calm for which she longed. They expected her to arrive in April of the following year, 1838.

Miss Dickinson and Anna corresponded several times over the next few months, and Anna was provided with a full description of her duties, information about some of the children, and encouragement to bring several lightweight dresses for the summer, along with proper boots, stockings, mittens, and a heavy coat for the winter weather.

Anna's family holiday celebrations were bittersweet. Many of the gifts she received from friends and family were appropriate, sensible items that they thought Anna might need to endure the primitive conditions during her journey and her stay at the Fort.

Anna's parents purchased her steamboat passage, and she was set to depart on January 30, 1838. When the first of the year arrived, it ushered in a new year far more different than Anna would have ever dreamt possible. A year earlier, she'd imagined she would be a newlywed who had been teaching for six months. Instead, she now stood on the precipice of a new life – a course she'd never expected her life to take.

At a party her parents hosted for her, her lifelong friends and acquaintances came to Cincinnati to see her off.

"We'll miss you, Anna," Mrs. Avery said with a hearty embrace. "Our prayers will be with you every day."

"Thank you. I shall count on that."

Anna mingled with the guests, graciously accepting their admonitions for caution and assurances that she'd be able to find employment closer to her home if only she could be more patient.

After the party was over, Anna was left alone with her parents; Caleb was worn out from the day's festivities and went to bed early.

"Dearest, *must* you go?" her mother asked.

Anna took her hand. "Mother, I've already committed to it, and they are awaiting my arrival and have invested much in preparing me. Don't worry. I'm an intelligent woman, a trait I gladly inherited from you."

"Aw, dear, you do flatter me. I want you to be assured that if at any moment – even in the midst of your travels – you decide to change your mind, you may return home without an explanation of any sort."

"Thank you, Mother, and I shall remember all you've taught me. I'll be careful, and I will make a difference to better the lives of the children at the Fort."

Anna's heart pounded within her chest. If not for the gloves, her hands, damped with nervous perspiration, would have lost their grip on the bag she carried. She fidgeted with her parasol while she waited with her family and gazed out across the dock to the river.

The lapping of the waves intensified the rhythmic hammering of her heartbeat. Anna closed her eyes tightly and tried to slow her pulse.

What am I doing? What was I thinking when I agreed to run off like this, to leave my home, my family, and my friends... and for what? Separation from Martin and the embarrassment his rejection caused me? And just what am I running off to? Desolation, danger... perhaps even death? The escalating waves of doubt washed over her and left her breathless.

God, what have I done? She prayed in silence with eyes closed. *If I'm mistaken, if I have made the wrong decision, please do whatever it takes to prevent my departure,* she pleaded. *Otherwise, I must take it for a sign that you want me to continue on this voyage.*

A touch on her shoulder caused her to open her eyes.

"Anna," said her father, who stood before her, "is all still well?"

"Yes." She sighed. "Yes, Father, other than a mere moment of wondering if I've lost my mind – and panic, I suppose. But other than that, I'm ready to go."

"Very well. Please remember your mother's offer. Any time, Anna, and for any reason, you can come back, and there shall be no questions. This is your home, and we are your family, and you are always welcome here, no matter what."

"Thank you, Papa." Though she'd called him 'Daddy' on occasion, Anna hadn't used that familiar name of endearment – 'Papa' – since her twelfth birthday, and her use of it now almost caused both to submit to their restrained emotions. "I've made my choice after much consideration and prayer, and I'm sure it's the course I'm to follow."

Mr. Collins nodded and took his daughter's hand. "You, my dear, are a brave, strong girl – one of the most intelligent women I know. Understand, of course, that this includes your mother," he added with a wink. "I stand here very proud of you." He hugged her and kissed her cheek. "All will be well, and I know God will bless your endeavors."

Mrs. Collins's footsteps interrupted them. "Have you succeeded in dissuading her departure?" she asked.

"Prudie," he admonished, "our Anna is confident that this path has been ordered by God."

"I know, but it doesn't hurt to offer her one last chance to change her mind."

The horn blast sounded and announced the beginning of the boarding process. Anna's luggage had been placed earlier in her cabin, leaving only a small carpetbag and parasol for her to manage.

The family looked at Anna, hoping she would exercise her prerogative to change her mind. When no announcement of such a decision came, they began their farewells.

Aunt Maggie embraced her. "Dearest, I'll never cease to mention you in my prayers. Always know that whatever happens in your life, a prayer will be your cover," she said, her eyes glistening with tears.

"Thank you, and thanks for coming back to see me off. Please let me know when you and Mr. Lynchfield set your wedding date."

Maggie blushed and nodded. "You will be one of the first to know, dear! You simply must promise me you will be there to see me walk down the aisle."

"I wouldn't miss it for the world," Anna said and hugged her aunt.

"Grandmother Sarah, Grandfather, I will miss you," she embraced her grandparents, who beamed with pride.

"You know we are so proud of you," her grandfather's voice wavered. "And God will be faithful to His promises."

"I know, Grandfather. Goodbye, Grandmother." Her grandparents, struggling with their emotions, welcomed their grandson's interruption.

"Anna, will you send me an Indian headdress?" Caleb asked, endeavoring to keep his composure. "And don't forget to get a coonskin hat for me. I know there must be lots of coons out there in Indian Territory, if the Indians haven't killed them all with their tomahawks."

Anna laughed; her brother was all boy. "I'll remember. If any Indians leave their headdress at the Fort, I'll be sure to retrieve it and send it off to you. You remember to behave and don't torment Mother and Father too much while I'm away. I'll write as often as possible." She hugged her little brother and tousled his hair.

Anna's mother hugged her so hard Anna thought she aimed to break her ribs so she would have to heal in a hospital bed and would be unable to proceed on her journey.

"Mother! I cannot breathe," Anna said, half-amused, half-annoyed at her mother's gruffness.

"I'm sorry, my love, but I'll miss you so much, and I –" she stammered, "I cannot help being frightened for your welfare. It's a mother's right!"

Mrs. Collins's voice cracked, and large teardrops fell upon her chest, marking the spot where her heart broke beneath the teal dress. "It will perturb you, but I must say it anyway. Please don't go, Anna. You can make a life here, and we will help you." Her imploring green eyes bore into

Anna's. "We'll help you find a job here or even outside of Cincinnati if you feel you must venture out. No-one will dare mention Martin's scandalous behavior ever again, if only you say you'll cancel your travel and stay here with us, where you belong."

Anna's father looked at Anna over her mother's head and winked. "Prudence, it's time for Anna to board now." He walked closer to Anna. "Dear, you must be off now." He hugged her and pressed several bills in her hand. "Take care, darling. We love you and are very proud of you. Now, get on that boat before you're left behind, and are forced to swim the river to catch up."

The family walked with Anna to the gangplank. On the boat, the band played a cheerful tune, but it didn't sound all that festive to Anna and her family as they bid their final farewells and she ascended the walkway all by herself. At the top of the plank, Anna turned and stood with the other travelers who waved to family and friends.

The crew began their departure procedures, untied the large coiled ropes, and drew up the plank. The horn blasted several short, piercing bursts and one final long sounding, which announced the separation of boat from dock and Anna from her family. She waved and blew kisses to each of them, trying not to look too sad and casting her mother a comforting half-smile.

Against the wall of the ticket office, Anna caught sight of a familiar form standing on the dock behind the crowd. She held her hand up to her eyes to block the sunlight and gasped. *Martin? Yes, that's him!*

When he realized she'd spied him, he simply tipped his hat and nodded.

Astonishment and anger filled Anna at his audacity to show up just as she was leaving to make a new life for herself out of the one that he'd so violently and needlessly stomped on. "That... why, you wretched, wretched man!" she said under her breath. "I'll show you – *and* those arrogant parents of yours!"

She was drawn back to her family as they waved. She watched as they slowly diminished in size and finally disappeared in the haze along the fading shoreline.

Chapter 9

Anna closed her eyes and tried to allow the cadenced pulsing of the steamboat engine lull her to sleep. Ever since the trip had begun, it seemed the moment sleep overtook her, she was too soon jolted back to consciousness. The boisterous cabin boys, bossy stewards, a crying toddler, or the horn blast as the steamboat arrived in a port to take on more passengers were all perfect triggers for insomnia, she'd come to find out.

Mrs. Devonshire, a portly woman who was on a return trip home from visiting her daughter in New York, guaranteed Anna that they would soon pass the scheduled stops; after that, they would presumably experience 'a quiet and peaceful trip to New Orleans', and Anna was glad to hear it.

Anna sat up in her bed. Her cabin was comfortable, though it was just seven feet by six feet and contained only a bed with small drawers underneath, a small closet, and a pop-up table that served both as nightstand and desk. The small window over the bed provided a view of the river and passing shoreline.

Anna turned back the covers, stood, and lit the hurricane lantern on the dual-purpose table next to her bed. She peered out the window and sat back down on her bed when she was unable to see anything other than darkness.

Outside, the voices on deck varied in volume from minute to minute. From what Anna could make out of the muffled conversations, the soldiers were enjoying an exciting game of poker. Their cries of joy and simultaneous shouts of dismay carried on the evening air long after most of the *Jewel Belle* passengers had retired for the evening.

Even with the rowdy laughter and noisy soldiers and the lack of any meaningful sleep, Anna had enjoyed the trip thus far. On the first day of her travel, she met many passengers at lunch. Entering the dining room, Anna held her head high to appear confident and at the same time inconspicuous while she searched for a place to sit and dine. Her foot had barely crossed the threshold of the doorway when she heard a shout.

"Yoo-hoo! Dearie, over here!" someone tooted to her.

Anna turned to see a lady waving her hankie at her.

"Dearie, sit with us."

Anna pointed to herself and mouthed, "Me?"

"Yes, yes. Come sit with us, dear. We have plenty of room, and that beautiful young face of yours will brighten our table." The lady stood and pulled a chair out as Anna jostled her way between the tables and patrons. "Here we are, all together now," the woman said. "I am Olivia Devonshire, but all my friends call me Livy." She held out her puffy, small ivory hand to Anna. "Let me introduce these lovely ladies to you."

Anna sat, smiled, and tried to make a mental note of each name and its respective face as Mrs. Devonshire rounded the table with her introductions.

"This is Grace Larsen from Pittsburgh. She is travelling to Tennessee to work as a nanny for a family who relocated there."

The petite blonde looked at Anna with a timid smile pasted upon her delicate face. "Nice to meet you," she said meekly.

Anna nodded to the pretty girl, who appeared too young to be in charge of herself, let alone small children.

Next was a beautiful, fair-complexioned, red-head, whom Mrs. Devonshire introduced as "Honora Malahy." She went on, "The poor dear is from West Virginia, travelling to Memphis to live with her sister in Tennessee after the tragic death of their parents."

Honora looked at Anna and rolled her eyes at Mrs. Devonshire's drama. It amused Anna to see how Mrs. Devonshire shepherded the pretty, attractive, young female passengers around her, much like a mother duck with a gaggle of baby ducklings. "So nice to make your acquaintance," was all Honora could manage to get out before Mrs. Devonshire continued.

The last two of her flock were Sylvia and Julia Norstrom from Philadelphia, on their way to Memphis to meet their uncle. The well-travelled, brown-eyed brunettes seemed rather reluctant and unhappy to be included among Mrs. Devonshire's wards. Between introductions at the table, Anna caught them eyeing every male who entered the dining room, and whenever a handsome man appeared in the doorway, they punched each other.

"Now, ladies," Mrs. Devonshire whispered with her head down so as to prevent any of the other diners from hearing, "you must be cautious. Yes, caution and vigilance must be exercised always, for they are of the utmost importance during your trip." She trembled with the importance of her message and continued, "There are rumors that a large assembly of soldiers will board at Louisville after lunch." Her eyes met each girl's and searched to see if they understood the seriousness of her lecture. "Soldiers are sometimes – how shall I put this delicately? – well, they are often lustful."

Grace gasped at the word.

"Mrs. Devonshire! Please!" Honora said.

"Oh, dears, I'm sorry, but I have only your best interest at heart. Men can be coarse, as we all know, and soldiers especially, since they have been rendered callous from the effects of battle and the harsh military lifestyle. We are all products of our experiences, you know."

"But Mrs. Devonshire," Julie said with a mischievous grin, "not all men are coarse, and certainly not all soldiers are vile and disagreeable."

"Yes, we're quite able to protect ourselves," Sylvia added. "Don't fret over us, ma'am. You should instead focus on enjoying your trip."

"There is no point in attempting to free me from what I consider to be my Christian duty, young ladies," Mrs. Devonshire scolded. "I will do what I must."

Anna saw the girls look at each other. Julia and Sylvia appeared troubled by Mrs. Devonshire's possible interference in their socializing. The notion of any potential danger dazed Grace, and it seemed to Anna that Honora took some strange delight in the others' reactions.

Mrs. Devonshire's attention was quickly diverted when the food was delivered by the well-dressed server, and the band played while the ladies finished their lunch.

Afterwards, they followed Mrs. Devonshire to the outside deck, where she took possession of the only empty chaise left. The girls sat on benches along the cabin walls and enjoyed the slight breeze and the sounds of the river as they glided over its surface.

"We'll stop soon in Louisville for the soldiers," Mrs. Devonshire said with her eyes closed.

"Mrs. Devonshire, please." Grace sighed, turned her head, and looked out over the river.

"Mrs. Devonshire, I am sure –" Anna began.

"Livy," Mrs. Devonshire interrupted, her eyes still closed as she snuggled down into the chaise.

"Livy? Very well then. Livy, thank you for your concern, but I am sure we will all be very cautious. There's no need to upset Grace any further."

Mrs. Devonshire nodded. "You're correct, dear," she whispered. "She's a very sensitive girl, but that is the very reason I feel I must be on constant lookout for her wellbeing."

"We'll be fine, ma'am," Honora asserted. "Please don't fuss."

The ladies grew quiet, each absorbed in her own thoughts as they were soothed by the lapping of the river, the cool breeze, and the fine meal they'd enjoyed.

Mrs. Devonshire promptly fell asleep to the rippling lullaby, and her unconscious state, confirmed by the slight snore she emitted with each exhalation, encouraged Grace to speak.

"Really!" Grace murmured. "I've never been so embarrassed."

"Oh, dearie," Honora exclaimed, "you're in for a shock when you settle in Tennessee. It isn't as genteel and civilized as New England, I'm afraid."

"Whatever do you mean?" Grace questioned.

"Simply that conditions in the newly settled West are not as comfortable as what many of us are used to, and proper behavior is not the status quo."

"Are you saying we shall be surrounded by brazen, uncouth, rowdy people?" Grace screeched.

A snort sprung forth from Mrs. Devonshire.

The girls muffled giggles.

"Grace," Anna whispered to interrupt Honora's description before the young woman became overwrought by fear and jumped the boat, "there are civilized people. It's just that some of the finer things enjoyed in the northern states aren't needful or practical in the southern parts of the continent."

"And how would you know?" Honora asked. "Aren't you from Ohio? That isn't exactly on the border of the wild frontier, with all due respect, miss."

"Yes, I'm from Ohio – Cincinnati, to be exact."

"And have you visited the untamed lands before?" Honora continued her interrogation.

"No, I haven't, but I have heard –"

Honora cut Anna off. "Then on what authority do you support your theory that civility reigns in those dastardly areas?"

"I have no intention of suggesting that I am any kind of authority or expert on frontier life because I haven't lived anywhere but Ohio," Anna said, incensed by Honora's condescending attitude, "but I have been in correspondence with a young lady of about my age who lives in Indian Territory, and she has convinced me that the settlers there aren't savages, nor are they as primitive as rumor would suggest. The mere lack of modern-day conveniences does not lower one's intellect, nor does it heighten the level of animalistic tendencies."

Honora shrugged her shoulders and rolled her eyes at Anna's speech. "I still think you believe too highly in the frontiersmen's genteelness."

"Where does this friend of yours stay?" Grace asked.

"She lives in a Fort on the southern edge of Indian Territory, north of the Red River."

"Goodness! A Fort?" exclaimed Grace. "Populated with the likes of the soldiers Mrs. Devonshire is afraid for us to meet?" She gulped.

"Yes. Her name is Mary, and she is a teacher at an Indian

mission located near the Fort. She is only serving as an interim, until her permanent replacement arrives," Anna answered. "Mary has told me that the soldiers are fine men who have their families with them. Grace, I assure you that you will not face as depraved a society as Mrs. Devonshire and Honora would have you believe."

"You said she is a teacher. There are *children* living within the Fort? Aren't they in grave danger from Indian attacks?" Honora asked.

"Miss Dickinson – Mary – wrote that the soldiers' children are well behaved and the Indian children are intelligent. Their families are like any other. They simply wish for their children to be properly educated. Those at the Fort are not in danger of attacks from the very people they live and work with."

"In any case, I hope they send a man to replace that teacher friend of yours. Any woman who would put herself in such danger on a permanent basis must be a fool," seethed Honora.

"Well, I suppose I am that fool then."

"Excuse me?"

"In fact, *I'm* on my way to replace Miss Dickinson as the teacher at Fort Towson."

"You? A city dweller – refined and ladylike? *You're* to live among soldiers and in Indian Territory? Have you gone mad?" Honora asked. "Any lady of proper reputation would refuse to live in such deplorable conditions."

"I resent your implication, Honora. My choice to live and work in a Fort is by no means a statement of my reputation or my morals. Miss Dickinson said the soldiers are not carousers. They are brave, hardworking family men, tasked with patrolling the country's border to protect its citizens. She feels quite comfortable and safe in and out of the Fort, and I am confident that I shall feel the same sense of security while surrounded with men of such high repute and courage."

"Does your family know what you are up to?" Grace asked, amazed that Anna – or any woman – would choose to leave a city to live in the wilderness.

"Yes. They've known of my intentions for quite some time. In fact, they saw me off when I boarded this ship."

"So they simply tolerated your rather insane desire to leave civilization for God-only-knows what kind of life?" Honora asked.

"They have worried some over the matter – my mother in particular – but we believe God *does* know what lies ahead for me and that He is well capable of taking care of me, whatever happens."

"Spare me your sermon. I've heard enough preaching from Mrs. Livy here," Honora said as she straightened her skirt and pulled a stray strand of auburn hair from her face, loosened by the quickening breeze. "Ooh. I'm afraid I'm catching a chill," she said. "I believe I'll go to my cabin before I catch my death in this draft." She stood and gathered her shawl tighter about her shoulders. "Are you ladies going to stay out here with Mrs. Slumbershire?"

"No." Grace shook her head. "My teeth start to chatter and my nose runs when I get cold, far from attractive or lady-like. Anna, are you coming in?" she asked. "And shouldn't we wake Mrs. Devonshire?"

"I'm coming, but you two go on ahead. I will help Livy into the cabin, and then I'll meet you for dinner tonight, if that's acceptable to you," Anna said.

"Of course, Anna," Honora said. "Come, Grace. Let's go fetch a hot drink to warm our bones."

Anna sat in contemplative silence for a moment, surprised at Honora's reaction and the fact that anyone would look down upon her in insult for her rather brave and selfless choice to teach at the Fort.

I will tell no-one else of these intentions, she thought. *The last thing I need is added discouragement to pile upon my occasional trepidation and doubt.*

The wind intensified, and intermittent sleet pellets and raindrops began to pelt her. All the other passengers had cleared the deck, and Anna realized it was time to follow suit. She nudged Mrs. Devonshire's shoulder. "Mrs. Devonshire! Mrs. Devonshire, it's beginning to rain. Wake up. We must go inside."

Mrs. Devonshire sniffed loudly and jumped. "Oh! I must have dozed off for a moment," she said, dazed.

"Yes, but we must head indoors now. The weather has taken a turn for the worse, and it seems it is beginning to sleet."

"Oh, you're right, my girl! It has grown much chillier." Mrs. Devonshire stood. "Let us go in before we catch our deaths."

She and Anna entered the hallway with the cabins located on each side, and Anna politely walked Mrs. Devonshire to her door.

"See you at dinner, Mrs –"

But the door closed before she could be heard.

In her cabin, Anna lit the lantern and removed her hat. She reached above the bed and retrieved her heavy shawl and socks from the bag. After she removed her boots, she put the socks over her stockings, threw the shawl around her shoulders and on top of her head, and crawled into the bed. Anna shimmied down into the bed and pulled the covers up to her chin to try and stop the shivering.

Outside, sleet peppered the lone window in her cabin, and the wind howled and whistled around the boat.

"Brrr. It's freezing," she said aloud. "I can't believe the change in the weather from yesterday... or from this morning."

Miss Dickinson had warned her to be prepared for varying climates on her journey. Anna had heeded her advice, and as she lay amidst the chill with her body warming beneath the layers of fabric, she thanked God that she was so well prepared.

When the boat entered Louisville port to allow the soldiers to board, Anna was stirred from her nap by the commotion. Dinner was an hour after the stop to provide the new passengers adequate time to settle in their rooms, so she needed to get ready to meet the others. She pushed back the quilt and stood.

Anna looked out the window, which was covered with a fine condensation that she wiped off with her sleeve. Instead of the brown shoreline and green trees she had seen before, she now saw only a white line along the edge of the river and the trees bent with heavy ice-laden boughs. She assumed the noise she heard outside was the result of the soldiers moving into their cabins.

She imagined Mrs. Devonshire standing guard at her

doorway with her arms folded across her ample chest, peering out on deck and quivering with anticipation at her self-imposed duty of protecting the virginal young women aboard from the wicked soldiers. It was a silly mental image indeed, but Anna was certain it was quite close to the truth.

Dinner was relatively uneventful since the soldiers were housed in the forward section cabin with the other gentlemen on the steamboat. They didn't dine with the passengers, much to the disappointment of Sylvia, Julia, and Mrs. Devonshire, who was always on the lookout for drama of any sort. Due to the frigid weather, all the women returned to their cabins immediately after eating.

Anna took a few pieces of fruit from the dining hall, along with a pitcher of hot water so she could nurture herself to sleep with a cup of hot tea. Nevertheless, the presence of the rowdy soldiers made it appear that another restless night was in store. She peeked out the cabin porthole at the grey, cloud-covered sky, which blocked any star shine or moonlight. The whining wind, like some evil specter in the night, rendered a sense of eeriness to the boat.

Having nothing else to do and no ability to sleep, she pulled her tablet from her bag and penned a letter to her family:

Mother, Father, Aunt Maggie, and Caleb,

I hope you're well and haven't endured harsh weather. The trip has been peaceful and the weather temperate until today. In the blink of an eye, it seemed, it went from a calm, mild day into a blustery, frigid evening, peppered with rain and sleet.

My cabin is quite comfortable. Though there is not much space, that is all the more a blessing, as it is much easier to keep warm between the narrow walls.

Aunt Maggie, I am very appreciative for the heavy woolen socks you knitted for me. If not for them, I think my feet might have suffered frostbite today. Thank you!

Please do not worry about me (and, Mother, I say this to you most especially)! I'm well and have been taken under the care of a very proper and conscientious chaperone. Her name is Livy Devonshire, and she has bundled all the young women around her. I am convinced Livy would pummel even the most intimidating of enemies to his death should anyone try to harm one hair on our heads. Send Grandmother Sarah and Grandfather my love.

Caleb, I do hope you've been a diligent student in Mr. Evans's class this semester. I haven't seen any Indians yet, but within a month, I expect to have ample opportunity. I haven't forgotten about the headdress you asked for, and I shall get one for you if I have the chance.

Mother, Father, everything is fine, and please know that I am still assured my plans are in alignment with God's will. I'll close now and send this at the next port. My love to all.

Anna put the tablet back into her bag, blew out the candle, and listened to the sounds of the night: the soldiers, the howling wind, and hoped sleep would come.

Chapter 10

I don't care what you think," Grace continued. "I don't think her mad at all. On the contrary, I believe she's one of the bravest women I've ever met." She slapped the pat of butter on the cinnamon raisin toast and looked Honora squarely in the eye, as if she was daring her to present a retort.

"I didn't mean to dishonor her. I merely suggested that perhaps she should reconsider her plans."

"Don't let Mrs. Devonshire get within hearing distance," Julia said, "or we'll never hear the end of it."

"You're correct about that," Grace said between bites. "And I've heard enough from her."

"I think the trees are beautiful," Honora said loudly, making an obvious change in subject as Anna approached the table. "Oh, good morning, Anna. Did you sleep well?"

Anna took the empty chair next to Grace. "Much better than I thought. I suppose my cup of hot tea helped."

"Tea? Would there have been anything else in that tea besides tea? Perhaps something a bit stronger?" Sylvia quipped. "Quite a ruckus onboard last night, if you ask me."

"Oh no. It was just tea." Anna smiled. "Where's Mrs. Devonshire?"

"Well, you missed her. She came in, ate quickly and furiously, and admonished us to stay put until she returns," Honora said. "As if we are ten years of age! Even my mother..." Honora paused as she realized what she was going to say. "When my mother was alive, she didn't treat me so strictly."

"I believe she's a kindhearted, if nosey, lady with a true concern for us," Anna said and looked over the breakfast. "Cinnamon raisin toast?" she asked.

Grace nodded excitedly, licking her lips. "My favorite!"

"Mine too. My grandmother makes marvelous cinnamon raisin bread."

The server delivered more juice and plates of fruit for the ladies just as Mrs. Devonshire dashed into the dining room, her blue striped taffeta skirt rustling with her gait. "Oh, the very creatures I warned you about have indeed come aboard our ship! You must remember what I said and heed my warnings, girls." Mrs. Devonshire's usually pallid face was flushed, and her broad bosom heaved with her breathlessness. "I've seen the likes of these scoundrels before, and I must recommend that you keep your distance, or you will be prey in their hostile claws, I'm afraid."

"Mrs. Devonshire, I'm sure we aren't in danger. They are just men," Sylvia said as two very tall, striking soldiers entered the dining room. "And very handsome in their uniforms."

Anna heard Grace gasp and watched as she hunkered down into the chair, a look of terror etched on her face. Grace slid down as far as possible so as to prevent the soldiers from seeing her. She certainly didn't want to be abducted by them after being overwhelmed with whatever decadent behavior Mrs. Devonshire was sure they were incapable of repressing.

"Grace," Anna asked, "are you all right?"

"They're... they're here." She trembled. "Whatever shall we do?"

"Nothing. Just sit there and be quiet," Honora said. "No-one is going to harm you. Even if Mrs. Devonshire wasn't in their way, they would not come after you. They're just men who are hungry, like all the other men on this ship."

"Yes, but hungry for what?" Grace asked, now on the verge of hyperventilation and as pale as the snow-covered banks of the Ohio River.

"Put your head down, Grace – down between your legs," Sylvia suggested.

"Why?" Grace cried. "Are they coming to get me?" She ducked and hurriedly bent at the waist, allowing her golden hair to sweep the floor like a makeshift broom against the planks. She began crying, and the tears fell to the floor. "What's happening?" she cried from below the table.

Anna bent down. "Grace, you are so pale that we were afraid you were going to faint, that's all. I assure you the soldiers will be no bother to us. I am sure they are good men, even though they seem a bit rough around the edges."

The soldiers walked to the bar and ordered lemonade under the careful watch of Mrs. Devonshire's suspicious eyes.

"Are you – are you sure?" Grace asked, weeping.

"Yes, dear. Everything's fine." Anna patted her back. "Just stay down until your head feels better."

"My head *is* better, but there are tears in my ears. Perhaps I should sit up now."

"Yes, yes, that would be best." Honora said, stifling a giggle.

Anna, Honora, Sylvia, and Julia surveyed the men as they finished their drinks, paid the waiter, and left the room.

"Thank the Lord above." Mrs. Devonshire gushed with her eyes lifted upward. "It was close, but I kept your honor safe... this time."

"Oh, I declare!" Sylvia exclaimed. "Our honor was in no danger whatsoever from men drinking nothing stronger than lemonade."

Grace lifted her head just as one of the soldiers tipped his hat to the ladies before he left the dining room. She swayed a bit and then ever so charmingly slipped to the floor in a crumpled heap of bronze satin.

Chapter 11

Anna sat and chatted with Honora as they watched over Grace until she recovered from her faint. A strikingly attractive girl of twenty-one years of age, Honora carried herself with a confident, aristocratic comportment, which only added to her natural beauty. Anna thought she would have fitted in well among the wives of Martin's associates at Jameson and MacGregor. *Strange. I haven't given that horrible man a thought since I saw him lurking behind the crowd at the dock.*

"Anna? Are you even listening to me?" Honora asked, snapping her fingers in front of Anna's face.

"Oh, I'm sorry, Honora," Anna said when she realized Honora was awaiting her response to a question. "I was just thinking about some things back home."

"Home? One doesn't usually look so angry when reminiscing of home."

"Yes, I suppose," Anna said, but she quickly changed the subject, as she had no desire to discuss Martin and his disgraceful behavior with anyone. Her past was her past, and that was where it needed to be left as she forged ahead down that river to her new life ahead. "Grace has more color now."

"Yes, but then again, even a shade of gray would be an improvement."

"Poor thing. I think Mrs. Devonshire had a great deal to do with her fainting. I know she has the best of intentions, but with all of her talk of –"

"Of course it's her fault!" Honora said. "That woman is

nothing more than a busybody, and it seems she delights in scaring us."

"I truly don't think she intends harm," Anna said in Mrs. Devonshire's defense.

"Perhaps not, but her meddling resulted in just that nonetheless. Perhaps we should try to keep away from her."

"Honora, I don't think that's possible. We are all fairly trapped aboard this vessel together, and it shall not be easy to hide from someone of Mrs. Devonshire's, uh..."

"Nosiness?"

Anna chuckled. "I think she'd call out the cavalry if we disappeared from her eyesight even for a moment."

"You're right." Honora looked down at Grace and moved a strand of golden hair from the girl's forehead. "She's a very sweet girl, isn't she?"

"Grace," Anna asked, "or are you referring to Mrs. Devonshire?"

"Of course I meant Grace."

"I think she'll make a great nanny for that family. She's not as much of a weakling as she takes herself to be, even if she does faint at the sight of soldiers."

"How do you mean?" Honora asked.

"Well, don't you think it would take a great deal of courage for such a timid girl to leave her home, travel to a new place alone, and live with a family she barely knows?"

"Truth be told, it shall be a much better situation than the one she left behind in Pittsburgh."

"Really? I thought she lived in fashion and comfort."

"Far from it, in fact. After her parents died in a fire in Philadelphia, she was taken in by a most wretched aunt and uncle. They had no compassion for poor Grace. All they loved was the inheritance left behind, her deceased parents' money."

"It's absolutely astonishing to me that anyone could know Grace without adoring her," Anna said quietly. "Do you think she will fare well in Tennessee? Will she be all right?"

"It seems as if it will be a good situation for her. The family she will work for is very prosperous and involved in politics. Grace says she is quite happy she left Pittsburgh to pursue such an opportunity. Look! I think she's coming around."

"Ow... my head hurts." Grace groaned and tried to sit up.

"No, no, sweetheart. Do lie back down," both Honora and Anna urged.

"You suffered a slight bump on the head when you fell on the floor," Honora informed the girl.

"But the ship doctor assured us you're going to survive," Anna added to prevent her any more anxiety. "Don't worry, Grace. He said there's been no significant or permanent damage."

"I'm sorry. I suppose I should be braver," Grace said and bit her lower lip to keep it from quivering. "That has always been difficult for me."

"Nonsense!" Honora said. "You're far braver than you think."

"Yes, that's true," Anna interjected. "In fact, we discussed your bravery while you were asleep," Honora said. "We both think you're quite a wonder, truth be told."

Grace shook her head. "A wonder? Me? How so?"

"Any young woman who leaves a secure situation to travel somewhere they know little about, in search of a better life for herself, is brave indeed," Honora said with a smile. "In fact, I believe the three of us are likely the bravest women – or maybe even the bravest people – on this riverboat. I'm sure we're even braver than those lemonade-guzzling soldiers Mrs. Devonshire insists are dangerous."

"I don't think –" Grace started, but Anna interrupted her.

"No, no, now don't argue. We're definitely the three most courageous creatures aboard this vessel. For once, I must concur wholeheartedly with Honora. We could overtake any enemy, even a soldier if we were forced to do so."

"Not to mention that we are also the loveliest of trios," Honora said with a swagger of her head.

"Surely!" Anna nodded in agreement

Grace sat up slowly. "I suppose you're right," she said and pulled herself upright against the headboard of the bunk. "I don't know why I let such silly things upset me so. Thank you for staying with me."

"You are most welcome. Now, when you feel ready, we'll

go to dinner."

"Maybe I'll just... perhaps I'll stay here in my cabin," Grace stuttered.

"No! You must gain your sea legs, go up on deck, and get some fresh air. The frigid temperatures will set you right and add color to those pale cheeks."

"We're to dock in Cairo tomorrow before we take to the Mississippi River. You must be well enough to go out tomorrow and have a look about the town," Anna said. "What is the point of a steamboat voyage if you aren't going to see the sights along the way?"

Grace looked at the girls. "Fine, let's go have dinner," she said in submission.

"Shall we?" Honora asked.

"Yes! Come, ladies. Let us brave women of the *Jewel Belle* go to dinner."

The girls helped Grace dress and walked with her to the dining room.

Diners filled the dining room, leaving only one empty table. Grace led the way and suddenly stopped dead in her tracks.

Honora came up behind and bumped into her. "Grace, why did you stop?" Honora asked as Anna brought up the rear.

"There are *soldiers* at the table next to the empty one," she whispered.

"And?" Honora asked.

"Nothing. I – I'm brave. That's right. We're the bravest people on this ship, aren't we?"

"Of course we are, dear," Anna said. "Go on."

Grace straightened her back, raised her shoulders, lifted her head, and walked to the table. She nodded to the soldiers, who stood as the girls approached. A soldier pulled out a chair for Grace and carefully scooted it under her as she sat down. He nodded to the other girls and returned to his seat.

Anna sat down and looked at Grace, expecting to see a pale, ashen face wrinkled with worry. Instead, Grace's eyes gleamed with an unmistakable victorious confidence. Anna suppressed her smile, and the ladies began their dinner and talked about their upcoming tour of the city.

The next morning Mrs. Devonshire found Anna, Grace, and Honora just as they were about to exit the boat onto the plank. "There you are!" she twittered. "I was afraid you'd gotten off without me to lead you safely through the town."

The girls stood still as Mrs. Devonshire toddled over to meet them.

"You've been to Cairo before?" Grace asked.

"No. I have never had this rare opportunity before," Mrs. Devonshire said, breathless from her short walk. "Why do you ask?"

The younger women smiled at one another, and all four walked off together.

"Well, from what you said, it sounded as if you know a lot about the city."

"I was simply referring to my duty as protector of you charming ladies. Besides," she continued, lowering her voice, "you never know how those soldiers will behave if they have a bit too much of the sauce now that we've made port, the rapscallions that they are," she said.

Grace stopped and stomped her foot. "Mrs. Devonshire," she snapped, "I will not listen to another ridiculous admonition again. You're wrong! Not everyone is out to cause us harm, and I am growing weary of being frightened by your ridiculous assumptions. Kindly abstain from speaking of such upsetting matters again."

Honora and Anna stood in silent amazement at the boldness Grace had asserted. Now, it appeared she was braver than even *they* thought.

"Now, ladies, shall we go into town, or are we going to stand here all day gawking at each other?" Grace asked.

Honora stepped up to Grace, raised her hand, and saluted. "By all means, Colonel Grace. We are humbly at your command. Let's go," she said. She hooked her arm into Grace's and walked off in front of Mrs. Devonshire and Anna.

"I believe we're leaving now," Mrs. Devonshire said, oblivious to what had transpired.

The ladies walked up the wooden stairs from the dock to the outer street of Cairo's downtown area.

Cairo's founders had strategically positioned their little

settlement at the convergence of the Ohio and Mississippi River waterways, certain the close proximity would benefit the many and diverse entrepreneurs who earned their living along the river edge. With their minds only on financial profits, they had paid little mind to the rivers' capricious natures. For instance, at the whim of those mighty rivers, the town boundaries changed monthly. Occasionally, even within a twenty-four hour period, the establishments on the city's southern edges would flood. Eventually, the eagerness of proprietors gave way to knowledge, and many moved their businesses closer to the heart of the city, away from the fickle rivers.

Many inns, stores, and eateries filled the city. It was a well-supplied burg, ready to please passengers disembarking from the numerous steamboats that travelled down the Ohio and Mississippi. Anna and the ladies made their first stop at one of the local millinery shops to look at the hats for sale. After trying on most of the large supply of varied styles and colors, Mrs. Devonshire chose a garishly decorated opera hat. On the side of the netted top, beneath a large, gray silk gardenia, three blue ostrich feathers fanned out above the small brim. It was the perfect accessory for someone of dramatic flair, which Mrs. Devonshire certainly was. Once her gaudy purchase was safely tucked into a hatbox, they exited the store out onto the boardwalk and continued their way down the sidewalk.

The morning air, although crisp and cool, held no hint of the previous day's inclement ice storm. The ladies toured several businesses and entered the general store.

"I have been looking for gloves in this color for quite some time," Honora said, holding up a pair of green leather riding gloves at Johnson's Mercantile.

"They match your eyes," Mrs. Devonshire observed.

"That is all fine and dandy," Honora said, "but I am more interested in matching them with my riding coat."

"You have a horse?" Grace asked.

"I did. I hope I can retrieve him from my home after I settle with Callie and John. She said they had plenty of room for Otis."

"Otis?" Grace snickered. "Your horse is named Otis?"

"Yes. What's wrong with that?" Honora asked.

"Nothing. I only assumed it would be something a bit more... sophisticated – like 'King's Ransom' – something noble such as that."

"Otis is noble. He's a beautiful horse, from a noble bloodline. I suppose his name is plain, but as far as horses go, he's quite on a pedestal," Honora said while paying for the gloves.

"Oh, dears, it's after six o'clock. We must make our way back to the dock before they leave us stranded in this quaint little town."

"I really enjoyed visiting here today," Grace said. "I have missed shopping more than I realized, and it is nice to plant our feet on solid ground after so long on the river."

"Your aunt and uncle didn't allow you to shop?" Honora asked as they entered a stage to deliver them to the pier.

"No." Grace snorted. "They do not believe such privileges should be given to a 'child', as they presumed me to be. Even though I was seventeen and made to work as an adult, I wasn't granted adult privileges." Grace's eyes filled with tears, and she cleared her throat. "I'm very excited about my future and living with the Marsh family. I intend to treat those blessed children with far more compassion and consistency and consideration than I was given by my horrible and greedy aunt and uncle."

Anna patted her hand. "In my opinion, you'll be a wonderful nanny. The Marshes are quite fortunate to have found you," Anna said.

"No, *I'm* the truly fortunate one."

"Where is our next stop?" Grace asked.

"I believe we won't dock again until we reach Memphis, Tennessee, and that should be in four or five days," Mrs. Devonshire answered. "Of course, that depends on the weather and the cooperation of the river and the boat."

"Oh. I'll have to leave you all then," Grace moaned. "I'll be so lost without you! We must keep in touch."

"Dear, I'd love to," Mrs. Devonshire answered quickly, which elicited muffled giggles and raised eyebrows from Honora and Anna.

Honora and Anna smiled and promised Grace that they, too, would write.

The ladies exited the carriage and walked up the gangplank onto the ship deck. They exchanged farewells and made their way down the ship corridors to their respective chambers. They were wearied from their sightseeing and shopping, and even though it was only six-thirty, they thought it best to retire for the evening.

Inside her cabin, Anna undressed and put on her sleeping gown and looked forward to a nice, quiet, long night's sleep.

Unfortunately for Anna, the night was not long enough. A noise roused her from her deep sleep, and she sat up in the bed, thinking perhaps she had imagined the racket or maybe even dreamt it. Outside her door, the sound of wood cracking, men yelling, and what sounded to her like a squealing pig confirmed that what awakened her was real. She threw back the quilt, stood up, grabbed her shawl, wrapped it around her, and tiptoed the short distance to the door. With her ear pressed against it, she listened. When the noises grew louder, curiosity forced her to throw her cautious nature aside. She unlocked the door and pulled it open only wide enough to allow her to peek out the door. She saw two soldiers down on their knees in front of the door of the cabin across from hers. In front of the kneeling men cowered a small pink piglet. Anna pulled the door open a bit more to catch a better glimpse.

The soldier closest to her looked up. "Ma'am, you'd better stay inside. This little fella's a might spooked, and there's no tellin' what's on his mind. We'll let you know when it's safe to come out."

"Oh, sure," Anna said. She quickly closed the door and leaned against it to listen. The creature squealed and snorted, and she heard more bumping and yelling in the hallway. Anna overhead the men discussing how they could get the creature into the burlap bag.

"Conner, get him!"

"I'm a-tryin'. This critter's a bit meaner than any pigs I ever dealt with."

"Whack him on the rump."

"You whack him! That end's on your side," the soldier said. "I ain't gonna get bit."

"Noah, get ready. I'm gonna shoo him over to you. Get

the bag opened."

"I'm ready. GO!"

Anna heard, "Get on, pig!" and a slap on what Anna supposed was the little pig's hind end, that elicited a loud squeal, several short snorts, bumping noises, shouting, and finally, "Got the little beast!" followed by muffled snorting and squeaking from the confined animal.

A knock on her door surprised Anna, and she shrieked and jumped back. "Ma'am," she heard through the door. "It's all clear out here. You can come out now if you'd like."

She opened the door a little, and when she saw the soldier with blond hair sticking up, his face red and streaked with perspiration, she couldn't help but giggle. "Did you gentlemen manage to apprehend the four-legged fugitive?"

"Yes, Ma'am, although I'm certain capturing a wild mustang wouldn't have been as exhausting."

The other soldier still wrestled with a writhing burlap bag. "Conner, come on! I don't think he's gonna put up with this bag much longer."

"Fine, Noah. I'm comin'!" He turned back to Anna. "I'm sorry we disturbed your evening. I think we need to get this little feller back to his pen. Goodnight."

"No problem. Goodnight, gentlemen."

Several of the other sleepy-eyed travelers stood at their open doors to check out the disturbance for themselves as the soldiers carried the unhappy prisoner off, mumbling their apologies to those awakened by the commotion.

Anna closed the door and checked the pedant watch she had stood on the nightstand. "Four o'clock! The days start so early on this boat," she exclaimed. She crawled back into bed, pulled the quilt over her, and closed her eyes.

Anna's mind whirled with the events of her journey so far. Although her heart still grieved over her losses, her journey to Fort Towson provided a focus. She hoped teaching could replace the pain she felt from a cruel acceptance that she'd likely never marry or have children of her own.

At six o'clock, Anna woke up and changed from her nightclothes into a mauve, cotton day dress. She brushed her hair and pinned it up, gathered her toiletry bag, and walked to the communal lavatory.

After she washed up, she returned to her cabin to find

Grace knocking at her door. "Good morning, Grace," Anna said.

"There you are! I thought you were still asleep."

"I don't think I've slept in late once since we began this trip," Anna said, unlocking her door and yawning.

"Did you hear about the wild boar that was loose in the cabins?" Grace asked.

"Wild boar? No." She rubbed her eyes sleepily. "Oh, wait. Do you mean the little piglet?"

"I don't know about a pig being loose, but Mrs. Devonshire told me a wild boar crated in the hold on its way from Asia to New Orleans escaped and went on a deadly rampage!" Grace plopped down on Anna's bed and took a deep breath.

Anna giggled. "Grace, Mrs. Devonshire is completely warped! She clearly embellished the story!"

"How do you mean?"

"Well, I saw it myself this morning. I *watched* the soldiers capture the little pink squealer in a burlap bag."

"Really? Was it fearsome? Weren't you frightened?"

Anna put her bag on the nightstand. "No, it was a little pig – just a pink piglet, about this size," she said, holding her hands apart. "Not some hairy ferocious boar!"

"Goodness. Our Mrs. Devonshire can wreak havoc with that tongue of hers, can't she?" Grace pouted. "I knew I shouldn't have listened to her. I think she considers it her duty to keep me upset and anxious."

"Yes, it seems that way at times, but I'm sure she means you no harm. Maybe it's her way of feeling important. Maybe she feels useless or ignored at home, and she needs a mission. I don't know enough about human personalities to venture a guess about her motives, but I can tell you I honestly do not believe they are malicious."

Grace rolled her eyes. "Perhaps," she said. "Have you eaten breakfast yet?"

"No," Anna said, "but I think I'm ready. Let's go." Anna grabbed her shawl.

"I imagine they'll serve ham today," Grace said as they left the room.

Anna laughed. "Oh, that's a terrible thought!"

The ladies entered the dining room, which was still filled with soldiers eating breakfast. The soldiers usually finished eating and left the dining room by six-thirty in the morning to make room for the other hungry passengers, but thanks to the shenanigans of the piglet taking up their time, everyone had to crowd into the dining room at once.

Anna noticed a small, empty table at the back of the room. She shepherded Grace to the table and tried to ignore the stares of some of the soldiers sitting at one of the tables. When Anna and Grace passed the table, a couple of the men whistled, and one made a remark about Anna's height.

"Should we leave?" Grace whispered, with a slight tremble in her voice.

"No. It will be fine, Grace," Anna whispered. "Just ignore the rude ones. The others seem fine, and they wouldn't dare bother two women with their commander in the room."

The waiter brought their plates, and Anna and Grace ate and talked quietly. Anna felt their stares against her back and shivered.

"They are so rude," Grace said when she noticed Anna's uneasiness, which echoed her own.

"Yes, some are, but please don't let them upset you."

The troop leader stood and signaled for his men to leave, and the tables emptied quickly except for the one with the leering men. After the other soldiers exited, the rude soldiers stood and moved out of their way to walk around the table where Anna and Grace were sitting.

"Good day, ladies," two men said in unison.

Anna kept her head up, looking directly at the soldiers, but Grace studied the napkin and silverware as if her eyes were glued to them. When they left, Grace sighed. "If I survive this trip, I shall never fear anything again," Grace said.

"You are a very brave woman, Grace, as we've told you. There is nothing on Earth you should fear because you are never really alone."

"How do you remain composed all the time?"

"Well, on the outside, I may appear calm, but sometimes I am shaking on the inside. Nevertheless, when those frightening moments come, I rely on the strength of someone greater than myself to steady me."

"You mean God?"

"Yes! Without His help, this trip would have been impossible for me."

"But you seem very confident and strong in your own right."

"That's because I know God is my very present help in times of trouble. He is my fortress."

"I wish I had such confidence."

"Grace, you can! His strength is always available to you if you'll only ask."

"I don't know. I'm not like you, Anna. I haven't been strong. I've been angry and bitter that my parents died and that my aunt and uncle were so cruel to me." Grace stopped for a moment to swallow back the lump in her throat; she didn't want to break out crying. "Would God be willing to help someone like me – someone who has carried around such fear, anger, and resentment?"

Anna nodded her head excitedly. "Of course, Grace! In the Bible, there is a story of a man who hid from a battle behind a winepress. God sent an angel to him, and the angel called him a 'mighty man of valor' even though the man was trembling in fear, hiding from his enemies."

"Trembling and hiding? Well, that certainly does sound like me!" Grace thought for a moment. "And anytime I ask, He'll be there to comfort and protect me?"

"Anytime and every time, Grace. God loves you so much that He sent His Son to die for the forgiveness of your sins, to give you day-to-day strength and an eternal life after your time on Earth is over. You only have to ask for it."

Grace's eyes filled with tears. "I've spent much of my life in fear. How I've longed to feel confident... and not alone. I always feel alone."

"The Bible says He will never leave us or forsake us," Anna said. "He knows the number of hairs on our heads, and we're always in His care."

"Oh, Anna, please help me find this peace and strength." Grace cried quietly.

Anna prayed with Grace and led her in a prayer for salvation and a special request for strength and courage to face her life challenges. When they were through praying and eating, the two of them walked away from their breakfast, filled and satisfied both physically and spiritually, Grace now armed with the breastplate of righteousness.

The *Jewel Belle* continued on down the Mississippi river way towards Memphis. The evening after the ship left Cairo, a ball was scheduled in the Captain's honor, and formal attire was expected.

Anna had seen the kitchen staff carrying several large flats of fruits and vegetables aboard the previous evening, before they left the Cairo dock. The crew decorated the promenade deck with flowers brought onboard from Cairo.

Grace, Anna, and Honora gathered in Mrs. Devonshire's stateroom to discuss the evening's events.

"Mrs. Devonshire, are you going to wear the new hat you purchased?" Grace asked, touching the beautiful rose-colored gown that she had laid out for the ball.

"No, dearie. I think it is far too elegant for an occasion such as this. I'm planning to wear it to my annual church festival next month though. It will be a glorious affair, and I wish to make a grand appearance!"

"I think *this* will a marvelous event," Grace said.

"Me too," agreed Anna. "What are you wearing, Grace?"

"The dress I wore to my cousin's inauguration into the Philadelphia assembly. I think it will suit the occasion fine."

"How about you, Anna?" asked Mrs. Devonshire as she twirled with her rose gown held up against her.

"I'm afraid the only thing close to a formal dress that I have with me is my... um, an old dress my Aunt Maggie and mother reworked and dyed pale blue." Anna's stomach turned at the thought of the dress. "Maybe I won't go. It simply isn't appropriate for the ball, and I'd rather not show up at all if I have to wear that dress."

"Are you all right?" Mrs. Devonshire asked. "You look upset, dear. Are you ill?"

"No – just a bit ashamed that I don't really have anything appropriate to wear. It's fine. I'll just stay in my room tonight. I've been meaning to write to my family, and I –"

There was instantly a clamor from the other girls. "But Anna, no-one will know it's not new," they protested. "You must come!"

Anna lowered her eyes. "I'm just not prepared to wear that dress."

"But dear, it's a beautiful dress. Perfectly appropriate for this event," Mrs. Devonshire said. "No, no! Absolutely not! You cannot desert us on a fine evening such as this, dear, and I won't have you holing up in that stuffy cabin of yours while we are out having a good time. Hmm... let me think," she said, her chubby finger drumming her dimpled chin.

"I..." Anna stammered. She turned to hide the fact tears filled her eyes. "It's... um... I was engaged and this was my... uh... wedding dress." She turned and gestured toward the dress. "But he changed his mind. So, you see..."

Anna did not have to finish her explanation.

"Oh!" Grace squealed and hugged Anna. "Oh, Anna, how awful."

Mrs. Devonshire stood in unusual silence.

"What a fool that man must be!" Honora proclaimed. She joined Grace in consoling Anna. "Do not give it another thought."

Mrs. Devonshire recovered her voice. "Honora, I think you are absolutely correct."

Honora released Anna and Grace and stepped back. "I have the solution!" she said. "You and I are about the same height and size. What if you wear *my* dress and I wear yours? Would it offend you for *me* to wear it?"

"Well, I do want us all to go to the ball. We don't have much more time together on this voyage, and – believe it or not – I think I'm going to miss all of you! So – would you mind me wearing your dress?"

Anna was truly not certain, but felt she must respond positively to Honora's kindness. "Of course not, and thank you so much. I brought a matching shawl you can also borrow, that will look nice against the blue of the dress."

"Oh, I'm going to miss you little darlings," Mrs. Devonshire said. "You are all my girls, and I do not know what I am going to do without you to look after!" Mrs. Devonshire cried as she gathered all three into a big embrace. "You girls make me feel loved."

"Mrs. Devonshire, we do love you!" Grace said, shocked at the older woman's words. "We've been together now for over a month and have had all sorts of adventures together.

It isn't any surprise we are fond of you."

"Enough of this drama!" Honora said. "We'll all be weepy and our complexions splotched if we don't put an end to this now."

"You're right. I'll get my dress and bring it to your state-room," Anna said. As she left the room, she looked back over her shoulder and announced: "This will be fun, after all!"

A t 7:40 pm, twenty minutes before the ball was set to begin, the ladies met together in Mrs. Devonshire's stateroom.

"That color looks marvelous on you, Honora," Grace said. "It makes your hair stand out."

"Well, that's a shame! I worked for thirty minutes trying to get it to stay pinned!"

"That's not what I meant," Grace continued, "I mean –"

"I know," Honora interrupted with a smile. "I was only teasing you."

The sight of her wedding dress nearly brought Anna to tears, but the delight and anticipation she saw in the ladies' eyes tempered her reaction to the painful memories. "Honora, you are so lovely!"

Honora blushed, adding to her beauty. "I do feel regal in this dress." She looked down and touched the lace inset. "Are you very sure I may wear it tonight?"

"Please, do. I'm quite sure... it wouldn't make feel as you do, if I wore it."

Honora smiled. "I hope you won't think of my compli-ment as being insincere, but you make my simple frock elegant, as well."

"Oh, please," Grace interrupted. "We all are beautiful, so let's go on before my hair falls down!"

The ladies and Mrs. Devonshire walked down the hall and into the foyer, then up the blue-carpeted stairs. The banis-ters shone, and the brass finials reflected the dancing light from the lanterns. Atop the stairs hung a tall mirror framed in golden filigree. In it, each lady took a survey of herself, a final inspection, then turned to the left and ventured out onto the promenade deck. Large floral arrangements in containers sat along the rails of the deck. The lanterns illuminated the deck, reflecting off the ripples of the river. The orchestra played a lively waltz, and the light breeze carried the aroma of roasted duck.

Several of the soldiers danced with passengers. Anna spied Julia and Sylvia dancing with two very handsome men dressed in three-piece suits; both men appeared older than the sisters. A waiter came up to Anna, Honora, Mrs. Devonshire, and Grace, and explained the buffet procedures.

The ladies joined the buffet line and filled their plates with some of the delicious roast and portions of the other many delectable items, then walked to the benches along the rail. The light apple fritters satisfied their yearning for something sweet, yet they were not too filling. Once they were finished eating, the waiter came by and took their empty plates and refilled their drinks.

Across the deck, against the railing, there stood the two soldiers who had disturbed Grace and Anna at breakfast. Anna again tried to ignore them, but even without looking, she could feel their foul stares.

Mrs. Devonshire finished her waltz with the Captain and joined the girls on the bench. "Whew! That Captain dances even better than he steers this ship!" she said, fanning herself. "Have you girls danced with anyone yet?"

"No," Anna said. "I'm happy just to watch the lovely ladies and sit in the calm night air."

"Me too," Grace agreed. "I'd prefer to watch the beautiful moonlight on the river and listen to the romantic music. This is the most fantastic event," Grace said.

Mrs. Devonshire stood. "I am parched," she declared. "Do you dears want to join me?" Without waiting for their reply, Mrs. Devonshire left for the buffet table.

"Well, I am going to dance with that tall blond soldier at the buffet," Honora said. "Now you can watch a real lovely lady!" She left the other three on the bench and strolled toward the man.

They watched his response as she talked to him, and when he took her arm, they snickered. Honora looked over her shoulder and winked.

"She looks very pretty in that blue dress of yours."

"I am thankful she traded with me," Anna said quietly.

"Anna, I don't want to pry, but is that why you are going

to Indian Territory? To get away from him?" Grace asked.

"Partly. Not only did I lose my fiancé, but shortly after that, I lost a chance at working as a teacher in a very fine school – a job I thought I was guaranteed to have."

"Oh no."

"Well, that's not all. To add more hurt to the situation, I discovered that was the work of my fiancé's father. He used his position to ensure that I would lose my teaching position – to keep me away from his son Martin."

"Goodness! I think I would have rolled into a ball and died. How have you managed to withstand all that disappointment and pain?"

"Well, Grace, as I told you before, it has only been with God's help." Anna shook her head. "There's no earthly way I would have maintained my sanity. If I didn't have God there with me, as well as the support and love of my family, I would have collapsed completely under the despair I felt."

"I guess you have reason to believe what you say, then."

"Yes. I suppose you could say I am an authority on disappointment."

"You are very kind, beautiful, and intelligent. I am sure you can find a man – a better one – without trying too hard, Anna!"

"Perhaps, and I thank you for the compliment, but that's no longer my priority. I want to make a difference, and I think I can do that by teaching children who need a compassionate and resourceful teacher."

"But do you have to go to the wilderness to fulfill that desire? Couldn't you have done the same in Ohio?"

"No. By the time I found out I had lost my teaching position, only the one in Indian Territory was open. Besides, I needed to remove myself from the situation, and this is what I believe God has chosen for me to do."

"Well, I think you succeeded in removing yourself from the situation all right," Grace said with a grin.

The girls stopped talking as Honora returned from her dance.

"Thank you for the waltz, Miss Honora," the soldier said as he bowed politely. "You're welcome," Honora said.

When the soldier walked off, the girls quickly began drilling Honora about him.

"I love this dress!" Honora exclaimed. "I believe it's my lucky dress," she said, blushing lightly as she fingered the lace on the sleeves.

"Well, in that case, it's yours!" Anna said.

"I was only joking," Honora said, shocked.

"No, please take it. I haven't any need for it. I don't... well, it will remind you of the time we've spent together after we leave and are out living our new lives."

"Thank you. I will always think of you and fondly of our trip when I wear it."

Grace patted Anna's hand. "That is very sweet of you indeed, Anna," Grace said.

As the band began to play another piece, Anna stood to make her way to the refreshments table.

While she refilled her lemonade, one of the soldiers from breakfast came up behind her. "Well, good evening, Ma'am"

Anna turned around to find the man standing so close that he was nearly leaning against her. "Excuse me, sir," Anna said.

"I thought I should introduce myself, as I believe the two of us are destined to get better acquainted. I'm Lieutenant Davies."

"Thank you for introducing yourself, sir, but I am on my way to rejoin my friends."

"Well, we could be friends if you'd just stand still for a moment," he slurred.

"Please, sir, step out of my way."

When Anna tried to move around him, he stepped in her way to stop her. He grabbed her hand. "What's the matter? You think you're too good for a soldier? Is that the problem?" he snarled.

Anna could smell the bitter odor of strong alcohol on his breath. "I'd like you to let go of me, sir! Move out of my way and leave me be."

The man squeezed her arm harder, causing Anna to squeal more from surprise than pain.

"Sir," said a voice from behind them, "it's clear that the lady wishes for you to leave her be. I suggest you do as she requests," the troop commander told the soldier.

"Yes, sir, Colonel Yarborough." Davies looked at Anna and sneered as he walked away from them.

"I'm sorry, Ma'am. Sometimes our men get cabin fever on these long trips. I am sure Lieutenant Davis will not bother you again."

"Thank you," Anna said, but she was trembling too much to say much else.

Honora walked up to the table just as the officer was leaving, unaware of Anna's altercation at the refreshment stand. "Did I see the Colonel speaking with you?" Honora asked naïvely.

"Yes, but it was nothing important – only casual talk about the long trip and the weather," she fibbed. "Would you like more to drink?" she asked to change the subject, trying to keep her emotions in check.

"Conner tells me that if the river cooperates, we will be in Memphis day after tomorrow."

"Conner?"

"The gentleman I danced with."

"Oh, him. Now I know why his name sounds familiar. I met him this morning during that little pig chase of theirs. He and his partner have quite a future in wild pig wrangling."

"Yes, he told me all about it. He's such a nice man," Honora said wistfully.

"I didn't know we were so close to Memphis," Anna said.

"Sadly, it won't be long before we'll be separated."

"I think I will miss even Mrs. Devonshire."

"Maybe, but it will be nice to be relieved of someone minding my business for me," Honora said.

They walked to the bench and had a seat. The rippling of the Mississippi and the cool breeze allowed Anna to relax and forget the episode with the belligerent soldier.

As the orchestra played a sonata, she closed her eyes and thought of her home and family, and her thoughts helplessly snaked to Martin. Even though she had willingly let Honora wear and keep her dress – her *wedding* dress, altered as it was – she couldn't keep dark feelings from coming to the surface again. As hard as she tried, she couldn't stop the escape of a few tears.

"Anna, what's wrong?" Honora asked and put her arm around her.

"Nothing. I'm sorry. I'm sure my moodiness comes from

lack of sleep. There's always some disturbance keeping me awake. I'm also homesick, missing my family, but I know it's silly and girlish for me to cry."

"Sometimes crying helps."

"I cannot believe you are saying that from personal experience, Honora. You do not seem like the type for tears."

"Me, cry? Never! But I *hear* it helps," she said with a coy grin, patting Anna on the shoulder.

The evening ended as beautifully as it had begun. Stars twinkled overhead, and the moonlight bounced off the slowly rolling river. The music faded, the lanterns were dimmed and extinguished, and all the passengers returned to their cabins, staterooms, and ordinary clothing. Anna, Grace, Honora, and Mrs. Devonshire left the promenade deck together. They walked to the ladies' cabins, and Anna left them at their rooms and continued on to hers, which was located further down the corridor.

As she neared her door, she saw someone going around the other end of the hallway. Anna stopped and hesitantly walked towards her cabin. She noticed an object in front of her door, and bent down to pick it up: a small brown package with a red rose attached. Anna looked around but didn't see the person who might have left it. As she stood, a piece of paper fell from underneath the rose.

For a beautiful flower. Next time, I will have my dance. D.

Chapter 12

Her hands shook as she handed the note to Captain Marston. First Mate Johan Brinter, a middle-aged man who resembled Anna's father, stood beside her and slowly patted her shoulder.

"Miss, do you know who sent this?" Captain Marston asked.

"No," Anna sighed and shook her head, "but at the Captain's ball, I did experience a rather uncomfortable incident with one of the soldiers. I believe his name was Daniels or Davies – something of that nature. Hmm... Lieutenant Davies. Yes, that was it!"

"An uncomfortable incident? How so?"

"He wanted to dance with me, but I told him as politely as I could that I didn't care to dance with him or anyone. He stood in front of me and wouldn't let me pass. He was rude and obtrusive."

"It sounds as if he's just a pushy man who wished to have a dance with a lovely lady – nothing very sinister. Seems a bit rude, of course, but certainly not a serious threat," he said. "Miss Collins, I'm sure you've dealt with this kind of behavior before."

"No, but even if I had, that should not excuse the soldier's actions. I felt threatened, and now I feel even more insecure. Why would any man be near the ladies' quarters anyway unless there was some sort of emergency going on? I thought it was off limits to anyone but female passengers."

"Well, yes, I suppose that would be a breach of ship policy, but it would be most difficult to prove that Lieutenant Davies placed the parcel at your door himself if there were no eyewitnesses, Miss Collins."

"But it refers to a dance and the fact that he didn't have one before. Please, Captain, could you at least make mention of this to his commander, Colonel Yarborough, I believe it is?" Anna begged. "The Colonel assured me that Davies wouldn't bother me again. If you mentioned this package and the note, perhaps he can prevent Lieutenant Davies from coming near me or my quarters again."

"To be honest with you, Miss Collins, I fear that going to his commander might anger Lieutenant Davies for getting him into hot water. If that happens, he might set himself on a course for revenge, and things could only get worse. All things considered, I think it is best to let the matter die down on its own. Some men do not take kindly to rejection, but the sting of it will likely wear off soon, and he'll move on to another object of affection."

"Captain Marston," First Mate Brinter interrupted, "it couldn't hurt to point out to the Colonel that someone was seen in the vicinity of the ladies' quarters. Perhaps he could go over the rules with his men again, allowing Lieutenant Davies to remain anonymous, of course."

The Captain nodded. "Fine. I'll summon Colonel Yarborough to my cabin and inform him about the incident and ask him to order his men to stay out of the passengers' areas and to stop fraternizing with the females onboard."

"Thank you Captain, and Mr. Brinter. I do not wish to cause any sort of ruckus or turmoil for anyone onboard, but I truly appreciate your help."

Anna stood and the First Mate opened the door to let her out. "If you have need of further assistance, please let me know, Miss Collins," Mr. Brinter said.

She thanked him and walked back to the stairs and down to her cabin hallway. At the corner, she cautiously looked around to be sure no-one was waiting for her or hiding. "At least Mr. Brinter seems concerned about my welfare more than his own reputation," Anna said to herself. She obsessively checked each shadowy corner and hall and doorway. "I need to calm down, or else the poor children at the Fort will be dealing with a rather neurotic teacher." She breathed a sigh and reprimanded herself for letting her feelings run wild – again.

Anna opened her cabin door, hastily locked it behind her, and looked around for something to place in front of it. *How silly this must look*, she thought, but she continued because it made her feel safer. The desk chair was the perfect height to place under the doorknob. With the door securely blocked, she sat on her bed and examined her work. "Dear God," she prayed. "Help me to find strength in You. Amen."

With her nightgown on, her hair let down, and warm socks on her feet, she climbed into bed.

Wait... what if there's a fire?

The lantern gave the room a comforting light, but Anna blew it out, knowing the danger of leaving it lit while she slept, and especially since she'd barricaded her door.

As the darkness filled the tiny cabin she prayed again for courage, protection, and wisdom and gave thanks for her friends and family. Moonlight from outside filtered into the room, calming her with just the right amount of light.

It took almost two hours for Anna to relax enough to fall into a fitful sleep. She woke several times, and eventually reached for her pendant watch to check the time. As she did so, she heard the doorknob of her cabin being turned.

Her heart quickened like a terrified bunny at the sight of a fox, and she held her breath and didn't move. After the knob jiggled a couple more times, whoever had tried to open her locked door gave up, and only then could Anna breathe again.

She lit the lantern and scooted her trunk over in front of the chair, still jammed tightly under the knob. Anna jumped back into her bed for only a second before she got back out and pulled the curtain closed over the small window, just in case the intruder was stubborn and wanted to try that next.

With her heart hammering in her chest, Anna pulled out her Bible. Too frightened to go back to sleep, she hummed her favorite songs from childhood, the ones her parents used to sing to her whenever the storms pummeled their home with violent thunder and lightning. She knew it wasn't the words of the songs that comforted her, but the fact that her parents cared enough to sit by her and her brother until the storms passed. In her parents' absence, she could only rely on God's presence to comfort and console her.

The brightening of the dawn sky relieved Anna, and she took a quick glance at her pendant watch. "Six o'clock," she said out loud. "Another short night and early morning."

She stood in the middle of the small room. The thought of going down the darkened hallway to the lavatory didn't seem sensible considering the events of the previous evening and night, so she sat on her bed, pondering what to do.

"God," she prayed, "I'm not even brave enough to leave this room in broad daylight." Tears trickled once again down her cheeks. "Please help me. If I can't find enough strength on this boat, what will happen when I'm in the wilderness?"

Just then, scripture words echoed in her mind: *My grace is sufficient for you.* If she'd learned anything over the past few months, it was the sufficiency of God's grace. She knew that even when God provided manna to the Israelites in the wilderness, they gathered enough only for the day. It seemed to her that God delivered grace and faith to her in amounts adequate for her tribulations, always at the moment when she most needed them.

Finally, she stood. "I'll take it step by step," she said to herself. "When I need to leave this room, His strength will be there." Anna nodded her head in agreement with herself and went to her little closet. She chose a dark, plain cotton dress, subconsciously hoping its drab color might conceal her from Davies or whoever had tried to open her door. If Honora or Grace didn't see her at breakfast, she knew they would certainly come looking for her, and she could walk to the dining room with them. "Unless God sends a large, fearsome angel to walk with me," she said with a giggle, imagining the angel's wings smacking against the ceiling of the hall as they walked.

She decided that after breakfast, she'd go again to the Captain and ask for his help. *Maybe he'll reassign me to a different cabin since someone has tried to break into my quarters,* she hoped.

About an hour later, someone knocked at her door.

"Who is it?" Anna asked through the door.

"It's me... Grace. Anna, why weren't you at breakfast?"

Her hands shook as she moved the trunk and chair from the door and unlocked it. She opened the door and began to cry.

"Oh, Grace, I'm so glad you came," Anna said.

"What's wrong?" Grace asked.

"Last night... someone tried to get into my room!"

"What? When?"

"Around 3:15. When I came back to my room last night I found a note by my door from one of the soldiers. After I came back from speaking with the Captain about it, I put the chair under the doorknob to make myself feel better, but I kept waking up, and I had just looked at my watch when I heard the doorknob being turned."

"Oh, my!" Grace said.

Anna sniffled. "I was so scared." She dabbed at her eyes with her shawl. "I hate feeling like this, so frightened and vulnerable."

"I'm sorry, Anna. Truly. Is there anything I can do?"

"I was afraid to leave my room and go to the lavatories, even, let alone breakfast."

Grace sat down beside her and put her arm around her shoulders. "We should go to the Captain together and tell him."

"Maybe later, after I've gained my composure and am not acting like an irrational, frightened little rabbit."

"No, Anna. We should go now. Perhaps he can speak with the night porters to see if they noticed anyone wandering around your corridor. I can accompany you. After all, I am one of the bravest creatures aboard this ship, remember?"

Anna grinned meekly.

"You and Honora told me that, and you weren't lying, were you?"

"No, Grace. We do think you are most brave," Anna said. She looked down at her trembling hands in her lap. Her fingers absentmindedly wrapped the shawl around them. "I guess we should go."

"Do you need to take anything with you? Your bag perhaps? You can stop by the lavatory and I'll stand watch while you freshen yourself."

"Oh, yes, I'll take my bag and my watch. I don't want to risk them being stolen if someone does manage to break in. They are really all I have of value."

They left the cabin and locked the door, and the two walked down the corridor very close to one another. Anna couldn't keep from looking from side to side; she was terrified that someone might try to jump out at her.

"I'm so embarrassed," she said a little later, as they climbed the stairs to the Captain's quarters on the hurricane deck.

"Whatever for, Anna?"

"For being so uncourageous after all that talk to you about faith."

"I, of all people, understand." Grace chuckled. "I fainted when I *thought* the soldiers were staring at me!"

"But now look at you," Anna said. "You're my brave protector!"

"Yes, I suppose I am amazing, aren't I?"

"I believe you are beginning to inherit some of Honora's ego," Anna said with a smile as she knocked lightly on Captain Marston's door.

First Mate Brinter opened the door. "Miss Collins! Good morning to you," he greeted, "and to you as well, Miss Grace," he added.

"Well, it hasn't been a very good morning," Anna said. "Not at all."

"I am so sorry to hear that. Please come in and tell me what you mean." Mr. Brinter sat in the chair beside the large desk.

"Someone tried to get into my cabin at about 3 o'clock this morning."

"It was blustery last night, Miss Collins. Perhaps it was the wind you heard?"

"The wind does not turn doorknobs, sir. Someone tried to open my door from the hallway."

"And I assume you've no idea who it might have been?"

Anna shook her head. "No. I was too frightened to get out of bed and certainly too scared to open the door. I couldn't even bring myself to leave my cabin this morning until Grace came looking for me when I missed breakfast."

He stood and took a deep breath. "I shall give this grim

news to the Captain immediately. Do you wish to disembark when we arrive at Memphis?"

"No, Mr. Brinter. I must go on, for I'm needed at my destination. However, do you think it would be possible for me to change cabins? Maybe if I were closer to the other rooms in the fore corridor, with all the people coming and going, whoever it was that bothered me won't do so again."

"I'm afraid that would mean an upgrade in your fare," he said. He turned to the logbook on the desk. "Yes, as I feared, an empty cabin or stateroom won't be available until we let off our passengers in Memphis, and that won't be until the day after tomorrow."

"I don't think I can stay in my room another minute, sir." Anna shook her head and sighed. The thought crossed her mind to pack up her bags and jump ship at the next stop, beg her parents' forgiveness for her stubbornness, and settle for a mundane, safe, secure life in Cincinnati rather than sleeping alone and feeling threatened night and day.

"Could she stay in *my* stateroom?" Grace asked. "My companion departed the ship at Louisville. Since I have no roommate, there is plenty of room, and I'll be getting off at Memphis anyway."

Anna looked at Grace and wanted to hug her. "Thank you, Grace," she said. "Would that be acceptable, sir?" Anna asked the First Mate.

"Absolutely, ladies," he said. "I'll have the porters transport your belongings to Miss Larsen's stateroom. I can't guarantee that whoever bothered you won't find you again, but while you are bunking with a roommate, it is likely they will stop with their childish harassing for fear of being caught."

"I understand. Thank you, sir. I will stay in the dining room until my things are moved. I am starving since I missed breakfast, and this news has brought my appetite back. I truly appreciate your help."

"Not a problem, Miss Collins."

"Are the soldiers in the dining room now?" Anna asked.

"No. They're in the hold with the officers, going over their assignment for New Orleans."

"Thank you," Anna said, glad to know she wouldn't have to lose her appetite again by running into Davies while she ate.

Anna and Grace left Mr. Brinter and headed for the dining room. She felt somewhat better walking with Grace, who planned to protect Anna by stomping on feet or hitting any suspicious characters on the head with her bag.

They chose a table close to the dining room door. No sooner had they taken their seats when Mrs. Devonshire swooshed in the room and enveloped Anna in a buxom embrace. "Oh, my sweet, precious darling! Are you all right? I just this very moment overheard Mr. Brinter ordering the porters to move your belongings. I marched right up to him and demanded to know what they were doing." She paused and placed her pale hand against her chest. "I did not care if they thought me nosey, for fear you were leaving the ship. Then of all things, Mr. Brinter tells me someone tried to get into your room! Oh, dear! That hooligan! How dare some brash, loathsome man treat one of my sweet doves in such a revolting manner? I know within my heart it was one of those soldiers. Did I not warn you girls? Right from the start, I told you that you should be careful, did I not? Darling, why did you ever get within an arm's length of those awful militant creatures?" She glared at the girls like an angry mother and did not allow them time to answer before she continued, "Now, because of your misfortune, maybe someone will pay heed to my words of admonition." She sat down in a splash of brocade.

"Mrs. Devonshire, this isn't the best time to reprim –" Grace started but was cut off midsentence.

"Did I not tell you those men are lustful, dangerous monsters incapable of restraining their sick carnal desires? Men like those could –"

This time, Anna cut off Mrs. Devonshire, more curtly than she intended. "I wasn't hurt, Livy. I was just a little frightened, and I'm fine now. I assure you that you no longer need to worry. The Captain and the First Mate, and the man's commanding officer are aware of the situation, and I shall be bunking with Grace in her stateroom until she gets off in Memphis."

"You poor, poor dear. I am sorry I was not able to protect you and keep watch over you girls more closely," she clucked. Her face wrinkled with contrition. "How selfish of me to let you fall prey to the wolves while I have been off gallivanting around!" She began to sob.

Grace rolled her eyes.

"Mrs. Devonshire, it isn't your duty to stand guard over us day and night," Anna said.

Mrs. Devonshire continued bawling with gusto. After one prolonged bellow, she took a deep breath. "Oh, darlings, I have failed you," she gushed, dropping her head to the table. "Mrs. Devonshire, please!" Grace nearly shouted to be heard over her thespian wails. "Everything's fine. Here... have a peach tart." She pushed the pastry before Mrs. Devonshire's lowered head and waved the aroma towards her.

Mrs. Devonshire slowly ceased her histrionics, raised her head, gathered her composure, dabbed her slightly moist eyes with her lace-edged handkerchief, and shook off the guilt. She reached for the delicacy. "I knew you would understand and forgive," she said with a hiccup.

This time, it was Anna who rolled her eyes.

Rooming with Grace in her cabin reminded Anna of her college days. She felt safer in Grace's company, and that allowed her to catch up on the sleep she'd missed the previous night.

Mrs. Devonshire stopped by their room to let them know about the mysterious new passenger travelling to New Orleans. Mr. Buerenger, the tall, handsome gentleman with coal-black hair and dark eyes, had captivated and dominated all Mrs. Devonshire's thoughts and conversations since his arrival on the boat at Louisville, which allowed Anna respite from her pity and overbearing attention.

Anna mentally prepared herself for the imminent departure of Grace, Honora, Sylvia, and Julia once they reached Memphis. She was sure she wouldn't miss Julia and Sylvia quite as much, since she rarely saw them, and even when she did, they were busy entertaining one of the wealthy male passengers. Mrs. Devonshire would travel on to New Orleans with Anna.

Honora, Grace, Anna, and Mrs. Devonshire ate their final dinner together, and then Mrs. Devonshire ordered a special dessert in celebration of their friendship and the start of their new lives. The rotund woman managed to keep her theatrics to a minimum, allowing all to enjoy a pleasant time together.

After dinner, they walked back to their cabins to retrieve their shawls before going up to the deck to enjoy their last shared evening on the river. After they gathered their wraps, the other girls met Anna and Grace outside their cabin.

"Oh no," Anna said when she looked at herself in the mirror at the end of the corridor. "I've lost Grandmother's brooch!"

"Where did you lose it?" Grace asked.

"If she knew that, it wouldn't be lost," Honora quipped.

"I'll go back to the dining room and see if I find it along the way."

"We'll go with you," Honora said.

Now, Anna, you cannot require someone to hold your hand all the time, she scolded herself, swallowing her fear of deserted hallways. *Be brave – like Grace!*

Anna shook her head. "No, you go on ahead. I shall catch up with you shortly. You don't want to miss the orchestra."

"Are you sure?" Grace asked. "Will you be all right?"

"Yes. I'm sure no-one will dare bother me now knowing I've got you as a bodyguard!"

"We'll meet you on deck then," Honora said, and they separated in the hallway.

Anna went to the left, into the main corridor towards the dining room. When she rounded the corner, she thought she heard a clanging noise. Anna stopped to listen, but when she heard nothing further, she continued on to the dining room, to the table where they had dined. There, under a chair, she found her precious pin. Just as she bent down to pick it up, the dining room doors closed. "Grace," she said, thinking her blonde guard had ignored her request and come to join her. When she looked up, however, she realized her visitor was a most unwelcome one. It was Lieutenant Davies who stood at the entrance, with a sickening grin on his face.

"What do you want?" she asked, trying to steady her voice.

"Only a dance, like I said before," he rasped. "You gonna dance with me friendly-like, or do I need to persuade ya?"

He rapidly closed the space between them.

Anna sidestepped around the table away from him, but he blocked her escape. "Please just leave me be, Lieutenant. I told you that I am not here for dancing, with you or with anyone else. Now go away or I'll –"

"You'll what? What... are you gonna stab me with that little pin of yours? Maybe you think you can scream for help." He looked around. "Go ahead, miss. Nobody's gonna hear you! With the band playin' and everybody up on deck, nobody'll hear a dang thing."

"Again, I'm asking you to leave me alone."

"And I'm a-tellin' ya that ya gotta dance with me first." He quickly stepped up and grabbed her arm.

"Stop it! Let me go!" Anna yelled.

He jerked her closer. The stench of alcohol and tobacco permeated his clothing and breath.

Nauseated by fear and the disgusting odor, Anna turned her head to keep the uprising bitter taste in her mouth from erupting.

"You think yer too good for me, don't ya?"

Anna started crying and struggled to loosen herself from his grip.

He pulled her towards him, trying to force her into a kiss. She ducked and stomped on his foot, and the pain caused him to momentarily let her go.

Anna tried to run, but he caught her arm and flung her backwards as if she weighed nothing more than a ragdoll, causing her to lose her footing and fall against a table. A glass vase filled with flowers crashed to the floor and shattered. Anna sobbed and struggled to get up. She could taste the salty blood oozing from her split lip.

"Well, now you gone and busted up that purdy little mouth of yours. Guess I should give it a little kiss to make it better." He walked to where Anna lay and grabbed her arm and jerked her to her feet.

Just then, the locked dining room doors shook, and someone yelled.

"Help! Help!" Anna screamed as loudly as she could. She writhed to loosen herself from her attacker's grip.

Davies slapped Anna so hard that her ears began to ring. The dizziness overtook her, and she fell unconscious, a helpless heap on the floor right next to where her brooch had lain.

When Anna awakened, the first thing she noticed was the ringing in her ears and the dull, throbbing ache in her head. As her vision began to come into focus, she saw four faces looking down at her: Honora, Grace, a short man who reminded her of her grandfather, and a tall man with black hair. Anna tried to pull herself up, but the room reeled from side to side.

"Lie back down, Miss, Collins," the grandfatherly man said. "You've suffered a concussion. You need to remain quiet."

Anna," Honora said, "the doctor says you should be still for the rest of the evening."

"Wh– what happened?" Anna asked weakly.

"That man, Davies, attacked you!" Grace answered. "He hit you, and if Mr. Buerenger hadn't come along when he did... well, it was a miracle he was there to help you."

"Who?"

Honora sat down on the bed. "Anna, this is Mr. Buerenger." She pointed to the tall stranger standing above her. "He's the one who came to your aid."

Anna strained to see the black-haired man. "Thank you, sir." She held her hand out.

"You're welcome, Miss Collins. I only did what any responsible person would have done. I am glad you're awake now. And please don't worry. That fiend Davies is in custody, holed up in solitary confinement. He'll be tossed off this boat in Memphis and held there on charges of assault and battery, as he should be. He will not bother you again."

Anna closed her eyes, overwhelmed by the events of the past hours. "I can't believe he hit me just because I didn't want to dance with him. He accused me of... truly; it wasn't because I think myself better than he! I just didn't..."

Her words were cut off by the threat of yet more tears. Honora took her hand. "Oh, Anna. It's all right now, you have nothing to feel badly about."

"Miss Collins, your friend is right. You weren't responsible for his behavior. He's been in trouble before for bothering people, especially after he's had a bit of the strong drink in him."

"Don't worry," Honora said, patting her hand. "After he leaves the ship, you won't have to be frightened anymore. Mr. Buerenger is staying on until you reach New Orleans, and he has promised Grace and me that he'll watch out for you."

"Oh, no. I don't need anyone to protect me," Anna countered, though she secretly thought a protector might be exactly what she needed.

"Oh, of course not," Grace laughed. "Mrs. Devonshire will still be aboard."

"Please, Grace! Don't upset me further." Anna snorted and then winced. "Ouch! The thought of that made my head hurt."

"Miss Collins, if you don't mind, I must leave you in the good hands of these most capable ladies. If you need anything, please let the Captain know. He sends his condolences about what has happened and his regrets that he didn't take the matter more seriously."

"Thank you... and thank the Captain for me too, please," Anna said.

Grace and Honora escorted Mr. Buerenger to the door.

"We appreciate your helping her," Honora said. "I'm afraid if you hadn't come to her assistance, she'd... well, she would have been much worse off in the hands of that drunken lunatic."

Mr. Buerenger nodded and opened the door, startled to find Colonel Yarborough there with his hand up, ready to knock.

"Duncan?" the commander said. "What are you doing here?"

"He rescued Anna from that awful soldier," Honora said.

"Really? You were the hero I heard about? Well, it's good to see you again," said the Colonel, and the men shook hands.

"Ladies, Colonel," Mr. Buerenger said and left.

"Ma'am, how's Miss Collins?" the Colonel asked Honora.

"She's awake now, but she's still a bit groggy. Her head hurts, of course, but the doctor assured us that our Anna will make a complete recovery, at least from the physical end of things." Honora grimaced.

"May I speak with her?"

"Let me ask if she feels up to more visitors."

In the bedchamber, Grace said quietly, in case Anna had fallen back to sleep, "Anna, Colonel Yarborough is here, the troop commander. Are you up to speaking with him?"

Anna sighed. "Yes, of course," she said.

"I suggest no more visitors this evening after the Colonel," Dr. Cameron admonished.

"Yes, Doctor. I'll go get him then," Grace said and started to leave.

"Grace, do I look a mess?" Anna whispered.

"No, dear. You're as lovely as always, only with some added color."

Anna groaned. "Thank you... I think."

Grace smiled and left the room.

A few moments later, Colonel Yarborough came in. "Miss Collins, I came to apologize for Davies's behavior." He cleared his throat. "If there's anything you need – anything at all – please don't hesitate to ask."

"Thank you, Colonel. I'm told I'll be fine, and I cannot yet fathom anything I might need other than some rest and peace of mind." She paused in thought for a moment and then muttered, "Well... there may be one thing."

"Yes?"

She tried not to give in to the fear and the pain. "May I have your promise the wretched man will not stay onboard? They told me he would be taken off, but I would like your assurance as his commanding officer."

He nodded. "Tomorrow Davies will be set off in Memphis to stand before the marshal for punishment. You will not collide with him again, miss."

Anna closed her eyes. "Thank you. In that case, I'll be fine."

"Very well, Ma'am. And don't hesitate to ask if there is anything further we can do for you."

Colonel Yarborough left her room and returned to the sitting area of Grace's stateroom. "I'm sorry your friend suffered such abuse at the hands of one of our men. Should there be anything she needs before you depart, please let me know. I will be continuing on to New Orleans with the troop, and I am happy to assist in any way I can."

"We certainly will," they both agreed.

"Good day then."

"Good day, Colonel."

The doctor followed the Colonel out as Grace and Honora returned to the bedroom area to sit with Anna while she slept.

When Anna awakened, they talked of lighthearted topics, purposely avoiding any discussion of the attack or their unavoidable separation.

Dr. Cameron checked on Anna later that evening. After he decided she had suffered no serious side effects from her fall, he prescribed her a sedative in case she had trouble falling asleep due to anxiety. "Now, Miss Collins, I want you to stay in bed until I check on you in the morning. If you cannot obey these orders, I shall have to call in the strictest, meanest medic on the ship to be sure you mind my commands," he said, wrinkling his forehead until his bushy gray eyebrows brushed the tops of his gold-rimmed glasses.

"The way I feel now," Anna said, "I don't think it will be difficult to follow those instructions."

"Fine," he said and packed up his bag, "but it wouldn't hurt to have Henrietta sit with you tonight. I have no doubts that the gal could easily lift you should you get up and take a faint or fall." He chuckled.

"Dr. Cameron," Grace said, "I'll be here. I'll watch after her and fetch anything she needs."

"As will I," Honora added.

"Well, Miss Collins, it seems you won't need Henrietta after all." He went to the door and shook his head. "Sure was looking forward to being alone tonight."

"Your nurse, Henrietta, sleeps in the infirmary?" Grace asked in disbelief.

"Yes, and after thirty years of marriage, I still haven't grown accustomed to that grizzly bear-like snore of hers. The strongest of sedatives won't allow me to sleep through that!"

The girls laughed.

"Goodnight, ladies," he said.

"Thank you, Dr. Cameron," Anna said.

Immediately after hearing of Anna's attack, Mrs. Devonshire bustled into Grace's cabin, brushed aside the doctor and the girls, and headed straight to Anna's side. At the sight of the unconscious Anna with the bruised face and cut lip, self-induced guilt and genuine compassion for Anna caused Mrs. Devonshire to hyperventilate. The doctor ordered her to bed – a remedy for both Anna and Mrs. Devonshire.

When Anna woke again, she and the girls talked late into the night and finally fell quiet. The medication Anna took calmed her body, but her mind continued to relive the horrible events in her dreams. Vivid nightmares plagued her, preventing her from the restorative rest she needed. In spite of the sedatives, she awakened several times, frightened and confused. Unable to light a lantern to read her Bible as she often did when she was upset, Anna prayed and remembered the scripture that had comforted her in the past: *I know the plans I have for you. Plans for good...*

Anna prayed for forgiveness for the soldier who had hurt her and for divine protection to keep her from further harm and distress. Tears filled Anna's eyes, and she shook with quiet sobs. Eventually, her prayer for peace was answered, and she fell into a calm, restful sleep.

Early the next morning the dining crew sent breakfast to Anna in her room, with an additional assortment of pastries, cakes, and Anna's favorite cinnamon raisin toast. The girls chatted gaily as Honora and Grace helped Anna recover physically and emotionally from the trauma. The Captain dropped by and checked on Anna, as did Colonel Yarborough, with a bouquet of flowers in hand. The company, the flowers, and the fine food helped Anna to feel much more at ease.

The mid-morning sunlight glistened off the rolling Mississippi. The number of shoreline establishments increased as the ship neared the bustling port of Memphis. The passengers who were disembarking had already packed up their belongings and placed them in the dining room, where the porters stacked and readied them for removal upon arrival at the dock. The excited passengers stood on deck, watching as they neared their destination.

Anna caught Grace dabbing her eyes as they sat waiting in the cabin. "Are you all right?" Anna asked her.

Grace chuckled. "Of course. Why?"

"I thought I saw a tear." Anna moved closer to Grace on the bed. "Are you afraid, Grace?"

A faint smile crossed Grace's face. "Not anymore, and I'm surprised about that. I'm only sad because I'm going miss you and our friendship. I feel like we have become sisters, of sorts. Do you think we'll ever see each other again?"

"Well, I imagine it's possible – someday."

"I never imagined my trip would give me three new and wonderful friendships."

Anna thought for a moment. "Three? I understand about Honora and me, but who else are you referring to?" she asked. "Mrs. Devonshire?"

"Anna!" Grace squealed in astonishment. "I mean my friendship with God."

"Oh, of course! I knew that." She laughed. "I have suffered a concussion, you know. I think I have that disease that makes one forget tidbits of information."

"Pneumonia?"

Anna laughed and then held her mouth, which was still painful and tender. "No! Amnesia! Perhaps you suffer from it also!"

Grace hugged Anna. "Oh, Anna, thank you for being my friend and for introducing me to another One. Because of you, I know He'll always be with me, even if the Marsh children get to be too much!"

"You're welcome, Grace, and those children shall be truly blessed to have you."

"You still believe that, don't you?"

"What? That God is always with me?"

"Yes," Grace answered.

"Why do you ask?"

"Well, after all that happened yesterday, I thought that perhaps you would question whether God really cares for you. I imagine that would shake anyone's faith. After all, if He controls all things, that means He allowed that horrible thing to happen to you. Aren't you disappointed in Him?"

"Grace, our faith in God doesn't keep us from all the bad things in the world or the actions nonbelievers take." Anna paused. "I believe that when something bad happens to me, He'll be with me *through* it, if not *around* it. I cannot blame God for that soldier's behavior, but I do credit Him for sending the man to help me."

The horn blasted three short bursts, announcing their arrival at the port.

"Oh, I'm going to miss you!" Anna said.

"I've written my employer's name and address for you should you have a chance to send a letter. If you are ever in Memphis, please come and find me for a visit!"

"I will, Grace. And I promise that once I've settled in at the Fort, I shall write to tell you about all my exciting adventures. Please take care of yourself – and of those children. I know God will bless your new life."

"It is so exciting, isn't it?" Grace said, gathering her bag and wrap.

They left the room, and Anna locked the door behind them. Walking down the corridor, they could hear the band playing on deck. Passengers stood along the railings of the three decks of the ship, watching as the ship approached the docks. Anna and Grace looked for Honora and found her waiting near the stairs.

"There you are!" Grace waved to her as they met. "Did you get your bags from your room?"

"Yes. I'm all ready. I certainly hope my sister isn't late. She sometimes gets sidetracked, and... well, I suppose I can admit I am feeling a bit nervous." Honora bounced up and down and grabbed Anna's hands.

"Me too, but in a good way." Grace giggled."I haven't felt this good in quite a long while, and I owe it to the two of you. You've made this trip wonderful – more pleasant than I ever dreamt it could be."

"That goes for me too," Honora said.

"Dear, I heard about your attack yesterday. Are you all right?" asked a middle-aged lady, her gloved hand resting on the arm of a tall, impressive man. She looked at Anna with concern and touched Anna's arm.

"Oh – yes, I'm recovering well, thank you." Anna smiled. "I am sure I look worse than I feel," she said when she remembered her black eye and swollen lip.

"What a horrible man! I hope the military provides an appropriate punishment for his actions. Justice must be served, or people shall never learn to behave properly."

"The Colonel told me he would see to it that my attacker is properly detained and tried."

"Well, dear, should you need legal assistance, my husband is a lawyer. Here's his card."

Anna took the card and thanked her, and the couple walked away. Anna rejoined Honora and Grace as she looked at the small yellow card: "Charles Abbott, Attorney at Law, MacGregor, Jameson, Morgan, & Abbott Law Firm, Cincinnati." Anna gasped. *Shall I ever escape these constant reminders of Martin?*

Grace took Anna's arm and linked her other arm with Honora's. "Here we are!" she yelled to be heard above the noise of the band, the ship horn, and the cheers of the passengers, which mingled with the cheers coming from the crowd that was situated on the dock, awaiting the ship's arrival.

"There's my sister – and John, and the baby," Honora screamed. "Look at them!" She waved and jumped up and down. "Callie! Callie!" she yelled and waved her arms high above the crowd, trying to get her sister's attention.

Grace looked out over the people standing on the pier. "I think I see Mrs. Marsh. There, the lady with the purple coat and large hat!" She pointed into the mass of people meeting the passengers. "See? Oh, there are the girls." Two blonde-haired girls aged about ten and eight waved at Grace.

The ship lurched and jostled the passengers as it slid closer to the wharf.

Mrs. Devonshire managed to find her little lambs before they departed. "You girls! I've been looking for you for hours, it seems! Ready to be off to your new lives?"

"Yes we are, ma'am," Honora said. "Thank you for your kindness during our voyage, Livy."

Mrs. Devonshire looked taken aback, since Anna had been the only one brave enough to address her by her first name till then. "You... well, you're welcome, dear," she stuttered. "I wish you all the best in your new home." She hugged Honora and then turned to Grace. "Dear, you be careful and don't let anyone mistreat you!" she said.

Grace giggled and embraced Mrs. Devonshire before she had a chance to initiate the anticipated enfolding.

Muscular men on the dock tied up the massive ropes that were thrown out by the ship crew, and the passengers began their descent.

Honora and Grace said their painful goodbyes to Mrs. Devonshire and Anna, and joined the others leaving the ship.

Out of the corner of her eye, Anna caught a flash of blue. She turned to see two soldiers escorting a shackle-bound Lieutenant Davies to the gangplank. His anger-filled eyes met Anna's, and he cast a nasty sneer in her direction, like a wild dog, foaming at the mouth. "I'll get you!" he mouthed to Anna and bolted against the soldiers, who jerked the chains tighter to keep him at bay.

Anna stumbled backwards. His threats panicked her but she quickly constrained her emotions, not wanting to create a scene that would set off Mrs. Devonshire. *Colonel Yarborough promised Davies will be punished and that I will never have to set eyes on him again*, she reminded herself. *He cannot touch me again, no matter what he thinks.* She relaxed when she remembered the Colonel's kindness and quick action to punish the man.

"I do hope they'll be well," Mrs. Devonshire said, unaware of the soldier's threats.

"Who?"

"Honora and Grace, of course."

"Mrs. Devonshire, I am certain they'll be just fine," Anna answered, touched by the genuine concern exhibited in Mrs. Devonshire's tone of voice. She took Mrs. Devonshire's arm. "What kind of passengers do you think we'll be taking on now?"

"I have no idea, dear, but I suppose we'll soon find out. I'm sure I'll know plenty about them by sunset!"

"Yes, Livy. That's another thing I'm sure of," Anna laughed.

Without Grace's lively chatter the room was quiet, but Anna didn't feel afraid or concerned for her safety. She had seen Davies taken off the ship, shackled and doomed by his own deeds, and she felt secure for the first time in several days. Mrs. Devonshire paid the extra fee for Anna to stay in Grace's stateroom. Anna obliged hesitantly but the comfort and security from the room stirred her into accepting the gift.

Mrs. Devonshire had spent all her time since their departure from Memphis scouting out the new passengers, gathering scraps of information about the new arrivals. To date, she knew that a family of three were travelling to New Orleans to acquire a plantation they had recently inherited; two young men were travelling to the southern United States in Mexican territory, hoping to receive land grants to settle new homesteads; and a young minister and his family were on their way to Shreve's Town, to start a new church.

The climate of the river area changed slowly due to the warmer air masses that surged upward from the southern part of the country and collided with cold air that survived its travel from the northern states. Such collisions sometimes spawned small thunderstorms with gusty winds, rain, and hail. Because of the more numerous showers resulting from such storms, the river flowed higher than normal.

Anna, who had despised storms since the time she was a little girl, noticed the tall, billowy white thunderheads piled high in the sky west of the river. The air felt heavy and humid. The Captain ordered the crew to secure all unstable items on the ship and warned the passengers that their river journey might, indeed, become a bit rougher as they weathered the storms.

On the upper deck, Anna watched the scenery pass by. She felt lonely since Honora and Grace had gone. After the other girls departed ship and the Colonel evicted Anna's predator, Mrs. Devonshire had felt somewhat released from her self-imposed role as Anna's protector. Even though Anna ate meals with Mrs. Devonshire and kept updated on the dossiers of the passengers, she often found herself alone, trying to pass the time.

Lightning crackled, and a thunderous boom roared above. Anna ducked and scurried into the stairwell. She giggled, embarrassed at how silly she looked ducking and running for protection from incineration by fiery lightning bolts. When she was little and begged her parents to sit with her and lullaby her through the waging storms, she had an excuse, but now she was a grown woman after all, and she needed to live up to her brave reputation.

On her way down the stairs, Anna bumped into the Captain and an older man going up to the deck.

"Ah, Miss Collins," Captain Marston said. "I'd like to introduce Earl Michaelson. He'll be traveling with us to New Orleans." The Captain gestured to the gentleman standing on the stairway next to him, face upward gazing at the sky. The man barely looked at Anna but managed to offer a polite nod of acknowledgment.

"My pleasure, Ma'am. Oh, what a fascinating sky," the man said, pointing to the boiling gray clouds overhead. "I love a good thunderstorm."

"Well, in that case, I think you're in for a treat," the Captain said. "Miss Collins, it is so good to see that you've recovered from your... uh, from the incident."

"Yes," Anna said and touched her lip, now only slightly bruised with a hint of the laceration. "I feel fine, thank you."

"It is such a shame that your voyage with us has been marred by such an unpleasant situation," said the Captain, shaking his head. "And as if you haven't had enough to worry about, it seems the wind's picking up. Perhaps I'd better get back to steering this old gal, miss, and you should head to your stateroom to get beneath the covers and sleep through it. If you need anything, Miss Collins, do not hesitate to have a porter contact me." He nodded to Anna.

"I will. Thank you for concern," Anna replied.

Another brilliant flash of lightning sizzled overhead, and a deafening boom roared from the skies, demonstrating Anna's strong sense of self-preservation and reinforcing her decision to go to her room.

As she unlocked the door, a fleeting moment of fright hit her. She shook her head, "He's gone, and I don't need to worry," she said to herself. Anna lit the lanterns to brighten her stateroom, which was quite dark without the usual bright morning sun that had been drowned out by the menacing clouds.

When a knock came on her door, it startled her. "Ah!" she screamed and then tittered from embarrassment. "Wh–who is it? Who's there?" she asked.

"First Mate Brinter, Miss Collins."

Anna unlocked the door and peeked out. "Well, good afternoon, sir."

"Hello. I am stopping by each cabin and stateroom to let the passengers know we're in for a rough sail over the next few hours. If you'd like company, some of the passengers are congregating in the dining hall to ride it out together."

"No. I'll be fine, thank you."

"Very good, Miss Collins, but you may want to watch your lanterns," he said, noticing Anna's flickering lamps. "Should it get really rough, it'd be best to blow them out and open your door to allow for light."

"Thank you, Mr. Brinter. I assure you I will be most careful and mindful."

Anna took a slice of the delicious bread she had saved from breakfast. She poured some hot water that was delivered to her by a helpful porter and made herself a soothing cup of tea. She opened the curtains all the way to allow as much light as possible into her room. Then, she settled herself upon the bed and listened to the shrieking howl of the winds.

She read the Bible and prayed aloud, "Father, I thank You for providing the opportunity to let me know Honora and Grace. Please be with them as they begin new chapters in their lives. Continue to guide Grace and strengthen her faith in You. Protect her, Lord! She's such a special girl. Touch Honora also, God. Ease her grief and help her to find You," Anna prayed.

She stopped, carried away from the prayer to thoughts of Davies's attack. Tears dripped onto her Bible. "Oh, God, thank You for saving me from greater harm and for letting Mr. Buerenger find me when he did. Help me, Father, to forgive the one who has wronged me and harmed me. Please forgive him," she continued. "Protect us on our journey and guide Captain Marston. Amen."

She felt it strange that praying that she would find forgiveness towards Davies was easier than finding it for Martin, but as she pondered, she realized that while the coarse, crude soldier had only physically hurt her, he held no place in her heart, as Martin had. Davies had assaulted her as a result of the effects of alcohol and bad nature, but Martin willfully and intentionally broke her heart and immersed her in intractable agony. He was far too sober and cruel to be relieved of blame, and it would be some time until Anna could take that step.

Anna mused about the incident with the lawyer's wife. "How odd that the man worked for the same firm as Martin," she murmured to herself.

Continuous thunder bellowed, and incessant lightning perforated the darkened skies, its brilliance illuminating Anna's room with temporary bouts of daylight. Hail pellets pelted the cabin windows, but in spite of it all, the ship still sailed smoothly.

With no further warnings from the crew, Anna decided the storm was over. *Surely if the storm posed any danger to the ship or the passengers, they would let us know,* she reasoned. She looked at her watch. "Five-thirty! My! I might as well take a nap," Anna said aloud. "I haven't slept much in the past week." Anna snuggled under a throw blanket, checked the lanterns to be sure they were stable, and closed her eyes.

Chapter 13

A loud clanging noise jolted Anna from her slumber. She jumped up from the bed and opened the door to see what the root of the noise was. Porters hustled up and down the corridors, shouting for the passengers to come out.

"Ma'am!" a small, black crewmember shouted. "Please move to the dining room!"

Anna grabbed her bag, slammed the door shut and locked it behind her, then joined the steadily moving line of passengers as they made their way to the dining hall.

About 150 guests stood against the dining room walls. The few children aboard cried, and one small baby wailed incessantly, much to the embarrassment and worry of his mother. The Captain stood in the middle of the room and shouted over the din: "Ladies and gentlemen, we've run into a bit of bad weather, as you can see! We're going to need your full co-operation just in case we start taking on water."

As calm as he attempted to sound, the announcement resulted in panic, and many of the women began to weep, clutch their husbands, and cling to their children.

"Please stay calm," he requested, though the request fell on far too many fear-deafened ears. "Folks, you will need to listen clearly to our instructions, to ensure everyone's safety!" He explained the evacuation plan to the passengers, as well as the procedure for loading the lifeboats in case the need arose. Thankfully theirs was one of the first of the river steamboats to carry such a luxury!

In the middle of the room, the crew lined the passengers up according to cabin location. Women with children stood at the head of the lines, followed by childless women, and finally the men. The First Mate prayed for protection, and the Captain returned to his post to navigate the ship as well as he could. Some passengers sat down at the dining tables and waited for further instructions. The ship rocked side to side with an occasional deep pitch forward. A few passengers complained of seasickness and decided to lie on the floor to ease the discomfort and prevent themselves from becoming ill in front of strangers.

Mrs. Devonshire waved to Anna from her line and mouthed the words, *"Isn't this exciting?"*

Anna raised her eyebrows, cast her a nervous smile, and waved back.

The lady next to Anna struggled with her young daughter's limp form, trying to balance the soundly sleeping girl upon her knees. She looked up and saw Anna watching her. "She's a handful when she's asleep," muttered the mother.

"Probably best she's asleep during the excitement, though," Anna said.

"Yes, you're right," said the lady as she swept strands of brown hair from the little girl's eyes.

"She's adorable. What's her name?"

"Thank you. This is my Hillary. She's a sweet little girl."

"Hillary. That's a beautiful name. I'm Anna."

"Cecilia Hayden. Nice to meet you, though I wish it were under more cheerful circumstances."

"Of course. In any case, it must be difficult to travel alone with a youngster."

"Oh, I'm not alone. My husband is with us, but they've sent him to stand with the other men at the end of the line. It's sad they don't allow families to stand together. It would be much easier for him to hold her than it is for me. She's growing bigger every day, it seems. Quite an armful."

"I could help you place her on the floor if you'd like. I'll gladly lend you my wrap for her to lie on, and you could fold little Hillary's blanket under her head for a pillow."

"Oh, that would be quite a rest for my tired arms, at least for a while."

Anna and Cecilia fashioned a makeshift fabric pallet on

the carpeted dining room floor. The little girl stirred when her mother put her down, but moments later, she quickly returned to her sound sleep.

Cecilia stretched her back and rubbed her arms. "I should have large muscles like a farmhand hauling that little thing around like this. Where are you from, Anna?"

"Cincinnati."

"We're from Memphis, Tennessee. My husband is taking us to New Orleans to visit his family. His father is very ill, and they haven't had a good relationship the last five or six years. Amatus, my husband, hopes to make amends with his father... before it's too late."

"Oh my. Well, it seems all families have their difficulties sometimes."

"Yes, especially ours. In choosing to marry me, my husband went against his family's desires. They preferred him to choose a woman of... well, a rich girl of a different religious persuasion, I could say."

"That seems honorable to me, that your husband chose you over his family's wishes."

"Well..." She paused. "Sometimes I wonder if it was a *wise* choice. He misses his mother terribly, and he was close to his sisters and younger brother before he gave his ring to me." She stopped and looked back at her husband, who smiled sweetly at her. "I often feel guilty for causing his estrangement from his family."

"I truly doubt he regrets his decision," Anna said. "It's obvious he adores the both of you. How could he not?" Anna asked, glancing down at the beautiful little girl. "Any man would consider himself blessed."

The storm's fury slammed the ship with a large gust of wind, pitching it forward. Squeals filled the air, along with a loud crash of thunder.

"Do you think we're in real danger?" Cecilia asked, biting her lip, her eyes feverishly searching for a comforting glimpse of her husband.

"I don't know much about travelling on the river, but I do know that our Captain is very cautious and well-experienced. I'm sure he wouldn't allow his passengers to remain in danger."

Lightning flashed for several minutes, lighting the sky

with brilliance and illuminating even the interior of the dining hall. Thunder rolled, and the rain fell more heavily.

Anna closed her eyes and prayed for protection. When she opened her eyes again, she saw the little girl looking up at her. "Hello, sweetie," Anna said to her. "You're awake."

"Mommy!" the little girl whined and looked up for her mother.

"Shh, baby. It's all right. Mommy's here." Cecilia reached down and pulled the girl up into her lap. Hillary leaned into her mother's chest and peeked shyly up around her mother's arm at Anna.

A loud crack of thunder frightened the toddler, and she started to cry. Anna picked up her blanket and handed it to her. With caution, the child took it from Anna and rewarded her with a very tiny grin.

"There. That'll make you feel better," Anna said.

Cecilia hugged her baby close and grimaced when the hail hit the ship with more fervor. Then, as if someone above had turned off a magnificent spigot, the rain and hail came to a sudden stop. Everyone held their breath, and the passengers' eyes widened.

"Oh no. That's not a good sign," muttered a woman across from them.

A sudden, much stronger wind blew against the ship, tilting it to the side like a toy in a bathtub. Passengers screamed, and Anna was sure a few men shamelessly yelped from fright as well. Anna reached over and grabbed the banister on the dining hall wall and held on. A few passengers who were standing lost their balance and tumbled to the floor.

As soon as the ship recovered from the bow to the left, it tilted to the right. The hail bounced off the windows, and lightning illuminated the storm's fury. Anna struggled not to scream. Frightened, she prayed for a quick end to the storm.

One more gust tilted the ship again, and Anna feared they would sink. After the vessel righted itself atop the violent wake, the rain eased and the thunderclaps decreased.

"That tells ya the storm's going away from us," said the woman who'd predicted the storm's escalation. "Thank God in Heaven," she added.

"Amen to that," Anna said.

Chapter 14

As far as Anna was concerned, coming through the storm unscathed added another 'jewel' to her 'crown of survival'. She had been through much in life, and she couldn't help imagining an exquisite, heavy tiara sitting slightly askew on her head with a large diamond positioned in the middle, the souvenir of her endurance of Martin's rejection. Situated next to that was an emerald, the spoils of the loss of her job. Neighboring the emerald was an impressive garnet, her reward for dealing with the separation from her family and friends and for exhibiting supreme gumption in heading to Indian Territory. Then, on the other side of the diamond there was situated a beryl, bestowed upon her when Davies attacked her. And finally, an opal – her latest jewel of resilience – was nestled in the glittering headpiece, a statement to the world that she had survived yet another of life's onslaughts, a horrible, tempestuous storm on a river, without so much as a scream of terror for her own life.

Surely, Anna mused, *this crown of mine is adequately decorated. Any additional gems would create a gaudy, pretentious, and flamboyant headdress, so I shall endure nothing more!*

If only that were the truth for Anna – or for anyone.

The stormy evening offered Anna the opportunity to become acquainted with Cecilia, her daughter Hillary, and – after the storm abated – Cecilia's husband, Amatus Hayden. Knowing nothing about him besides the fact that he chose his fiancée over his family's desire, Anna could only look on him with awe. He was a handsome, compassionate, friendly man, and Anna seriously doubted that he lacked for other marriage prospects that would have suited his family's criteria. Nevertheless, he still chose Cecilia. Why? Simply, and most importantly, because he loved her.

Humidity left over from the storm still hung heavily in the air. A yellowish-green hue colored the morning skies in the dawning daylight. Off towards the east, the dark gray clouds that had earlier borne down upon them with such a fury lumbered on, grumbling, as if they were looking for more victims on which they could unleash their dreary and frightening vehemence. Along the shoreline, cracked boughs of trees hung limply in the water. The river flowed quickly and carried with it all matter of debris, wrenched from the storm-battered land. In the early morning, the passengers on deck watched many small animals rooting around the ground on the water's edge. Uprooted from their usual habitats by the storm, porcupines, rabbits, snakes, and squirrels searched along the riverbanks for any morsel of food; the slithering vipers occasionally trying to make a meal of the less fortunate rodents.

Anna encountered Mr. Hayden early in the morning, but Cecilia and the baby were nowhere to be seen. "How is Hillary after the storm, Mr. Hayden?" Anna asked as he walked by.

"Oh! Good morning, Miss Collins. Our little one did not fare too well, I'm afraid." He shook his head. "Cecilia was awake most of the night, and Hillary is cranky and intolerant of anything other than being constantly held by her mother."

"Poor Cecilia. She must be exhausted," Anna said.

"Yes, she is. Cecilia falls asleep holding the child, but when I try to take Hillary and put her to bed elsewhere, she screams and sets Cecilia off in a panic." He chuckled. "I decided it best to leave them be."

Anna smiled and returned to her book as Mr. Hayden walked off. She sat on the deck and enjoyed the sounds of the rippling river and hoped to settle her queasiness by taking in the panoramic view of the landscape. The book she clutched was one her father had given her from his personal library to read during her long trip. Annoying mosquitoes, stirred by the warming air and the heavy humidity, hovered over, irritating Anna. One particularly persistent mosquito landed on her hand and prepared to take a bite.

Slap!

"Ah-HA!" Anna said as the pesky insect quieted its incessant buzzing and died with an almost undetectable flicker of its transparent wing. "There! You've tormented me long enough!" Anna declared, as if it were the conquest of a nation rather than the annihilation of a defenseless insect. "Mother and Father warned me about bothersome individuals I might meet on the river, but they neglected to mention I'd see the largest insects known to mankind!" she grumbled.

Although it was only the first of March, the climate of the Mississippi waterway served as the perfect environment for such vexing creatures to propagate unchecked. The river meandered and cut through lands thick and fertile with various species of trees, thick underbrush, and large, colorful flowers. The wildlife was no less varied and abundant with squirrels, deer, possum, rabbits, and snakes. An occasional fish popped up out of the river, much to the delight of the children aboard the steamboat.

A group of ladies who had boarded in Memphis had welcomed Mrs. Devonshire into their circle, and kept her entertained with their account of plays, music, and fashion updates. Mrs. Devonshire's involvement with them allowed Anna some quiet time to herself, and Anna changed her focus to her fellow passengers.

A family of four was traveling to the recently built Shreve's Town, Louisiana – the new and bustling community named for Henry Shreve. His 'snag-busting' watercraft had boosted steamboat travel by opening the southern waterways to the larger passenger boats. If not for his invention Anna's river journey would have been impossible, and she would have been left to face an uncomfortable and dangerous overland trip to the territory.

Anna saw the pastor and his family a few times in the evenings and at meals, but the mother had ventured out on deck only once since boarding in Memphis. The pastor's children, however – a ten-year-old girl with golden hair tied with gingham ribbons, and an eight-year-old, towheaded, lanky boy – loved sitting on the deck throwing anything they could find into the water, taking delight in the ripples left behind. From what Mrs. Devonshire had been able to garner from eavesdropping and chatting with the other passengers, the lady of the family begrudged the relocation to the growing settlement and the calling to a new congregation, whether it came from God or not.

The tall, handsome, mustached Mr. Buerenger stood by the post. He seemed mysterious, and he intrigued Mrs. Devonshire's curiosity. Anna shuddered when she thought about the fact that if not for him, her encounter with Davies might have ended in far more dire consequence. Although she was grateful for his help, she couldn't help feeling it was best to keep her distance.

Mr. Buerenger flicked his cigar into the ripples of the Mississippi; he had caught a glimpse of Anna's studying stare. He tipped the rim of his black felt hat to her and with an alarmingly charming Southern drawl greeted, "Mornin', Miss Collins. Mighty fine day on the river, don't you think?"

"Yes, yes. It is a beautiful day." Anna blushed with embarrassment at being caught staring at him. She quickly cast her gaze to the other end of the massive steamboat deck, to a group of soldiers involved in a heated game of poker.

According to Mrs. Devonshire, the soldiers had brought aboard a large cache of weapons, ammunition, and whiskey. Anna didn't know how the woman had come upon such juicy tidbits of gossip; Mrs. Devonshire was blessed (or perhaps cursed) with a most inquisitive nature, and Anna was convinced that she could successfully pry a bevy of information from even the tight-lipped soldiers, if the occasion arose.

Anna returned to her father's book in her lap, but the words on the page blurred into a swirl of meaninglessness. Sometimes she questioned her sanity in choosing to leave all she knew and loved, forsaking her family and friends to teach in an untamed country so far from home. But the doubts that resurfaced occasionally eased when she remembered how much she loved teaching children. Fortunately her parents had booked her passage on a newly constructed, modern steamboat with luxuries and lavish decorations, making the difficult journey as pleasant as possible.

And it would have been a great trip thus far if not for Davies and that horrendous storm, Anna said to herself. *I cannot fathom which was worse.*

Recalling the attack, she wondered for a moment what her parents would do about it if they knew. The thought of it sent her into an absolute panic. *What if Mrs. Abbott – whose husband works at Martin's law office – tells Martin, and he mentions it to Papa or Mother? Oh! Papa will embark on the very next steamboat, or swim if he has to, so long as he rushes here to take me back to Cincinnati, whether I want to go or not.*

Another mosquito ignored its cousin's corpse and flitted around her, interrupting her disquieting thoughts. *Davies, that storm, and these annoying insects!* Anna added, swatting the bloodthirsty creature that was attempting to nibble on her hand.

"How do people tolerate these horrid creatures?" she asked out loud.

"Sassafras, Miss Collins," advised Mr. Buerenger. "Excuse me for eavesdropping, but sassafras oil has long been used by Southern ladies to avoid being eaten alive."

"Sassafras? Well, thank you for your kind advice," Anna said, and her cursed blushing returned.

Mr. Buerenger smiled and nodded politely, then strode to the other side of the boat and leaned against the railing. Colonel Yarborough walked over and joined him, and the two engaged in quiet conversation. Anna took notice of their animated discussion. Mr. Buerenger shook his head at a remark and the Colonel used his hands as if to plead or try to change his mind. After a minute, the Colonel straightened, his face set and red with anger. Mr. Buerenger again shook his head, and the Colonel walked off. Anna hurriedly looked back down at her book before he passed. *If only Mrs. Devonshire was here, she'd have all this figured out in a second,* she thought.

Reverend Wheeler and his children came up on deck. His daughter, with a little basket in her arms, sat down in the *chaise longue* next to Anna.

"Hello! How are you?" Anna asked her.

"I'm fine, thank you."

"I'm Anna. And who are you?"

"I'm Elizabeth," the young girl said, "but I like to be called Beth. My mother sent me out of the cabin. She says she needs some peace and quiet to think about things."

"Ah, yes. I have a mother as well, and I know mothers sometimes need quiet," Anna said.

"My mother needs a *lot* of quiet." Beth opened the basket and removed a white linen cloth. She took a strand of embroidery yarn and threaded a needle.

Anna said, "That's lovely. What is it you are stitching?"

"It is a tea towel for my hope chest." She held it up carefully for Anna to admire. "This is called a *fleur de lis*," she said and returned to her stitching.

"You are very good at embroidering."

"Thank you. My mother taught me. It's a good thing, too, because it's boring on this big old boat."

"My mother tried to teach me to sew once, but after I poked myself with the needle time and time again, she thought it best that I not be allowed to play with sharp objects."

Beth giggled.

"But I do know what you mean about being bored. My father sent a book for me to read for that very reason."

The little girl face crinkled into a smile. "Was he afraid you'd get into mischief? That is what my mother was trying to avoid."

Anna laughed. "I believe that's exactly what he thought!"

"Where are you going?" the girl asked while completing a knot.

"I'm travelling to Indian Territory."

"Indian Territory?" Beth cried in wonder. "With Indians? My mother once said that is a dangerous place full of savages. Why would you want to go there?"

"Well, yes, it can be dangerous, and there are Indians around, but I'll be teaching the children who live in the military Fort."

"Aren't you afraid?" The girl's eyes were wide with curiosity, and her eyebrows rose almost to the top of her blonde bangs.

"I do worry sometimes."

"Oh, I'd be too frightened to go to where Indians live."

"Not all Indians are frightening. Some are very nice, just like you and me," Anna said. "I know you've heard that they are mean and wild, but I know someone who lives where I am going, and she said they are very nice people once you get to know them. They are just a little different to us, that's all."

"We're going to Shreve's Town," Beth said with her face wrinkled, as if she was none too impressed at the thought.

"You don't wish to go?"

"No. I loved my home and my friends, and I didn't want to leave. Now, I'll have to miss them forever." Her eyes dampened.

"I miss my friends and home as well, but I'm excited to go somewhere and visit a place I've never seen before. Besides, I'm sure I'll make a new bunch of friends there." Anna looked deeply into the little girl's blue eyes. "Beth, I'm sure you'll make plenty of new friends too. You can teach them how to embroider their own tea cloths!"

"That's what Papa says, and Papa is a very smart man. He talks to God, even."

"Well, your father is a pastor, and I think ministers must be intelligent."

"He knows almost the whole Bible by memory."

"Really? That's astounding! Most people cannot even remember a few verses or a chapter by heart."

"I know. Papa hardly has to use his Bible when he preaches." She looked back down at her work. "Mama says it's amazing he can remember the words of the Lord but cannot remember what she tells him."

Anna stifled a giggle. "Well, men are funny like that when it comes to their wives."

"That is exactly what Mama says!"

The two grew quiet, and Anna returned to the same page she'd been trying to read for over thirty minutes.

Just as Anna reached the bottom of the page, still uncertain what she'd read, Beth's brother walked up. "Beth, are you going to sit here fooling with that sewing all day?" he asked.

"I just might, William. What else is there to do?"

"Well, you could chase me... but you'll never catch me anyway."

"William," she said in as authoritative a tone as a young girl could muster, "Papa specifically told us we cannot run or chase each other anymore, and I'm not going to get a whipping because of you."

"You're no fun, Beth." He plopped down on the chair beside her. "This is boring. I do hope we arrive in stupid old Shreve's Town soon. I'm tired of being trapped on this boat with all of these old people." He sighed and put his head in his hands, then reached down and played with a twig trapped underneath his foot.

"William, this is Miss Anna. She's going to live in an Indian fort!"

The boy's eyes grew large, and then he wrinkled his face, "Nun-uh," he said, shaking his head. "Stop telling fibs, or I'll tell Papa."

"She is too! Miss Anna, aren't you going to live in a Fort?"

"Yes. I am going to Fort Towson in Indian Territory, to teach in the school there."

"Really? How exciting! I'd love to live in a Fort with all the soldiers and Indians and cowboys. I bet it'll be much better than dull, stupid Shreve's Town."

"Well, I'm excited about it as well, but I am sure Shreve's Town will be its own adventure for you."

William kicked at the twig. "Maybe, but for now, anywhere'd be better than this wretched boat."

"Tomorrow we'll be docking in Greenville, Mississippi, while the ship crew restocks the boat supplies. I hear from the crew we will be there for a couple of days. I'm sure you'll have a chance to stretch your legs a bit then," Anna encouraged.

"I hope Papa won't make us stay in the room and study or do the washing, like he usually does." He pouted and tossed the twig into the river.

The dinner bell rang, and the children's father came to fetch them. "I do hope they haven't been a bother," he said and tousled the boy's sandy-brown hair.

"No, sir. I enjoyed their company."

He nodded. "Good," the pastor said. "Well, you two, let's find your mother and round up some dinner."

Beth gathered her sewing and put it into her basket. She turned to Anna before they departed. "Thank you for letting me sit by you. I will be very lucky if all my teachers are as nice as you."

"Well, thank you, Beth. It was nice to meet you as well."

"Are you going to dinner?"

"Yes, but I must wait for my friend."

"Maybe I will see you again later," the girl said before she scurried off behind her father and brother.

Anna watched the three walk away, picked up her book and left the deck, heading down the corridor to find Mrs. Devonshire.

Chapter 15

On the way to her cabin, Anna saw the minister's wife coming out of their stateroom. Her dark-print dress matched the gloomy expression on her face, in direct contrast to their happy children, who were skipping ahead of their parents. The lady took the minister's hand and, with reluctance, followed her little ones to the dining room. Anna wondered how it was possible that a woman with such a precious family could appear so glum.

"Sweetie!"

Anna heard Mrs. Devonshire behind her and turned around.

"I've had the most delightful afternoon with the guild ladies," Mrs. Devonshire said, her voice bubbling with giddy glee.

"Really?"

"Yes, yes. My, they are the gayest and most lively women I've met in such a long while."

"I'm glad you enjoyed your time with them," Anna said. "What have you and the ladies been up to?"

"Oh, we discussed all manners of entertainment... oh, and their families, of course. What a lovely group. I so wish I could be with them more, but I told them I must not neglect my young friend, and they seemed to understand." She pushed her lip out and lowered her eyes.

"Mrs. Devonshire, please don't stop visiting with them for my sake. I'm just fine. We're near the end of our trip, and you should enjoy yourself."

"Are you sure? Will you not feel neglected and woeful?"

"No, no!" Anna said. "I've met a couple of families, and I enjoy the chance to sit and plan my lessons."

"Oh, I'm so relieved," she said sheepishly. "I did take the liberty to ask the ladies to dine with us tonight. I hope that is acceptable to you?"

"Why of course! I'd be glad to eat with you and your friends tonight," Anna said. She wasn't certain how she *really* felt about it, as she tended to keep to herself most of the time, but she knew there was no way to turn down the invitation without hurting dear Mrs. Devonshire's feelings – or, worse, causing Mrs. Devonshire to feel forced to be with her instead of the ladies, which would result in an evening filled with brooding and martyrdom. The choice was very evident to Anna: to dine with a group of eccentric women rather than spend an evening with a petulant and moody Mrs. Devonshire.

When they entered the dining room, a table with eight ladies of the most varied shapes, sizes, and personalities sat waiting for Anna and Mrs. Devonshire to join them – a far cry from the group Anna had first encountered with Mrs. Devonshire. Most of these ladies were widowed and all from very affluent homes and families in Memphis, and the leader of the guild, Mrs. Beatrice Bordenau, introduced the other ladies one by one.

Mrs. Bordenau herself, the petite widow of a prominent Washington politician and the mother of an up-and-coming industrialist, was ivory-complexioned, and her black hair was streaked with platinum strands. Anna thought her appearance to be the direct opposite of the pale, plump, and proper Mrs. Maria Crittendon, who sat beside her.

Next to Maria sat Mrs. Eleanor Wixom, who laughed with a disconcerting abandon. The first time Anna heard her boisterous guffaw, she expected the poor woman to fall face first onto the floor, dead from choking or as a result of a deadly convulsion.

Then, there was Miss Victoria Kennigh, never married, never courted, and never concerned about that situation and circumstance. A tall, large-boned woman in her late forties, Miss Kennigh had formerly served as the head librarian in a large Eastern university and could recall a stockpile of information on almost any subject one cared to discuss. Anna imagined her as the social delight of many parties attended by self-important, cigar-smoking men who wished to discuss politics, husbandry, and military strategies – all subjects upon which Miss Kennigh could pontificate, and punctuate with hundreds (if not thousands) of meaningless, trivial statistics heretofore unknown.

A garishly decorated woman sat near Miss Kennigh. Mrs. Constance Vanderhill, mercifully widowed early, her reprieve from a philandering tobacco plantation owner, wore an elaborate gown of gold taffeta. A large ornate amethyst and ruby pin, which screamed of wealth and cried of the absence of financial woes, secured a rich, scarlet cape that draped around her shoulders. When Constance spoke she tilted her mouth to the side, as if everything she said was a secret meant for the person sitting to her right.

Mrs. Valencia de Cortenay, the largest and most bodacious of the guild members, sat beside Mrs. Vanderhill. She had styled her silver hair in a voluminous French bun, and she was garbed in a dark mauve satin gown, highlighted with mauve velvet ribbons along the puffy sleeves, emphasizing her large stature. A gold chain dangled from her thick neck and flowed over her deeply cleaved bosom. Valencia, or 'Lady de Cortenay' as Mrs. Devonshire called her, was a previously well-known *coloratura soprano* in the opera houses of Northern and Eastern cities. She committed to every move an air of drama and forethought.

Two shy sisters sat beside Lady de Cortenay. They looked as if they could not bear to be beyond touching distance of one another. The older sister wouldn't speak without looking at the other, as if asking for her blessing to utter a word. Anna wondered if they could read each other's minds and if the younger was telling her sibling what to say. Eunice, the youngest, talked with a slight lisp and took great breaths between sentences. Her head seemed too small for her body, and her complexion was nearly translucent. On the contrary, Mildred, the older of the two, had a small body that seemed to wobble underneath her larger head, piled high with a beehive of flaming red hair, from which a few tendrils fell and framed her bronzed face. Neither Eunice nor Mildred spoke a word without first consulting each other. When asked if they were enjoying their trip, Eunice looked at Mildred and echoed, "Are we enjoying our trip?" to which Mildred nodded affirmatively before Eunice answered, "Yes. Yes we are."

The guild ladies chatted quietly amongst themselves while waiting for their food to arrive. Mrs. Devonshire kept the ladies entertained with her tales of the previous passengers and an embellished account of Anna's attack – much to Anna's embarrassment. The ladies coddled and cooed over Anna, but when the food came they quickly changed their focus and settled into devouring the piping-hot delicacies brought to them from the ship's kitchen.

Anna watched and listened to the ladies with amazement, wondering if she would ever be like them. *Will there come a day when the most important discussion I can muster will be lumpy and cheesy cream sauce?*

After dinner, the orchestra played on the deck, and the passengers retired for an evening of Schubert and Haydn. A few of the passengers danced, creating something of a festive ambiance. Mrs. Devonshire and her guild toddled off to find the best seats from which to listen to the concert. Lady de Cortenay, ever ready to take the stage, graciously succumbed to pleas to sing an aria for the pleasure and entertainment of the evening guests.

On the way to her cabin after dinner to retrieve her fan, Anna heard someone crying. She stood in the hallway, listening for the source of the pitiful sobs, and she decided it was coming from the minister's stateroom. Anna walked on by so no-one would see her eavesdropping. She strolled slowly by the door after leaving her cabin again, but the weeping had either stopped or had grown too faint to be heard through the door.

Whatever is making the woman so sad has consumed her, Anna thought, whispering a prayer to God that her grief would be eased.

Out on the deck, the soprano notes of Lady de Cortenay flew high above the sounds of the river and flitted off into the night air. Anna giggled, imagining animals along the shoreline scurrying for cover and then peeking out from some hole of comfort and security to see what could possibly be tormenting this poor, wailing creature so greatly.

Anna came up behind the crowd as they listened to the ongoing concert. She found a seat at the back of the audience; Colonel Yarborough arrived to take it at the same moment, but immediately graciously bowed and offered it to Anna. She mouthed a thank you, and sat down, feeling his presence behind her.

The lady next to Anna scooted over and offered the Colonel a seat beside her. As he sat down Anna caught the scent of vanilla, and ventured a guess that it was the amalgamation of vanilla and the sassafras Mr. Buerenger had suggested for repelling the ever-present mosquitoes and gnats.

After the end of an extremely arduous operetta by Lady de Cortenay, the crowd erupted into cheers and applause. She bowed with aplomb and appeared spent, as if she'd waged a great battle.

Colonel Yarborough leaned over to Anna. "What a relief!" he whispered into her ear.

Anna's neck tingled from his nearness. She managed a faint giggle and continued to applaud the diva.

The orchestra started another piece. Lady de Cortenay jumped in on a high note and continued to ascend further up the scale. The Colonel tried to remain composed but with subsequent and higher pitch, his hands grasped his knees until the knuckles on his tanned hands blanched. When Lady de Cortenay completed a prolonged arpeggio littered with trills, he exhaled. "If she doesn't stop soon," he whispered, "I shall need a good doctor to set my fractured bones."

Anna smiled in sympathy. A few minutes later, Lady de Cortenay finished the torturous piece to a flood of applause, cheers, and cries of "Bravo!" and "Encore!"

"If she takes them up on the encore, will you accompany me for refreshments at the other end of the ship?" he asked.

"Yes," Anna said. "I believe I would like something to drink."

They made their way to the refreshment table just as Lady de Cortenay began to wail again. Anna picked up a glass of lemonade, a few pastries, and some delightful-looking finger sandwiches. After the Colonel had made his selection of food and drink they chose seats as far away as possible from the melodious soprano.

The boat's movement upon the river stirred the thick, warm air, and a slight breeze allowed them some comfort in the evening heat.

"Have you travelled by ship much, Miss Collins?" Colonel Yarborough asked.

"No," Anna said. "Only short trips on smaller steamboats."

"Have you enjoyed the trip thus far?"

"For the most part, it has been comfortable and very pleasant."

Colonel Yarborough took a bite of his sandwich, and a large chunk of chicken salad fell on his leg. "Gracious! I'm not very genteel, it seems," he said as he picked it up with the napkin.

"The sandwich was too full," Anna said kindly.

When he smiled back at her the handsome gleam of his grin caught her off guard. She caught herself staring at him, helplessly blushing again.

"Just where is it you are headed, Miss Collins?"

"Fort Towson," Anna said, still a little flushed.

"Really? Why the Fort?" he asked.

"I've accepted a teaching position there."

"You weren't able to find a safer environment in which to teach?" he asked.

"Actually, no." Anna grimaced. "I applied for a couple of them, but they were already filled. The only one I could find still vacant is at the Fort." She looked down at her food, then back at him. "I'm excited about teaching there, though."

"I think excitement at the Fort is a certainty, Miss Collins."

"How do you mean?" Anna asked.

"Well, it is on the boundary of the country, with somewhat primitive conditions, which may prove treacherous and difficult for a lady such as yourself, Miss Collins."

Anna blushed at the compliment and smiled. "I'm sure I'll be fine, Colonel."

He sat back in the bench, considering her. "I guess you will." With a tilt of his head, he smiled at Anna. "Just be careful," he said with warmth in his voice, something she hadn't noticed from him before. "It *is* the wilderness, full of hidden dangers." He took a deep breath and continued: "But as long as you keep your eyes and ears open, your guard up, and your wits about you, you'll be fine. Well, that, and carry a big gun and learn to run really, really fast."

Anna laughed. "Thank you. I'll remember your advice." She liked him; he seemed a very nice man. "Where are you going, Colonel Yarborough?"

"Nate," he said with a coy grin. "Well, it's really 'Nathaniel Evan Yarborough', but the people I care about call me Nate."

Anna felt a thrill at the comment, but aimed to keep it hidden. "Well then, Nate, are your plans secret, or are you just naturally evasive in your answers?" Anna asked.

"I assure you, Miss Anna, that I am not involved in any clandestine operations. My troops and I are traveling to the southern part of the country, close to Fort Towson, in fact. We're setting up a boundary just south of the Red River to keep watch on the Mexican army. They've been slowly moving northward. Talk is they're becoming more interested in the land south of the river, so we're being posted to prevent any further encroachment on our lands."

"Mexicans? I assumed the Fort and the military personnel were to keep the Indians in check?"

"Well, we are generally tasked with keeping the peace, and protecting the Indians who were moved to the area from the southeastern states."

"Protecting the Indians from the Mexicans?" Anna asked, surprised that no-one else had mentioned the imminent danger.

"No. As it turns out, the territory's native Indians, those who were there before it became the repository for the removed Indians"

"It does sound exciting, indeed."

"Too much excitement for you?" Nate asked when he saw the change in Anna's composure.

"I'm not sure, at this point." Anna sighed. "But it's too late to reconsider my plans now. There aren't any job possibilities for me at home, and there are reasons I think facing

Indians, soldiers, and Mexicans will be easier than returning to Cincinnati."

"Hmm. It would take a mighty big problem indeed to make me run South, away from my kinfolk. Did you rob a stage, or commit some other heinous crime? Is there a reward to be collected for your capture, my dear?" He laughed.

"Do I look like a fugitive to you, Colonel?" Anna shook her head, laughing with him.

"No, but I can only assume a very serious or desperate situation would be required for a beautiful lady like you to scurry off to such a wild and unknown environment."

"Well, I have my reasons." Anna could feel her face beginning to blush.

"Are you trying to prove something to someone – or to yourself?" He sat forward and looked down at the deck. "I hate to be the one to tell you this after you've come so far, Miss Collins, but proving someone wrong – even yourself – is not worth risking your life for." He looked back up at Anna with a very stern gaze.

"Are you this philosophical when dealing with your men?" Anna asked.

"I have my moments."

"Why did you become a soldier?"

"To please my father, General Yarborough."

"Really? And isn't that the result of trying to prove something to someone, good sir?"

"Touché, mademoiselle," he said with a sheepish grin. *"Touché."*

"Did your father force you to enlist?"

"No. I think the military is a reputable endeavor, and I believe in this country. It's a grand land, and we must do what we can to protect our investment on all sides."

"So you're a philosopher *and* a politician."

The concert by the *soprano diva* ended, and Colonel Yarborough slapped his hands on his knees. "Finally! I thought she'd never stop."

Anna looked at the Colonel, lit by the moon and the flickering glow of the lanterns. His sandy-brown hair curled at the base of his neck. The firm line of his jaw and his slightly angled nose reminded Anna of the portraits she'd seen in her ancient Greek textbooks.

He caught her studying him. "And what is it you are looking at, Miss Collins?" He smiled faintly. "Do I have more chicken salad on my face?" He reached up to wipe his chin.

"No. I was thinking... I'm sorry. I didn't mean to stare."

"I have grown accustomed to it." He grinned.

"Women stare at you often?"

"I can only give the credit to the uniform," he whispered, "or those occasions on which I have food on my face, which are far too frequent."

Noticing that the other passengers were beginning to leave the deck, Anna sighed. "I suppose it's time to go in," she said. "Thank you for the diversion from the concert."

"'Tis I who should be thanking *you*, Miss Collins," Nate replied. "I believe you saved my life tonight. One more high note from that woman, and I might have been inclined to hurl myself over the railing into the quiet depths, to be eaten by fish." He touched her arm as he led her to the hallway and the stairs. It surprised Anna that she didn't feel uncomfortable at his touch. "Thank you again for keeping me such wonderful company this evening. Good-night, Miss Collins."

"And a good night to you, Colonel Yarborough."

They parted in the hallway, and he headed down the stairs to his stateroom.

As Anna walked slowly to her cabin she once again heard weeping coming from the minister's room. In her own stateroom, Anna locked the door and removed her dress, which was now wrinkled from the humidity and from sitting so long during the concert. The night air, still oppressive from the heat, caused Anna to choose a lightweight sleeping gown and to open the cabin window for fresh air. A slight breeze flapped the curtain in the small window, a relief from the nearly unbearable heat.

Anna pulled the coverlet back and crawled into bed. The night's events ran through her mind: the entertaining and interesting dinner with the Ladies' Guild of St. Louis and Mrs. Devonshire; the concert; and sitting with Colonel Yarborough – with Nate – which topped the evening with a dollop of pleasure.

She thought of the minister's wife and her sorrowful

appearance. Anna decided that the next day, she would seek the poor woman out. *Perhaps I can be of some help to the reverend's wife, as I, myself, am no stranger to despair.*

Anna sat alone at the table and chose from the usual breakfast fare of toast, eggs, soufflés, ham, and flapjacks. She missed eating with Mrs. Devonshire, who had opted to sit with her friends from the Ladies' Guild; only a wave from her fleshy hand signaled she had noticed Anna.

The waiter brought coffee and water; Anna removed the napkin from the table and placed it in her lap. She saw the minister, his wife, Beth and William at the door, searching for a table. When Beth saw Anna sitting by herself, she headed in her direction.

"Miss Anna, are you by yourself?" the girl asked, standing by her chair.

"Yes, I am. Would you and your family care to join me? I don't think there's another table with enough room for all of you."

"I'll ask Papa." Beth ran back to her parents and pointed to Anna.

The lady shook her head, but the minister took her arm and cautiously led her forward with Beth and her brother leading the way.

"Thank you, Miss Anna," Beth said as she sat down. "We were getting hungry waiting for Mama to dress."

"Miss Collins, are you sure you don't mind our intrusion?" the minister asked.

"No, please have a seat. I'll feel less conspicuous with your family sitting with me."

The minister pulled a chair out for his wife next to Anna, and then he took a seat on the other side of her.

"I'm Anna Collins," Anna introduced, holding her hand out to the minister's wife. "Thank you for joining me."

The pale lady smiled – or at least Anna thought it was a smile. "My name is Rebecca. Thank you for your hospitality."

"You're very welcome." Anna thought it an amazing coincidence that the unhappy woman was sitting beside her, since she had decided only the night before that she would try to befriend her.

"I'm Reverend Wheeler. This is William, and you've met Beth already."

"Nice to see you again. Yes, Beth and I sat on the deck together the other day, and I met William also. She is very good at her embroidery, Mrs. Wheeler. She said you taught her." Anna felt pity for the woman, who was obviously uncomfortable in the situation.

"Th– thank you Miss Collins," she stuttered. "She does a good job."

The waiter brought the family's food. They bowed their heads, and Reverend Wheeler prayed to bless the meal.

"Mama, Miss Anna is going to live in Indian Territory and be a teacher," Beth said as she buttered a slice of toast and lifted her glass for the waiter to fill it with orange juice.

A look of astonishment flashed momentarily on Rebecca's face, and the disbelief moved her beyond discomfort and forced her to question Beth's statement. "Is that correct, Miss Collins?"

Anna dabbed her mouth with the linen napkin. "Yes. I am to be the new teacher at Fort Towson."

"I have an associate in the ministry down there with the Choctaws," the minister remarked. "Reverend Wright. I believe he's somewhere down south, isn't he, Rebecca?"

She merely nodded.

"In fact, he's working in a girls' school there. What's the name, Rebecca?"

"Wheelock, dear. I think its Wheelock Academy, or something like that."

"He'd been out in the southern part of the country, perhaps Mississippi. When the Indians were forced to move, he and his wife went along with them. I heard he's doing well, and he's helped the Indians to settle in to their new habitat."

"I've corresponded with Miss Dickinson, who I'm replacing at the Fort. Maybe she'll be at his school."

"It's possible, but it's been a very long time since I last spoke with Reverend Wright. He and I met in Connecticut at a ministers' gathering."

"Beth told me you're moving to Shreve's Town."

At the mention of their move, Rebecca dropped her knife on the table with a loud *clunk*. "Excuse me," she said. "It just slipped. Must have been a little damp from my water. My apologies."

The minister put his hand on his wife's shaking hand. He signaled to the waiter and asked him to bring his wife more juice. "Yes, we took a parish there. We lived in Illinois before, but I heard of the town's growth, and I truly feel led by the Lord to move there so we can reach some of the new inhabitants."

Rebecca sat with her hand under his for several moments. When Reverend Wheeler removed his hand she began again to eat, her shaking less noticeable than before.

They continued eating and chatting about the weather, ship passengers, and the trip to Greenville, Mississippi, where *Jewel Belle* would dock for two days to replenish supplies for the remainder of the journey.

"I can't wait to run around," William said, his legs swinging back and forth under the chair until his father cast him a stern look that stilled him.

"Yes, I think we're all getting a little weary of the tight quarters," agreed the Reverend.

"Papa said we're going to find a big park, and he's going to let us run until we're exhausted and fall right to sleep," William said, ready for any physical activity.

"Mama and I are going shopping to buy dresses," Beth said excitedly. "Mama hasn't been shopping since baby Charles got sick and –"

She was cut off by Reverend Wheeler's admonition. "Enough, Beth."

Rebecca closed her eyes and took a deep breath. A lone tear slid down her cheek.

Anna pretended she didn't notice anything, but now she knew the reason for Mrs. Wheeler's sad countenance. Anna's heart ached for the woman who was leaving everything behind, including a child that she'd seen put to rest. "What color dress are you going to buy, Beth?" Anna asked, trying to change the subject.

"Mama and I think a blue dress would be a good choice for the spring and summer weather in... where is it, Papa?" she asked, wrinkling her nose.

"Louisiana."

"Loosiannia." She giggled. "That's much harder to say

than Illinois."

"Blue is my favorite color," Anna said.

Beth beamed and smiled at her mother. "My mama is very beautiful when she wears blue. It makes her eyes twinkle."

Rebecca smiled faintly at her daughter. "Thank you, sweetie."

"Well, Miss Collins, thank you for letting us join you for breakfast," the minister said. He put his napkin on the table. "Come on, children. We must pack for our jaunt into Mississippi. Want to try that name, Beth?" he asked, teasing his daughter.

"No, Papa. I have enough problems with Loo... whatever it is!"

The family stood to depart Anna's company.

"Thanks, Miss Anna," Beth said.

"Bye, Miss Anna," William said, trying to get out in front of his father before he caught him.

"Miss Collins, I enjoyed meeting you," Mrs. Wheeler said with a slight tremble in her voice. She held out her small hand to Anna.

Anna took it, thinking how bony and cold it felt. "My pleasure, Mrs. Wheeler. I appreciated you sitting with me. Please join me again sometime, won't you?"

"Thank you."

Rebecca and her husband walked off, his arm wrapped around her, as if something had to hold her up and keep her from falling.

"Father, please touch Mrs. Wheeler and heal her heart," Anna prayed.

After lunch many of the passengers disembarked to tour the small hamlet during the ship's two-night stay in Greenville. The Wheeler family joined the passengers who left the ship. Although many went ashore hoping to shop and dine at the fine restaurants, the Wheelers left to give their restless children room to run and play.

Anna and Mrs. Devonshire arranged a dinner date for the first evening at a certain restaurant, but as they walked down the wooden dock to enter the city, they met the women of the Ladies' Guild.

"Oh, Livy," said Mrs. Vanderhill. "We hoped to see you before you made your way into the town.

The ladies chattered and giggled and invited Livy and Anna to join them for the evening. Anna decided she would rather tour the city and eat on her own so she wouldn't be required to dine with Mrs. Devonshire's opulent new friends, who made her slightly uneasy. She said goodbye to Mrs. Devonshire and the ladies and walked along the cobbled path alone to the veranda of a stately, ornate hotel where she took a seat in a large wicker chair. A waiter from the hotel's café brought sweet tea, a few scones, and cherry jam to Anna. The first sip of tea shocked her; the sugary drink seemed more like a dessert than a beverage.

Anna watched the action on the street. Horses and buggies plodded by. Genteel men escorted ladies with large parasols. Laughter and pleasant sounds filled the late afternoon air.

Across the street at the Hotel Arthur, a group of soldiers exited. They stood for several minutes and talked and pointed, and then they took off in the direction of the majority's choice. As the men left, one soldier was left standing alone. Anna squinted and recognized Colonel Yarborough. He put on his hat and worked his way across the street, dodging buggies, wagons, and galloping horses. When he stepped on the boardwalk, he looked up and down the street.

Anna didn't want to appear forward, but she pitied him because his men seemed to have deserted him. "Colonel Yarborough!" she called, trying not to be too loud; she didn't want the others sitting on the veranda to think her rude or improper.

He looked several different directions, trying to find the voice.

"Here, Colonel!" Anna stood up from the chair and waved.

His face lit up with a big smile, revealing perfect white teeth. "Well, hello. Are you dining here?" he asked as he walked up and tipped his hat.

"No, Mrs. Devonshire and I were to dine, but she and some of her friends from the boat are dining together. I stopped here to sit and watch the townsfolk and decide where I would go next."

"So you're alone this evening?"

"Yes, it appears so." Anna shrugged.

"That's terribly unkind of your friend." He walked up the steps.

"Not really. I'm glad she found new friends closer to her age and situation. I'm afraid I've become too boring for her!"

"I don't imagine your company could ever be construed as boring, Miss Collins. Have you eaten dinner yet?" Nate asked.

"No, but I have enjoyed a few delicious scones, cherry jam, and sweet tea, although I'm not sure about the tea."

"Different than you're used to? A little too sweet, perhaps?"

"Yes, but I will try it again sometime."

"If you'd rather not, I won't be offended, but would you care to join me for dinner? I know of an excellent restaurant which serves the finest steaks this end of the Mississippi, and perhaps their tea will be a bit easier to tolerate."

"That sounds grand," Anna said. "Do you mind if I step into the hotel for a moment?"

"That will be no problem at all." He opened the door for Anna. "I'll just wait here."

"Wonderful. It'll take me but a moment."

Anna went to the indoor lavatory. She checked her hair in the mirror and let out a little squeal. "Oh, I can't believe I'm going to dinner with the Colonel! Mrs. Devonshire would just die to hear it." She smiled. "I wish Grace and Honora were here. They'd be beside themselves!"

She waltzed down the hall and at the end, stopped and looked for Colonel Yarborough, but he was nowhere to be seen. "Well, how about that?" she mumbled. "I've been abandoned twice in one evening."

Just then, he came up behind her, carrying a small bouquet of roses. "Sorry."

Anna turned to see the Colonel and his beautiful petite bouquet.

"It took longer to pry these from the boy on the corner than I thought it would," he said.

Anna smiled. "Thank you for going to the trouble." She sniffed the exhilarating scent and closed her eyes. "I absolutely adore roses."

"Good. I thought you might. Are you ready?"

"Yes," Anna said.

"I have a coach waiting outside." He opened the hotel door, took her arm, and led her down the steps. He helped her into the coach and touched her hand when she was situated inside it. "I do hope you don't mind going to dinner with a soldier, as I know your experiences with such may have caused you to wonder if we're all such horrid creatures."

"Colonel, if I were wary of going with you, I wouldn't be sitting here."

"Nate. It's Nate."

"Fine. Colonel Nate, if I'd been –"

He laughed. "You can leave the 'Colonel' off unless we're in a Fort. Then, 'Colonel Nate' would be fine. Well, I suppose it'd be best if you addressed me as 'Colonel' on the boat, too." He shook his head. "Just call me whatever you wish."

Anna laughed. "I'll be sure to address you with the appropriate title when we're on the ship."

The coach travelled down the street and into a beautiful section of the town. The scent from the large, fragrant, white blossoms on the trees wafted about the air all around them. The twinkling street lanterns added a romantic aura to the setting.

Anna sensed something she hadn't felt in a long time, and she found that somewhat alarming. She didn't know much about Nate, but from what she did know and what she had seen, she was beginning to like him very much. He was courteous, but not patronizing; humorous, without being crude or hurtful; and to her surprise, she felt safe with him.

The coach stopped in front of a restaurant. The horse neighed and tromped in place, not ready to finish his stroll.

Nate helped Anna down and paid the horseman.

Inside, they were led to a secluded table nestled beneath a gardenia garland. The restaurant was perhaps the most sophisticated she had been in, and she was delightfully surprised; it was so different to the usual eateries.

Nate ordered their dinner and sat quiet for a moment. He sighed. "I love this restaurant."

"I can see why," Anna said, taking note of the pleasing French décor, the toile curtains, and the violins serenading the diners. The owners had gone to a great deal of trouble.

"It's very charming."

He looked into her eyes. "Thank you for accepting my invitation."

His gaze made Anna blush, and again she was nearly overcome with those disconcerting feelings. "Oh, no. Thank you, Nate. I planned to dine alone this evening, so this is a wonderful unexpected treat. I truly appreciate your kindness."

"Good," he said as the waiter brought their drinks. "Properly sweetened tea, milady!" he said, as he lifted his glass, smiled, and took a drink.

Anna grimaced after she took a drink of hers. "I'm not sure what *properly* means to you, Nate, but *sweetened* is certainly the word for it!" she jested.

Anna thought the meal was the best she'd eaten since leaving Cincinnati, even better than the wide variety of cuisine she'd enjoyed on the boat. She loved the slightly rare, tender steak and the potatoes, seasoned with a pungent blend of cayenne and paprika. She also loved the coconut cake they ate for dessert, which she thought might have rivaled her grandmother's in taste and appearance.

After the two finished their dinner, Nate paid and held the door for Anna. "Do you mind if we walk back to the pier? Would it be too far for you?" he asked.

"No. After a meal like that, I should think a walk would be nice. The weather's pleasant, the town is charming, and the company is –"

"Perfect? Dashing?"

Anna laughed. "Well, I was going to say delightful, but I suppose those work as well."

"Wonderful. I need a chance to work off that rich cake." Nate offered his arm, and Anna slid hers through it.

The two strolled down the walkway, making small talk, until they came to a park. Several little yellow ducklings quacked as they followed a female mallard around a pond, kicking their tiny webbed feet behind them.

Anna watched the park lights reflected in their wake. When she looked up again, she realized the Colonel seemed far more interested in watching her than he was in watching the paddling feathered family.

"What is it, Colonel?" she asked.

He bent down and gave her a gentle kiss then immediately sprung back up and said, "Um... I do hope that wasn't too forward."

Anna blushed, and tried to remain composed, but her heart was pounding against her ribs and her skin tingled from their brief contact. "No. It was – it was quite all right."

She watched a family toss bread pieces into the pond to the ducks. Their laughter caused Anna to miss her parents and Caleb, and she heaved a saddened sigh that didn't escape Nate's notice.

"Shall we sit and talk in the gazebo for a moment?" he said.

"That would be wonderful," she said.

He took her hand and smiled at her as he led her to the bench in the gazebo. Anna had to admit that she enjoyed holding Nate's hand, especially since it was coupled with the complete absence of guilt, concern, or shame.

They discussed the state of the country and the chance for expanding its boundaries, and as they did, deep inside her head and her heart, Anna savored being thought of as desirable once again. She smiled secretly to herself, remembering his warm lips on hers.

When the family feeding the ducks left the park, Nate pulled out his watch. "I do believe it's almost too late for refined ladies to be out alone with men."

"Especially with soldiers such as yourself," Anna teased. "You are a rough and rowdy bunch, you know."

He chuckled at her gentle sarcasm and took her hand to help her stand.

As graceful as she tried to be in his company, Anna still tripped on her long skirt and fell abruptly against his chest. "Oh! I'm so sorry. I am so clumsy, and I –" Anna started, but he interrupted her with kiss.

"Well, Miss Collins, this has been a lovely evening."

"Anna. Please call me Anna, Nate."

"Well, Miss Anna, we –"

This time, it was her kiss that interrupted their conversation.

Chapter 16

After returning to the steamboat, Anna and Nate continued to socialize. Anna enjoyed his companionship and friendship and welcomed their discussions. They talked about all sorts of things, all manner of topics that Martin had never cared or bothered to discuss with Anna, counting her for a fool who would have nothing valuable to contribute to any conversation of substance. If Martin ever brought up a subject to speak of, Anna was painfully aware his motives for doing so were not to solicit her opinion.

Getting acquainted with Nate opened her eyes to the truth: *Martin never even really knew me, and he never tried to. Looking back, I see that he didn't want to be with me anymore after I completed my education and obtained my degree. That was why he was acting so odd at my commencement. For the first time, he realized he was to be wed to a woman he never imagined me to be.*

Contrary to her reaction to thoughts of Martin, whenever she thought of Nate she smiled. She noticed his demeanor as he instructed and interacted with his troops. He asserted authority speckled with kindness, and he commanded respect without tyranny. He respected his men, and they, in turn, honored their worthy and compassionate commander.

The evening Mrs. Devonshire spent with the Ladies' Guild had forged a strong bond betwixt them all. Other than a cursory nod, wave, and one "Toodle-doo," Mrs. Devonshire said little to Anna and spent the majority of her time with her new friends. In spite of Mrs. Devonshire's shallow loyalties while the Ladies' Guild was present, Anna did not spend all her time alone. She ate breakfast every day with the Wheelers, and that began to give her a clear picture of poor Rebecca's broken heart.

One morning, Nate waved to Anna when he and the soldiers entered the dining hall. He walked over to the table with a smile on his face.

"Reverend Wheeler, allow me to introduce Colonel Nate Yarborough," Anna said.

The minister politely stood to shake Nate's hand. "A pleasure to finally speak to you face to face," Reverend Wheeler said. "Anna has told us quite a bit about you."

Anna smiled sheepishly. "Nate, this is Beth and William, and this is Rebecca, the Reverend's beautiful wife."

The Colonel gently took Rebecca's delicate hand and looked directly into her eyes. He could tell by the waif-like spirit lingering there that she was a fragile, broken creature indeed. "Very nice to meet you, ma'am," he said, "and what a pleasure to meet these adorable children of yours."

"Thank you," Rebecca smiled faintly as a blush appeared on her pale cheeks.

Even though she'd yet to have a lengthy conversation with Rebecca, Anna felt she'd soon have the opportunity to learn more about her – to find out if the loss of their baby was truly the only fuel behind the deep inferno of sorrow that burned visibly in her soul. Because of the woman's mental and physical frailty, Anna knew she had to be careful not to pry. In time, she was sure Rebecca would open up to her. Meanwhile, Anna watched as Rebecca's husband continued to shepherd her around. It appeared to Anna that if it were not for his strong support, she would collapse and fade away, although Rebecca seemed more at ease now during their breakfast meetings than she had when Anna had first met her.

Later that morning Anna sat on the promenade deck reading her book. Engrossed in the story, she didn't notice when someone slipped quietly up behind her. When her mysterious stalker covered her eyes from behind, Anna panicked. She screeched, threw the book at her would-be attacker, then fell off the chair and onto the deck. In spite of the brave face she'd put on for everyone around her, and in spite of the fact that she wanted desperately to trust Nate's promise to keep Davies at bay, she had subconsciously been waiting for that moment when Davies would somehow make his way back onto the ship, and now she was sure he'd found her again. Anna scampered backward towards the rail, frantic, frightened, and sure Davies was there to follow through with his sadistic threats.

"Anna! Anna, it's only me!" Nate said and bent down in front of her. "It's me, Anna. It's just Nate." He reached out to her, but she had covered her face and was sobbing hysterically.

Nate stopped his attempt to touch her. "Anna!" he shouted to be heard above her crying, and slowly inched towards her. "Anna?"

She recoiled but looked fearfully between her fingers at him.

"Anna," Nate said quietly. "It's me, Nate. Anna, Davies isn't here. You're safe. I'm sorry I frightened you," he said, reaching out to her. "I was just playing a bit of a prank. How foolish of me. Anna, please forgive me."

Several passengers gathered to see what had caused the disturbance. Nate held up his hand and whispered to the gathering crowd. "It's fine. She's fine... just frightened. Thank you."

Rebecca ignored the Colonel's warning and went to his side. "Colonel, may I help?" she asked.

"Mrs. Wheeler? Yes, yes, please," he said.

"Anna, it's me, Rebecca – Rebecca Wheeler, dear," she said. "I'm here to help you." She reached out to Anna. "Take my hand, Anna, and we'll talk."

Calmly, the minister moved his children to the other side of the ship and helped keep the other passengers from interfering. Still frightened and semi-hysterical, Anna continued to cry, her shaking hands still covering her face.

Rebecca reached for Anna's hand again. "Anna, dear, take my hand. Let me help you up."

"Please – help me!" Anna sobbed.

"I am here to help you, Anna. Just take my hand, darling."

Anna grabbed Rebecca's hand, and the woman pulled

Anna closer and held her.

"Let's sit right here on this bench," Rebecca said as she helped a shaken Anna get to her feet and shepherded her to the bench.

Rebecca sat beside her with her arm around her. Anna nestled into her embrace and kept her head down, still weeping and murmuring.

"Anna, are you all right? It's me, Rebecca – Mrs. Wheeler," she said. She kept her thin arm around Anna and gently raised her chin. "Anna, can you hear me?" she asked.

"Yes," Anna muttered. "Is he...?" Anna's wide, unblinking eyes darted from side to side in terror.

"Who, dear?" Rebecca asked as she looked at Nate. When he shook his head, she continued. "No, Anna. He's not here at all. It's just you, Nate, and me. No-one else is here, love," she said.

"Nate? Nate's here?" Anna asked, still shaking but becoming more lucid.

"Yes, Anna." Nate knelt down in front of her and reached up to touch her hand. "I'm right here," he said.

"Nate, he was here – Davies! He came back, Nate!" she said, and started crying again.

Nate held her hand, trying to soothe her. "Anna, he's gone. He was taken off the ship several days ago. In Memphis, remember? He was even shackled and escorted by military guards. You're safe, Anna," he said. "I'm here to keep you safe."

"But... but he grabbed me, and I couldn't get away."

"Anna, dear, it wasn't that man, whoever he was. He's far away, and you're safe here with us," Rebecca said, looking at Nate for some explanation.

Anna slowly came out of her daze and quieted for a moment.

"Anna, Davies is nowhere near here." He rubbed her hand. "Anna, I'm so sorry. It was me. I put my hands over your eyes, but I never meant to frighten you. Please forgive me."

She turned to Rebecca. "Mrs. Wheeler?" she said wonderingly.

"I saw how upset and frightened you were, so I came to help you."

Anna's mind cleared at last, and she regained her senses. Tears fell down her cheeks. "When he got off the boat he said he would get me." More tears slid from the corners of her eyes and dripped to the deck floor below. "I'm sorry," she said. "Truly, I thought he was back, and I –"

"Shh, Anna, darling," Nate said softly. "It was only me, and I can't express how sorry I am for upsetting and frightening you."

"Oh, Nate." Anna leaned forward and hugged him.

He let her cry against his shoulders. "Please forgive me, Anna," he whispered. "Please let us walk you to your cabin so you can rest for a while. We'll meet for dinner, and I'll apologize all over again. I'll apologize every day for the rest of my life if that will make you feel better," Nate said as he wiped the tears from Anna's cheeks, and smiled faintly at her. "I am such a fool sometimes, Anna, and I am truly sorry."

Anna looked up at him and sniffled. "You're not a fool, Nate. But I would like to rest now."

"Mrs. Wheeler, would you help me escort Anna to her cabin?" Nate asked.

"Of course," she said. She stood and helped Anna to her feet. "Come, Anna."

"Would you mind staying with her until dinnertime?" Nate whispered to Rebecca.

"No, not at all," she said. "Could you tell my husband that Miss Collins will need me for a while?"

"Certainly. If you or Anna need anything, ring for the porter to send me a message."

"I will. Don't worry. I'll take good care of her."

Rebecca and Nate led Anna down the stairs to the cabin area. Rebecca found the key in Anna's bag and opened the door, and Nate took his leave of them.

Anna, recovering herself slowly, walked to the bed and sat down. "I am so sorry, Rebecca. This is not like me at all! It's just – well, I..."

"I understand," Rebecca soothed her. "I, too, have dwelt in a fear and... well," she confessed suddenly, "I've been drowning in sorrow for months now." She poured a glass of water for Anna. "Do you have any headache powder?"

"Fortunately, yes." Anna laughed nervously. "There's

still some left from my concussion, after Davies attacked me. You will find it in the desk drawer, I believe."

Rebecca found the packet and poured the white powder into the glass of water. "This will help you feel better. Even if you don't have a headache, a fright can make a person feel poorly," she said as she handed the glass to Anna.

Anna drank the bitter liquid and twisted up her face. "Blegh! That awful taste adds to my appreciation that I don't often suffer headaches," she said.

"Would you like to lie down?"

"Yes, I think I will." Anna removed her boots. "Rebecca, doesn't your family need you? I'll be fine now that I've taken the medicine and am safely in my bed."

"They'll be fine without me for a while. It will free them from having to worry about me or look after me."

"I feel terrible to inconvenience you all. Please return to them. I really will be fine now."

Rebecca sat in the chair next to the desk. "Unless you're absolutely against it, I promised the Colonel I'd stay with you until he can take over at dinner. If I leave now, I'm afraid he'll arrest me for abandoning my post!" She smiled, and Anna smiled faintly back.

"Well, I don't wish you to be punished for dereliction of duty. You may stay then, even though I fear you will be bored while I'm napping."

Rebecca retrieved a coverlet from the chest and placed it over Anna. "Rest assured I will not be bored, dear," Rebecca said and sat back down. She sighed. "This is the first time I've felt useful in a long while, and it shall do as much good for me as for you."

"Are you sure your family doesn't need you?" Anna asked, wondering how a family with children could go without a mother's guidance and love, even for a little while. "Beth and William are still so very small."

"No doubt they still need my assistance and comfort, but that is something I haven't been able to give them lately." She looked up at Anna. "I hate to keep you awake. Please rest, Anna."

"Rebecca, I don't wish to pry or make you feel uncomfortable, and there is no obligation, of course, for you to discuss anything you don't wish to talk about, but I'm willing to listen if you need to talk about anything – about anything at all. It seems to me that you always carry a heavy burden on your mind and heart, and sometimes it helps to talk about it."

"How very sweet, Anna. I appreciate your kindness to me and my family, and I know you have nothing but sincere concern for us."

"It's odd. I've met so many people aboard this ship who have rescued me in so many ways," Anna said. "Mr. Bueren-ger and Colonel Yarborough came to my rescue when Davies attacked me. The ladies who became my friends earlier in the trip – Honora and Grace were especially precious to me. And now I have you. I guess God's Word is right. All things do work together to bring about good for those of us who love Him. I wouldn't have met all those wonderful friends if the bad things hadn't happened to me."

"I took you for a Christian right from the start, Anna. Strange isn't it?"

"What?" Anna asked. "That I'm a Christian?"

Rebecca smiled. "No!" Rebecca said. "No, of course not. What I mean to say is that I boarded this boat full of resentment and anger. I was furious with my husband and furious with God. I didn't think I'd find anything good on this journey. But, Anna, I know now that God arranged our meeting. Being able to help you like this has reminded me that there is a reason for all things." She closed her eyes. "Even the bad things in life can work together for good, just as you said." She stood and walked to the small window. "Lately, it's been most difficult for me to continue on – to walk, to eat, and even to live."

"Yes, I've noticed your deep sadness, Rebecca."

Rebecca put her hand up to her quivering lip. "Sadness is only a very small part of the heavy burden I carry in my heart, I'm afraid." Her voice trembled.

Anna sat up in the bed. "Rebecca, if you wish to confide in me, I promise I won't divulge anything to anyone."

"Oh, but I haven't spoken of..." She gasped to prevent herself from crying. "I shouldn't burden you." She turned back to Anna. "After all, you've been through quite a bit this morning – and on the earlier part of this voyage, it seems. It would be most selfish for me to talk of *my* problems when you're resting after your awful scare."

"Don't worry about me," Anna said, waving her hand. "Trust me when I say that I'm very sturdy! I may be young, but I've weathered many battles, and God has strengthened me through them."

"It would be helpful to talk with another woman. Are you sure you won't feel taken advantage of?"

"No, Rebecca. I consider you a friend, and I would consider it a privilege to lend you a listening ear if that will help you."

"Well, I know Beth has probably told you some things about me. She doesn't mean to be indiscreet, but she's been concerned for me, and she has missed our relationship. I haven't been a good mother to her, nor to Will, as of late."

"Beth hasn't mentioned any disappointment in you, only in your sadness."

Rebecca smiled. "Such a sweet angel. And my Will's a very intelligent and industrious lad. I'm afraid the attention I've needed from my husband has taken much of the time that he would have spent with Will."

"Reverend Wheeler doesn't seem resentful that you need him."

"No, but he does resent my hesitance at moving from our home in Illinois to live in Shreve's Town and start a church. He says we should quit looking at our own situation and think of others who have needs and sorrows greater than ours." Fresh tears fell from her eyes. "He says we must move on after – even after we lost our baby."

"Oh, Rebecca!" Anna stood and walked over to her. "Your baby died?"

She nodded and cried harder. "And to think I thought I was incapable of crying another tear," Rebecca said.

"It's understandable. The death of a child must be a horrible ordeal."

"Yes. Not only do I grieve over my baby's death, but I must also deal with the heart-wrenching guilt of it."

"Guilt?"

Rebecca sat down. "It was..." She coughed, almost unable to continue. "It was because of me that our baby Charles died." Rebecca wept harder and began sobbing and heaving deeply.

"I'm sure that's not true, Rebecca. What happened?"

"Charles died after I put him down to sleep. I was relieved when he didn't wake me up fussing in the middle of the night. I woke and listened for him stirring, and when I didn't hear anything, I thought he was finally sleeping through the night, so I went back to sleep without bothering to check on him as a mother should. If I had dragged my lazy bones out of bed and gone into his room, maybe I – maybe our baby boy wouldn't have died!"

"Rebecca, I know you blame yourself, but has anyone else blamed you for his death or told you that your attention in the middle of the night might have saved him?"

"No." Rebecca wiped her face with her hands. "In fact, the physician who came to look at him discovered that our dear boy had a defect in his tiny lungs. I had taken Charles to the doctor just the week before because he began to tremble and turned blue after I had nursed him. Dr. Cunningham said it was probably because he was an impatient eater, and that was all. After he died, though, Dr. Cunningham told us he'd suffered from either a heart or lung problem. I thought he just said that so I wouldn't feel so guilty."

"I doubt that, Rebecca. Physicians are held responsible to tell the truth in physical matters. Did the doctor give you any other reason to disbelieve what he told you?"

"No. It was only my suspicion. My husband was overwhelmed with my guilt and our grief, and I assumed he asked Dr. Cunningham to offer some sort of reason that would comfort me and allow me to carry on."

"I'm so sorry, Rebecca." Anna put her arm around her.

"Here we are, two weeping women. Aren't we a sight?" Rebecca said feebly.

"I know you are a woman of faith, Rebecca. Have you prayed that God would deliver you from your sorrow and guilt?"

"It's been difficult to pray for anything. I have been so angry at God for allowing my baby to die and for calling my husband off to a new place, with my children and me in tow. I feel like God demands more from me than I can give. I had to leave the place my baby is buried and deliver the

'Good News' to people, all while I feel nothing is good at all. All I feel is sadness and anger and loss."

"You know, Rebecca – and I know this may seem odd to say especially after what happened on deck – but I've learned it is in the midst of our deepest struggles that God will come most vividly to our aid. When we're beyond our own strength, He has promised to give us His."

"I know the promises, dear. They are lodged in my head, though, and I cannot seem to force them to dwell in my heart."

"I know one thing for certain."

"What's that?" Rebecca asked, her voice shaky.

"God feels our distresses and understands our inability to bear life's sorrow. Why, Rebecca, He Himself lost His Son and watched Him die. He grieved at the sight of Calvary just as you do now."

"Of course. I believe He knows how I feel, but if He knows how painful such a loss can be, why would He allow that to happen to me, especially when my husband and I have dedicated our lives to lead others to Him?"

"Trusting in God as our Father doesn't make us impervious or untouchable to life's agonies, Rebecca. We have Adam and Eve's sin to thank for that."

"Oh, how my heart longs to feel faith and joy again," Rebecca said as she turned to face the window, "but I'm afraid it's not possible for me."

"Well, it may be beyond you – that's true – but it isn't beyond the God who loves you." Anna approached her and put her hand upon her shoulder. "Ask Him, Rebecca. He won't deny you the peace for which you yearn."

Rebecca wept. Anna sat next to her and prayed that God would give Rebecca peace, joy, and freedom from her guilt and sorrow so that she could go on living and taking care of her beautiful family.

Just as Anna said Amen, a knock at the door interrupted them.

"Oh, I kept you from resting!" Rebecca said. "If that's Colonel Yarborough, he'll be disappointed at how I've carried out my assignment." She wiped her eyes with a handkerchief and smoothed her hair.

"I won't let on that we haven't done anything but rest

and sit for this whole hour."

Rebecca opened the door. "Good evening, Colonel Yarborough."

"Am I disturbing Miss Collins?" he whispered.

"No, sir. She's up if you wish to speak with her?"

"Yes, if it is possible please."

"Do come in then."

"Anna, how are you?" The concern in his voice nearly moved Anna and Rebecca to tears again.

Anna sat on the edge of the bed. "Nate, I'm so sorry about all the drama I caused."

He took the chair from the desk and sat down. "I feel awful about the thoughtless prank I pulled on you. Can you ever forgive me?" he asked.

"Yes, of course. No more apologies are necessary."

"Here. These are for you." He held up a small bouquet of flowers.

"Thank you, Nate," she said, taking them gently from him and admiring their colorful petals and their fresh scent, "but where did you find flowers on the ship?"

"Well, seeing as though I'm of highest authority on the boat, next to the Captain and the First Mate, and that I've made a friend of the head porter, it wasn't too difficult a mission."

"You *stole* them?"

He laughed. "I'm shocked you think so lowly of me," he said.

"Only for a moment. Thank you again for all your attention and kindness."

"Anna, you're not just *any* passenger," he moved forward. "I truly care about you, and I never want to frighten you again."

In an instant, Anna could feel the heat rising to her cheeks. She knew if she were able to look in a mirror, she'd catch a glimpse of a pinkish hue decorating her face and neck. "And I care about you also, Colonel," Anna said.

Rebecca smiled and cleared her throat, feeling a bit awkward to be in their company. "Well, do you suppose we should head to dinner?" she asked.

Anna leaned to the side to see around Nate. "Thank you for taking such great care of me, Rebecca. If there's anything you need from me, just ask."

"Of course I will. Colonel, will you join us for dinner?"

"Absolutely. Anna, do you feel well enough to eat in the dining hall?"

"I'm fine, Nate."

He smiled encouragingly, and after Rebecca helped Anna put on her boots on, Nate helped her stand and took her arm.

Anna and Nate followed Rebecca out of the cabin. The couple went on to the dining hall and Rebecca went quickly back to her family's room, to her children and husband, feeling hope for the first time in months.

Chapter 17

Anna and Nate met for lunch and dinner the following day. He seemed very talkative, jumping in and out of conversations about everything and anything that popped into his head. Anna could only assume his chatty tactics were to try and keep her mind off the previous day's incident.

She wanted to share the conversation she'd had with Rebecca, but she knew it wouldn't be proper – and she was no Mrs. Devonshire when it came to flaunting rumors and gossip. Even more importantly for Rebecca, it would let Nate know that she'd failed to keep her promise to ensure that Anna got some rest. All things considered, Anna's lips remained sealed on the matter – a most private matter indeed.

The kindness and attention Nate had shown Anna after her embarrassing behavior only rekindled Anna's desire for a deeper relationship with someone. If she had any say in the matter, she decided that Nate would be the perfect man to fulfill that role in her life, though she wanted to make sure that she didn't incautiously go down the wrong romantic path again.

"Nate," Anna said quietly. "What will happen when you go to Shreve's Town?"

"What do you mean?" he asked, taking a sip of his coffee and looking at her over the rim of his dainty cup – which looked quite ridiculous being held by a man of such military prowess.

"When we're apart, will you think of me again?" Anna

toyed nervously with the lace corner of her linen napkin.

"Of course," Nate said and chuckled. "Once you've nearly scared a woman to death, she's not easily forgotten."

Anna smiled in response. "I guess I am a bit worried about what lies ahead for me at the Fort. I won't have anyone to save me there if I get into trouble. I am excited about getting there, though. It has been such a long journey, and I'm ready to start teaching. Still, I would like to hear from you after we leave the ship." As soon as the statement crossed her lips, Anna regretted it.

"Hmm. I'm not sure when I'll be able to write," he said. "I'll be far from any established towns most of the time."

"Well, seeing that you're a soldier, maybe they'll let you stop by Fort Towson sometime?"

"If our detail's enlisted in securing the border, there is a slim chance I'll be able to do any traveling, but as of now, we are not yet sure what our assignment is. We never really know until the last minute, I'm afraid, as political and military conditions are often difficult to predict."

"My friendship with you and the other passengers I have met has been the only positive experience I've had in the last year," she said as she sat back in the chair.

"Even my frightening you half to death?"

She laughed. "Yes, even that."

"Well, in that case, my dear, you must have had a very dismal past year."

Anna sat quietly for several moments. "I'm not asking for any sort of promise or commitment on your part." Anna looked down at her hands. "It's... well, I guess I'm just feeling a bit insecure knowing that soon, I will lose touch with all the friends I've made here, including you." Tears threatened to appear, but she managed to keep them at bay in the corners of her eyes.

"Anna, I will promise you that I will send a note as soon as possible, but the assignment will keep us busy. Besides, I doubt you'll have either the time or the energy to miss me once you start teaching at the Fort," Nate said. "Please don't worry. You'll be fine. In the meantime, let us just enjoy the few days we have left before we are forced to go our separate ways."

"Will the passengers get off the ship and stay in Simmesport for the night?"

"Yes. I think everyone will disembark so the ship crew can replenish stores. We'll load our supplies that we have to transport to the settlements and military posts in the southern region of the country."

"Mrs. Devonshire and I plan to dine at a little restaurant she heard about once. I believe she said it's called *The Jolly*."

"If I finish loading supplies in time, I'd very much like to join you. Perhaps we could walk about the town and say our farewells there? Assuming that I am invited, of course."

"You never need to ask for an invitation, Nate, and while I'm not sure what else Mrs. Devonshire has planned, that does sound nice."

"Fine. I'll check on you after we're finished."

The soldiers and Nate exited the ship at the dock soon after they pulled into the wharf at Simmesport. The small establishment served as a harbor for ships ascending the Red River, and others continuing on down the Mississippi to New Orleans.

The passengers stayed in a quaint little hotel. Mrs. Devonshire shared a room with Mrs. Bordenau, leaving Anna to herself in a small, cozy room with a veranda that overlooked the lively street. The hotel restaurant offered an array of delectable vegetables, Creole entrees, desserts, and beverages.

In the evening, Anna sat on the balcony. Magnolia trees, heavy with large saucer-shaped, ivory blooms, swayed and dipped in the delicate breeze. The thick scent of blooming flowers and trees filled the air.

Across the wide street, a small park interrupted the row of narrow storefronts and private businesses. In the center of the park sat a very beautiful garden filled with crocuses, irises, tulips, and rhododendron bushes. An orchestra of instrumentalists: guitar, banjo, clarinet, fiddle, and bass viol, accompanied a very smooth baritone gentleman singing great songs of the South. Several people danced, laughing as they twirled to the lively beat.

Anna looked up at the dark sky, littered with twinkling stars and a white sliver of a moon sparkling like the crown jewel of nighttime. She held her quivering lip and wiped away the lone tear that fell down her cheek.

At lunch the next day with Mrs. Devonshire, Anna pushed her food around the plate.

"Aren't you hungry, dear?" Mrs. Devonshire asked. "Is this café not to your liking? It isn't as elegant as *The Jolly*."

"Hmm? Oh, no, it's not that – not really. I mean, the café is lovely and the food is delicious. I just think I've eaten too much during this trip," she said. "Soon I'll be too large for the few dresses I brought with me! And I don't want to spoil myself, as I'm sure rations at the Fort will be far less luxurious."

"Well, I think you should eat to keep up your strength. Such a young girl as you going to teach in the wilderness," Mrs. Devonshire clucked. "It's absurd, if you ask me. You should gobble up as much food as you can now. Maybe that will lessen the likelihood of some wild animal or some cannibalistic savage gobbling *you* up in the wilds," she said, trying to sound funny but sounding ominous nonetheless.

Anna looked at the chipped beef, asparagus in Hollandaise sauce, and the yeast rolls. She sighed. It seemed odd to Anna that nearing her destination resulted in such confusing emotions. *I suppose I'm just being moody and… . well, silly. That's it. I'm just being a silly, silly girl.*

With a 'hmph', Mrs. Devonshire placed her silverware across the gilded plate.

"Dear, it's getting late and if you aren't going to finish your lovely meal, would you mind if we left now?" she asked.

Anna's irritation with Nate threatened to contaminate her usual tolerance with Mrs. Devonshire. She looked at the café's doorway, hoping to see Nate saunter in.

"I suppose…" Anna paused to give Nate one more second to appear and improve her attitude . "Yes, Mrs. Devonshire. I am ready to leave."

Mrs. Devonshire waved her pudgy hand and the waiter brought their dinner check. Even knowing Nate was not going to join her, she couldn't help but gaze at the door once more while Mrs. Devonshire paid for their fare.

As she and Mrs. Devonshire stepped through the café door onto the stone pathway, the bright evening sun stood at a position which made it nearly impossible for Anna to see. She reached her hand up to pull down the brim of her hat and to shade her vision, and what she suddenly saw made her gasp.

Across the street, a tall and elegant brunette stood beside a man – Nate! The woman held his arm in a very familiar grasp, and Anna's heart fell. Her stomach seized into an all too familiar knot.

Oh, Nate. I thought you were different!

Chapter 18

Anna felt so forlorn that she allowed Mrs. Devonshire to coo and coddle her, albeit under the guise of a minor illness rather than revealing her emotional pain. She prayed, and searched her heart. She cared for Nate, but he hadn't promised her anything. He did care for her, just not in the way she'd hoped he would. She reprimanded herself for losing focus. She made herself recover from the disappointment and embarrassment as she came to the realization that she had simply mistaken Nate's feelings for her.

Mrs. Devonshire was right. Soldiers aren't to be trusted after all – not even Colonels.

The next day, as Mrs. Devonshire stood on the deck waiting to leave the boat and travel to her home in New Orleans., Anna realized the importance of Mrs. Devonshire's friendship. "Livy," Anna said, embracing her, "I have truly enjoyed travelling with you these past several weeks. I want you to know how much your friendship means to me. Thank you."

"Oh, dear, you needn't thank me. It was my pleasure, and I have considered it my duty to watch over you." She looked into Anna's eyes. "Anna, please be careful out there."

"You're such a sweetheart to care so much. Know that I will be fine and that I shall always take your warnings and advice to heart," Anna said.

"After I return to New Orleans I'm going to move to St. Louis to be closer to my daughter. The St. Louis Ladies'

Guild has invited me to join their group." Her eyes twinkled. "Mr. Devonshire left me a large plot of land in Louisiana, and if I sell it, I'll be able to set up a new home in St. Louis."

"I'm glad to hear of your new friends," Anna said. "That sounds wonderful."

"My new home will be spacious enough that I may entertain the Ladies' Guild as often as I like. Dear, you simply must drop by to visit anytime when you're in the area. Consider it an open invitation. Besides, I should love to hear tales of your wilderness exploits."

Anna chuckled, imagining the dramatic flair Mrs. Devonshire would add when retelling her stories to the Ladies' Guild. "I will. If I make my way to St. Louis, your home will be my first stop." Anna patted her hand.

The ship horn blasted.

"Oh, dear, it's time for me to leave you now," Mrs. Devonshire gave her one last corpulent embrace. "Do take care and don't forget my invitation to visit."

"I won't. Goodbye, Livy."

Mrs. Devonshire and the few passengers continuing on down the Mississippi to Baton Rouge and New Orleans left the *Jewel Belle* to board another ship. The remaining passengers travelling to Shreve's Town via the Red River stayed on the *Jewel Belle,* waiting to join the snag-busting boat in Shreve's Town to travel inland.

The fact that Nate was busy with his men was a relief to Anna. Several times since she'd seen him with the mysterious lady, she'd chided herself for letting someone get close to her again. It seemed their relationship had no future, and she was frankly growing weary of falling for men who had no room in their futures for her.

Chapter 19

The ship began its ascent up the Red River, and the Captain directed its route to prevent being caught on sandbars or large masses of timber and other debris held captive by the river. The water flow now wore a dusky rose shade, as it carried the silt and dirt washed away from the upper lands of Louisiana and the Indian Territory. The Red River traipsed through the lush lands of the purchase and etched deep, high-walled chasms, exposing the orange-red soil from which the river took its name. Blackjacks, elms, cedars, and a vast assortment of other foliage grew along the riverbanks.

Anna noticed the weather now stayed warm throughout most of the day. With the improvement in the weather, the Captain felt at liberty to tell the passengers that, barring any unforeseen difficulties, the ship would reach Shreve's Town by the end of the week.

Anna spent most of the days up on deck. She sighed a lot in the quiet solitude of her loneliness. Although she didn't miss the opera diva's ear-piercing melodies, she did miss the festive evening concerts. Mrs. Devonshire and the ladies of the guild had added an air of aristocracy, and their departure had left the ship immersed in a wake-like somberness.

In Alexandria, Anna sat on the upper deck and watched the crew load cotton bales, barrels of flour, and sugar off the pier. A group of thirty soldiers entered the boat under the watchful eye of Mr. Buerenger, who stood with his brow wrinkled and his arms crossed while he studied each soldier who stepped over the gangplank.

A large, hefty man with a handlebar mustache walked onto the ship last. Three military men escorted him, one on each side and one behind, all dressed in uniforms decorated with epaulets and stars. Long silver swords swung at their thighs.

The man nodded recognition when Mr. Buerenger saluted. "Buerenger, how've you fared on your trip thus far?" he asked.

"Well, General. Very well indeed."

All the pomp intrigued Anna, and she followed the entourage to the dining hall, trying to be inconspicuous. She stifled a giggle. *Mrs. Devonshire would be so proud!* She slipped in behind them and took a table next to the window, hiding behind a large column.

Across the room at the counter Mr. Buerenger ordered a round of drinks for the men and then joined them at the long table. The waiter brought the drinks shortly thereafter, along with a platter of food. The men hushed their discussion until he walked away. Their conversation echoed off the dining room windows, allowing Anna to catch a few words.

"Are the plans in place for the land acquisition, Buerenger?" the man asked.

"Yes, according to Colonel Yarborough. The deed was signed. It is in his possession and he plans to deliver it to you today."

"Excellent." He nodded. "We can no longer delay our plans. According to Houston, Mexicans are congregating near the Rio Grande. At the smallest opportunity, they will surely advance to overtake the boundary."

He tossed a fried shrimp into his mouth and chased it down with a gulp of his drink. "We must be on the offensive when it comes to those Mexican forces. We've got to get the land in our coffers; keep the assets where they belong – to us."

"Well, King's your man for the job. I'm merely the mediator between you, the government, and the men down there fighting for your desire to lengthen the country's southern boundaries."

The wooden chair creaked under the General's heavy,

muscular physique as he lit a cigar and puffed on it ponderously. "Yes, I suppose you're right. He and Houston have their fingers on the pulse of the activity down there. I think we need to keep 'im happy. Send 'im all the men and supplies he needs. He's our key to stabilizing the area."

Just then Colonel Yarborough entered. Under his arm he carried a leather pouch tied with a strip of thin leather. He nodded to Buerenger as he walked over to the General's table.

Anna repositioned her chair to remain hidden while still being able to see. She was interested to see that Nate's usually calm demeanor had disappeared. His face was red, and his jaw muscles twitched. He saluted the men, then plopped the pouch down on the table.

"Sir. Your document authorizing your theft of the land from its rightful owners."

The General grunted. "Got a burr under yer saddle, Colonel?"

"Only the fact that you think it's your job, your *right*, to steal property out from under the men who worked hard, shedding their own sweat and blood, to own it. It's not right, even if your motives are to make this country larger and stronger."

"Now don't go meddlin' in politics, Colonel," the General growled. He snuffed out the fat cigar. "You don't need to worry about those poor people. They'll be compensated nicely for their land – probably with more money than they'd ever see in their lifetime otherwise."

"Wrong, General. You know as well as I do that your so-called *compensation* is merely a pittance, a fraction of their investment. You're robbing them of their homes to gain notoriety for yourself, and I'll want no part in it ever again. Buerenger," said Nate, and tipped his hat before he stomped out of the dining room, muttering under his breath.

Mr. Buerenger started after him, but the men called him back.

"That Yarborough, getting all riled up about the *poor* little land owners," the large man mocked. He turned to the tall soldier next to him. "Stop his meddlin'," he barked. "If he interferes in any of our work, he'll be sorry."

The man nodded.

"Really, General, I doubt there is any call to sit on Yarborough," Mr. Buerenger said. "He's been working with the ranchers and feels he's betrayed their trust. I'll take care of him." Mr. Buerenger stood, saluted the men, and left the dining room.

Anna waited a few moments and then followed him to the promenade deck. Even if Nate didn't care for her as she wished, she didn't want to see him hurt.

She peeked around the door and saw Nate bent over the forward railing. He looked up as Mr. Buerenger approached, then straightened up completely, his face still red and lined with anger, and faced Mr. Buerenger. Anna couldn't hear anything they said, but from the animated gestures she knew they were involved in a serious disagreement. She slipped to the other side of the ship; Mr. Buerenger raised his voice to Nate, and Anna could finally catch an earful.

"Leave it be, Nate. He won't listen, and the only thing you'll accomplish is being ostracized from the group, unable to do any good whatsoever."

"Duncan," Nate said, pointing down the stairs, "that man is a wretched, vile thief who's stealing land from hardworking family men for nothing more than his own pathetic advancement and pride. I can't stand by and let that happen, and I refuse to be involved again."

Mr. Buerenger turned to look down the stairs and spied Anna. He paused and motioned with his head to where Anna stood. Both men nodded to her, and Mr. Buerenger turned on his heel and made his way to the stairs, tipping his hat to Anna. "Goodnight, Miss Collins," he said, and stomped down the stairs.

Nate leaned again on the railing with his head bowed down, gazing angrily into the river below as if he wanted to throw someone into it.

Anna walked up to his side and placed her hand upon his back, causing taut muscles to bulge beneath his uniform at her touch. "Nate?" she said uncertainly.

He took a deep breath, exhaled loudly, and banged his fist on the railing. The outburst frightened Anna. She removed her hand as if stung, and stepped back.

Nate straightened. "I'm sorry, Anna. I didn't mean to

startle you." He blew out.

"Nate, are you all right?"

"No, Anna, I'm not. I'm angry. I've been used and manipulated into a duplicitous act that sickens me – all in the name of an honorable and decent plan, when it is, in fact, nothing more than a deceptive, disgraceful lie that hurts innocent people."

"Well, as long as you're not angry with me," Anna whispered.

He chuckled. "No. I'm not mad at anyone except that pompous pretense of a politician sitting in the dining room." He walked to the bench and sat down with a *plunk*.

Anna stood still, waited a moment, and then looked over at him.

He looked pitiful, like a puppy who'd been reprimanded for some misbehavior. When Anna didn't follow and sit with him, he looked up. "What? What are you doing?" he asked.

"Looking at you."

"Well, what do you see?"

"A very angry man who needs an understanding and kind ear to listen to him."

"That's probably not a very interesting assignment."

"Maybe not, but if you'd like to talk, I'm willing to take it." Anna joined him on the bench.

For a moment, they sat together in silence. Nate took a deep breath, blew it all out, and then took another.

Anna looked at him and raised her eyebrows. "Well? Are you going to just sit there holding your breath?" she asked him.

"Phew!" He let it out. "It's a technique I learned to release tension."

"Does it help? Are you more relaxed now?"

"Might be if I could continue without interruption."

"Oh, I'm sorry. Please continue to suffocate yourself to your heart's content."

"So kind of you."

Anna stifled a laugh and sighed.

"Now you're mocking me," Nate said.

"What?"

"You're breathing loudly to mock my tension-releasing exercise."

"I am not. I sighed... deeply."

"To mock me."

"You're ridiculous."

"Fine. I feel better, though. Thank you."

He took her hand and tried to speak.

"I'm sorry, but I can't discuss it with ..." He stopped.

Anna was afraid he would add a unflattering word such as 'silly', or 'ignorant girl'.

"Civilians," he concluded, which lessened her angst a little.

"Well, I'm glad you're all right now,"

"Yarborough!"

Anna and Nate looked to see who had called out.

Mr. Buerenger signaled to Nate.

"Excuse me, Anna, I'm needed. Thank you for offering your ear." He gave her a stiff smile and stomped off to join Mr. Buerenger.

Anna stood and walked to the side of the boat. The murkiness of the swirling river seemed to Anna to resemble her own emotional state. She sighed. The odd beauty of the riverway encouraged her to be thankful instead of slipping into the usual self-pity when events didn't fall in with the perfect pattern she planned.

"Father," she prayed, "forgive me for my petulant and spoiled ungratefulness. Especially when men are involved. I am thankful for this opportunity to have experienced all I have on this journey – I guess even the emotional and physical pain. I'm sure You might wonder if I meant that, but I do. I know Your plans are for my good and You order my steps. If I am to walk in my journey alone, or with unfulfilled desires, I will, with my hand in Yours. Amen."

Anna walked to the stairs and down to her room. She readied herself for the night, crawled into the bed and fell asleep resting on the arms of her Father, comforted by the knowledge that even if no earthly man could, He at least considered her the apple of His eye.

Chapter 20

The *Jewel Belle* continued to plod its way up the Red River. At times the low water level concerned the Captain, and he feared they might find themselves hung up on a sandbar in the shallow flow if they attempted to further navigate the waterway. Therefore he ordered that they tie up at Natchitoches, Louisiana, and wait for the river to rise, and he assured the passengers that there shouldn't be a long delay before they could continue on.

A light spring rain started falling after they docked at the landing, and the Captain predicted the steady rainfall would hasten their departure by raising the water level. However, the rain had ceased by nighttime.

After the first week of waiting for the river to rise, it appeared the Captain had misread mother nature. The crew removed the passengers to the settlement to bide time while the river decided when it would comply with the Captain's plans.

The passengers toured the little settlement, shopped, and dined, as they waited for the crew to return for them so they could continue on their journey.

Anna kept her distance from Nate, who had continued to be moody and angry since the dining room meeting with the military assembly. That was not her only reason for avoiding him, but it did provide a sufficient excuse.

Anna also suffered from foul moods most of the time while in Natchitoches. She decided the confusion with Nate's relationship, the weather, or a combination of the two, coupled with a bit of anxiety over her impending arrival at the Fort, were responsible for the black cloud that seemed to hover over her head. The end of her steamboat journey would bring the beginning of her new life, along with all its insecurities and questions. She would no longer be able to enjoy the sanctuary of the ship, nor the camaraderie of the passengers. Neither Nate nor her family would be close by to help her, and neither the wise Captain nor the charming and humorous First Mate would be within quick reach, just up the stairs. All of these thoughts stirred together to create a rather unsettling stew in Anna's mind.

Anna and Rebecca had talked a few times since their evening together. Rebecca's face radiated, for a change, and she looked on her husband and children with a rediscovered joy.

One morning, Beth had skipped up to Anna and hugged her. "Miss Anna, thank you!"

"For what, darling?" Anna asked.

"For helping my mommy. She's all better now," she whispered.

"I'm so glad. I prayed that God would touch her heart, and it seems He did."

Beth shook her head. "Just like Papa says, God hears the cries of our hearts and answers our petitions."

"Again, your father is right. He's a very wise man."

Just when the passengers began to lose hope their travel would commence before the third week at dock, a gentle rain started and continued, accompanied by cooler temperatures. When the horizon grew gray, the Captain predicted a snowstorm.

Anna looked at the skies. "I think the Captain's a bit off in his prognostication," she told the First Mate.

"Well," he said, raising his head, "I've never seen him wrong in the six years I've been his First Mate, but I suppose anything is a possibility. We shall soon see, Miss Collins, one way or the other."

When Anna and the passengers returned to the ship, a steady sleet fell, complemented by a strange duet of thunder and lightning. She shook her head. *I won't doubt the Captain's weather predictions ever again.* She stood looking out the dining room windows. The icy rain quickly coated the railings, posts, and ropes with a thin, glassy layer. "How is it possible to have sleet, ice, thunder, *and* lightning at the same time?" she asked Mr. Brinter.

"This area is constantly plagued by unexpected weather changes. One moment it will be a nice, sunny day, but within an hour or so that can disintegrate into a full-blown gale of hurricane-force winds with lightning, rain, and hail." He shook his head. "Adds to the charm and mystery of the land, I suppose."

"How do you prepare for such drastic changes and downturns? How do you know whether to dress for warm weather or to wear all the winter clothes you possess?"

He laughed. "That takes time. If you pay attention to the wind flow and the behavior of the animals, you'll be able to read the signs within a few months' time." He rubbed his stubble-covered chin. "Although, to be honest, even an occasional upheaval of that method does happen. Like I said, it only adds to the charm."

"I'm afraid I'll be caught out in a sudden snow storm wearing only a cotton dress and light bonnet."

"I don't think it's quite as bad as you imagine," First Mate Brinter said with a smile.

"I trust not, Mr Brinter."

One cold morning, Anna saw Rebecca on deck reading her Bible. When she came inside, Anna met her at the door. "Rebecca, why were you sitting out there in that frigid air? You could catch pneumonia."

Rebecca shivered a bit. "I'm tired of being cooped up in the cabin. How funny that I think that way now! I love the weather, no matter what it's doing! And the cold is just... well, I find it absolutely invigorating!"

"Aren't you worried you'll become ill in such a chill?"

"Anna, *cold* doesn't make one ill! It's a tiny particle of an illness that causes one to become sick. In fact, some people think the cold stimulates the body to fight off illnesses more effectively."

"Do those people live long?" Anna asked.

Rebecca laughed. "Oh, how I'm going to miss you and that wit of yours, Anna," Rebecca said.

"And I shall miss you as well, Rebecca Wheeler – you and your adorable family."

By the end of March, the water level of the river had eventually risen to an acceptable depth, so the ship was able to resume its travel to Shreve's Town. Since Natchitoches, Anna and the Wheelers had dined together at every meal, and considering Nate's continuing absence and involvement with his men, the family's companionship served to lessen Anna's loneliness.

Nevertheless, when she was back in her cabin again Anna cried herself to sleep on more than one occasion, in spite of the fact that she knew her disappointment in Nate's platonic view of their relationship was unreasonable, if not a bit selfish. Several times, Anna scolded herself for being silly and petty. Nate, a soldier, considered the military to be his life. Teaching was hers, and she was just at the threshold of beginning it.

In certain moments, when she mused on the situation, she knew she really didn't want anything – or anyone – to get in the way of her plans. Anna's calling was the one thing she was certain of, and she resolved to continue and finish what she started, alone if she had to.

Chapter 21

On Sunday, the ship tied up at a small settlement between Natchitoches and Shreve's Town. The Captain allowed Reverend Wheeler to deliver a short sermon to the passengers and a few crew members. The orchestra played hymns, and the old familiar words and melodies comforted and encouraged Anna's heart.

In the afternoon the crew bundled up the supplies for delivery in Shreve's Town. The Wheelers crated up their belongings, all except for items and clothing they would need the next day. The ship was scheduled to dock in Shreve's Town on Tuesday, around three o'clock in the afternoon.

That morning, Anna ate breakfast with the Wheeler family and once again enjoyed their lively banter. Beth's and William's eyes shone when they talked with their mother, the woman who for so long had answered their questions only with monosyllables or a nod.

After breakfast, Beth and William hugged Anna and told her goodbye. Rebecca gave Anna a long embrace, wished her well, and told her she'd pray for her safety and success every day.

After his wife and children walked out of the room, Reverend Wheeler shook Anna's hand. "Miss Collins, I can never truly express my gratitude for your kindness towards my wife. Your encouragement gave her back to us."

"Oh, Reverend, I'm the one who has benefited from our friendship."

"Perhaps you have as well, but if you hadn't befriended

my darling Rebecca, I'm afraid she never would have recovered her faith or her will to carry on. Your friendship has reignited the spark in her eyes, and I feel she's once again connected to us."

His concern for his wife touched Anna. "I'm glad I could help Rebecca. She's an amazing woman, and I consider myself blessed to know her."

"If you are ever in Shreve's Town, please stop by the Elliot Street Church."

"Yes, sir, I most certainly will. Goodbye, Reverend. I know God will bless your work and your family here."

The time for their departure came too soon for Anna. She stood with the family on deck as they waited to leave the ship. A few moments later, the ship pulled into the pier and the crew lowered the ramp. The Wheelers exited the ship and walked down the gangplank while Anna waved to them. A family met them on the pier, and Anna watched as they escorted her friends down the street, out of her sight. She wiped a tear from her eye – again. Farewells were becoming all too frequent for poor Anna, it seemed, and none of them were easy to bear. She knew that the next day, Nate and the troops would leave the ship, too, separating her from the one remaining friend she'd made on her trip.

Nate had sent a note earlier in the morning via the porter, inviting Anna to meet him for dinner in that evening.

"Surely he's not too busy to ask me in person," Anna mumbled crossly, and then: "Lord, please help me," she prayed. "I fear I am allowing bitterness to take over again."

She folded the note and stuck it in her pocketbook, then picked up her small bag and carried it to the deck, where she joined the remaining passengers of the *Jewel Belle* and disembarked with them.

Once they were off the ship they all made their way to the large hotel in the center of the city, where they would stay until they started the final leg of the trip up the Red River. This settlement resembled the other southern towns Anna had visited during her eventful trip. The wispy branches of tall weeping willows hung close to the ground, shrouding the enchanting streets in a grayish-green canopy. Large, sprawling homes lined the avenues. Lofty magnolias graced the sky with their blossoms and lent their aroma to the air.

After Anna checked into her room at the Hotel Belanforte, she hired a coach to take her to the restaurant to meet Nate. She paid the driver and looked for the Colonel as she exited the cab and walked up the steps of the restaurant, onto the terrace.

The door opened, and a small black man's cheery smiling face welcomed her. "Good afternoon, miss. Dining alone tonight?"

"No. I'm meeting someone here – Colonel Yarborough. Is he here yet?" she asked, looking around.

"Why, yes, miss, he is indeed. Allow me to escort you to his table."

Anna followed the waiter to Nate's table. When he saw her, he smiled and stood.

The waiter pulled Anna's chair out, and she sat down without looking at Nate. She found it difficult not to be angry with him. "Good afternoon," she said coolly. "I haven't seen you in quite a while. Are your men ready to finish your trip soon?"

"Yes, almost. We still have a few loose ends to tie up, but then we'll be finished." He could sense her disdain and continued, "Anna, I'm sorry I've been so busy with my job."

"Well, like you said before, it is your job, and no-one can fault you for performing your best. If that means putting off your friends... well, who can blame you?"

"Anna, are you angry with me?"

"Yes, Nate, and frankly, I can't believe that you have to ask, or that it has taken you this long to figure that out," Anna said.

"Because I'm working and... and not paying attention to you? Is that the reason?"

Surely he isn't as daft as that, Anna thought. *Surely he's only pretending he doesn't know the real reason.* "Colonel, who was that woman?"

"Woman? What woman?" He looked around. "Here?"

"No. The woman in Simmesport." She tried to remain calm, but the man was totally ignorant of her feelings.

"When?"

"The tall brunette who... who... clung to your arm like she was drowning!

"Katherine? You must mean my sister, Katey?" Nate wrinkled his forehead. "I did meet her in Simmesport for lunch..."

Anna suddenly felt ashamed at her ridiculous assumptions. "I – I don't know. Your *sister*? You've never mentioned her before, and I –"

"Well, Anna," he said, cutting her off, "there are a few facts you probably don't know about me yet, as we haven't really known each other all that long. You've been angry with me because you saw us together? Because you saw me walking with another woman? You mean you assumed that I... oh, Anna, if I'd seen you, I would have introduced you. In fact, we went into the restaurant to find you, as arranged, but you had already left... we were later than expected because Katey had delayed in getting herself ready, I'm so sorry."

She was mortified. "You must have missed us by only minutes. I'm sorry, Nate," she said. "Sometimes I think and do the stupidest things." Truly, it wasn't the first time she'd embarrassed herself in front of him, but she sincerely hoped it would be the last.

Nate took her hand. "I'm sorry you were hurt and... well, I must admit I'm a bit flattered by your jealousy."

"Ugh. That sounds pathetic," Anna moaned.

"Well, thank you for meeting me this evening, in any case. Even though you were angry, you still came, and I find that most admirable – and brave."

"It's kind of you to find some virtue in my jealous nature." She smiled at him, shamefaced. "So, is everything ready for your assignment?"

He took a deep breath. "Yes. It has been hectic since we reached Natchitoches. The government is attempting to realign our assignment, but I've been fighting that on behalf of my men. Sometimes I wonder what our leaders are up to, what they're thinking – or if they're thinking at all."

"Are you still to be positioned along the southern border?"

The waiter interrupted Nate's answer and asked for their order.

"Would you like steak again?" Nate asked Anna. "They're

just as good here as in Greenville."

"I think I'd rather try the roast with vegetables. My girth is expanding as quickly as our country's, I'm afraid. But please order me a glass of that sweet tea. I've developed quite a taste for it, just as you said I would. I shall have to introduce it to my family the next time I travel back north for a visit."

Nate chuckled, and after the waiter left with their order, he folded his hands on the table. "Well, I'd have to say yes to your previous question. So far, we're to stay down south, but I'm afraid it could change any day. How do you feel about your trip? Are you ready to complete your journey and get into teaching?" He buttered the roll Anna handed to him.

She wiped her mouth with the gold linen napkin. "I feel more ready now than when I first left home," Anna said.

"Where are you from?" Nate asked. "You mentioned that you're from somewhere north, which I would have guessed anyway by your accent and your lack of knowledge about sweet tea, but we haven't discussed your home or your life before the boat."

"I believe you're right! In all the other excitement, I guess it just never came up." She took a drink. "My home is Cincinnati, Ohio. I have a mother, father, and a brother named Caleb. My father's sister lives with us as well. My father's parents own a bakery in the city. Truly, I have a very nice family, and I miss them dearly."

"They sound delightful, so why would you choose to leave them?" he asked. "You've already denied that you are a fugitive on the run, so what was it that sent you off on such a journey that few women would dare to take?"

Anna sighed. "It's a very long story that involves a man, a broken promise, and betrayal of trust."

Nate raised his eyebrows. "You left your family, your home – because of a man?"

"Well, in a way. I felt I needed to prove to myself that his opinion of me was wrong. He convinced me that I am not capable of doing anything. He crushed and ruined all my dreams." She cut her roast in an exaggerated sawing motion. "I really shouldn't discuss it. I decided long ago that I need to put it behind me and carry on with my plans and goals. What happened in the past is just that – the past."

He put his hand over hers, a brave gesture because she was angry at her thoughts of Martin and still holding a knife. "I'm sorry I brought it up. In all fairness, would you like to now torture me with questions about my past to get even?" he asked and smiled at her. He let go of her hand and drank his coffee.

Anna giggled behind her napkin. "I appreciate the offer to denigrate and humiliate you, but it's not necessary."

"I have something for you," he said and reached into his jacket pocket. He pulled out a gold box and gave it to Anna.

"Oh, Nate, you shouldn't have! We've only known each other a while, and –"

Nate interrupted Anna's refusal with his upheld hand. "Please. It's merely a little gift to remind you of our friend-ship."

Anna untied the bow and lifted the lid. Inside on a satin pillow sat a gold, heart-shaped brooch, studded with several blue sapphire stones. She gasped and looked at Nate. "Oh, Nate! It's beautiful, but I'm afraid I cannot accept such an expensive gift."

"Please, Anna. I wanted to express how much I've enjoyed our time together. Besides, a beautiful girl deserves beauti-ful things."

"Thank you," she said. "It's such a wonderful gift. I will always cherish it as much as I've cherished our times together." She held the beautiful pin in her palm. "Oh, I have something for you too." She bent to retrieve her bag.

"After you balked at my gift? What hypocrisy!" he laughed.

"Yes, I suppose you're right," she said and pulled out a parchment tied with a green velvet bow. "I know it's some-thing you'll treasure always," Anna said with a mischievous look on her face.

Nate looked at Anna with suspicion, pulled the bow, and unrolled the paper. After a moment, he broke out into a loud laugh. "Anna, this is cruel!"

"Perhaps, but I know that every time you see it, you'll remember our first meeting."

"No doubt," he said. He smiled as he held a page of the

sheet music to Rossini's *Elisabetta, Regina d'Inghilterra,* autographed by Lady de Cortenay. "I shall carry it with me always."

With a shocking abruptness, he suddenly returned to his meal. "Let's finish this fine meal, while it's still hot."

Anna sat stunned for a moment, but then resumed eating her dinner.

Several minutes into their entrée, Anna summoned up enough courage to discuss their future. "Nate, what are...?" Anna stammered, looked down at her food and pushing a carrot around with her fork as she continued. "I am so confused about our, our... relationship, or friendship, or whatever you would like to call it. I... Nate, what will happen to our friendship after we part?"

Nate stopped mid-chew and looked at Anna. He finished his bite and swallowed. "Well, I suppose we'll remain friends. You'll go on to Fort Towson to teach, and I'll serve with my troop, as both of our duties demand."

Anna looked down at her hands, which now gripped the gold napkin that she'd mindlessly twisted into a knot, resembling how her heart felt.

"Let me explain," he said, and cleared his throat. "I'm commissioned to remain in the military for at least another year, but not more than two unless the rebels in the south make moves to attack the citizens there."

"I see," Anna said.

"If I don't wish to continue in the military after that time elapses, I'll go back to mapping out the new lands."

"You're a cartographer?" Anna asked.

"Yes. It would mean long treks across the wilderness and lands, long periods of exploring the territory, far from any settlements. If I became involved with a woman, it would... well, it would mean that correspondence and visits – if any – would be brief and sparse." He stopped. "I'm afraid no woman would accept the life I will have to offer her, and I don't wish to become something I'm not, or take on an occupation I'll despise, simply to keep someone else happy."

"Nate, I –" Anna started but was interrupted by Nate.

"I know it may seem very selfish, but I am trying to be frank with you – first, to let you know of my plans and second, to tell you I understand if you can't accept my situation."

Anna struggled to keep the disappointment in Nate's revelation from showing on her face. She stared at the dessert, at first tantalizing, but now unappealing and bland. Her fork slipped from her hand and clanged hard against the china plate.

"I'm sorry," Nate said. He reached to take her hand. "I didn't mean to hurt you."

Anna pulled her hand back and pretended to pick up the fork to use again. "No, I'm fine. I understand, and you are right. We both have our lives carefully planned, and we shouldn't allow circumstances between us to interfere." Deep inside, the sense of rejection crawled back up and gripped her vulnerable heart in a vice-like hold. She took a deep breath. "Like you, I have a plan and want to see it completed. I'd like to continue our friendship, but it appears I thought our relationship deeper than I should have assumed. It's just that it seems one moment you are fond of me, and the next – well, I'm just a friend for this journey. It's confusing."

Nate forced her to let him hold her hand. "Anna, please. You must be reasonable. Don't let your emotions negate all we have shared on this trip."

"I thought you were sincere and that you cared for me as I've grown to care for you. I suppose I have allowed my feelings to overtake me."

"If you want a solid, unbreakable promise from me of a permanent relationship, I'm afraid I cannot offer you that. If you want a promise that I will never forget you, you have that," Nate explained. "I don't wish to lose you, Anna."

"It appears you never had me," Anna said as tears trickled down her cheeks. She wiped them from her face with the gold linen. "I'll go on and finish my journey. I am ready to get started with my teaching, ready for my new life."

"Anna, we –" Nate started but Anna stopped him.

"Nate, don't worry. It's fine, and I *have* enjoyed our friendship." She refused to let him see how deeply wounded she felt. She would go on and prove to herself that she was important to someone, even if only to the students of Fort Towson. She fought back disappointment in Nate and anger with herself for allowing another rejection by another man.

They chatted of trivial things – the abundance of mosquitos, the odd weather – intermingled with an occasional uncomfortable silence, until the waiter came and delivered the check. Anna smiled at the man out of habit, but in reality, she never even saw his face.

They left the restaurant, and Nate escorted Anna back to the hotel in a carriage. Quiet and subdued, Anna chose to respond with only an occasional nonchalant, "Really?" and, "Hmm," while Nate chatted of the city's rich history.

At the hotel, he helped Anna from the coach and walked with her to the hotel veranda, though Anna tried to stay a step or two in front of him.

When they reached the door, Nate took her hand. "I've enjoyed spending time with you, Anna," he said as he bent to kiss her.

Anna stood stiff and responded only enough to keep him from seeing how hurt she felt. Her heart was so hardened now that even Nate's kind words couldn't pierce the armor she'd placed around it, nor did she allow his parting kiss to move her.

Chapter 22

The next morning began with a heavy heart for Anna. A slight fear edged into her mind. The last time she'd suffered a man's rejection, the loss of her job had followed. Again, Anna prayed for help and comfort.

Back on board, Anna headed for her cabin ready to end the trip and move on to another chapter in her life.

The *Jewel Belle* waited at the dock to join an entourage of ships led by Henry Shreve's new boat. Able to bust through the large and sometimes massive logjams that blocked the way on the Red River, it opened the waterway for delivery of commercial cargo for settlements and supplies for nearby military installments.

Three ships sat in the wharf: the *Burgess,* a smaller steamboat than the *Jewel Belle,* and a slightly larger ship, the *Heroine,* lay waiting for Shreve. About midmorning, Shreve's boat, which was outfitted with a large grid on the front, had easily cleared the tangled debris blocking the entrance to Red River. The first boat struggled over a sandbar and broke loose just as its Captain and pilot readied to concede defeat. The next boat, the *Heroine,* broke through effortlessly and continued up the river.

The *Jewel Belle,* a heavier craft than either of the previous boats, groaned and squealed as it approached the sandbar. The pilot and Captain barked orders and admonitions to the boiler crews. A few curses expedited immediate action. The men, sweating and blackened by the soot expelled from the fire, stoked the boiler with as much wood as was possible without causing an explosion.

People stood on the banks and held their breath as the gallant girl skirted the bar and swirled to the other side, belching black smoke from her twin smokestacks. On the ship, bells rang and the orchestra hailed the success with a lively march, accompanied by the cheers and screams from the onlookers standing on the banks and docks.

Anna returned the wave of the handsome Colonel standing on the southern shore. With tears clouding her vision, she watched him shrink into distance. Then she determinedly turned her attention to the river way.

The three ships made good time. The Captain kept the passengers apprised of what lay ahead for their journey. If all continued as well as it had to this point the *Burgess* and *Heroine* would reach their destinations within a day, with the *Jewel Belle* making its arrive at Fort Towson in two days at the most.

Large, jagged walls of red dirt, gouged out by previous high and swift water flows, stood high alongside the river. The rust-colored soil surprised Anna. The bare roots of many trees stuck out from the edges of the banks. Today the two ships would leave the *Jewel Belle* to continue on to the Fort, and Anna felt excited for the arrival. The thought of being on solid earth for more than a day or two at a time thrilled her. The confines of the ship began to close in on her and she longed to run and walk for more that the length of the boat. Her thoughts were interrupted as:

"We're roundin' the Skyler bend. Keep her stoked!" the pilot yelled.

More thick black smoke bellowed from the innards of the *Jewel Belle* and was forced through the vents. The *Burgess* made it through the bend, and the *Heroine* managed to climb through the eyelet, its boilers at full blast, before disaster struck.

Several long horn blasts sounded, and the *Heroine* pulled to the port side. There was a terrifying *boom;* the ship tilted violently to the starboard side, then righted herself before discharging another plume of black exhaust. Anna could see the panic spread through the passengers lining the *Heroine's* railings. The boat juddered in a great wave from its stem to its stern. Its occupants screamed and yelled for help. A brief lull in the violent shaking quieted the screams; then, with another sudden tilt to the starboard side, the boat flung its passengers across the deck. The ship paused – as if holding her breath. Then abruptly she broke in half, as the forward section of the dining room crashed inward. The other portion of the ship emptied its passengers into the swirling, crimson murk of the Red River and then sank beneath the water.

Cries of terror and horror resonated from the watchers on the decks of the other ships, and Anna's hands flew to her mouth. "Oh, God! Help those people!" she screamed.

Along the riverbanks, many onlookers who'd come to see Shreve's snag-busting craft witnessed the *Heroine* descend into the maroon depths. Several men jumped off the sinking ship as it went under and swam to the *Burgess,* where they were pulled aboard to safety. One soldier struggled as he towed the limp form of an unconscious man from the water, to the side of the *Burgess.* As the men pulled the wounded man to the deck, Anna prayed he would live. Plucked from the river, the rescuer fell exhausted upon the deck.

The *Heroine's* tall smokestack poked from the water like a tombstone, marking its resting place. The Captain pulled the *Jewel Belle* as close to the river banks as possible to avoid catching her on the wreckage as they passed the sinking ship. The somber passengers of the *Jewel Belle* stood on her decks as she continued upstream to the Fort Towson landing. All talked only of the tragedy they'd witnessed, and many whispered prayerful thanks for their own ship's safety.

"Shame about that ship," the Captain said. "Over twenty barrels of pork, several crates of ammunition, meal, corn, and wheat stores for the Fort went down with the *Heroine.*"

"But no-one died, did they?" Anna asked.

"Well, I can't say for sure, miss. I wouldn't doubt it, although most were on deck I think, not down below, thankfully. There was that one fellow who they pulled out. From where I stood, he didn't look too good."

Anna's heart went out to the man, and she prayed again for his safety and gave thanks that her own vessel had made it through the treacherous path unscathed.

She knew without a doubt that the cold hard horror of that day would remain with her forever.

Chapter 23

A day and half later, on April 1, 1838 Anna stood on deck, clutching the rail as the ship pulled up to the Fort Towson landing. The *Jewel Belle* chugged up to the weather-worn dock that protruded from the riverbank. For the first time since she'd begun her journey, no cheering crowds hailed their arrival. She grabbed her bag and waited until the crew lowered the ramp.

"Miss Collins, I hope you have enjoyed your ride with us," the Captain said.

"I have, sir. Thank you for all your kindness and for getting me here safely."

"Will you be taking the ship back to Cincinnati soon?"

"No. I haven't planned a return trip," Anna said with a gulp, "but when – *if* I do, I'll be sure to take passage with you again."

"Fine, fine. Goodbye, Miss Collins."

"Goodbye, Captain."

Anna strode down the wooden walkway lined with small rosebushes until she reached a building. Miss Dickinson stood at the edge of the boardwalk, and relief washed over Anna at the sight of a familiar face in that strange new environment. Even though she'd only met Mary once, it was nice to look upon her again.

"Miss Collins!" Miss Dickinson said and took her hand. "I'm so glad you arrived safely. I heard about a steamboat wreck, and I prayed it wasn't your vessel."

Anna sighed. "No. Thankfully, my boat made it through without any problems. The trip through the area where the other boat sank frightened me. Our ship had a little trouble getting around the bar, but the Captain held it steady," Anna said, biting her lip at the memory of the shipwreck. "We saw a man pulled from the river, but we didn't know about any other injuries. I pray he survives. The Captain said he would be brought here by wagon."

"We heard there were no deaths, but some did survive several minor injuries, and one man suffered serious wounds," Miss Dickinson said. "Perhaps he's the man you saw rescued."

"That's good news, but why bring anyone here when a larger settlement would surely have better facilities?" Anna asked.

"Well, fortunately for the military men and their families, the Fort has a well-trained physician and an infirmary ready to treat anything from a headache to broken arms. The government brought Doc in when the Indians arrived after their transfer from the eastern states. Kinda to protect the soldiers and settlers already here."

Anna hoped the condition of the hospital did not match that of the dock as she stepped cautiously so as not to catch the heel of her boot in the numerous wide gaps between the wooden slats.

"Miss Dickinson said. "Was the rest of your trip better?"

"Yes. It was very exciting and – well, to be honest, a little frightening at times. In any case, I'm thrilled to be here now, and I'm all yours. What shall I do now?"

Miss Dickinson took Anna's arm and led her to a wagon. "Well first, let's retrieve your baggage from the office, and then we'll be on our way."

A large man with glowing red hair and skinny arms walked up.

"Seamus," Miss Dickinson said, "would you please bring Miss Collins's belongings to the wagon?"

"Ah! Here's that little lady you been waitin' for," said another man, who stood next to the small wagon.

"Miss Collins, this is Mr. Gaither," Miss Dickinson said to Anna.

"Good to meet ya," he said.

Miss Dickinson climbed up into the wagon seat, and Mr. Gaither took Anna's hand to help her into the seat beside her.

After the men piled Anna's trunks into the back of the wagon, Mr. Gaither climbed up into the seat, and the other man, Seamus, hopped onto the back. Mr. Gaither took the reins of the team and slapped them. "Yaw!" he cried, and they trotted off, bumping along on the uneven, rutted path.

Anna sat in silence as the three bantered back and forth about crops, insects, and the largest skunk they'd ever seen in Indian Territory.

"Miss Collins has travelled all the way from Cincinnati, Mr. Gaither," Miss Dickinson said to the wagon driver.

"That so?" He peered around Miss Dickinson and smiled at Anna. "Well, we're mighty glad to have ya in the terratory now, miss."

"Thank you," Anna said.

"In the back is Seamus O'Malley. Seamus, say hello to Miss Anna," Miss Dickinson said.

"Yep. Mighta fine yer 'ere nah."

Anna wrinkled her brow and looked at Miss Dickinson for the interpretation.

"He says he's glad you're here now."

"Oh. Nice to meet you, Mr. O'Malley," Anna said, wondering if everyone in Indian Territory spoke in such a strange dialect.

"Seamus came from Ireland and lived in Mississippi for a while, but when the government forced the Indians to move here, he came with them. He figured this area could use a good blacksmith, and he was sure right about that. Isn't that true, Seamus?"

"Ya, 'tis!"

They continued their ride for about ten minutes through flatlands covered with thick green grass, dotted with yellow flowers. Large dragonflies hovered over white flower-laden bushes. A rabbit hopped out of the horses' path. To the east of the trail, tall trees stood along the edge of a winding creek. Various sizes of blackjacks, oaks, maples, and several trees with pale lavender-reddish flowers sprinkled the land.

"How far is the Fort from here?" Anna asked.

"Well, reckon it's about a mile north of the dock. Ever been to a fort before, Miss Collins?" Mr. Gaither asked as he slapped a bug on his leg. "Those mosquitoes are nasty this spring. Big as houses, them blood-suckers!"

Anna wrinkled her nose at the thought of dealing with mosquitoes yet again. "No, I've never been to a fort, or any other military establishment. I'm looking forward to the experience."

"Well, if experiences is what yer after, you're in for plenty of them!" Mr. Gaither said with a chuckle.

"Please don't frighten Anna, Mr. Gaither," Miss Dickinson begged as she patted the top of Anna's hand.

A large grasshopper, disturbed from the grassy path by the trotting horses, jumped onto Miss Dickinson's arm. Anna shrieked and scooted away from her. Without any emotion or change in demeanor, Miss Dickinson calmly flicked it off.

"Pay Mr. Gaither's teasing no mind," she instructed Anna. "If you listen to him, he'll make you think we live in a rube town filled with yahoos and crazy folk!"

"And that'd be lying to her?" he laughed.

How lovely, Anna thought. *Large insects, mosquitoes, and insane people shall now be my new neighbors.*

"There is one thing I should like to ask about," Anna said to Miss Dickinson.

"What's that?"

"You mentioned, when I met you in Montgomery, that the Indians don't capture or harm the white people in the area."

"Yes, that's true."

"Well, on the trip – I think it was near a town called Toadville – the soldiers told me some Indians had captured a woman."

"Whoo boy! They saw you comin'! Miss Anna, they just wanted to spook ya," declared Mr. Gaither, laughing.

"It wasn't true?" Anna asked.

"No, Anna," Miss Dickinson said and put her hand on her arm. "They likely made that up to see your reaction. And the town is Frogville, not Toadville."

Anna shook her head. "I'm sorry, but I see nothing funny about relaying a frightening story just for the sake of upsetting someone!"

"Miss Coal-lins, don't let 'em scare ya off. This here's a

byouta-ful place," Seamus broke in.

Mr. Gaither nodded back towards Seamus. "Better listen to good ol' Seamus back there. If he thinks it's great here, miss, then I reckon it's the truth."

Anna decided to hold her opinion till she had settled in rather more.

They made their way up a small incline and joined a dirt trail that swung to the west. As they rounded the bend, Anna saw the cantonment. On the north side of the road sat the Fort, which formed a large U-shape that opened to the dirt road. On the northernmost edge of the compound, three large buildings housed the headquarters and offi-cers' rooms. From the front of the barracks, a large green beltway ran to the open road. On a tall pole in front of the officers' buildings, a large flag flapped in the warm breeze.

The area bustled with activity. In the 'marching green', as Mr. Gaither called the grassy area, Anna watched perfectly formed lines of soldiers walk, their steps synchronized to perfection. The sight of women and children walking freely about the camp caused her heart to sing.

Anna took a deep breath. *Finally!* she thought. *After all this time, I've finally made it.*

After almost nine weeks of travel on water and a short trip by wagon, she felt ready to start her career; to find redemption from her failures right there in that Fort.

Dust swirled around the wagon as it pulled up to the barracks on the left side of the compound, and Mr. Gaither yanked the reins. "Whoa, now!" he yelled. When the wagon stopped, he jumped off and reached up to Anna to help her down from the seat.

Anna stood, wondering how to get off the wagon without exposing any of herself, and still survive the fall.

Miss Dickinson pointed to Mr. Gaither. "Put your hands on the top of his shoulders. He'll grab your waist and swing you down."

Anna stared at her. "What?" she asked. *Surely Miss Dickinson doesn't mean for me to jump down, of all things!*

"Here – I'll show you." Mr. Gaither walked to the other side of the wagon and stood in front of Miss Dickinson. She placed her hands on his shoulders, and Mr. Gaither helped her down off the wagon. She plopped feet-first down on the ground and looked up at Anna. "See? It's not as difficult as you think."

"All right." Anna scooted over to the edge of the wagon seat and followed their instructions. "Ah!" She squealed and giggled from embarrassment when her feet hit the ground.

Mr. Gaither patted her back. "There ya go. See? Nothin' to it."

Miss Dickinson led Anna to the third building and opened the door. Anna gasped with surprise at the wonderful space. Eight tables and benches sat in the center of the room, and a flag adorned the front.

"This is our classroom – or *your* classroom, rather," Miss Dickinson said.

Anna couldn't believe she was finally standing there, in a classroom all her own. "It's quite charming," Anna said.

"Yes, it's a fine schoolhouse. We're fortunate to be blessed with this spacious accommodation. I'm sure you'll find that your students are just as charming. They're quite a grand group."

"How many are there?"

"Well, at present, we have eight"

"Only eight? Is that the usual number?"

"No. Most of the time there are ten, but in springtime, when the planting begins and in fall, during harvest time, we lose a few of the boys. They have to help their families with the farming."

"They're allowed to miss school because of farming?"

"It's a different life here, Miss Collins. The farms and ranches are everyone's source of survival, so it's imperative that everything is harvested at just the right time in order for the farmers to earn the most from their crops."

"Don't the student farmhands fall behind in their studies?"

"Some do, but these folk are just happy to have any opportunity for education – even if it must be sporadic."

Anna nodded her head with the strange realization that the children faced so many impediments to their education – not only their dangerous environment, but also the necessity of helping out with chores.

"Come on. I'll show you your quarters."

Anna and Miss Dickinson walked to the rear of the classroom and into a smallish back room. A window dressed with striped gingham cloth curtains allowed just enough light in.

"It's not fancy, but it'll meet your needs for shelter, privacy, and proximity to the school."

Anna sat down on the bed, which creaked under her weight. "It'll be nice to sleep in a bed instead of the cabin bunk on the boat."

"It might not be the most comfortable bed, but perhaps when the cook kills a chicken, you can ask for the feathers to plump your mattress. I like mine nice and firm, so I haven't bothered with that."

"Oh. Well, I've been sleeping on a hard cabin bed for some time now, so there's no need to sacrifice a chicken just for me."

Mr. Gaither and Seamus entered the classroom carrying Anna's large trunk and her two smaller bags. Miss Dickinson stood from the desk chair.

"We'll let you get settled into your new home. The privy is out the classroom door around to the right, down a little slope. Just follow the path. You can't get lost. If there's anything you need, Seamus lives just down the way at his blacksmith shop. It sits behind the Captain's Quarters, directly north of the flagpole. Also, Mr. Gaither lives in the cabin off to the right of the grounds. He'll be glad to help you with anything you need, and his wife Lillian is a wonderful woman who is most excited to have you here. I'm staying at the parsonage until I leave. Mr. Gaither can fetch me if you need me."

"Thank you." Anna stayed seated on the bed as Miss Dickinson left her alone with her sparse belongings and an empty, darkened room.

Anna knelt by the bed upon the rough-hewn wooden plank floor. "Father, thank You for protecting me on my trip, for the friendships I made, and for the comforts You've given. Guide me and assist me in this endeavor to be a teacher to these children. Oh God, give me strength."

Exhausted and uncertain, she went on. "I pray I've followed Your leading," she petitioned fervently, hoping her plans weren't simply the result of the mad rantings of an embittered and lonely woman. "I hope I've done the right thing, God!"

She stood and wiped the stray tears from her cheeks, drying her hands on her dress.

Her small room began to warm, and Anna opened her trunk and removed one of the cotton dresses she had packed for hot weather. She secured her door with the sliding bolt and made sure the curtain was closed. The heavy dress she'd been wearing on the boat and the wagon ride clung to her sweaty skin. After she wrenched free from it, she stood in only her camisole and petticoat and let her skin breathe for a moment.

Anna raised her hands over her head to stretch and relax her tight muscles, then dug through her bag for the perfumed talcum powder her mother had given her for Christmas. Patting her damp skin with the powder puff propelled white particles into her tiny room. Grudgingly, she dressed. "Can't stand here all day in my undergarments," she told herself. The scented talc eased her regret at having to put clothes on again, and she pulled the lightweight dress over her head and pinned her hair up off her neck.

She separated the curtain panels and opened the door to allow a flow of fresh air into the room. Then she emptied her trunk and bags and hung her dresses and coat in a walnut wardrobe in the corner. Her boots and flats fit nicely at the bottom of the wardrobe, and her other clothing items filled the drawers of the dresser beneath the window.

Anna scooted her trunk to the end of the bed. In it, she left her winter clothing. The thought of putting on a coat nauseated her. *Maybe a coat and gloves won't be needed here after all,* she thought.

A wave of homesickness washed over her after she'd unpacked the small amount of her personal items. At the bottom of her carpetbag she found the sapphire brooch Nate had given her on their last dinner date. Anna clutched it tightly in her hand and closed her eyes. She remembered his touch, and how she had felt when he kissed her...

"Oh, Anna, don't go making yourself miserable so soon," she mumbled. "Ugh!! Men! They get into your head and heart and leave you crazy!"

Atop the little dresser she created a vignette of pictures

of her parents and Caleb. The pin from Nate lay beside her Bible and notepad.

Anna's reverie was broken by the clanging of a bell, and she looked out the window to find a reason for the noise. The window framed a view of tall grass waving in the slight breeze around a large tree, its triangular leaves glistening in the sunlight, but presented no answer for the clanking. She turned around and stood still in the middle of her room, unsure of what to do.

Well, I guess it would be best to ask someone what that means. I wouldn't want to be left out of any excitement! She giggled at the thought. Perhaps Mrs. Devonshire had rubbed off on her a little more than she'd hoped!

Picking up her hat and closing the bedroom door, Anna stepped into the classroom. She walked through the room and outside onto the boardwalk which connected the buildings together.

A group of men stood in the middle of the field. They looked calm, unfazed, and apparently not worried about the clanging bell. After waiting watchfully for several moments, she walked to the other side of the field to find Mr. Gaither's house. Miss Dickinson had told her he would be the one to ask if she needed anything, and what she needed now was a bit of explanation.

The men began marching around the field in lines, and it seemed Anna kept getting in their way. She quickly scampered out of their path to the farthest southern end of the grassy area, across to a small cabin on the right behind the other line of barracks.

Anna knocked on the door and waited for a response from inside. She jumped back when the door opened. A boy of about seven years old looked up at her enquiringly.

"Umm... is Mr. Gaither here, please?"

"Yep." The little boy remained still, without offering any further information or making any move to fetch Mr. Gaither.

"He's here?"

"Yep," he answered. Again, that was all.

"Would you mind asking him to come and talk with me?"

"Who are ya?" he asked.

She smiled, gathering herself. "Would you please tell

Mr. Gaither that Miss Collins is here and would like to speak with him?"

"All right." Finally, he turned on his heels and sprinted off inside the house. "Pa! Pa!" he yelled at the top of his lungs. "Some lady's here fer ya!"

Anna heard talking from inside the house, punctuated by more of the little boy's loud and boisterous shouts.

Another voice joined the cacophony. "Josiah! Stop that yellin' or I'm gonna hafta whoop ya." Anna heard the voice getting louder as someone neared the door. Finally a petite woman stood before her.

"Howdy. My name's Lillian," she said. "How can I help ya?" She wiped her hands on the apron perched atop a rounding abdomen that appeared to be harboring a future sibling of the noisy Josiah, and then offered her hand to Anna.

When Anna gave her hand to Lillian, the woman grasped it firmly and pumped it with gusto. Taken aback for a moment by the vigorous handshake, Anna stuttered. "Um... uh, I'm Anna Collins, the uh... the new teacher. I was wondering if I might have a word with your husband, if he's here. Is he here? Mr. Gaither, I mean."

"Dear, you're as skittish as a worm in a pond full of catfish. Sure, Mr. Gaither's here. And yes, Jordan *is* my husband. Come on in and have a seat. No use standin' there sweatin' in that heat while you wait for him."

She led Anna into a small main room. Anna looked around at the surprisingly tidy space (considering the number of children that decorated it), sparse except for the blue silk-covered settee that seemed as out of place in the room as Anna felt in the territory. "Jereboam, scoot on out of Miss Collins's way and let her have a seat. Jedediah, go fetch your pa from out in the shed and tell Josiah to get the wood for the stove. Tell 'im Miss Collins is here to speak with him. Boy, don't stand there gawkin'! Get on an' do as I say." She swatted the child on the backside, and he took off outside.

Lillian sat down hard in a rocking chair next to the stone fireplace. She rubbed her back. "Ya got any young'ns?" she asked.

"No, no. I'm not married."

"That so? Well, this here baby'll be my sixth time in the family way. Lost one baby a couple years ago to the influenza. I told Jordan I wanna have ten or 'leven of 'em, but that's all I can handle." She patted her stomach. "As long as this old body holds out, that is."

Anna heard heavy footsteps enter the back of the house as Mr. Gaither entered the main room.

"Miss Collins! Good ta see ya again, miss. Did ya get all settled in?"

"Yes, I did, thank you. The schoolhouse is wonderful."

"Is there anything we can do for you?" He walked over to his wife and patted her shoulder.

"I am a little confused about the protocol in a military establishment. The bell that sounded earlier, what does it mean?"

"Bell? Oh, yeah! That's just the signal for the next squad of soldiers to meet in the field and start their military exercises. We've all gotten so we hardly hear the thing anymore. You'll get used to it."

Anna smiled faintly. "I didn't know if it signaled an emergency. I mean – I – just didn't know what to think," Anna said, stumbling over her words.

"Honey, it is a little overwhelmin' comin' from a big city to this little rinky-dink Fort town out in the middle of Indian Territory, but I'm sure you'll be fine in a little while," Lillian said, smiling at her.

"I'm sure you're right," Anna said. She rubbed her forehead and realized for the first time how badly it was throbbing. "I'm a little tired. It's been a long, long journey. Once I rest up a bit, though, I am sure I'll get used to the activity here."

Lillian smiled and took her husband's rough, calloused hand. "Now don't go getting' all worked up. There's nothing wrong with a little concern and a few questions. It's a whole new world out here, and things are a little different than what you're used to. Would you like to have dinner with us tonight?"

Anna couldn't imagine being surrounded by all those boisterous children, when she was so weary. "That's very nice of you, but I'm afraid I'd be poor company, with this headache. Please don't think me rude, but I'm very tired –

if you don't mind, I'll just eat dinner quietly in my room."
Then Anna realized she had nothing more than a few slices
of bread and tea that she'd taken from the ship. "Oh! I
haven't brought anything with me... Is there a restaurant
or diner here?"

"Across from the schoolroom, there's a little cantina.
Bessy'll be glad to rustle up some food fer ya," Mr. Gaither
said. "I'll walk ya over there and introduce ya if you like."

"Sure, you take Miss Collins to Bessy. Supper's 'bout
ready, so it'll be all rounded up for ya by the time you get
back."

Mr. Gaither walked with Anna to the cantina. As they
opened the door the aroma of food awakened Anna's
stomach, causing it to growl in greedy anticipation.

A large, heavyset black woman peeked around the
doorway. "Jordan? Something wrong at home? Tell me that
wife a yers ain't in the middle of birthin' that baby while yer
over here gallavantin' at my cantina!"

"No, Bessy. Lillian's fine. I've just brought someone I'd
like ya to meet."

Bessy came out of the back room and smiled a big grin
that instantly warmed Anna's heart. "Why, hello, miss. I'm
Bessy Standingdeer."

"I'm Anna Collins, the new schoolteacher."

"Well, mercy me! They fine-ly got somebody to come all
the way down here? Amazin'! Now – don't get me wrong
– this is a great place, but it's purdy far from everything
civilized."

"Bessy, ya got anything fer this little lady to eat?"

"Sure! Ya know that be the truth, Jordan."

Mr. Gaither waved and headed off home, and Bessy
turned to Anna. "Miss Collins, you go on and have a seat
over there, an' I'll bring ya some vittlins. Ya like squirrel?"
Bessy stood still, with her wide eyes unblinking and stared
at Anna, waiting for her answer.

"Um, well... I – I don't really think... um... maybe just a
drink will do," Anna stuttered.

Bessy slapped her chubby thigh and cackled. "Mercy!
Honey, ya gonna hafta get less serious 'round here, or yer
gonna get pranked day an' night. Folks in this Fort love ta
pick on big-city folk!" She shook her head. "Now, how about

some beef stew with roast taters, sweetened tea, biscuits, and sand plum jelly?"

Anna closed her eyes in quiet relief. "That sounds absolutely heavenly, Bessy."

When the lovely woman scurried off to make her dinner, Anna sighed. "Bessy *is* an angel! Thank you, Lord, for her... and for not making me eat squirrel!"

Chapter 24

Anna sat up in her bed, confused. Where was she? As her mind cleared, she realized that she'd slept all through the night and it was now quite late.

Probably the fatigue – and that most filling meal from Bessy's cantina! she decided.

Anna washed and dressed, read a passage of her Bible, and went into her classroom. She squealed with delight. "*My* classroom!"

She swept the schoolroom and prepared notes on her tablet for the lessons. Miss Dickinson had agreed to sit in during classes for the first week until Anna got her bearings and became better acquainted with the students, the procedures, and the curriculum.

According to Miss Dickinson, the students consisted of five girls between the ages of seven and thirteen, and six boys ranging from seven to twelve. One of those students was the talkative Josiah Gaither.

School started at ten o'clock in the morning and ended at approximately four in the afternoon, until harvest in late August. At that time, classes were suspended until after the first frost, which Mr. Gaither, Miss Dickinson, Bessy, and Seamus all guessed would be anytime between November 16 and December 1. With such an irregularly scheduled school term, Anna wondered if there would be enough time to teach anything of substance to her students.

Miss Dickinson assured Anna that all the students progressed well in their classes except for one boy, twelve-year-old Eli Grainger. His father was a soldier patrolling in Mexican territory with the military, and his mother had died as the result of an infection from a cut. With his father away and his mother passed, little Eli was a bit of a make-shift orphan, left to live alone in their cabin. Miss Dickinson warned Anna about his moodiness and his desire to get into as much trouble as he could. Nevertheless, Anna's heart went out to the boy.

With Miss Dickinson's help, Anna outlined lessons for her students according to grade or age level. She was sure her plans would allow the students to learn as much as possible in the short time she had to teach them.

School was scheduled to commence on Thursday of the week after Anna had arrived at the Fort. Until then, she used her time to check out the Fort and the small, busy community.

A sutler's store sat to the west of the Fort compound. It was operated by Mr. Gooding, and he was most proud of his assortment and the variety of wares he offered; his latest addition was sarsaparilla extract. From the sutler's store, Anna purchased tea and sugar for her one extravagance: sweet tea.

She also bought some trinkets to send to Caleb, and mailed a letter to her parents and Aunt Maggie to let them know she had arrived safely and was settling into her new environment. She didn't mention the troubling events of the trip, nor did she say a word about the fact that she'd witnessed the sinking of a sister steamboat on the Red River.

A letter from Nate arrived soon after Anna had. She carried it unopened to her room, threw her bonnet on the bed and sat with the envelope in her hand. She closed her eyes and exhaled deeply. If it carried upsetting news, she felt ready to deal with it, so she ripped open the end and pulled out the paper.

Her eyes quickly scanned the note, and when she found nothing to hint at bad news, she began to carefully read each word.

In his letter, Nate summarized his activities since he'd last seen her in Shreve's Town. He mentioned the sinking of the *Heroine* and expressed his thankfulness that her boat was not damaged. For the rest, he talked about the weather, their arrival at the Mexican boundary, and his hopes that she was settled in and growing accustomed to life at the Fort.

Her eyes clouded with misty tears when she read: *Love, Nate.* Even though she knew he wanted nothing more than a platonic relationship, she longed for his company.

That night, as Anna crawled into bed, her head was filled with thoughts about her first day of teaching, her lesson plans, the children she would meet, Nate and his letter, and her parents and Caleb. They all swirled together in a massive, oppressive cloud hanging above her.

The heat didn't help calm her mood. The sultry day began with uncomfortable humidity and ended with over-whelming temperatures. Tall, fluffy white clouds – thunderheads – piled higher and higher in the western sky.

Anna threw back the cover, jumped out of bed and opened the curtain wider to allow in even a whisper of the very slight breeze. Outside, she heard the clattering of a speeding wagon and the *galumph* of horses' hooves as they entered the compound.

Anna stood on her tiptoes and looked out the window. She saw three soldiers running to the wagon, from which they extracted a stretcher. Atop the stretcher lay a motionless form, and the soldiers made haste to carry the man to the infirmary. Anna couldn't help but wonder about the injured man who had been taken into the medical center. Was he a soldier who'd been wounded in combat? She crawled back into her stifling bed and whispered a prayer for the injured man.

She closed her eyes and tried to doze off, but the antici-pation of her first day as a teacher kept her mind whirling.

"Anna, you must go to sleep!" she ordered herself. "Maybe I'll recite one of those boring poems Professor Noah required in Literature. They seemed to have no problem sending me off to slumber, even in the middle of class." She giggled. "Hmmm," she sighed. "How far I've come! Tomor-row *I* may be the teacher hypnotizing students!"

She drifted off eventually into a fitful sleep, interrupted by dreams of standing in front of the class without anything planned, and another in which she stood before the children dressed only in her camisole and slip!

If I survive tomorrow, Anna thought during one brief span of consciousness, *I can survive anything!*

Chapter 25

Anna awakened before the soldiers' morning bell sounded. Her stomach churned with nervousness for what the day would hold, and she hoped she wouldn't get sick and embarrass herself in front of her students – especially on her first day!

Anna dressed in a pretty cotton shift that matched the blue in the sapphire pin Nate had given her. She pinned her hair tightly up off her neck and pulled a few strands of her dark brunette hair loose to soften the frame of her face.

The evening before, Bessy had prepared a light lunch for her, but now she wondered if she'd even be able to eat a morsel of it without falling ill. She prayed for peace, guidance, a calm stomach, and a cool breeze, before leaving her room.

In the classroom she straightened her desk and the benches one last time, and smoothed her dress. Then she stepped outside the school and grabbed the rope attached to the silver bell atop the arched pole. She took a deep breath to calm herself, and pulled, ringing the bell punctually at ten o'clock. With excitement, she watched as the students – *her* students – came running up the path to the schoolhouse, many of them without shoes.

Each child eyed her with caution, some with suspicion, some with amusement, and one boy with total disregard. Anna presumed him to be the Eli Grainger she'd heard so much about.

When it appeared to Anna that the last of the students had arrived, she stood in front of the class, as calm and composed as possible. She cleared her throat, and the class quieted – a silence so thick one could have heard a moth's wings in the tree across the field.

"Good morning, students. I'm your new teacher, Miss Collins. I will be taking over from Miss Dickinson here at the Fort so that she may return to her students at the Indian school in Park Hill. Miss Dickinson is here and will be with us for a while to help me become acquainted with you," Anna said.

The class craned their necks to look back at Miss Dickinson, who'd come in after them. Mary walked to the front of the room and stood beside Anna. "Young ladies and gentlemen," she started, "I expect you will be as courteous and respectful to Miss Collins as you have been to me. She is an exceptional teacher, and she has many exciting and fun lessons in store for you."

Eli Grainger moaned and rolled his eyes.

"Eli," Miss Dickinson said, "you will sit up straight and keep quiet unless you are asked to speak."

The boy sat up, but he insisted on rolling his eyes again, this time in a more animated fashion.

"You know that you are all excellent, well-behaved students," Miss Dickinson said, glaring at Eli, "and I trust that you will continue to be so."

Eli slid back down in his seat the second Miss Dickinson stopped speaking. Anna decided it was best to deal with his poor attitude later, in private, thus denying the boy any attention he wanted to gain from his behavior.

Miss Dickinson sat at the desk while Anna taught the spelling lesson. The students enjoyed the game Anna had created to help them learn the new words. They were so entertained by it that after they'd gone through all the words, several children wanted to continue.

"No," Anna said. "We'll do more tomorrow, but right now it's time to eat lunch and take a break."

The students cheered and lined up at the door, ready to wash their hands and retrieve their lunch baskets from the coat closet.

After lunch, Anna began their arithmetic lesson. Several of the students were at the same achievement level in math, so that made teaching the concept of division easier for

Anna. While they completed their assignments, Anna gave the younger students simple addition problems to work out on their slates.

Before she knew it, the school day had come to an end, and she breathed a sigh of relief. She had, indeed, survived – and more importantly, she'd enjoyed it right from the start.

One little girl named Susan hugged Anna before she left. "Miss Collins, thank you for comin' to teach us," she said before she skipped off with her pigtails bouncing at the sides of her head.

Miss Dickinson smiled at Anna. "You did it!" she said. "I must say I haven't seen them take to spelling as they did with your game. That was ingenious! How did you come up with it?" Miss Dickinson asked as she picked up her satchel.

"Well, my professor at Oberlin used creative and innovative methodologies for stimulating interest in subjects, even those considered tedious and boring by most students."

"Hmm. I guess that answers my question! Anna, you don't have to work at convincing me that you are a capable and wonderful teacher. I'm already convinced."

"I can't believe I did it! I really just taught my first class," Anna said and smiled.

"And no-one cried – not even you!" Miss Dickinson said with a laugh.

As they walked out of the schoolroom, Anna caught Eli standing at the corner of the building. "Hello, Eli," Anna said. "May I help you?"

"Naw." He stuck his hands into his baggy trouser pockets. "See ya in the mornin'."

"Good day, Eli."

"That was odd," Miss Dickinson said, watching the boy plod off across the field with his hands in his pockets, his shoulders slumped, and his head down.

"How so?"

"Well, in the two years I've been teaching here, not once has Eli ever mentioned seeing me in the morning." She looked at Anna. "You indeed have a gift for teaching, Anna – even for those previously thought unteachable."

"I suppose that's because it's a passion of mine. Thank you for your help, Mary."

They walked from the schoolroom across the marching

green towards the cantina.

Anna smiled. "I am excited! I really feel ready for this, Mary."

Mary laughed. "I believe you are, Anna!"

After she and Miss Dickinson had eaten dinner at Bessy's cantina, Mary returned to the parsonage and Anna to her new home and school.

The day for Mary to leave the Fort came and the children made their farewells. The little girls pouted and some cried. The boys shook her hand and offered her odd gifts to carry with her to her new school – a dry, shriveled apple carved into a face was presented by the second oldest Grainger boy, and a stick whittled to a point, adorned with a feather and leather strings, from Sherman Smith.

"Thank you very much," Mary said to the children surrounding her. "I will never forget my time here with you and I am quite sure you will continue to learn and behave as well as you know you should." Mary eyed the boys pointedly and they shuffled their feet and had the grace to blush.

The children left and Anna turned to Mary. "Best wishes for your new position."

Mary embraced Anna. "Thank you, and to you also." She let go of Anna. "Are you ready? They're all yours now?"

Anna nodded. "I am!"

"Alright, I'll be at church Sunday, should you think of anything we haven't discussed yet. I know you'll do fine, Anna. I'm relieved to know the children will be taught by someone who genuinely cares about them."

"Goodbye, Mary. Please keep in touch, and I'll send notes about the children's progress," Anna said.

"I will. Take care," Miss Dickinson said. She hugged Anna and left her standing on the steps of the school – Anna's school.

"I *am* a good teacher," Anna said to herself

She cleared away the day's lessons, swept the room, and prepared for the next day. After finishing those daily tasks, she wrote to her parents and Caleb again. She prayed and thanked God for her successful day and prayed for each child in her class. *All need a special blessing,* she thought, *and maybe Eli most of all.*

She chose a bright yellow calico dress for the following day, and she laid out her petticoats and hose over her chair before she let down her hair and washed her face.

Anna climbed into bed, and easily fell asleep, overcome with a sense of peace and happiness.

Friday, the western skies again filled with the voluminous, towering clouds. Before sunset even more clouds formed in the southern sky.

"Looks like we're gonna git a bit of bad weather," Bessy said.

"Because of the clouds?" Anna asked.

"Not just that. The critters are all actin' fidgety and skittish-like. Now, honey," she warned, "if a cyclone should plop down upon us, you get into that little closet in the schoolroom. And fer goodness sakes, honey, put a piller or two on that pretty little head a yers and hang on. You'd be surprise what them clouds can kick up out here."

"I've had my fill of wretched storms," Anna said.

Thinking back on the conversation later in the evening, she shook her head. *Oh Lord, please don't let one of those come down*, she prayed silently.

As if in denial of her request, lightning flashed in her window, followed by the crack of thunder.

"I asked You, Lord, to *postpone* that for a spell, if You'd be so kind," she said aloud, surprised and somewhat upset that God didn't answer her prayer for divine weather adjustments.

Another clangor of thunder followed several lightning strikes that appeared to Anna to be striking ominously close to the camp. Heavy rain fell and dripped off the edges of the roof. After nearly forty minutes the stormed eased, leaving only an occasional flash of lightning and thunder booming off in the distance.

The storm left the air cool and fresh and gave Anna a pleasant respite from the recent string of overheated days. She drifted off into a comfortable and sweet slumber, thankful that God had His reasons for ignoring her prayer; clearly, the cool air and the fresh scent were on His agenda all along.

Anna and her students continued to bond. All improved in their studies, and Eli's attitude showed gradual improvement. Anna knew he was dealing with much at his young age, including sorrow at his mother's death, loneliness in his father's absence, and the heavy responsibilities of caring for himself while he was without parental care. In light of his home situation, she thought learning might seem trite and unimportant. Each night Anna prayed for Eli and for wisdom to help him.

Anna spent the weekends working on lesson plans, sewing, and mending the few dresses she brought. She checked the mail every time it came in, always looking for a letter from her family or Nate.

On one trek to the sutler's building, Anna saw soldiers scurrying into the infirmary. She guessed that the man who had been taken into the hospital several weeks earlier still required constant care, for she'd seen no sight of him, or of his body being taken out of the infirmary.

At the store, Anna found a peach-colored floral fabric. Mr. Gooding told her it was newly arrived from Boston. She bought several yards of it to make a dress for the Harvest Festival that would be held in October at the Fort.

A soldier rushed by Anna to the counter. "George, did you get that medicine yet?"

"Well, I don't know. A crate came in earlier. Lemme look right quick." Mr. Gooding bent over the box and began moving items around, searching for the bottle.

"Yes, Micah, it's here. I forgot all about it. Got that shipment of yard goods in, and the womenfolk have been pestering me all day." He chuckled and handed the brown bottle to the man. "Sign here, would ya? Is the feller gonna make it after all?"

The soldier raised his eyebrows and shrugged his shoulders. "We aren't sure yet. His infection's a stubborn one. It hasn't eased up much, and it's been a few weeks now. Doc can't make up his mind to amputate or leave it be – 'less he gets worse, o' course."

"Awful. Just awful. Is he conscious?"

"In and out. Makes no sense whatsoever when he tries to talk though. Can't get his name outta him, nor the names of any of his kinfolk. Lieutenant Dalton thinks he was on his way to Houston. Doc found an itinerary in his pocket. Looks like he had a meeting with some Texas land men down there, but we just can't get enough information from 'im to help any."

"'at's a shame. Just let me know if ya need anything. Always glad to help if'n I can."

The soldier nodded at Anna as he left the store. "Miss," he said politely.

She walked up to the desk to pay for her material and the tea she'd chosen. "Thank you, Mr Gooding."

"George, please Miss." He smiled widely at her.

"George." She smiled back and paused for a moment, hoping she wouldn't sound as nosey as good ol' Mrs. Devonshire. "If I may ask, what happened to that man? The one in the infirmary?" she asked.

"Oh, him. You know that boat, the *Heroine,* that sank down there on Red River?"

"Yes."

"That fella was on it. Got his leg trapped under the paddle wheel in all the commotion. He's been in a bad way since he arrived about a month ago." He shook his head and frowned. "Mighty sad situation. They don't got his name or nothin', so they can't find any kin to notify in case he don't make it."

"Didn't the ship have a passenger log?"

"Yes, but that went down with the ship. They're hopin, to find the Captain next time he makes his way down here so they can question him, but that probably won't be for another week or so."

"That is awful," Anna said. She left the store, saddened by the whole thing. *How terrible it is that a wife, a mother, a sibling is out there unaware that their husband, brother, or son is here, lying unconscious, wounded, and near death.* "God, be with that man and his family," she said under her breath.

She carefully balanced the cumbersome bundle of fabric with the package of English tea she had purchased from George's new stock. Anna bought it specifically to have with Bessy's gift. Earlier in the week, she'd mentioned to Bessy that she missed her grandmother's scones. Early this morning, Bessy had met her at the school with a basket of freshly baked wildberry biscuits.

"Bessy!" Anna cried when she saw the little cakes. "Thank you for the scones."

Bessy smiled, a little embarrassed. "I know they aren't like those fancy scones your grandmother makes, but out here, that's 'bout as fancy a biscuit as yer gonna git!"

"They look delicious." Anna laughed. "My mother's biscuits never looked like these, Bessy. Thank you." Anna's eyes twinkled. "I planned to purchase some of Mr. Gooding's special tea today, and now I can drink it while I gobble up these delectable little jewels." She hugged Bessy.

"Now, don't be gettin' all smarmy over some simple little cakes, missy... but you're very welcome."

Now, back in her room, Anna dropped the material on the bed and removed her bonnet and shoes. Pouring out a cupful from her large jug of stored water, she set the small pot on the stove, added a few bits of tinder and struck the flint to ignite the wood. When the water boiled she made her cup of tea with it and then poured more water into a basin, with some sweet smelling salts. Her feet had ached incessantly since her arrival at the Fort, more than she ever remembered them hurting at home. She sat and placed her achy feet in the water basin, sipped Mr. Gooding's special tea, and devoured Bessy's delicious biscuits.

On Sunday morning, Anna walked to the little church located about a quarter mile north of the Fort. Enjoying the walk, she thought of the children. Anna was rather amazed by how easily the transition from Miss Dickinson to herself had gone. She felt the children accepted her, and even Eli seemed more receptive to her help with his schoolwork.

Since it was now the middle of May, the other children who worked with their families planting crops would return to the schoolroom. With Miss Dickinson's help, Anna organized their study plans after she first arrived. She hoped she could get the new students caught up without interfering with the ongoing lessons of the others.

Anna entered the small white building.

"Good Sunday morning," the minister said. "Have you had a good week?"

"Well, yes I have," Anna said and smiled.

"Well, you're all my little daughter talks about. She came home last week saying, 'Miss Collins said this' and 'Miss Collins said that'! We haven't needed to bribe her to get up and ready for school since you arrived!"

"That is a wonderful compliment! Thank you."

Anna walked up the aisle, filled with a satisfaction and encouragement to go on. She took a seat next to an uncomfortably pregnant Lillian and her four bored, squirming children.

"Mornin', Miss Collins," the children and Lillian greeted her.

Lillian straightened and rubbed her back.

"Are you all right?" Anna asked.

"Yes, but I'm very ready for this little one to come. His foot is doing a jig on my back, and I swear, if I get any bigger, I might possibly be the first woman to *actually* pop."

Anna giggled. "You must be uncomfortable, especially in this heat, but surely you don't have much longer, do you?"

"No. The way I figure, I still have about five weeks or so to go."

The littlest Gaither child tried without success to climb up on Lillian's nonexistent lap, and wailed loudly when his efforts failed.

"Jonathon! Mommy cannot hold you, sweetie," Lillian said to him.

The little boy screamed louder.

"May I hold him, Lillian?"

"If you'd like. I think he'll drop right off to sleep as long as he gets comfortable and still."

Anna held out her hands to him. He looked at his mother, and when she didn't hold her arms out for him, he took Anna up on her offer. As soon as he was in her lap, he plopped his head against her shoulder, held his little blanket tightly, and closed his eyes. Holding him felt nice to Anna. The little boy smelled like lilac soap, and his soft golden hair brushed against her cheek. She hugged him a little tighter, remembering how she felt when her mother and father held her.

The minister delivered a sermon on the scripture, "Whatever you do, do it as unto the Lord." Anna thought applying such a principle would make a menial or difficult occupation hold purpose and become tolerable. She remembered talking with Gideon, Miss Dickinson's cousin, about his job and sighed. As far as she was concerned, that conversation had initiated the healing of her emotions.

This sermon punctuated her belief that she could make a difference in the Fort by teaching the children, perhaps even in the community as a whole. Several ladies had befriended her, and even those without children enjoyed her company. Anna hadn't interacted much with the soldiers or other men of the Fort, except for George at the sutler's shop, Mr. Gaither, Seamus O'Malley, and the boys in her class.

Now she was more familiar with the Fort's activities, she managed to stay out of the soldiers' way. The few men who remained in the Fort were often busy with their duties and their families, so Anna didn't have to work at keeping away from them. One night she dreamt about Davies, and that only reinforced her desire to stay away from the men – in case another soldier such as Davies lived in the cantonment.

On Monday morning, Anna rang the bell to start class and noticed three boys she hadn't seen before walking up to the main road. They were older than the other boys, and that shook her self-confidence for a moment. "Good morning," Anna greeted each of the boys.

Two acknowledged her salutation and responded politely, but the third stared her hard in the eyes and walked past her into the classroom without a word. The rest of her students followed, and after they'd all arrived, Anna pulled the door to and entered the room.

Two of the new boys sat on the front benches.

"Welcome to class, boys," she addressed the new students. "If you wouldn't mind, please sit in the back row. These seats are for the younger students, so they can see better without having to look over everyone's heads."

One immediately nodded his head and moved to the back. A small girl, Casey, took his seat. The other boy remained seated.

"Sir, I asked you to move."

"Babies," he grumbled. He slapped the desk, stood, and created as much noise as possible. He sat down on the back row only after forcing the other boy to scoot over.

"Thank you. Now, class, we finally have the rest of our students with us. I'm Miss Collins. I've taken Miss Dickinson's place so she may return to the Indian Mission School at Park Hill. Now would you gentlemen please introduce yourselves?" Anna looked towards the back, where the three new boys sat.

The polite boy stood. "I'm Clinton Arnold."

"Nice to have you with us, Mr. Arnold."

The boy sat down. The other two sat still, with no obvious intention of obeying Anna's request.

"I asked you other boys to introduce yourselves." The dark-headed boy next to Arnold finally gave in and stood. "Miss Collins, I'm Adam Matthews."

As he sat down Anna thanked him, but the belligerent boy remained seated and ignored her request. She walked to the back of the room and stood to the side of the bench where they sat. Anna prayed silently for God to keep her inward shaking hidden from the student. "I asked you to introduce yourself. If you do not comply now, you will sit in the detention seat for the remainder of the day. Do you understand?"

The boy threw his head back and turned it to look at her. Anna thought it odd that someone could stand so slowly and not fall over. "Name's Daniel Miller, and I do not like school, or babies who have to sit in the front row... or teachers." He plopped down on the bench and resumed his slouching posture.

"Well, with an attitude such as the one you are exhibiting now, I doubt many people enjoy your presence either." Anna turned and walked to the front of the class. "If any student causes disruption by further disobedience and outright insolence, he or she will be punished here in the classroom, and I will meet with his or her parents to discuss further punishment at home."

Anna looked at the students. Fear showed in the younger students' faces, while the older ones seemed only mildly concerned. Daniel Miller's face held a scowl that Anna could interpret as nothing other than a dare.

Chapter 26

Surviving the first day with her new students paled in comparison to Anna's making it through the first week. Exhausted after four hours, she relished the thought of bidding the children farewell at the end of the school day.

Anna appreciated the transformation of Eli's previously morose and sullen disposition into a cooperative and helpful attitude. With the addition of Daniel Miller, she needed that sense of accomplishment to encourage her. She wondered how to effectively deal with the rebellious boy without destroying any hope of connection with him, and continue teaching the others at the same time.

After the long afternoon wrestling with Daniel and trying to teach geometry, Anna walked wearily to the cantina. In her peripheral vision she thought she glimpsed someone hiding behind the building, but she couldn't see anything when she turned to look.

Anna scolded herself for her paranoia and continued on, but near the end of the walkway she heard footsteps crunching on the gravel. She quickly turned and caught sight of a boy running between the barracks. Daniel Miller – trying to frighten her, no doubt.

She could do nothing other than pray: *Lord, please help me.*

The week continued with each day more tedious and stressful than the previous. Daniel, intent on disrupting the class, prevented the other students from learning and managed to intimidate Anna and the younger children. Anna felt as if she was nearing the end of her wits and her patience. She decided if he disobeyed or misbehaved just one more time, she would have no other choice but to meet with his parents.

His defiant attitude and sneaking behind Anna as she left the school to go to the cantina, or the sutler's, disturbed her. She decided to speak with Mr. Gaither at the end of the week and ask for his advice about dealing with the boy.

Fortunately the other two boys adapted well and caught up with the other students in their respective grades. Clinton was exceptionally gifted in math, and Adam's grasp of science astounded Anna. She searched through her trunk for notes from her college biology class to add to the lesson plan for Adam.

Friday finally arrived, and by the time it did Anna felt as if she'd battled a giant. Daniel continued to be as obnoxious and disrespectful as possible, right up to the last second of class every single day, even that very afternoon. After all the students had left, Anna sat down at the desk in the classroom. Her head hurt, her feet throbbed, and the week had been the most trying since she'd arrived at the Fort, if not the most trying since she'd left Cincinnati.

Honestly, she felt frustrated with and fearful of Daniel. Even though he was just a boy, he insisted on taunting and frightening her, the younger children, and even some of the older boys with his father's tales of Indian scalpings. That morning, she'd caught Daniel whispering the gory details of a scalping to a group of students. Before Anna could stop him, the minister's daughter had burst into tears, and ran to her and cowered in her skirt.

"Daniel Martin!" Anna screamed. "Stop talking and sit in the detention seat... NOW!"

He sauntered to the stool with a sinister smirk spread across his freckled face, and flopped his lanky form on the chair; unfortunately with his mission of terror accomplished.

Thinking of the day's battles caused her head to pound. She rubbed her temples. "No more," she said. "I must follow through with my words."

She finished cleaning up the room, left the school, and

walked to the headquarters to ask for directions to Daniel's home so she could speak with his parents about his attitude at school. She planned to discuss his incorrigible behavior, and she was sure they would set him right once they heard what he was up to.

A couple of men stood when Anna entered the office. She walked up to the tall counter asked the officer for assistance.

"Oliver Miller, miss," he told her. "His wife ran off about a year ago."

Disappointed that she wouldn't be able to appeal to the boy's mother for help, Anna bolstered all her courage and begged God to give her a lot more as she followed the directions to the soldier's post. Daniel's father stood guard at the confinement building, over two men who had recently been caught in a drunken brawl in Frogville.

Anna took a deep breath and opened the door. "Mr. Miller?" she asked the soldier sitting at the desk.

"Yeah? Whaddya want?"

Immediately, Anna realized where Daniel had learned his manners – or lack thereof.

"I need to discuss something with you – your son Daniel's behavior in school."

"What'd that boy do wrong now?"

"Well, Mr. Miller, I'm afraid I have to tell you that Daniel is disruptive, surly, and uncooperative. Since his return to class after the harvest, I have to place him in the detention corner most of the time, for his disrespectful behavior and outright rebellion."

He sneered at Anna. "Well, ain't that just terrible?" Mr. Miller's disrespectful demeanor had obviously passed down to his son. "Reckon' I can't do much to help ya, miss. The boy's got a terrible attitude. Got it from his old lady." He spat a tobacco laden stream into a cuspidor on the floor.

Nauseated by Mr. Miller's nasty habit, Anna breathed deeply and looked away. She was growing weary of the man's rudeness and lack of concern. "Honestly, sir, the problem is his misbehavior in class. While your son is there, he must be respectful and not disruptive. His antics prevent the other students from learning, so I've come to ask your assistance in changing his behavior."

"Miss, I'll have a word with him, but I ain't promising nothing."

"Thank you, Mr. Miller. I'm sure it will help."

Anna's headache had worsened with the heat, and the frustration in dealing with Mr. Miller. When she reached the school, inside her room, she poured water from the pitcher and took a drink, then froze with the cup in mid-air.

Hanging outside her window was a bloody strip of flesh with hair.

Anna screamed. She dropped the pewter cup and backed away from the window, out of her room, and ran to the Gaithers' home.

Lillian placed another wet cloth on her head. The coolness relieved the pounding in her temples, as did the freshly made chicken soup, which eased her queasiness. "You poor, poor dear," she said as she refilled Anna's cup with tea. "I hope ya don't think all our children are scallywags like that Daniel Miller. He and his pa have a pretty bad reputation in this part of the territory."

"I can understand why." Anna took a drink of the cool tea. "Thank you, Lillian. I hope I haven't put you out too much."

"No worries, dear." Lillian stood and stretched her back. "I'm always 'put out' these days," she said with a smile, patting her ever-growing stomach.

Mr. Gaither came in with Seamus and a soldier.

Lillian stood by Anna and put her hand on her shoulder. "What did ya find out?" Lillian asked.

"Well, it's not a human scalp," the soldier, Lieutenant Baker said. "Looks like a bobcat or fox hide, something like that."

"Who'd do such a thing to an animal?"

"It was probably killed during a hunt or by another wild animal. I'm sure whoever tacked it on your window just happened to come on it."

"I'll inquire around to see if anyone may know who did this," Lieutenant Baker said as he left them.

Anna looked gratefully at her hosts. "Thank you, Mr. Gaither, for your help. I should go back now and clean –"

"We already took care of that fer ya, Miss Collins. There's not a sign anything was ever there."

"I keep having to say it, but thank you again." Anna stood and started for the door.

Lillian pushed her husband, and he responded immediately. "Miss Collins, may I accompany you back to your room?"

Anna nodded. "Yes please, I would appreciate that. Goodnight, Lillian," she said.

"Goodnight, and God bless you."

Monday classes convened with no sign of Daniel Miller. Mr. Gaither and the lieutenant had spoken with Daniel, and he had denied being involved, but the men weren't absolutely sure he was being truthful.

The children entered the classroom subdued and with an unspoken anxiety. Clint and Adam chatted and joked with each other and tried to lighten the mood in the class. The children had completed their assignments from Friday, and their exemplary behavior surprised and relieved Anna.

Little Susan Newton raised her hand midway through their spelling lesson.

"Yes, Susan?" Anna could see her eyes fill with tears and her lip quiver.

"Miss Collins," she sniffed, "is it true an Indian left a white man's scalp on your window?"

Anna knew small communities were hotbeds of rumors, and this appeared to the case at the Fort too. "No, Susan that isn't true. Someone wanted me to think so, but it was just an animal skin, probably taken from a trapper before it was cleaned. Don't worry. There aren't any murderous Indians on the loose in our area."

"All right, Miss Collins," Susan said, wiping her eyes little blue eyes on her sleeve.

After their lunch break, the students were taking turns reading from Homer's *Iliad* when Daniel opened the door, shut it hard, and skulked across the classroom. With a defiant grin on his face, he flopped down noisily on the bench.

Anna took a deep breath. "Daniel, you're very late today. Do you have a note from your father explaining the reason?"

"Naw. Pa don't care if I come to school or not."

"Daniel, I am required to notify your parents when you are tardy. Please have him write a note explaining why you were late and bring it tomorrow, or else you will be punished with splitting wood for the winter woodpile."

Anna realized the scowl on his face showed only a glimpse of the fury and anger within the belligerent boy's being.

After the students finished their recitations and read poems, she allowed an outside break. They walked outside into the fresh air. A few of the boys ran to the green grass in front of the building.

Anna followed them and stood to watch over them, and suddenly, she heard a scream. She looked to see Casey pointing at the school. Another bloody mass of flesh hung on the post, but this time it was held in place by a two-foot arrow with several feathers and beads attached.

Chapter 27

Anna held Casey against her. The other students stood around her, shocked, but not one face held a trace of guilt. She sent the older Gaither boy to run to his house and bring his father. She ordered all the rest of the students inside and led Casey and the other small children by the hand, covering their eyes to keep them from seeing the mass again. She knew she needed to keep her composure, worried that if she appeared upset, she'd lose the children's trust and respect. Bringing up children in such a wild and cruel environment now seemed insane to Anna.

Mr. Gaither came within a few minutes, with Lieutenant Baker and Seamus in tow. The men removed the carcass and the mess it left. Mr. Gaither stayed with Anna and the students for the rest of the day, and at the end of class, he and Anna carefully watched the students as they left for their homes. Daniel left with the others, and Anna kept an eye trained on him until he walked past the bend of the road. She waited several minutes to be sure he didn't sneak back.

After Mr. Gaither left she went back into her classroom and tidied up the desks and papers. As she did, she thought back on the past year. It seemed that every situation she had faced was tainted with complications and fear!

In the evening, she dined with Lillian, Mr. Gaither, and the children. They danced around the subject of the animal skins and arrows until the children had finished eating and were tucked in bed, safely out of earshot.

Mr. Gaither sat down on the bench next to the stone fireplace. Anna and Lillian sat on the settee, and Lillian propped her swollen feet up on the top of the trunk.

"Miss Collins," Gaither said, clearing his throat, "the skin was another pelt, but the arrow was a genuine arrow from a warring tribe in the southern part of the territory."

"What does that mean? Why would they... why would any of the Indians want to scare the children or me?"

"I'm sure it wasn't put there by the Arapaho, but whoever did it must have some inner connection to the tribe. There's no way someone could get one otherwise." He looked around to be sure the children were still up in the loft. "It's an arrow used only by Eagle Scout, the Arapaho's meanest warrior. The man's reputation travels far beyond Indian Territory. His arrows are usually found in one place – lodged inside one of his dead victims."

Anna gasped, and Lillian grabbed her stomach.

"Where's this Eagle Scout now?" Lillian asked.

"Well, the military intervened in a skirmish between Eagle Scout, his warriors, and some Choctaws. He threatened the Choctaws with total annihilation if they didn't leave. Of course that ain't gonna happen, so he planned to eradicate the tribe one by one. That didn't set too well with the Choctaw or the government, so the army's been on the lookout for these men since."

"Is this threat coming from them, or from someone who's trying to intimidate the families of the Fort?" Anna asked.

"I reckon someone who knows about the warning decided to use it to his advantage. I am sure it ain't the work of Eagle Scout himself."

Lillian sat upright to move the baby off her bladder. "Oh!" she moaned.

"Are you all right?" Mr. Gaither asked, rubbing her back.

"Oh, sure – just a little uncomfortable. The baby's moving around quite a bit tonight. Anyway, do you think we need to worry about this arrow and old Eagle Scout?"

"Naw." He yawned. "Like I said, it most likely ain't the Indian himself, but someone using the threat to scare everyone in the Fort and surrounding areas."

Anna stood up. "I should get back to my room. This week hasn't been any better than last week, and I think I'm going to need all the rest I can get." She patted Lillian's shoulder. "If you need anything, like with the children some evening so you can rest, just let me know. I'd be glad to do it."

"You are the sweetest," Lillian said. "I think it won't be much longer before this little guy decides to come out into the world. I hope so, anyway!"

"Just let me know. I don't have any experience or expertise in childbirth and newborns, but I could wrangle the kids for a while."

Mr. Gaither stood and kissed his wife. "Stay put, ya hear me?"

Lillian nodded in compliance. "I don't think I have the energy to move right now."

"Goodnight," Anna said and waved to Lillian.

Anna and Mr. Gaither walked to the schoolhouse. She unlocked the door and entered the schoolroom. In her room, she lit her lamp and made sure things were the same as when she'd left. "Everything looks fine, Mr. Gaither. Thank you."

"You're most welcome. Just holler if you need anything."

"You too."

After he left Anna locked the schoolroom door and went back to her room. She made sure the curtains were closed and then undressed for bed. After reading from her Bible and praying for help and courage, she blew out the lantern and fell asleep quickly, utterly exhausted.

Sometime in the middle of the night, Anna heard noises outside her window. Her heart beat so fast and hard that she wondered if it could be heard through her chest. She held her breath in hopes that she could better hear what was going on outdoors. When she heard footsteps on the gravel, she climbed quietly out of bed and tiptoed to the window, where she peeked out around the curtains.

In the faint moonlight, she caught sight of a bare-chested man. His long, black hair hung down his back in wild strands. Bands of red cloth were wrapped tightly around each of his biceps. Several long feathered arrows poked from a leather quiver hung over his shoulder.

She stepped back away from the window but leaned forward again to peek around the side of the curtain. This time, she caught a glimpse of his face. Yellow and orange paint lined the man's angular nose and strong jaw, and a band of beaded leather encircled his head.

Anna grew faint when she realized that an unfamiliar Indian stood within fifteen feet of her window. She backed away and sat on the floor beside her bed. She daren't even try to leave the room and run for help!

In her terror, her fervent prayers continued until at last she took another peek, and saw him retreating into the distance. Then she cried from the overwhelming fear.

What have I done to myself? Am I crazy for leaving Cincinnati and coming to this place, a place where murderous Indians war with peaceful Indians, children threaten adults, and each night some new life-threatening occurrence arises?

She didn't need to vocalize the answer.

Chapter 28

After the wretched week Anna and the children had endured, Anna decided to suspend classes for a week during the Rendezvous. This was a yearly event at which all the people in the area gathered to show their wares, crafts, and expertise in tomahawk-throwing, jousting, hog-racing, and other competitions. During the week-long break she hoped to have some time to recover from the stressful events that had taken place in the previous two weeks.

Anna took the opportunity to check in on Lillian, who was miserable from the heat and the ever-growing baby inside her taut abdomen. One evening, Anna kept the boys while Lillian rested and Mr. Gaither spent the evening doting on her. The Fort surgeon examined Lillian and proclaimed her to be in excellent health and the baby was positioned perfectly. The pronouncement irritated Lillian, who blamed the baby's stubbornness on his father and complained about the doctor's diagnosis. "I don't know why people think he's such a great medical man," she pouted. "Didn't tell me a thing I didn't already know."

On the first day of the Rendezvous, Anna walked among the tents of fur-traders, soap- and candle-makers, wagons, plows, fruit, vegetables, corn, and assortments of goods available for purchase by the inhabitants of the Fort and the nearby community of Doaksville. She bought a large, round, green-striped melon of some sort after sampling a bite of its sweet, watery, pink insides dotted with black tear-shaped seeds. She tasted Mrs. Mark's tart and sweet green apples. A man with a silver beard even gave away bites of his bison jerky, hoping to make a sale as he shared stories of snowstorm survival with the aid of his delicious leathery meat.

In the evening Anna checked on Lillian again, who had finally gone into labor earlier in the day. Bessy stayed with the Gaithers, and Mr. Gaither puttered around doing whatever Lillian told him to until she changed her mind and bid him to complete some other task instead. Anna took the Gaither children to the schoolroom to keep them occupied, and to prevent them from worrying too much about their mother. She tried to distract them by playing games and telling stories.

Since the Indian sighting, guards had been stationed at strategic spots around the Fort, and that helped Anna to relax a bit when she was alone. At first Lieutenant Baker had hesitated to believe Anna's story, but after her description of the Indian and later finding moccasin prints on the path behind the school, he paid her warnings more attention. Her description matched Eagle Scout's appearance and raised questions as to why he was in the Territory. His presence *inside* the Fort compound concerned the soldiers even more. The Choctaw Indian agent gathered information from Anna and wrote to the government agency, informing them of the Indian's arrival in the Territory.

Bessy came to the school around eight o'clock with the news that the 'little guy' was, in fact, a 'little gal,' as beautiful as a baby could be. The Gaither children desperately wanted to see their mother and new baby sister, so Anna gathered their things, locked the schoolhouse door, and followed Bessy to welcome the newest Gaither into the world.

Sophia Angelina Gaither was as beautiful a baby as Bessy had said. Her hair was blonde, like her brothers' and mother's, and her little hands were perfect. Small as she was, those lungs of hers were quite capable of emitting a profoundly audible wail.

Anna stayed the night with the children in their loft so they could be close to their new baby sister and mother while not being too taxing upon their recovering parents.

Bessy stayed to help Lillian tend to the baby until she got her strength back.

Mr. Gaither, worn out from the excitement and Lillian's hard labor, slept, sitting upright in the rocker next to the fireplace, snoring like a bear.

Anna loved being with the children. She enjoyed their excitement for the new addition, and the novelty of having their teacher's undivided attention. Truly, the Gaithers were a wonderful family, and she was happy to be part of their lives and share those precious moments of little Sophia's first days in the world.

The next morning, Anna borrowed the wagon and took the Gaither children for a ride in the countryside – which was still heavily guarded by the soldiers, and so she felt quite safe. Bessy supplied the group with a picnic basket of freshly fried chicken and lemonade. A half-mile northwest of the Fort, the Doaksville cemetery was located on a rise. A little stream flowed on the west side of the cemetery, and golden flowers lined the edge of the gate.

They spread a quilt on the ground between the trees, which rustled in the breeze and offered the group shade. An occasional curious grasshopper hopped close by, and more frequently, hungry flies would buzz around near their opened picnic basket, wanting a taste of Bessy's fried chicken for themselves.

Anna loved that part of living in the territory – the wide open spaces that offered so much fresh air and quiet. After eating, the children played and waded in the stream. Before sundown, Anna and the children headed back to the Fort, proud of their bounty: an unfortunate crawdad and some minnows captured in a bucket.

Anna noticed a flurry of activity as they entered the Fort compound, including several soldiers running towards the guard shack. "Children, let's get on to see how your mom and baby Sophia are doing," she said to distract the children from the commotion. "We should be very quiet when we go into the house in case they're resting," Anna said when they pulled the wagon to the barn.

The children immediately hushed, and with exaggeration tiptoed into the house.

Lillian sat in the rocker with the baby in her arms. She held her finger up to her lips. "Shh," she whispered.

The children quietly approached the sleeping infant and cooed over her for a moment before they ran off outside.

"What's all the commotion about?" Anna asked.

"I'm not sure. Jordan just ran out of here after Lieutenant Baker dropped by. He said not to worry, but he'd tell me that even if a cyclone fell down on us."

Anna took a deep breath. "Well, will you be all right if I go see what's happening?"

"Sure." Lillian gently stroked her baby's cheek. "We'll be fine. Before you leave, though, please tell the children to be quiet when they come back in. I've had an awful time getting her to sleep, and we both need a nap."

"Sure. I'll come by later and see if you need me to take command of the little guys again."

Anna walked out the back of the house and told the children she was leaving and to keep their voices down when they went back inside. Then she walked to the cantina to ply Bessy for information.

At a large table, four well-dressed men drank steaming cups of coffee. She approached the counter where Bessy stood, arms folded over her chest. "What's going on?" Anna whispered.

The scowl on Bessy's face warned Anna that whatever it was, she wasn't happy. "I ain't got no idea. These men barreled in here all flustered-like, demandin' to talk with the Fort commander, waving some papers around like they are royalty of some sort. I told 'em they better start talkin' a little nicer or they was gonna get kicked outta here by me. I don't go wavin' papers much, but a big black fist does *my* talkin'."

Anna smiled, assuming Bessy's threats had done some good because the men seemed to be sitting quietly.

The commander entered the cantina, and Anna recognized the man with him as Mr. Buerenger.

After the two men took their seats, Mr. Buerenger looked up and instantly recognized Anna. He acknowledged her with a tip of his hat.

"That's odd," Anna muttered.

"Ya know that handsome one?" Bessy asked, astounded.

"Yes. Believe it or not, I met him on the trip here."

"Girl, you must've had one excitin' trip on that ship a yers."

Anna raised her eyebrows. "Yes, you could say that."

Anna and Bessy sat at the counter and drank tea as they watched and listened to the drama unfolding before them.

The men rose and left the cantina, but Mr. Buerenger lingered behind. He approached Anna and held out his hand. "Miss Collins, what a pleasant surprise to see you here in this wild place. Are you being held captive?"

Anna smiled, hoping the heat of embarrassment she felt on her neck wouldn't soon reach her face, where he might notice it. "No, sir. I'm not a prisoner." She laughed. "I'm the teacher here."

"You *chose* to come here?" he asked, surprised.

"Yes, of my own free volition."

"And what do you think about Fort life?"

She chuckled. "Well, it's been unbelievably... uh, I guess I could say I've had some amazing experiences thus far. What brings you to Fort Towson?" Anna asked.

"I'm here as an agent of the government to pick up a lawyer who journeyed to Texas on behalf of some of our financial backers. I'm afraid he was critically injured when his ship wrecked on the way up here."

"Oh, yes. I saw when they brought him in. How is he? Is he still... alive?"

"Yes, his condition has improved somewhat but it seems he has continual set-backs. The doctor isn't sure what's going on, but as soon as we can get him stronger, we'll take him back to his home. They sent more medications with me to see if it would help. His father asked us to come and take him home. He spared no expense in finding his son, getting better drugs and making arrangements to return him to civilization."

"The last I heard, no-one knew who he was. They have been waiting for the Captain's return to see if he might be able to identify him."

"Yes, it took us a while, but we have finally located him. When he can travel, the men will take him home and I will go on to Texas territory to complete the transactions he began."

"Well, it's been a pleasure seeing you again, Mr. Bueren-ger. I hope the man recovers soon."

"My pleasure, Miss Collins, it's been nice to see you again."

It seemed that since Anna had arrived at the Fort, new and surprising events happened daily. She sometimes thought she'd like a week of boredom and lazy days, sitting around yearning for excitement, but she doubted she'd have such a lackluster day anytime soon.

A nna stopped by the sutler's store the next morning to purchase a gift for Lillian and the new baby. Lillian recovered quickly and proved to Anna that her impression of Lillian was correct: she was, indeed, a very tough woman. Living in the wild territory with four children was Anna's proof, and Lillian was a wonderful mother, wife, and now Anna's friend.

George wrapped her purchases in brown paper. "Anything else, Miss Collins?"

"Yes. Would you please send these letters to my family?"

"Of course." He bent down and added them to the leather pouch of outgoing mail. "Miss Collins, could I impose on you?"

"Well, I guess that would depend on what it is," Anna answered. She always thought it best to inquire about people's requests, especially since one student had recently tricked her into eating some distasteful rubbery food called a 'mountain oyster'.

"Nothing illegal, that's for sure. More of that fancy medicine arrived for that wounded man in the infirmary, and I don't have time to run it over there. Would ya mind carryin' it to the doc for me?"

"I'd be glad to help, George." She took the package and tucked it carefully in her arm.

"Thank ya kindly."

"And thank *you,* George. I will see you next week. I'm looking forward to that shipment of new fabric." She smiled and left the store.

Although Anna and the children needed and enjoyed their break for the Rendezvous, school would resume

Monday. The heat had been increasing and Anna was looking forward to the cooler climate, and everyone frequently reminded her of it when she complained of the oppressive heat. "You'll be a-wishin' fer some of this heat right about January," they'd say while she fanned herself, and she hoped they were right.

Anna walked up the boardwalk that connected the infirmary and the row of barracks. She opened the infirmary door, allowing the pungent medicinal odors of the clinic to escape. A mixture of heat, sulfur, and lye caused her stomach to lurch, if only for a moment.

"May I help you?" asked an attendant.

"I brought the medicine from the sutler's store for the injured man." She handed the package to the private.

"Thank you, miss. I hope it helps. That guy sure could use a miracle drug to get him well." He pointed over to a still form lying on the cot, being tended to by another medic.

When the medic walked away, Anna looked at the injured man and blinked her eyes. She looked again. The silver cup for baby Sophia clanged as it hit the floor.

Chapter 29

Martin!

Disbelief filled Anna's being. *What is the likelihood, the infinitesimal probability, that Martin would ever end up here, in Indian Territory, of all places – where I came to escape the heartache he caused me?* Anna doubted the possibility existed to calculate such an improbable value.

She sat in the infirmary with her head in her hands, shaking with incredulity.

"Ya know this man?" the medic asked.

"Y-yes," Anna stammered.

"But how?"

"I'd rather not go into it now." Anna's voice trembled.

"He's delusional and incoherent at times," the attendant said. "Then he'll perk up, seem to know what's going on, and then go backwards. Ain't never seen anything like it."

Torn between compassion for Martin in his awful condition, and anger at the fate that had brought him into her life again, she shook her head. "I just... I can't believe he's here," she said.

"It is amazing he's *still* here," the attendant said. "Not many a man could survive such a wreck, and it's even more uncommon that a man will overcome the debilitation the illness will inevitably cause." The attendant looked over at the cot. "He's on shaky ground, to be sure. If he does survive, it'll be only by the grace of God Almighty."

Anna left the infirmary and walked aimlessly. She didn't know where to go, just wanted to remove herself from the situation.

How can this be!?

She stomped her foot on the boardwalk and stormed off to the cantina. When she tromped inside, past Bessy who was standing behind the counter, she threw herself into a chair, put her head down on the table, and moaned audibly.

"Miss Anna? Everything all right with ya?"

Anna wallowed in her arms and shook her head. "No," she mumbled into the table.

Bessy walked over and sat across from her. "What's the problem?"

She lifted her head and blinked. "He's here, Bessy."

"That Southern gentleman? Ya already knew he was here, honey. 'Member?"

"No," she moaned. "Not Buerenger. I mean Martin."

"Who's Martin?"

"He's the real reason I came here." She leaned back in the chair and ran her hands through her disheveled hair. "I travelled a thousand miles to get away, and he ends up here. Here, Bessy, in this territory. I don't know how this is possible."

"Honey, I don't know who this Martin fella is, but I'm a-guessin' it ain't good he's here."

"Well, your guess is correct. I'm sorry he's injured, but why did they bring him *here*, where I am? Is God playing some kind of cruel prank on me?"

"I doubt that God's up there in Heaven just waitin' to see what turmoil He can wreak upon you."

Anna raised her arms up. "Bessy, that man broke my heart. He cancelled our wedding two weeks before the date because his father or his mother or someone didn't think we should marry. Then, on top of that humiliation, his father arranged for my teaching position at a very prestigious school to be revoked. He made my future disappear into thin air."

"No!" Bessy was appalled. "What a swamp rat!"

"Exactly." Anna put her head back down on the table. "I need tea, please Bessy, sweetened, and lots of it," she mumbled.

Chapter 30

Since Anna had discovered Martin was in the Fort compound, she'd decided to remain remote and check on him only occasionally, without his knowledge of her presence. Pain and anger still lay beneath the bravado and courage she piled upon her wounded feelings.

The posse hired by Martin's father to find him had split up, leaving half of the group at the Fort and the other three to return to Cincinnati and update his family on his whereabouts and condition. No doubt, Anna surmised, the pompous chauvinist would hire the fastest boat or coach, or both, to come down to that uncivilized primitive hovel and make things right for his boy.

During their few and brief conversations, Anna never revealed to Mr. Buerenger that she knew Martin. She didn't want to discuss Martin, or anything that concerned him, with anyone again.

Since the medication had arrived, according to the steward and Mr. Gooding, Martin's condition had miraculously turned around. He was coherent and was on the mend. Anna continued her intermittent and covert assessments of him, never getting close enough for him to see her.

Classes resumed and Daniel's incorrigible behavior had lessened at least to a more tolerable level. But during one exceptionally hot, humid, unbearable afternoon, while Anna shared the mathematic facts theorized by Pythagoras, and the philosophical ideologies of Plato, Daniel breached the invisible line of Anna's patience and understanding.

Without breaking a stride in her lessons, she sentenced him to the wood pile, where his penitence included splitting thirty logs into firewood.

The class listened as he strained with the axe and grunted with each strike of the metal blade into the logs.

"Miss Collins," Eli said, "ya think it's safe lettin' Daniel alone with an axe?"

The other children's eyes held the same question and watched Anna for her answer.

"Yes. Don't worry. I'm sure Daniel's too exhausted to get into any mischief."

At the end of classes, the children followed Anna outside.

She approached Daniel, who was still swinging the axe. His beet-red face and perspiration-soaked clothing moved Anna to compassion. She poured a mug of water from the bucket, and he gulped it down.

"Thank ya, miss."

His appreciation took Anna aback. *The boy* **can** *express thanks and communicate without sassy retorts!* "You've done a fine job on that wood pile, Daniel. That'll be enough."

"There're only two more logs. I'll chop them."

"Sure," Anna said, shocked.

He swung the axe and split the remaining pieces and added them to the pile of neatly stacked wood.

"I never expected you to complete the task. In all honesty, I thought when I told you to chop the wood, you'd just run off."

"I thought about it, Miss. But my pa thinks I'm like momma... ain't no good." The boy managed to look recalcitrant, sulky, yet uncertain too. "I... I done some thinkin', an' I don't think that's true. I *am* good. Ma was good, too."

"That's admirable, but I hope your new way of thinking involves better behavior and no further disruption in class, Daniel."

He stood and stretched and wiped his forehead. "Yeah, guess so."

"Just one thing I'd like to know. Did you put the animal skins on the door and my window?"

His face showed honest horror. "No, miss. I hate huntin', and bloody stuff makes me sick as a dog."

"Thank you, Daniel. Now you run on home, and we'll see

you next week."

Anna watched Daniel walk around the bend in the road. This time, it wasn't to protect herself, but to stand in awe of the change in the boy.

A new worry crossed her mind: *If Daniel didn't hang the skins nor dress as the Indian, then someone else tried to frighten me. Who was it... and why?*

Chapter 31

Word that the injured man from the *Heroine* had regained consciousness spread through the camp. He asked for food and water and managed to sit upright for a while each day. The mangled condition of his leg would cripple Martin for the rest of his life.

The next week began with Daniel ready to learn, and by the end of the week, he was reprimanding the younger students when they bickered over who would ring the bell. He even argued when one student asked to dust Anna's desk. Anna had hoped her influence on Daniel would result in his metamorphosis into a model student, and it seemed to be working in leaps and bounds.

Thursday after school, Anna walked down the boardwalk to the cantina. She passed the infirmary and saw two men sitting on the porch. Not wanting to stare, she walked across the field to get a better view without being conspicuous.

The hunched-over, pale man sat with his leg propped up on a chair. His shirt hung limply from his emaciated form, but even in his feeble and frail condition, Anna recognized Martin. Her heart skipped beats, and she argued with herself as to what she should do. She didn't know whether it was best to keep her presence a secret or face him and wave her accomplishments – the ones she'd managed in spite of him and without him – in his pompous face. *Maybe revenge would be too sweet or mean spirited,* she decided, and she chose to stay hidden and went on her way to visit Lillian and the other Gaithers.

According to Mr. Gaither, little Sophia now weighed

about the same as a 'sack of taters.' Anna gave Lillian the little hat she had ordered from George. She cooed at the baby and laughed when Sophia smiled.

"She's beautiful! ... I'm afraid the hat's a little big on her."

"The way she's growing, it'll fit fine just in time for the winter. I think she's pretty, too, and her daddy thinks she's the best lookin' gal this side of the Mississippi."

"How have the children adapted to having another baby around?" Anna let Sophia wrap her hand around her finger and try to pull it into her mouth.

"They just ignore her bawlin', but when she smiles at 'em, they're sure she's thinkin' they are the best brothers in the world."

"That's only normal."

"I heard Daniel Miller said he didn't put the animal skins on the school to scare you."

"Yes, and I believe him."

"If that boy's tellin' the truth for the first time in his life, ya gotta find out who did it."

"I hope the chief officer and your husband can get to the bottom of it."

Lillian stood to soothe the fussing baby. "I think she's getting' hungry."

"Well, Lillian and Sophia, I'd better be going. Take care, and don't hesitate to let me know if you need anything."

Anna managed to evade the infirmary. She went around it, behind it, or anything other than where she'd see anyone outside. Still unsure of whether or not to face Martin, she chose to put off the decision indefinitely.

Anna prayed for help. She needed help to understand why God had allowed Martin into her citadel – the one place where she found herself, her potential, and her success in teaching. Now he sat within a few hundred feet in quiet mockery of her and her accomplishments.

The summer heat peaked in Indian Territory, and with the passing of the rainy months the air stayed hot and changed the previously lush brush to dry and brittle tinder. Several nights, distant wildfires painted the skyline orange and scented the air with the heavy odor of burning plant life. Bessy told Anna the grass often became so dry it crunched underfoot. With the ending of July, the heat intensified, and the drought became just another topic for conversation and reminiscing. Anna heard about every known drought in the Indian Territory, and each new prairie fire dredged up more horrific tales of burned homes, lands, and losses of human and animal life.

The locusts sang in the trees, and the prairie clicked with grasshoppers jumping from the plants they devoured, traveling on to find more fodder. The cattle hid under the trees or stood in the low water of previously full ponds, endeavoring to lessen their misery. Even the flies considered their annoying buzzing a waste of their energy.

The lack of any breeze and the oppressive heat drove everyone from their barracks and rooms. Anna gave in and joined the others who were sitting on the porches to try and catch any light winds that happened to come their way, though the breezes were few and far between. The medical attendants sat outside the infirmary with their long-term patient propped up on a chaise.

Anna knew she'd more likely than not have to face Martin eventually and deal with his presence, but she decided it would be better served on a night when the heat was not quivering off the rooftops and the rocks.

Over a month had passed since the last sighting of the Indian sneaking around the Fort and the animal hides tacked to the schoolhouse. It relieved Anna to walk outside without looking over her shoulder or fearing what she'd find tacked to the school building, and keeping the doors shut or her curtains closed for protection would have been most torturous in the unbearable heat.

August came with no waning of the sweltering heat, and three months had passed without any rain. Many cattle died from exposure and thirst, and often soldiers teetered on the verge of heat exhaustion after performing drills. Life, and the occupants of the Fort, moved slowly.

The end of the school session neared to allow students the freedom to assist their families with the harvest – if there was anything left to harvest. Many of the crops that had survived the wretched heat and drought served as food for the insects.

In the middle of August, a cloudbank formed on the western horizon. Old and young alike held their breath and prayed that the cloud carried precipitation and respite from the blistering temperature. The mid-afternoon heat rose from the ground and heated the atmosphere; the tall thunderheads grew higher on the forward edge. High, white, anvil-shaped cloud towers created a beautiful contrasting picture against the darkening sky and the sparse plots of ripened golden wheat.

Anna sat outside after her class had ended. The day had gone well, but the heat was as draining on the students as it was on their teacher, and they grew lethargic soon after lunch. She'd sent them outside for quick drinks and splashes of water from the well. It surprised Anna that she had no appetite, but the thought of expending any energy to walk in the oppressive heat squelched the desire for food.

In the early evening, Anna heard the first distant growls of thunder. The skies darkened, and the wind picked up and carried the refreshing scent of rain. Those who sat outside endeavoring to cool off thrilled at the promise of rain, as long as it wouldn't evaporate as soon as it hit the hot air and steaming ground.

A loud roll of thunder followed a bright white streak of lightning. The heavens opened, and *a toad-floatin', gully-washin'* (as Bessy put it) torrential rainfall cooled the citizens of the Fort and watered the land. The evening sun dimmed, and the air held a fresh, just-cleaned aroma. For the first time in several weeks, the curtains in Anna's window fluttered in a cool breeze.

The climate and temperature continued to improve after the welcome rain, as did the farmers' outlook on their chances of reaping a profitable harvest. Their conversations now centered on rounding up enough help to bring in the crops, rather than on the dismal bounty of their efforts.

Early Monday, a group of soldiers from the cantonment in east Arkansas Territory rode into Fort Towson. The flurry caused by their arrival sent shivers up Anna's spine. High-ranking officials of the Fort scurried to greet the men.

The occupying soldiers of Fort Towson convened to the parade grounds, quickly lined up in military files, and stiffened to attention as the officers saluted each other.

Anna watched the ceremonial greeting in silence. The previous week, at dinner with the Gaithers, Jason had told Lillian new forces would soon arrive to monitor the Indians' activities. The government had assigned the troops to protect their newly acquired lands and to buffer the ongoing aggression between the native Indians in the Red River territory and the newly transported Indians from the eastern states. Still worried someone might want her frightened or harmed, Anna welcomed the soldiers who had been sent to protect her and the other inhabitants of the Fort.

Anna enjoyed the break from teaching, even though she tutored Daniel in the afternoons during his father's guard duty. This prevented Daniel's father from seeing him study and spared Daniel from his father's ranting and raving about the uselessness of education. Anna added more demanding coursework, and Daniel managed to keep up, just as she had anticipated he would as long as he put his mind to it. At times, living in the territory and the Fort proved wearisome and difficult for Anna, but the thrill of seeing a young boy learning and bettering his future far exceeded any discomfort or problems she experienced.

One night, Anna lay in her bed after visiting with Lillian and her family. Mr. Buerenger had stopped by the cantina that morning to speak with her and bid her farewell before departing the next day. Anna thought Mr. Buerenger very charming with his accent and good looks, but he was undeniably somewhat mysterious. She decided it was best to keep her emotions in check when he was concerned.

Since she had discovered that Martin was recovering within the very walls of the Fort where she lived, she couldn't help thinking often of Nate, but he didn't seem to reciprocate such attention to her. Since Anna had arrived in Indian Territory he had sent only two posts, both very brief. The last note mentioned a possible opportunity to travel to the Red River area in late September, but only for military work. It was no matter, though. Before, Anna had wished for more out of their relationship, but now she felt that in order to help the students and succeed in her job, it was best to forget her own romantic desires.

As she tried to fall asleep, she heard the soldiers laughing and talking in the commons. It reminded her of her first encounter with soldiers on the *Jewel Belle,* when their banter and laughing kept most of the ship passengers awake. Then her thoughts wandered to Martin, her reason for being aboard the ship.

"Humph!" she moaned, and turned over in the bed. "Men cause such problems."

Maybe soon I'll get the nerve to confront Martin.

She'd watched him limp on the boardwalk in front of the hospital, but had never approached him. Even from a distance, Anna saw him wince in pain with each step. Selfishly, she found requital in his obvious pain. He deserved to suffer some agony, some despair, some sense of losing control – as she had. *Maybe this will open his eyes to the pain he's caused,* she thought, but she doubted it.

During another dinner evening with the Gaithers, Anna stayed late to play with the children and watch baby Sophia turn over all by herself. When she left Lillian's house, a breeze stirred the leaves, and in the darkened sky twinkling stars splattered around the faint outline of the moon.

Anna heard a rustling in the bushes as she walked past the guard shack on the southern edge of the Fort. She stopped and looked around but saw and heard nothing. She moved again and realized that the noise had gone away, and Anna shook her head at her own silly paranoia. "Probably some critter looking for food," she said to herself. She continued walking and rounded the curve in the road towards the western edge of the Fort compound and buildings.

Just as she stepped beyond the first barracks, someone jumped behind her and grabbed her. The hand clamped over her mouth, muffling her scream amidst the reek of whiskey and tobacco. "Gotcha," he growled, his fetid breath hot against her ear. "Told ya I'd find ya, didn't I?"

Even without seeing his face, Anna knew from the stench and the harshness of his vengeful touch that Davies had somehow, someway, found his way to her again.

Chapter 32

S he fought against him as best she could, but he wrenched her arm behind her back, sending a sharp pain through her and stars to her eyes. Afraid she would faint if she continued to struggle against him, she went limp.

The man tried to drag her behind the barracks, but the dead weight of her body slowed his progress. His hand loosened from her mouth only for a second, allowing her time to manage a loud shriek. Her punishment for that was a hard slap and a powerful push against the building wall. He mercilessly slammed her head into the window frame.

Anna kicked him and swung her hand at his head. She knew he would overpower her at any moment. *Oh God! Please help me.* Blood from the cut on her forehead trickled down into her eyes, and her head swam from the throbbing pain. Her vision blurred, and she felt her strength fading away. She knew he would kill her at any moment, and the faces of her mother, father, brother, and grandparents crossed her fading consciousness.

In her dimming vision, she saw a commotion to the side. Her ears roared, but in the darkening abyss of unconsciousness, she heard a man moaning loudly.

Davies suddenly released his grip on her arm and waist, allowing her to collapse to the ground, coughing and struggling to breathe. In the next instant, Anna saw her assailant lying on the ground, a garden hoe resting beside his still body. She wept, trying to hold her ripped bodice together. Someone reached down to her, and she took the hand and listened to the voice.

"It's all right. He's not going to hurt you now."

Anna let the man help her up and hold her close. The touch seemed strangely comfortable, familiar somehow. Through her swollen eye, she looked up into Martin's face, grimacing with pain.

"Miss, are you hurt?" he asked. His expression of concern and pain changed to shock when he realized who she was. "Anna? Is that you?"

"Yes," she said.

The thought that now was a good time to tell him she was there flickered through her mind just before she lost consciousness.

The doctor checked Martin's leg, and the attendants helped him back to the infirmary. They settled him into a cot.

Once again, Davies was behind bars, this time unconscious and with company: Oliver Miller, Daniel's father, who had teamed up with Davies to attack poor Anna. In fact, Mr. Miller had hired Davies to harass, frighten, and drive off the new teacher who had filled his son's head with ridiculous thoughts that school was important. The threat of being hung on the spot coerced the two to reveal their conspiracy.

Miller had met Davies on a trip for supplies in Vicksburg after his release from jail in Memphis. Drinking together, Miller mentioned his need to get rid of the teacher who was filling his boy's head with foolishness such as math and reading, turning him into a lazy, useless nothing.

When Davies realized the teacher's identity, he quickly joined Miller in his plans. Spurred by his desire for revenge upon the 'snooty lady on the boat who caused him to be kicked out of the army', Davies and Miller conspired together to accomplish their devious goals of revenge.

Using whiskey and army weapons, Miller had enticed a warrior from a rebel tribe to appear as the murderous Eagle Scout in order to terrorize the teacher. When the gruesome pelts failed to drive Anna away, Miller and Davies took their revenge further and planned Anna's permanent removal from the territory.

Anna sat by Martin's cot. He struggled to stay awake until the surgeon checked Anna and assured him she would be fine. He held her hand even after he fell unconscious from the drug.

Her throat burned and made her voice raspy. The surgeon stitched and bandaged the cuts on her head and arms. She consented to the doctor's pleas to stay in the hospital overnight, for her sake as well Martin's, and that of his other patient.

The doctor ordered Anna to bed after Martin fell asleep. She pulled her hand gently from his, and he stirred and mumbled a little but managed to stay asleep.

The attendants placed Anna's cot next to his, and she watched him as he slept. He moved for a while, apparently dreaming, and muttered several times. Once, she heard her name.

What am I doing? All this time working to get over you, and now, here I am beside you again!

Early in the morning, Bessy dropped by the infirmary when she heard Anna had been mauled by some wicked soldier, as the rumor went. "Darlin'," she said quietly as she approached Anna's bed, "ya gon' be all right?"

"Bessy," Anna said. "Oh, I'm fine. It takes more than a drunken soldier to get me down, apparently!"

"What happened, honey?"

Anna relayed the events to Bessy. When she told her it was Martin who rescued her, Bessy's jaw dropped.

"Girl, ya got some kinda excitin' life, don't ya?"

"I guess you're right, Bessy. I guess so." Anna shook her head in wonder. "I guess so," she repeated.

Martin slept the remainder of the day and started to rouse about dinner time.

The doctor felt his forehead and shook his head at the warmth. "That's good. No fever."

When Martin opened his eyes, he searched for Anna and muttered her name.

Anna sat up in the cot. "I'm here, Martin," she said as she started to stand.

An attendant rushed to check on her. "Miss," he said,

"you best be careful. That head injury of yours might render you a little unsteady for a bit. Sit here," he ordered and pulled a chair close to Martin's bed.

"I thought I dreamt the whole thing," Martin said weakly. "What are you doing here?"

"I think I should ask you that first. Did you follow me here?"

A look of confusion crossed his face, and he shook his head. "Follow you? No. I didn't know where you were – only that you left Cincinnati."

"I saw you at the dock when I left, Martin."

"I was at the dock to board the *Heroine*." He coughed and grimaced in pain. "The firm acquired clients who wanted to purchase land in the Mexican territory. I was on my way to sign the land deeds when the *Heroine* hit a snag and sank. The day I saw you at the Cincinnati dock, I left for a rendezvous with a military convey who would escort me to the land." He groaned and tried to get more comfortable. "Why are you here of all places, Anna?"

"Well, Martin, it seems I managed to become a teacher after all, with or without your father's help and in spite of his efforts to derail me. I am the teacher here at Fort Towson."

"I suppose I deserve all your animosity."

"I meant to hold it back, but sometimes, I... I'm afraid after what I've gone through, it's difficult to quiet my emotions sometimes."

"Did you know that man?" He closed his eyes when a stabbing pain shot up his leg.

"Unfortunately, yes. I encountered him on the steamboat trip here. He attacked me on the ship, so they kicked him off the boat in Memphis. They assured me I'd never see him again. He threatened me when he left the boat, and it seems he meant to follow through on that threat."

"I'm sure he'll never hurt you again. I heard the attendants mention a prison somewhere in the upper states, and that is where he'll be sent to rot."

"I don't care... as long as I don't ever have to see him again."

"I saw your family at the dock before I left."

"They didn't tell you where I was going, that I had left for the Indian Territory?"

"No. I tried to engage them in polite conversation, but they wouldn't even acknowledge me."

"Good for them, and I can't say as though I blame them, can you?" She saw a slight flicker of remorse in Martin's face. "I should go. You need to rest, and so do I," Anna said as she stood. "Goodnight, Martin." She started to leave.

"Anna..."

She looked back at him.

"Will you come back tomorrow?" he asked feebly.

"I... um... I'll see. Rest well," she said and left the room.

Chapter 33

Martin continued to improve and by the end of September, he began walking in the front of the hospital under the watchful eye of the attendants. The men his father sent searching for Martin had contacted his family. They relayed his mother's demands for his rescue from the primitive conditions that had nearly cost him his life. Martin's father sent his men back down the Mississippi armed with medical aid, drugs, food, and money to buy anything that might speed up and facilitate Martin's recovery so he could promptly return home.

Anna visited Martin only when she received a request from a steward. During one visit, she heard the attendants make mention of the remarkable amount of money and supplies that Martin's father insisted on sending, and it angered her beyond belief.

If not for his father, she and Martin would have been in Cincinnati, married, quite possibly planning a family of their own. Instead, because of her would-be father-in-law's interference, meddling, and self-righteous attitude. How Martin failed to see the damage his father had caused was beyond Anna's comprehension.

In their visits, neither she nor Martin ever mentioned their previous relationship. He did, however, openly answer her questions about friends in Cincinnati and other common acquaintances, but hearing news from home only made Anna more homesick, so she eventually stopped asking.

The harvest began with a splendid cool front. The leaves on the tall trees gradually changed from lush green to lemon yellow, orange, and brilliant reds, before they fell to the earth in piles to be swept together by the wind. Pumpkins and leaves decorated the cantina, and Bessy made her famous sweet tater pies and breads. Tall corn sheaths, bundled together by the harvesters, dotted the fields. Most of the farmers barely eked any profit from their crops, but all expressed gratitude for whatever they earned.

Martin's recovery sped up, and he walked with an attendant farther into the Fort compound. One afternoon he made his way to the cantina, attendant in tow.

Bessy and Anna sat at a table discussing the upcoming festival. As he limped in, Bessy stood and met them. "Can I he'p ya, gentlemen?" she asked

Martin looked over at Anna and smiled faintly. "I'd like a cup of coffee. You have coffee, don't you?"

"Sure do. I think it's marvelous. Some folk have mentioned it tastes a bit like swamp water, but I reckon they're just funnin' me."

"Well, I'll give it a try." Martin sat gingerly upon the stool at the counter and reached down to massage his calf, while the attendant fetched a paper and sat down opposite him, after having declined anything from Bessy.

Bessy plopped down a cup of black coffee and a piece of pie. "I know ya been under the weather. This oughtta start a-settin' ya right."

"Thank you, ma'am."

Bessy went back and sat down with Anna. "Ain't ya gonna go over an' sit with 'em?" Bessy whispered to Anna.

"Bessy! I told you."

"I know what ya told me, and I asked, ain't ya gonna go an' sit with 'em?"

Anna sighed. "Fine. I'll sit with them," she said and made a face at Bessy. "Martin, Private West, may I join you?"

Martin pulled his leg over to allow Anna room to sit next to him. "Yes, please do." Private West nodded politely at her and stood.

"Please excuse me, miss." He dipped his head at her, and at Martin, and discreetly left.

"You're looking well. How are you feeling?" Anna asked.

"Much better since I've eaten a bite of this pie. What is it?"

"Sweet tater!" Bessy hollered from the other side.

"Yes, some sort of potato," he said. "Quite unusual, but it's good."

"When do you expect to return home?"

He finished his bite of pie. "The surgeon assured me I'll be up to travelling in about a week." He drank a sip of the steaming coffee.

"You'll return to Cincinnati?"

"Yes, and after I've recovered completely, I'll continue my duties with the firm."

Anna looked at Martin's profile. The injury and illness had drained his usual dark complexion and left his face, pale, thin, and strained. She remembered thinking he was wonderful, thinking she was so fortunate to find such a marvelous and kind man. Now the memory pained her.

He turned to see her looking at him. "Wretched, aren't I?"

She blushed slightly. "No, just a little thinner than before."

He cleared his throat. "Anna, are you... have you met... I mean, have you made any close friends since you left your home?"

"Are you asking me if I am involved with a man? Why would you ask?" Anna asked, stunned.

"I didn't mean to offend you. I was just... just curious."

"It's none of your business, Martin." She stood. "I have no obligation to answer to you or anyone for anything. You gave up that right a long time ago. Remember?"

"I'm sorry; I didn't mean to anger you."

"I knew it was a mistake to... to let myself –"

"Please, Anna. Can't you forgive me for what happened?" He took her hand. "Isn't there any feeling left for me? I know you haven't forgotten what we had, how much we loved each other."

Anna shook her head and tore her hand from his. "What are you saying? I am supposed to forget what we had? What you destroyed? I bore the agony, shame, despair, and sorrow all by myself after you rejected me, Martin. Then your father ruined the only hope I had of an occupation in my hometown. How dare you suggest I don't have feelings?"

"Surely you can see that I'm different now." He looked at her with eyes that pled for understanding.

"I know one thing. I know you left me for love of a career forced upon you by a manipulative and chauvinistic man, and that career nearly cost you your life. I've fought to recover from the wounds you inflicted upon me, and my recovery hasn't been as grand as yours."

"I truly am sorry. I was wrong. I loved you. In fact, I still love you, and I want us to be together again. We can go home and make a life there. You don't have to stay here. You deserve more than this... this wild place, Anna."

Martin stood slowly and moved towards her. He took her in his arms, and she gave in to his kiss for just a moment.

Then suddenly she jerked away. "No! Martin, don't. Please, I can't go back. You hurt me so much," Anna said. "I loved you once," she cried, "but I don't think I could ever trust your love for me again."

"Anna, I know, but now... well, now I see I was wrong. You are the wife I need, the wife I want. Please, Anna! Please try to forgive me."

"Please leave me be." She walked out of the cantina crying softly and ran to the schoolroom.

Bessy wiped the counter with a defiant air.

"Girl, you gonna be all right," she said quietly into the air.

Chapter 34

The next morning, Anna stayed in her room instead of going to the cantina. She wrote to her parents and told them everything – good and bad – that had happened to her on her journey to the Fort and since her arrival. Hot tears rolled down her cheeks and dropped onto the pages, smearing her ink in places. She sobbed while she wrote of the soldier attacking her on the ship and reminisced of Mr. Buerenger and Nate coming to her rescue. She told them about her relationship with Nate and her friendships with the ladies on the boat, and Mrs. Devonshire.

She laughed when she wrote about Bessy and her wisdom, Lillian and all the Gaithers, and the joy of seeing baby Sophia grow into a sweet toddler. All the fear of the Indian Eagle Scout came to mind when she recounted the carcasses and arrows tacked on her school. Her successes with Eli, Daniel, and the other students in her classes filled two pages. Anna wrote about Daniel Miller's plans for a new trade for his future; he wished to become a minister to the Indians and became an apprentice at the nearby church for the Reverend Wright and Cyrus Byington.

Then, she came to the most difficult part of her tale: Martin's arrival in her sanctuary and all which resulted from his presence. Anna closed her eyes and cried. "Oh, Father! I know all things work together for good for those who are called according to Your purpose," she prayed. "But still, I don't understand why these awful things had to happen to me, or why Martin had to reappear in my life. I thank You for the wonderful events that I have been blessed to be a part of and I ask that You, in Your divine wisdom and mercy, would heal my heart, fill my longing, and remove the desire I have for a relationship so that I may continue my work here and fulfill Your plan for me, fully reliant upon You for *all* I need. Amen."

She sealed the envelope, addressed the letter, put on her bonnet, and left to place it in the mail at the sutler's. The bare trees created a canopy under the cerulean sky as she made her trek. She entered the shop and greeted the women who were looking wantonly at the dainty china cups. She picked up the fabric she had ordered earlier from George; it would make up a pretty dress appropriate for the Harvest Festival the following week.

"Miss Collins, I nearly forgot," he said. "You got a letter." He handed Anna the envelope.

"Thanks, George," she said as she gazed down upon the familiar handwriting that had penned her address. It was from Nate.

She hurried back to her room and made a cup of hot tea. Winter would soon return to Indian Territory, and Anna found that a hot cup of tea helped to stifle the chill in her bones and bring her some comfort and reminders of the teas she'd shared with her family and friends back home.

As she unfolded the letter, which carried his scent, she realized how much she missed Nate. *Perhaps Martin's presence has caused me to think of him more often,* she guessed. But again, even after her prayer and decision to go on without a romantic relationship, Nate's letter arrived, stirring her desires.

Anna fell upon the bed and cried.

On Friday, Martin knocked on the schoolroom door. Anna opened it and endeavored to be cordial. He limped in, leaning on a fancy carved wooden cane that his father had sent from home. The ornate detail reminded Anna of Martin's office desk, and a sickening remembrance of the day he'd released her wafted into her mind.

"Anna..." he began uncomfortably. "Umm..." He stepped closer to her. "I'm leaving with the men for Shreve's Town, and then we will take a packet up to Cincinnati." He looked down and took her hand. "Please come with me, Anna. We will gladly wait for you to pack – or, better yet, you can take only what you desire, and I'll buy you new clothes and any personal items on our way home. I need you," he said, looking into her eyes. "I'm sorry I hurt you before, but I've changed. We'll be happy together now, Anna, and if I have you in my life... well, it'll make my life better," Martin said.

Yes, she wanted a happy life next to someone, but that someone wasn't Martin. "I – I can't go, Martin. This is where I belong."

"No, Anna! You can't mean that. This is certainly an adventure you can talk about to your friends and to our children, but there is so much more for you back home. I need you, Anna. The doctor said it will be a long recovery for me, and I can think of no-one else in the world that I would rather have by my side. Please come back with me. I don't know how I'll make it without you. Seeing you again now, after all this time, I've come to realize that... I know I have always truly loved you, Anna, and I know we'll be happy together. Come with me and you'll see! You'll meet the society women in Cincinnati, and once I've made partner in the law firm, I assure you that you shall never lack for friends – or for any of the fine things you deserve. Surely I have more to offer you than this wretched place!"

"You still do not understand," Anna said. "You never did. I don't need the same things you need, Martin. I have no use for prestige, authority, reputation, and high-minded acquaintances. All I want is a home, a husband who loves me, and an occupation through which I can make a positive impact on the lives of children. I have what I want here. Believe it or not, I find society wretched, and I am much happier without all your material possessions and shallow friendships based on nothing more than income and clout."

"Just give up this nonsense and return with me," Martin said gruffly. "Your family will never forgive you for abandoning them."

"I have not abandoned them! And they have nothing to forgive me for – they have supported me every step of the way. I did what I thought was right and what God wanted me to do. When you left me with nothing, I found a way to be happy and productive – without you. I don't need to go back to the way things were." She stopped. "I forgive you,

Martin, for breaking my heart, even though I thought at the time that you had ruined my life." She paused and looked into his eyes. "You actually saved my life. I wouldn't have been happy with you, and now I know that for sure. Your version of happiness is far different to mine, Martin. We do not belong together."

Martin took a deep breath. "Fine. Goodbye, Anna. I wish you the best."

"Goodbye, Martin. I hope you find God, for you need Him if you are to ever be truly happy beyond your temporal, material gains." She kissed him gently on the cheek.

This time, it was Martin who limped out of her life.

Chapter 35

Sophia pulled up on Anna's leg.

"Look, Lillian!" Her excitement startled the baby, who plopped back down to the floor. "Oh! You missed it. She stood up!" Anna said.

"Those babies are sneaky. Just when you think you're gonna catch 'em doin' somethin', they stop, until you're not lookin', and then they do it again and you still miss it."

"Well, I'm sure she'll do it again – maybe she'll even walk and talk someday. If you're just patient, perhaps she'll do it while you're looking." Anna giggled. "What do you have planned for the Harvest Festival?"

"Me?" Lillian laughed. "Same thing I always do. I'll chase children, try to keep up with my husband, and every once in a while look at something. How about you?"

"I plan to walk among all the booths and sniff and taste the foods and buy gifts for my family and buy myself something I don't need. Maybe I should stay in my room and prepare for next week's lessons instead. The boys have caught up with my plans, and I need to add more challenging material to hold their interest."

"You can't go hidin' in your room the rest of your life, Anna. Ya wanna be one of those school teachers no-one talks to but always talk about? One of them odd, eccentric schoolmarm types?"

Anna laughed. "What's gotten into you, Lillian? You're a bit sassy today, aren't you?"

"I know, but it isn't just today. Ask my husband. He says I have a mouth on me like no other woman in the territory." She paused and folded more baby clothes. "I'm sorry that Martin fella didn't work out."

Anna looked up at Lillian. "It never had a possibility of working out. He ruined our chances long ago, and I've finally accepted that for the blessing I didn't see it to be at the time. I would never have been truly happy with him as my husband, but I'm content now. I love this wild country with all its wildfires, tornadoes, droughts, floods, cold weather, hot weather, and the people who'd do anything to help a neighbor in need."

"I never thought I'd hear ya say a thing like that," Lillian said.

"Well, I mean every word of it."

"I'm sure you do," said Lillian, "one sassy woman to another."

Anna strolled through the hastily constructed Harvest Festival kiosks that were set up on the greens of the Fort compound. She smoothed her fingertips over oddly-shaped objects called 'gourds' and examined the baskets filled with shiny golden apples and a variety of pumpkins in every shape, size, and shade of orange.

She picked up a few corncobs and bought a coonskin hat for Caleb. The leather pouch she purchased for her father would hold his change, and whenever he withdrew it to pay for something, he'd be able to tell the story of his brave daughter who lived inside a Fort filled with soldiers, in a land filled with Indians, wild and untamed animals, and people of a hardy and stoic nature. Anna could picture him going on and on about it, and the thought brought a smile to her face. Mrs. Clotcher's lace and Indian beadwork pouch would thrill her mother.

Aunt Maggie wanted only one thing from Anna, and that was for her to return to Cincinnati for her and Mr. Lynchfield's wedding in the spring of the following year, 1840.

Her shawl slipped off her shoulders and fell. She bent down to the leaf-covered ground to pick it up, and saw a boot standing in front of her. She looked up to see Nate's smiling face.

Gasping, she dropped her basket of purchases and immediately reached up to grab his arm. "Nate! I can't believe you're here!" she squealed.

"I am. Seems you may have missed me a bit, haven't you?"

Anna took his face between her hands and planted a kiss on his lips.

"I'll take that as a 'yes'."

Embarrassed, Anna pulled back. "I'm sorry. I *have* missed you, and it's just so nice to see you!"

"Join me for a walk," Nate said, offering his arm.

At the end of the rows of the merchant tables, Nate looked at Anna. "Is there somewhere we can sit and talk?" he asked.

"Yes, surely. How about over by the well?" Anna said. "Follow me."

"How's life here in the Fort?"

"Oh, Nate, you wouldn't believe everything that's happened since I arrived. The beginning of the school year was terrible. So many awful things happened that I had to question if I did the right thing by coming here."

Nate pulled out a piece of jerky and offered it to Anna. "Awful things?" he prompted.

"Well, do you remember Davies, the man on the boat who attacked me?"

"Yes, of course. That is how we met, after all, and you are rather unforgettable, in my estimation. What of that nasty old Davies?"

"He did it again!"

"Anna!" he said, looking confused. "He came here?"

"As unbelievable as it sounds, he found out where I was and conspired with the father of one of my students to force me from the region. When they couldn't scare me off, they resorted to trying to kill me."

"Oh, Anna," Nate said and took her hand. "I told you it would be rough here."

"Yes, but Nate, there've been so many wonderful things that have happened to me as well! I love teaching, I've met so many wonderful new friends, and I finally feel I have a purpose in a place I adore."

Nate sighed heavily. "Perhaps I've waited too long, then," he said.

"For what? To visit? Yes, but I forgive you now that

you're here."

"The last few months, I have been tromping around the country, working for the government. I saw the Indians forced from their ancestral lands, property taken from the citizens who struggled and sacrificed to own it, and I can't continue to be part of it, Anna. I have decided to resign my commission and become a civilian," he said. He took her hands in his. "Like you, Anna, I have been searching for purpose in my life. I thought I would find that in the military. Also like you, I prayed for guidance when I became dissatisfied with the direction my life was heading."

"But we never talked about my faith – or yours," Anna said.

"I've always thought one should live it and show others the right way by their actions. That's why the assignments became so bothersome to me. How could someone look at me and believe me to be an upright Christian man when, in all reality, I allowed myself to be used as a pawn in the theft of their livelihoods and properties?"

"I knew something was bothering you when those men met with you and Mr. Buerenger on the *Jewel Belle*," Anna said.

"Well, that was the beginning of my introspection. I examined myself and realized that I needed to change either my faith or my occupation. There wasn't really a choice."

"So what will you do now?" Anna asked.

"That's why I'm here, Anna."

Anna's heartbeat quickened. "Why?" she asked.

"I want to spend my life with you, Anna – that is, if you think you want that too. I realized while I was out walking through those muddy rivers that I love you. I want us to be together, Anna. Wherever I walk from now on, wherever God takes me, I want you to be with me."

"Nate, that's exactly what I want too!" Anna said as she embraced him and wiped away her tears behind his shoulder.

He kissed her, and it was a kiss she most willingly returned. "I suppose I can take that as a 'yes' as well, Miss Collins?"

"You most certainly can, Nate. You most certainly can!"

The wagon jostled down the road, and a string of people followed behind the couple. The students yelled and threw flower petals and rice upon the newlyweds. Nate leaned over and gave his new bride a kiss.

Anna stood in the wagon. She tossed her bouquet of wild daisies over the crowd to a chorus of delightful squeals and laughter. She and Nate looked to see who would be the next bride of Fort Towson, Indian Territory.

Bessy was beaming from ear to ear, waving the daisies mercilessly in the air. "I'm-a gonna get me a man too, honey – wait an' see!"

THE END

ABOUT THE AUTHOR

Cheryl Riley Cain began writing for others when asked to create humorous biographies for birthday and anniversary celebrations and character sketches for friends' baby showers. Since then she has written numerous plays for children's vacation Bible schools, and Christmas presentations for churches. Cheryl's love for history, and for her home state of Oklahoma, combined with her desire to share God's love with others, culminated in her first novel, *Redemption on the Red River.*

Cheryl lives with her husband, Mark, two sons, Micah and Matthew, daughter-in-law Casey, and precious and beautiful granddaughter, Sophia. Sherman T., a mix breed dog rescued by Cheryl, adds to the excitement in the Cain household.

THE MOUNTAINS
BETWEEN

A searing and powerful novel from
one of Wales' best-loved authors

Julie McGowan

THE MOUNTAINS
BETWEEN

Julie McGowan

Part One

1929 ~

Jennie

J ennie heard Tom's voice calling her, but she ignored him and scrambled over the gate into the ten-acre field. She ran head down, forcing her legs to go faster and faster, her breath coming in great racking sobs, until she reached the corner of the field where the land sloped down towards the railway line, and she would be hidden from the house. As she flung herself face down onto the grass and the sobs became bitter, painful tears, Mother's words echoed in her head, refusing to be quelled.

You were never wanted! You were a mistake!... A mistake... a mistake!... Never wanted... !

The day had started so well. The Girls were coming home and Jennie had been helping Mother in the house – as she always did, but more willingly this time, excitement tightening her chest because her sisters would soon be here and the summer holidays would then have begun in earnest. Mother, too, seemed happy; less forbidding, and the crease between her brows that gave her such a disapproving air had been less pronounced.

Never wanted!... A mistake... Your Father's doing!

Eventually there were no more tears left to cry, but the sobs remained; long drawn out arpeggios every time she inhaled. And the more she tried to stop them the more it felt as if they were taking over her body.

She sat up and wrapped her arms around her knees in an effort to steady herself. A small girl dressed in a starched

I

white pinafore over a blue print summer frock, with two mud-brown plaits framing a face whose eyes looked too large for it. She stared at the mountains – her mountains, her friends, keepers of her secrets. But today she wasn't seeing them, could draw no comfort from the gentle slopes of the Sugar Loaf which stretched out like arms to encompass the valley. Today the mountains were majestic and aloof, wanting no share of her misery. In her head the scene in Mother's bedroom replayed itself endlessly before her.

She'd been returning a reel of thread to Mother's workbox – a sturdy wooden casket kept in a corner of the bedroom. Inside were neat trays containing all Mother's sewing things, and one tray full of embroidery silks, the colours rich and flamboyant as they nestled together. Jennie had lifted the silks up and let them run through her fingers, enjoying their smooth feel and the rainbows they made.

Then, for the first time, she'd noticed that what she thought was the bottom of the workbox was, in fact, too high up.

She lifted the rest of the trays out and pulled at the wooden base, which moved easily to reveal another section underneath. There was only one item in it; a rectangular tin box with a hinged lid on which was a slightly raised embossed pattern in shiny red and gold. She traced the pattern with her fingers. It was an intriguing box. A box that begged to be opened.

Jennie had lifted the tin clear of the workbox when suddenly Mother appeared in the doorway, her face bulging with anger.

"What do you think you're doing? Put that down at once!"

Taken unawares by her mother's arrival and the harshness of her tone – excessive even for her – Jennie turned suddenly and the box had fallen out of her hands, the hinged lid flying open and the contents scattering over the floor. Had she not been so frightened by Mother's anger, Jennie would have registered disappointment, for the box, after all, held only a few old papers.

To Mother, though, they seemed as valuable as the Crown Jewels. With an anguished cry she'd pushed Jennie aside and scrabbled on the floor to retrieve the documents.

"I'm s-s-sorry," Jennie stammered, "I didn't mean ..."

But Mother wasn't listening. She was too busy shouting.

"Why don't you ever leave things alone? This is mine! You had no business! You're always where you're not meant to be – always causing me more work! Either under my feet or doing something you shouldn't!"

Her voice had grown more shrill as she spoke, with a dangerous quiver in it, so that Jennie didn't dare offer to help – or to point out that the things her mother was accusing her of were grossly unfair. She'd given up doing that a long time ago. "... It's not right – I didn't want... Three babies were enough!"

Mother had been looking down, thrusting the papers back in the box, continuing to exclaim about the unfairness of her lot as she did so, almost as if she were no longer addressing Jennie. But then she'd snapped the box shut and swung round to face her daughter.

"You were never wanted, you know! It was all a mistake! All your Father's doing!" She turned back to the workbox, her shoulders heaving with emotion.

There was a moment's silence.

"What did Father do?" a crushed Jennie had whispered.

Mother's hand had swung round and slapped Jennie across the ankles. "Don't be so disgusting!" she'd hissed. "Get out of here!"

Jennie knew, as she sat on the grass, that Mother had meant it. She was used to her mother's tempers, her insistence that the house, the family, and at times the farm, were run exactly as she wished, but this was different. The expression on her face as she'd spoken the dreadful words was one that Jennie had never seen before. It had been full of a strange passion – and something else which Jennie, with her limited experience, couldn't identify. But it had frightened her.

Never wanted! A mistake!

It changed everything. Nothing in her world would ever be the same again. Her eight years thus far had been secure ones; lonely at times, being the youngest by so many years, and hard when Mother's standards were so exacting. But happy, too. Happy in the knowledge that she was well-fed, clothed and housed; well-cared for (didn't that mean loved and wanted? It appeared not). Happy on the farm, surrounded by her mountains, and in the company of her beloved father.

Father! Jennie's heart beat faster in alarm. Did this mean that he didn't want her either? That he too saw her as some sort of mistake? Her relationship with her mother always held uncertainty, but Father's affection never seemed to waver.

A kaleidoscope of images of herself with her father rushed through her mind. Making her a wheelbarrow all of her own, so that she could 'help' him on the farm, when she was only four. Holding her in his arms when she cried because a fox had got in and wreaked havoc in the hen-house; comforting her because she'd been the one to discover the terrible decapitated remains. Letting her help to make new chicken sheds, safely off the ground – not minding when she'd splashed creosote on the grass. Urging the cows to milking, his voice kind and gentle, calling each cow by name and helping her to do the same until she could recognise each one.

Surely he loved her! He had to love her!

Panic was rising inside her and she wanted to run to her father and beg him to tell her that it wasn't true; that she wasn't simply a mistake. But fear stayed her. There was the awful possibility that he might tell her even more dreadful things that she didn't want to hear. It would be the same if she asked The Girls, and as for Tom, well! – he had never disguised the fact that a sister six years younger than himself was fit only for endless teasing.

The words were still playing in her head when suddenly the panic eased. What else had Mother said? ... *All your Father's doing!* She didn't know what her father had done, but surely if he'd done it then he must have wanted her?

She lay back on the grass and closed her eyes. Perhaps if she went to sleep she would wake up and everything would be just as it was. She could go back to the house and carry on as usual and the lead weight in her chest that was making breathing so difficult would be gone.

The hot July sun soothed her. Mother would be cross if her skin burned, but Mother being cross about such a thing didn't seem quite so important at the moment. Convincing herself that her Father loved her and wanted her was, she instinctively knew, the only thing that would help her to push her mother's awful words to the back of her mind.

Katharine Davies sat on the edge of her bed, her shoulders sagging uncharacteristically, her breathing rapid and shallow. The papers were safely stowed away again but the episode had unnerved her too much for her to return downstairs just yet. Jennie was too young to have understood the implications of what the papers contained, but what if she told the older children of their whereabouts? A hot flush spread over her anew as she considered what they would think of her. She tried hopelessly to calm herself, but memories of nearly seventeen years ago refused to go away.

"Edward! Oh Edward!"

The voice was her own, urgent, pleading as his hands caressed her, explored her; and she wasn't urging him to stop. Oh no! To her everlasting shame she wanted him to go on, to satisfy the craving that had taken over her whole body. And he had: gone on and on until she felt she was drowning; until she had screamed her ecstasy.

I love you Katie. I'll always love you! Edward had held her afterwards, murmuring into her hair, promising to take care of her. And he had. But it hadn't been enough.

The memories sent prickles of shame up her spine until her neck was on fire. Yet, unbidden, the feeling was there again; that same burning physical wanting that had gnawed away at her in those early years, trapping her with its demands, its insatiability.

She stood up abruptly, angry that her body should be betraying her after all these years when she'd thought she had it firmly under control. She clenched her hands tightly in front of her. She must, she would, maintain that control.

She forced herself to think of what must still be done, which chores in the dairy or in the garden would best exercise her treacherously unreliable body.

She thought fleetingly of Jennie as she moved swiftly out of the bedroom. She shouldn't have spoken to her as she did, but doubtless the child would get over it – would probably look at her with those sheep's eyes for a day or two and then it would pass.

v

But you meant it, nagged the mean voice of Conscience.

She clutched the crucifix hanging round her neck, as if gathering strength to push the voice away. *I'll pray about it tonight,* she vowed, making for the stairs.

"Bessie! You'd better see about scalding the milk or it will turn in this heat! Then come and help me clean the dairy."

The girl, plump and homely, turned from the large stone sink where she was peeling potatoes, ready to make a cheery remark until she saw the expression on her employer's face. Best not look in the churn, madam, she thought, or the milk will turn never mind the heat.

J ennie saw her mother in the dairy as she entered the back of the house and tiptoed up the back stairs. She didn't want Mother to see the grass stains on her apron.

She'd thought long and hard once she'd finally stopped crying, and had decided that if she tried, really tried, not to let Mother see her doing anything wrong, and not to argue with her ever again, then perhaps Mother would forget that she was 'a mistake' and decide that she was the best-loved and most wanted of all her children.

She sighed as she reached her room. It would be hard work. There seemed to be so many things that Mother had definite and immovable views on. Take her apron, for example. Aprons weren't meant to get dirty. Mother's aprons always stayed spotless – except for the apron she wore over her apron to do 'the rough'.

Not that Mother ever did the really dirty jobs. They were done by Bessie, the latest in a long line of girls who stayed until they could take Mother's demands for perfection and her sharp tongue no longer.

She put on a clean apron and went to the recently-installed bathroom to wash her hands and face, careful to wipe the basin clean afterwards and replace the towel just so. The bathroom was a sufficiently new addition to be treated with exceptional respect. Then she returned to the kitchen by the front stairs so that Mother would think she had been in the house all along.

"May I go now, please – to meet The Girls?"

Jennie didn't want to look Mother in the face; instead

she fastened her gaze on the shiny gold crucifix.

The crease between Mother's brows deepened as she surveyed her daughter. She opened her mouth as if to speak, but closed it again. Then her shoulders dropped a little as she appeared to relent from whatever it was she had been going to say.

"Very well. But wear your sunbonnet – and keep your apron clean!"

Jennie went meekly to the little room behind the kitchen and fetched her sun hat before letting herself out through the back door, forcing herself to walk sedately in case Mother was watching her as she crossed the farmyard – immaculate as ever because the cows weren't allowed to cross it lest they make it dirty.

Once round the corner of the barn she ran again to the gate of the ten-acre field. But she didn't climb over it this time. Instead she divested herself of her apron and sunhat and hung them on the gatepost before turning to a smaller, iron gate which led to the lane running parallel to the field.

She began to skip along the lane, sending up little clouds of dust as she went. It was impossible, somehow, to walk once you were out-of-doors and alone, even when you were feeling pretty miserable. Had she been feeling happier she would have tucked her skirts up into the legs of her knickers and tried a few cartwheels. But as she thought this, the awful words bounced up at her in time to her skipping... *Not wan-ted... not wan-ted... not wan-ted...*

The engine hooted as it pulled out of Nantyderry Halt, diverting Jennie. No need to think about anything else now The Girls were home! She broke into a run as they appeared at the end of the lane. They were each wearing their school uniform and carrying a small case; Tom would take the van down later for their trunks. Their uniforms bore the badge of the convent school at Monmouth, which they attended not because they were Catholic but because it was the best school in the area, and they boarded, not because it was far away but because that was what the best families did.

Jennie threw herself into the arms of her eldest sister, sure of a rapturous response.

"Steady on!" laughed Emily, swinging her round. "You nearly knocked me over! Let me look at you! You've grown again while we've been away! Laura! Don't you think she's grown?"

Laura, a year younger than sixteen-year-old Emily, but inches shorter and already more buxom, hugged Jennie more steadily.

"At least an inch taller," she agreed.

"Does that mean I can use your tennis racket this summer?" Jennie asked excitedly, turning back to Emily. "I've been practising like mad against the barn wall with the old one, and you promised me yours when I was big enough."

"We'll see," came the reply. "You'll have to show me how good you are."

But Emily's eyes held a merry promise and suddenly she caught hold of Jennie and danced round with her again.

"Isn't it wonderful? I've finished school for good! My very last day! I can hardly believe it!"

"It won't be so wonderful if we're late for dinner," Laura reminded her, picking up her bag and beginning to walk up the lane. "Jennie, your dress is terribly dusty – Mother will have a fit!"

"It's alright," said Jennie, "I can cover it up with my apron – I've left it on the gate."

But as they reached the gate, there was Tom, Jennie's sunhat perched ridiculously on his head, and the apron held aloft.

"Give it back, I mustn't get it dirty!" Jennie cried, hers arms flailing wildly as Tom held her easily at bay with one gangly arm.

"Please, Tom!" Laura sounded as urgent as Jennie, as the gong for lunch sounded from the house. "You know she'll get into trouble."

Emily sauntered through the gate behind her sisters. "Give her the apron and the hat, Tom, and carry these bags in for us." Her voice sounded almost lazy, but Tom was aware of the authority behind it. He was taller than both his sisters, but Emily always managed to make him feel small.

He relinquished the garments to a relieved Jennie, tweaked each of the long brown plaits hanging over her shoulders, and then grinned. "Better not spoil the homecoming, I suppose."

But he didn't move to embrace his sisters. Instead they all hurried in for dinner.

C ome along! Come along!" said Mother as Father stopped to kiss and hug his two elder children. "This dinner will be getting cold."

Jennie contrived to sit between Father and Emily and at once felt happier, although tears threatened again when Father asked her in his gentle voice what she'd been doing all morning. Fortunately Mother began speaking to Emily, and as it was unwise to talk at the same time as Mother she didn't have to answer.

Edward Davies surveyed his family with a degree of pride as they sat round the large, scrubbed kitchen table. All four children well-grown and healthy – no mean achievement when you compared them to the malnourished rickety children over in the valleys, many of whom would be lucky to survive infancy. He would have liked another boy, for the farm, but he loved his daughters nevertheless.

Not that Katharine would have been happy with another boy – there'd been enough fuss as it was when Jennie came along, so he'd thanked God that He had seen fit to bless them with another girl. For some reason Katharine saw girls as a blessing and boys as a kind of blight. *Poor thing,* she would say whenever she heard of a mother being delivered of a son, no matter how longed-for. She treated Tom well enough for all that, Edward allowed, although he never saw the look of pride in her eyes that he had seen other mothers bestowing on their sons. But then, he reflected, Katharine was not like other mothers in a good many ways.

He watched her now, talking to Emily. She was still a handsome woman, despite her nearly forty years, with no hint of grey in the coils of rich brown hair which she wore piled high like Queen Mary. She'd kept her figure too, which was petite, with delicate wrists and ankles, but her body had always curved in and out in the right places.

Beautiful she'd been, when he first met her; beautiful with no idea of her beauty, which was what he'd found so appealing. Large grey-green eyes, more green when stirred to anger or passion, had beguiled him, and a relentless determination to set the world to rights according to her own view of things had been particularly attractive in one who looked as if she should languish and be pampered all day.

They first met when she was only eighteen, and had returned home from being a children's nanny to care for her younger brothers and sisters following the death of both their parents – her father having discreetly drunk himself to death after losing his wife from septicaemia.

Edward had watched her over the next few years as she struggled valiantly to prepare her siblings for adult life, while he himself was struggling to make a go of his first smallholding. But it had been some time before he'd plucked up courage to court her formally; there had always been an elusive quality about her that held him back, whilst at the same time tantalising him. She was twenty-three before the demands of her family had ceased and she had begun to take Edward seriously and allow him any degree of familiarity – and then, to his joy, what sensuality had been unleashed! And he had loved her! Oh, how he had loved her!

And I still love her now, he mused sadly. But it had been many years since the passion which had simultaneously driven and mortified her had been given rein. The determination which had enabled her to take over successfully from her parents had been channelled into 'getting on' in the world – or at least in the important bits of the society in which they moved, while the passion had been supplanted by a strange mixture of worldliness and godliness.

And, he thought with a sigh, *if cleanliness really is next to godliness, then she'll have a special place reserved for her when she gets to the other side.*

END OF SAMPLE CHAPTER
*"The Mountains Between" by Julie McGowan
can be purchased from all good online stores,
or better still, ask for it from your local independent
or chain book store.*

About

THE MOUNTAINS BETWEEN

by Julie McGowan

Despite its physical comforts, Jennie's life under the critical eye of her tyrannical mother is hard, and she grows up desperate for a love she has been denied. As she blossoms into a young woman World War II breaks out. Life is turned upside down by the vagaries of war, and the charming, urbane Charles comes into her life – and he loves her … doesn't he? …

On the other side of the scarred mountain, in the wake of a disaster that tears through his family and their tight-knit mining community, Harry finds the burden of manhood abruptly thrust upon his young shoulders. He bears it through the turmoil of the Depression years, sustained only by his love for Megan. But his life too takes many unexpected turns, and the onset of war brings unimaginable changes. … Nothing is as it was, or as it seems …

Blaenavon and Abergavenny surge to life in this vibrant, haunting, joyful masterpiece – a celebration of the Welsh people from the 1920s to the 1940s. It's the saga of two families and their communities, and the story of two young people who should have found each other much sooner. It's the story of the people of the mountains and the valleys who formed the beating heart of Wales.

*The Mountains Between became a regional best-seller almost immediately. Now in its 3rd edition, it was author Julie McGowan's first book, and is based in her much-loved homeland of Wales. Her second book, **Just One More Summer**, is a wonderfully intricate read based in Cornwall, while her newly-released third book, **Don't Pass Me By**, is also a Welsh spectacular.*

SUNPENNY PUBLISHING GROUP

ROSE & CROWN, BLUE JEANS, BOATHOOKS, SUNBERRY, CHRISTLIGHT, and EPTA Books

MORE BOOKS FROM the SUNPENNY GROUP
www.sunpenny.com

A Little Book of Pleasures, by William Wood
Blackbirds Baked in a Pie, by Eugene Barter
Breaking the Circle, by Althea Barr
Dance of Eagles, by JS Holloway
Don't Pass Me By, by Julie McGowan
Far Out, by Corinna Weyreter
Going Astray, by Christine Moore
If Horses Were Wishes, by Elizabeth Sellers
Just One More Summer, by Julie McGowan
Loyalty & Disloyalty, by Dag Heward-Mills
My Sea is Wide (Illustrated), by Rowland Evans
Sudoku for Christmas (full colour illustrated gift book)
The Mountains Between, by Julie McGowan
The Perfect Will of God, by Dag Heward-Mills
The Skipper's Child, by Valerie Poore
Those Who Accuse You, by Dag Heward-Mills
Trouble Rides a Fast Horse, by Elizabeth Sellers
Watery Ways, by Valerie Poore

FROM OUR ROMANCE IMPRINTS:

Uncharted Waters, by Sara DuBose
Bridge to Nowhere, by Stephanie Parker McKean
Embracing Change, by Debbie Roome
Blue Freedom, by Sandra Peut
A Flight Delayed, by KC Lemmer

SUNPENNY PUBLISHING GROUP

ROSE & CROWN, BLUE JEANS, BOATHOOKS, SUNBERRY, CHRISTLIGHT, and EPTA Books

COMING SOON:

30 Days to Take-Off, by KC Lemmer
A Devil's Ransom, by Adele Jones
A Whisper On The Mediterranean, by Tonia Parronchi
Brandy Butter on Christmas Canal, by Shae O'Brien
Broken Shells, by Debbie Roome
Fish Soup, by Michelle Heatley
Heart of the Hobo, by Shae O'Brien
Raglands, by JS Holloway
The Stangreen Experiment, by Christine Moore
Sudoku for Bird Lovers (full colour illustrated gift book)
Sudoku for Horse Lovers (full colour illustrated gift book)
Sudoku for Sailors (full colour illustrated gift book)
Sudoku for Stitchers (full colour illustrated gift book)

Lightning Source UK Ltd.
Milton Keynes UK
UKOW05f0158211114

241949UK00004BA/263/P